Terrorist Harvest

by

Michael J. Benson

PublishAmerica
Baltimore

First printing

ISBN: 1-4137-1109-X
PUBLISHED BY PUBLISHAMERICA, LLLP
www.publishamerica.com
Baltimore

Printed in the United States of America

To Patricia, my wife and best friend, and my mother Nell.

Acknowledgements

Gordon and David Benson
John Strain
Stephen Quinn
Andrew Stewart
Eric Morris

1

SEPTEMBER 22ND, ENGLAND

The group of seven men sat in a quiet area of the restaurant on the M6 motorway service area, just North of Birmingham, England waiting for the arrival of John Strain, the team leader. The motorway service areas were conveniently placed on all motorways throughout the UK to act as rest stops and cater for the needs of drivers and passengers. They normally included a restaurant, store, restrooms and re-fueling areas for cars and trucks. The team always chose a quiet area out of earshot of other restaurant patrons, especially when they knew that there might be a briefing. The briefings they had at these locations were normally very quick and wouldn't make any sense to anyone that was listening. If anyone had the audacity to sit near the team the looks on their faces would make people find a friendlier seating area.

One of the men known as Shadow got up from the table and walked outside the restaurant to the parking lot. He positioned himself where he could keep observations for the arrival of Strain. It was something of a habit for Shadow to do this whenever the team were expecting a briefing about an operation. Under normal circumstances keeping observation on your own team leader would be most unusual behavior; however, this is how Strain's team tried to stay one step ahead of him. Shadow did not have to wait long when he saw Strain's vehicle searching its way through the lines of cars, looking for a parking space. Shadow could hear the music Strain was playing in his car—*Mission accomplished*, he thought to himself. By knowing what music he had playing in his car the team would know how easy or difficult the operation was going to be. The music prior to a job was always opera, Strain's preference when he had to give his thoughts totally to the job ahead, or, as he called it, his calm down music. Calm down music, the team always smiled at that expression; yes, he was calm, but this was when Strain was at his deadliest, totally focused, knowing exactly what had to be done, good or bad.

Shadow calmly walked back into the restaurant without Strain seeing him. As he reached the area where the team was sitting he paused before speaking.

Shadow always did this, as he knew how impatient Bulldog (Matt Grantham) was, and he liked to agitate him whenever possible. He looked down at the faces of the team members, who were keenly waiting for the news.

"Come on, spit it out," said Bulldog.

"*Nessun Dorma*," replied Shadow. Although none of the team members listened to opera they all knew the names of certain songs, as they called them. The fact that they called them songs would have made most opera purists weep.

"It must be a bad one, we haven't had *Nessun Dorma* since Frankfurt," said Stan.

He was referring to an operation they performed six months previously with the assistance of a covert SAS team. They went to Frankfurt to detain four Neo-Nazi skinheads that had been in hiding for almost a year after they had set fire to four synagogues in England. To add to their enjoyment, as they saw it, they beat to death a Rabbi and his wife in one of the synagogues. The caretaker of the synagogue discovered the bodies soon after the murders. The description of a suspect vehicle was circulated to all police officers within an hour of the murders. Two uniformed police officers saw the suspect vehicle parked in a side street only a mile from where the murders took place. They called for backup and approached the vehicle, which contained the driver, one front and two rear passengers. The officers separated and approached the vehicle from both sides, one officer engaging the driver in conversation.

Ignoring the instructions given by the police officers to stay in the vehicle the occupants got out of the vehicle and started to argue with the officers. A sawn-off pump action shotgun was produced by one of the skinheads, he shot one officer in the chest at close range. The second officer immediately grabbed the shotgun and tried to wrestle it away from the skinhead, within a matter of seconds the shotgun blasted again, blowing off the officer's left leg just below the knee. Apparently the skinheads gathered around the wounded officer lying in the road and laughed out loud at the sight of him screaming in pain. They left him lying in the road but not before they administered a number of kicks to his head and body. Mercifully the officer had passed out before they had finished. The same group of skinheads was involved in the supply of weapons and drugs to other Neo-Nazi groups in Europe and IRA members in the UK—hence the interest of the SAS.

The successful capture and deportation back to the UK of the individuals responsible for the murders was received with great applause by the press and public.

The team watched through the restaurant window as Strain walked in from the parking lot outside. Strain was not a tall man, 5'10", short black hair, thickset and broad across the shoulders. Strain had the look of a typical Rugby player, which he had enjoyed playing in the past.

"Hello lads," said Strain as he walked in. "What's the sad faces for? Cheer up, I will get a coffee and be right back, anybody want a brew?" Nobody did and he went off to the service counter.

"He's too bloody chirpy," said Stan.

"We will find out why soon enough," Shadow replied.

Strain was always upbeat when he had finally worked out exactly what the team had to do to complete an operation. The fact that he was so upbeat made the rest of the team anxious to know what was going to happen.

Strain returned to the table. "OK lads, we are going to complete our present job tonight and provide free accommodation for the participants." He meant that the subjects involved would be arrested and taken to jail.

"About bloody time," Bulldog whispered.

Strain knew that each member of the team was ready, fully aware of the individual parts they had to play. They had rehearsed the procedures over a dozen times for entry into the apartment of Peter Foy, the brother of their target Alan Foy. They found an empty apartment in the next road that was exactly the same layout. The team had used this apartment as a command center for the previous two weeks. Basically a simple front and rear entry into the apartment was all that was required. Arrest Foy and his girlfriend and convey them to police H.Q. Strain concluded the briefing by emphasizing once again that Foy may have arms in the apartment, although he had never been known to carry or use a weapon.

With the short briefing over Strain excused himself and headed for the restrooms. As he came out of the restaurant he saw a group of five soccer fans displaying their Everton soccer club scarves, walking out of the room containing the slot machines. They were exchanging profanities with two burly truck drivers as they left. The soccer fans must have been nineteen or twenty years old and were very intoxicated. As they barged their way out of the slot machine room they knocked down an elderly woman who was walking towards the exit doors. Strain immediately went to the woman's aid, as did the two truck drivers. Strain stooped down to help the woman up, when he heard one of the soccer fans say, "The doddering old bitch shouldn't have been in the way," which his friends thought was funny and laughed as they walked away.

This lack of respect and disregard for his wife was too much for her husband. Although in his late seventies he wanted to teach these lads a lesson and he lunged at the group. One of the truck drivers held him back and told him to take care of his wife. Strain watched them out of the corner of his eye and saw the individual that had knocked down the elderly lady walk into the restroom as his friends went into the store. Strain asked the truck drivers to take care of the man and woman while he went to the restroom. The biggest of the two looked at Strain and immediately saw who was going into the restroom and said, "Go on, mate, we'll take care of them."

As Strain went into the restroom he could see that he was alone with the youth. Strain walked up to the urinals where the youth was standing relieving himself, he stood at the urinal next to him. Strain looked at the youth and said, "When you have finished I would like you to go outside and apologize to that elderly man and woman."

The youth looked at him as though Strain had lost his mind and said, "Fuck off and mind your own business or I'll fuck you up as well." The youth looked at the restroom wall in front of him and smiled, proud of the fact that he had put this interfering bastard in his place.

Strain zipped up his trousers and said, "I'm sorry that you feel that way."

Before the youth could say anything Strain grabbed the hair on the back of his head and smashed his face into the tiles on the urinal wall. Blood immediately appeared from the youth's nose as he fell to the floor still urinating, soaking the front of his trousers. This was a technique Strain had been taught by his grandfather, who was a well-respected man in the pubs that he frequented around Liverpool.

As Strain turned to leave two of the other soccer fans walked into the restroom to see their friend lying on the floor. The taller of the two pulled out a knife and said, "We are going to do you in, you bastard," and they both moved towards Strain.

"Do you need any help, mate," the voice said. Strain looked past the two youths; he could see one of the burly truck drivers.

"Fuck off, this is nothin' to do with you," said the youth with the knife.

It was too late, the truck driver had a hold of him and picked him up like he was a rag doll. The youth screamed at the truck driver to put him down, to which he replied, "OK," and dropped the youth headfirst into the urinal, knocking him unconscious. The second youth ran past the driver out of the restroom screaming to his friends to come and help. The truck driver shook hands with Strain and they both walked out, leaving the two youths on the floor. As they came out of the restroom the three remaining youths stood waiting for them. The courage of the youth that ran out of the restroom was now restored as he had his friends supporting him.

"OK, we are going to show you that you can't fuck with us," he said.

He should not have wasted time talking because Strain was at him before he could think, butting him in the face. The truck driver moved well for a man of his size and punched one of the other youths so hard it knocked him backwards six feet. Strain was already seeing to the third youth by kicking him in the crotch. As he obligingly bent forward in pain Strain added his knee to the youth's face, lifting him off his feet and onto his back. The head butt was not enough to deter the first youth and Strain saw him jumping at him. Strain stepped slightly to his left, turning his shoulders and hips towards the youth, at the same time forcing his elbow into his face. The youth did not know what hit him. He crumpled to the floor, his face a bloody mess.

Strain's team observed everything that was going on outside of the restroom from where they were sitting. Not one of them moved to offer assistance to Strain, they just enjoyed the show. Knowing that Strain really didn't need their help, especially with that huge truck driver next to him.

"Christ, look at that poor bastard," said Bulldog.

He was pointing to the first youth that Strain had followed into the restroom. He was walking out of the restroom holding his face with a blood-soaked wad of paper towels. The evidence that he had urinated down the front of his pants was obvious by the large wet patch around his crotch area. This sight delighted two teenage girls that were leaving the store and they pointed at him giggling, as did several other people watching. This only embarrassed him further and he hurried towards the parking lot, followed closely by his friends.

"I guess the boss must have had one of his talks with that one, Animal strikes again," said Shadow. Animal was the nickname given to Strain by one of his fellow officers after a riot at an industrial dispute in the town of Warrington.

Strain shook hands with the truck driver and returned to the restaurant. He always had a certain presence when he walked into a room that made people look at him. The incident outside the restroom made even more people look this time. As he got to the tables where the team were sitting Bulldog got out of his chair. He dusted the seat of the chair with a napkin and indicated to Strain to sit down, saying, "Please sit in my chair, it would be a great honor for me to have a real live knight in shining armor to sit in my place."

Strain called Bulldog an asshole as the rest of the team bowed to him, saying, "We are unworthy, we are unworthy." Strain started laughing at the team and told Bulldog that as he had started this show of disrespect for authority he could buy everyone dinner before they left.

Bulldog replied quietly, "With respect, boss, you can go fuck yourself," he bowed at the waist as if greeting a member of royalty and walked to the self-service food area.

SEPTEMBER 22ND, FRANCE

Mohammed Ali Gahi was very proud of the reward on his head, offered by both governments in Algeria, his native country, and France in the early nineties. Gahi had been instrumental in the development of the guerilla activities in Northern Algeria, particularly those which involved attacks on government oil facilities.

Sonatrach, the Algerian national oil company, had become increasingly frustrated with these attacks and had requested the assistance of the French government in combating the terrorists. France was somewhat sympathetic to the request, as they had invested many millions in oil and gas exploration in the country. In addition to the direct financial investment, French companies exported hundreds of millions of francs worth of vehicles and other goods to Algeria. At first the assistance offered by France was a comparatively small supply of weapons and limited training for the troops. In return the Algerian government got deeper into debt with France by ordering more equipment for the military. A vicious cycle that the French designed to keep the Algerian government forever reliant. This practice by the French was not unusual, they performed the same act throughout North and West Africa, as well as in the Middle East. France was very good at this game of dangling the supply or political carrot in front of these nations, much to the bemusement of their allies. Not that France really cared what their allies thought—they always positioned themselves so that they could continue the game to their benefit.

One example of this was in 1988 when the U.S. and Britain wanted to bomb Libya to punish Col. Gaddafi for his alleged role in the support and training of international terrorist groups. France refused the U.S. and Britain permission to fly through French air space to perform the bombings, making the mission logistically more tedious, forcing the midair refueling of aircraft in order to reach the targets in Libya and return to base in the UK. Why would they do this? One school of thought was that the French had once again put the arm of friendship and support around the shoulders of what they publicly announced was a nation being wrongfully intimidated by these aggressive nations. Yes, the arm around Libya's shoulders was showing some sympathy even though it was manufactured and not in the least genuine. As a result of the support the French would tie Libya down for over a decade, forcing them to purchase French goods and services over those of other European nations. Obviously when this school of thought was presented to the French government they spoke of their disgust and shock that anyone would think of them in this way. They only saw Libya as a friend and did not agree with the oppressive tactics being used by the U.S. and Britain. Did anyone believe this public display of shock and disbelief? No, not even Col. Gaddafi, as he knew what the game was. He needed the support of a friendly nation to show his Arab brothers, especially those who did not support him, that they were wrong not to give him support.

After the beheading of several foreign oil workers at an isolated rig-site in the northern region of Algeria, security intensified. Foreign companies operating in Algeria who were investing billions of dollars and francs into the Algerian oil and gas economy demanded more government help. The Algerian government and military authorities again called for assistance from France. Members of the French foreign legion already operating in Algeria as advisors were reinforced with several groups ordered to evaluate the security and training of the Algerian soldiers.

Foreign oil and gas companies were stunned by the news of the beheading and in some cases they too re-evaluated their security. The increase in cost to them would eventually run into the millions. The Algerian government offered troops that would end up being fed and watered by the oil companies at no cost to the Algerian government. The increased pressure on terrorist groups by the government caused Gahi along with three of his closest and best soldiers to leave their homeland for France. His absence caused a lot of in-fighting with the remaining fundamentalist chiefs in Algeria and a bloodbath ensued, resulting in 3,000 Algerian dead in the first year. The situation would not improve for many years.

Gahi and his soldiers started a campaign of terror in France six months after his arrival. The financial support for the campaign coming from extreme left-wing political opponents of the French government and ETA, the Basque separatist group. A series of bombs announced the start of the campaign, targeting the underground rail system in Paris and various government buildings in Marseilles and Lyon. These attacks were weak and infrequent but proved to be an irritant to the French government. The effects of the attacks would not be felt for a number of months, not until tourism started to decline.

The French government applied great pressure on the criminal families operating in Paris and other major cities around France, to assist them in locating the people responsible for committing these acts of terrorism. The tactic worked and Gahi and his soldiers went into temporary hiding in the mountains of Southern France and Northern Spain with members of ETA before returning to Algeria.

Two years had passed and it was time for the French and Algerian governments to hear from the great terrorist Mohammed Gahi once again. The bombing campaign he had designed would be widespread and devastating. Gahi called ETA for support and offered them a part in this glorious rebirth of terrorism. Initially ETA was not interested, but Gahi had access to weapons in France and England, a member of ETA saw this as a way of using him to start a new campaign.

This marriage, though temporary, would prove to be disastrous for both groups of terrorists.

The captain of the Dover-Calais ferry stood on the bridge of his vessel looking down onto the French dockside. He was completely immersed in his thoughts about the weekend ahead. Captain Morris had promised his wife that he would spend his three days off with her. This would be the first weekend he had off work in six weeks thanks to the start of the tourist season. Captain Morris had been on the cross channel ferries for twelve years and never really got tired of his job. He enjoyed watching the faces of his passengers, mostly tourists, as they boarded the ferry. He often wondered what their final destination would be, who where they visiting, a family member, friend, or secret lovers stealing a weekend together. The ferry was already running an hour and a half behind schedule due to a problem in the engine room, which the chief had fixed in double quick time. With the problem fixed and all of his passengers on board, he was ready to cast off. His moment of peaceful thought was broken as he heard the sound of a loud explosion that rocked the whole vessel.

"What was that?" he said out loud and immediately thought that there was a problem in the engine room. He was about to call the chief when he heard a second explosion and a third. He picked up the telephone but soon realized that it was dead. Smoke started to appear around the deck where some passengers were standing. He could now hear the chaotic shouts and cries of fear from his passengers.

"Stay here, George," he said to his second-in-command, George Lane.

"What do you think it is, a boiler?" he asked. The captain did not answer he had already gone, ignoring the normal procedure to stay on the bridge.

On the deck the passengers were pouring out of every door, some calmly and others screaming. He could hear the fire alarms ringing from inside the vessel. A crewmember ran to the bottom of the steps where he stood.

"Captain, there has been an explosion on the car deck. There is a lot of black smoke and fire, the fire fighters are in there."

"Thank you," he said, "Go to the bridge and tell Mr Lane to lower the ramp doors and evacuate the passengers."

Morris opened the door marked, 'CREW ONLY', and took the vertical metal stairs down to the next level. As he reached the bottom the lights went out and the emergency lights immediately took over. Two crew members, faces black with the effects of the smoke came up the ladder from the deck below. Both men were fighting for air and coughing violently.

"You can't go down there, Captain, we have secured the inner doors to the vehicle deck, the heat is intense and the smoke thick. The fire team had to back out on the starboard side and there are too many vehicles starting to burn." He covered his mouth as he started to cough again.

The second crew member spoke, "I think it was a fuel tank that blew up on one of the heavy goods vehicles (HGV). I saw the driver jump out of the cab, he didn't have a chance. He was engulfed in flames, and I could hear him screaming. He was waving his arms around trying to put out the flames."

"How many vehicles are on fire?" asked the captain.

"It's hard to say because of the second explosion at the opposite end of the deck. Within fifteen or twenty seconds the whole deck was filling with smoke. Almost at the same time a third explosion went off about three cars behind the HGV that was already burning. We had to leave," the crewman answered.

"Wait, you say there was an explosion at the opposite end of the deck just after the HGV blew up?"

"Yes, sir."

"That doesn't make sense, why would we get two explosions at the opposite ends of the deck to each other? Go on deck and help evacuate the passengers."

Morris was now convinced that this was no accident. He ran across to the starboard side of the ferry and climbed the metal ladder down to the car deck level. He could feel the heat rising past him as he worked his way down the ladder. At the bottom the heat was as intense as his crew had described, with thick clouds of black smoke pouring through the door where he stood. He could hear a woman crying for help on the deck somewhere to his right. Morris got down on all fours and crawled out onto the deck to see if he could spot the woman. He squinted, his eyes peering through the smoke, trying to see her. There she was, about twenty feet away from him, lying on the metal deck semi-conscious.

Again the woman called out, "Help me, someone please help me."

"OK, I'm coming, stay calm, I will help you." In a crouched position he quickly shuffled along to where the woman lay. He saw that the woman, in her mid-50s, had a large open wound on the back of her head that was bleeding badly.

"OK, help me to get you to your feet and we will be out of here in no time." He used his most calming and reassuring voice in an effort to keep the woman from panicking. He didn't know it but he was wasting his time because at the precise moment there was another explosion from the stern of the deck. Morris looked up, only to see a huge red and yellow fireball racing towards him. Neither of them would survive as the fireball consumed both of their bodies.

It was chaos on deck as the crew helped passengers escape the vessel. Many dockworkers and passengers of vehicles waiting to board the next ferry were lending a hand. The scene was a nightmare with people running in every direction. Smoke was now pouring onto the deck, adding to the confusion.

On the bridge the number two was opening the watertight doors leading into the vehicle deck as instructed. The effect of the door opening and the sudden rush of air only added to the intensity of the heat. Flames and smoke billowed out onto the dock setting fire to some of the escaping passengers' clothing and the clothing of their rescuers.

Mohammed Gahi watched from the roof of a building across the street from the dock entrance. He showed no emotion as the vessel was engulfed in flames and people burnt to death as he watched. The police and fire services started to arrive to offer assistance to those who were already fighting the fire and rescuing passengers. Another giant explosion took place on board the ferry. Gahi had seen enough; he saw no reason to hang around. He returned to his car and headed south to Spain.

It would be several days before the real reason for the disaster was discovered and before the authorities had a true count of the dead and injured. The cost to the ferry company would be several hundred million dollars. Gahi had done well, French and international governments were calling the attack an atrocious act of cowardice and vowed to hunt down those responsible.

2

SEPTEMBER 22nd, ENGLAND

Peter Foy's apartment was in an area of Birmingham known for its seedy rental accommodations, an ideal place for someone to remain anonymous. This was one of the reasons why he had chosen the location. The bed-sits were old terraced-style houses that were originally very expensive properties for people to own. Now the owners had divided the houses into individual apartments to make them profitable, renting them out to students and low-income workers.

The four police surveillance vehicles had two team members in each with their normal pairings. Strain always kept everyone in the same pairing, as they had come to know how each other operated and almost what the other was thinking. The vehicles were strategically located around the bed-sit building to gain the best possible advantage of any movements in and out of the property. They had been watching the movements and activities of Peter Foy and his girlfriend for four weeks. The girlfriend was still unknown and the surveillance photographs sent to Scotland Yard did not produce her identity. The only thing they found out about the girlfriend was that she was a stunning redhead with a Belfast accent.

The Mask team had been keeping observations on Peter Foy's apartment for an hour when he returned home as usual at 7.30pm with his girlfriend. Four more hours passed without any sign of movement in or out of the apartment, the team was starting to get restless. The boss did say that they were going the finish the job tonight and they all wanted to get it over with and go home.

"What are we waiting for, it's midnight, we know they are in there!" Bulldog was showing his usual keenness to go into action. They were both watching the windows of the first-floor bed-sit, which was illuminated by the light inside. The lights went off and came on again briefly, then went off again.

"Plenty of time, Bulldog, let them have an hour's sleep first and then we will surprise them," said Strain.

"What's with the lights flashing on and off?"

"Most probably got his sticky little fingers caught on the light switch," Strain replied.

Bulldog huffed and slipped a little further down in the carseat, looking up at the now darkened windows. He had received the name Bulldog from the team leader, who had eventually given everyone on the team a nickname. The nickname given to a team member generally related to something about the individual's character or their professional ability. Bulldog got his because of his sheer power and strength for a man that was only five feet eight inches tall, 'built like a brick shit house,' was a common observation.

Strain held the rank of Detective Inspector in charge of the special ops team code-named 'Mask'. The team of detectives that Strain had working with him were hand picked with an average of twelve years service in the British police. All members of the team were firearms trained and always armed, ready to respond to any incident requiring their talents. All team members had served in the past on the Serious Crime Squads or Drug Squads in their respective police forces. Only their Chief Constables, the Prime Minister and a handful of Home Office staff knew of the real reason for the Mask Team.

What was the reason for Mask? A simple remit: Locate known mainland IRA active unit members, sympathizers and arms caches, bring individuals to justice by any means, weapons to be destroyed or utilized to effect the success of future operations.

The remit for the team was against normal police operating procedures, hence the secrecy. This ability to operate without restriction made the team very successful, bringing no fewer than eight IRA active unit members and thirty sympathizers to justice in the first twenty-one months. The loss of so many active service members, supporters, weapons and explosives really rocked the IRA chiefs back in Northern Ireland. Although they did not want to admit it, they felt that they had a mole within the organization. Mask had been equally successful in Europe in locating and arresting various UK-based terrorists/activists. The terrorists belonged to Muslim extremist organizations, Animal Rights activists groups etc. and were in hiding from the UK authorities. The extradition process of these individuals back to the UK was proving to be a lot slower than the British government wanted. Some cases were still being appealed by the legal eagles representing the detainees for the third and fourth time.

Capturing these individuals and then bringing them to justice were two completely different things. This process always frustrated the Mask Team as they had located and arrested the criminals quickly, only to be slowed down by the judicial system.

Prior to the team going operational three years previously all eight team members spent three grueling months at the SAS base in Hereford.

The SAS were considered to be the finest military counter terrorism group in the world by their peers. This training was to help prepare them for the relatively unknown world of counter-terrorism, relatively unknown to the team members that is, old ground for the SAS instructors. The training included fitness development, going through the rigors of jogging every day with backpacks and attacking the assault course, or should it be said the assault course at Hereford attacked you. Weapons training, tactics and familiarization of known Irish Republican Army, (IRA) members and their operations was also high on the training agenda.

The IRA terrorist organization dated back as far as the 1860s to the Fenian Movement in Northern Ireland. The objective of the movement was to create an independent Irish republic, ending British rule. The IRA name had been used ever since in various conflicts with the British government. In 1972 the Provisional IRA (PIRA) was formed, becoming the most feared and recognized IRA group of modern times. Through terrorist acts in Ireland and in mainland Britain they hoped to force the government to withdraw British troops from Northern Ireland.

Strain particularly enjoyed the hands-on training with the SAS, as they knew far more individually about close quarter tactics in a terrorist situation than his whole team combined. The team was under close evaluation by the SAS as directed by the Prime Minister, to locate the key players and leadership potential. Strain as a result of this scrutiny came out on top, showing great leadership ability, calmness under pressure, and basically soaking up everything about the training like a sponge. The whole team received excellent reviews by the SAS instructors, who were genuinely impressed by the group, which in itself was an achievement. The evaluation given by the instructors on Strain gained him promotion to Detective Inspector, putting him in charge of the team and future operations, this was a popular decision with the whole team.

This gave the SAS a great deal of confidence as they were to be assisted by the Mask Team on a number of operations, locating and arresting targets. This was another way in which the SAS could operate covertly but have the assistance of an outside group to bring the operation to a conclusion without revealing who they were. The two teams were excellent together and over the three-year period the Mask Team were becoming more and more respected at Hereford. They were now going to the SAS base in Hereford every four months for a one-week refresher course. They even had the Prime Minister at the last training session observing them going through their paces. He was particularly vocal about how well the team was doing, but then he would be as 'Mask' was *HIS* idea, *HIS* team. When in fact the idea came from the Home Secretary, Adrian Bowles.

The silence enjoyed by the team was suddenly broken.

"One, this is Four, over."

The sudden sound of a voice in their earpieces made Strain and Bulldog pay attention as they were supposed to be on radio silence.

"Go ahead, Four, this had better be good, over," Strain replied.

"We have a subject walking down the alleyway at the rear of the property, white male, 5'8" to 5'10" tall, slim build, wearing jeans and a black jacket. He is carrying a large holdall type bag, over."

Strain paused a moment before he replied, "Where did he come from, over?"

Stan Cartwright, nicknamed Sleepy because of his droopy-looking eyes, knew Strain wasn't going to like his reply, "He just appeared out of nowhere, we did not see him enter the alley, Shadow is following him, over."

Shadow was Steve Jones, Stan's partner, he was known as Shadow because he was so damn good at keeping observations and following people. He could be next to you and you would not even notice him. The dark alleyway made it even easier for Shadow to do his job. He followed the subject at a reasonable distance along the dark, damp brick walls of the alleyway.

Before Strain could respond Four came back, "He has entered the yard at the rear of the target's property, it looks like he is using the external fire escape, over."

The radios went silent for what seemed to be an eternity, when in fact it was only a few seconds. All four teams were now fully alert, sensing something was about to happen. The adrenaline started to pump around their bodies like some illicit drug.

Alan Foy opened the wooden gate leading into the yard at the rear of the bed-sit. The gate did not make any noise, which he thought was unusual as the hinges on these kinds of gates normally squeaked when opened. Alan walked silently into the yard and made his way up the fire escape. He stopped halfway up the metal fire escape and took two empty beer bottles out of his bag, carefully placing them on one of the metal steps. He tied a piece of fishing line to the top of each bottle and separated them until the fishing line was straight. Foy had used this technique many times over the years, particularly in Northern Ireland, to warn him of the presence of uninvited guests. He also liked this warning method because the fishing line normally became entangled with the person's feet, making it difficult for them to move quickly or quietly. The fact that it was completely dark at the rear of the bed-sit made his trap even more likely to work. Foy made his way up the fire escape and tapped twice on the window of the apartment where his younger brother was staying, his hand in his jacket pocket ready with his faithful Beretta. As the window slid open he saw Peter, his brother, who beckoned him in, he lifted the heavy bag through the opening and climbed through.

"Four, he is entering the property through a window in the subject's apartment, which someone opened for him, over."

Shadow left the surveillance car to see where the suspect had gone. As he approached the rear of Foy's bed-sit he could hear Stan talking in his earpiece to Strain, telling him that the suspect was going up the external fire escape. Shadow kept himself concealed in the dark and observed the suspect. He saw a white male climbing through a window and within a minute a light came on inside throwing a beam of light out into the dark where he was standing. Shadow threw himself against the alley wall and moved further into the dark so as not to be seen.

Both brothers immediately hugged each other, Peter being the first to speak. "It is good to see you again, big brother, you're looking great." Peter always looked up to his brother, who, apart from their father, was his idol.

"Good to see you as well, it has been too long."

The two brothers had been apart nearly two years, mainly due to the fact that Alan had been in hiding in Holland for nearly eighteen months after he shot and killed a policeman and his wife in their home in Belfast. At twenty-two years old he was already one of the IRA's most ruthless and experienced soldiers. The murders happened at a time when the IRA where debating amongst themselves about a possible deal with the British for a cease-fire and peace talks. Some members of the IRA did not want peace with the British, the hatred for them running back generations to the 1920s and the days of Michael Connolly, a true IRA hero in the eyes of some and a traitor in the eyes of others. The murder of the policeman and his wife in front of their children enraged the British government and local police. The murders did the trick and cancelled any thoughts of peace talks with the British for some time, which was the reason why the murders were carried out. Not that Alan knew this—he was just acting under orders. Alan was forced by his father to leave the country until things calmed down. It was his father's strong influence over the IRA Army Council that stopped them from punishing Alan by taking his life. Without Alan's father knowing it the main advocates for sending young Alan Foy to an early grave were the same people that gave him the orders to carry out the murders. A very good ploy, which made Alan's father believe that he had secured his son's safety through hard bargaining. Foy senior was a walking legend in the IRA, only forty-two years old and very fit, he was still very capable of active service for the Irish cause.

"Would you like a Tullamore Dew to warm your insides and celebrate your return?"

There is nothing like a good Irish whiskey, thought Alan. "It took you long enough to ask," he replied.

"Well, look at you two like children in the school playground," Maureen said as she walked into the room.

Maureen walking into the room startled Alan, as he did not expect anyone else to be there, causing him to instinctively reach for his Beretta in his jacket pocket.

"Easy, big brother," Peter said, putting his hand gently onto his brother's arm, "Put the table lamp on," he said to Maureen.

The light was bright due to the fact that there wasn't a shade on the lamp, which made Alan squint in order to see who was there. Maureen stepped away from the light, where Alan could focus on her.

"It can't be, Maureen Donnelly, is that you?"

"Yes it is, Alan, in the flesh."

"I hardly recognized you, give me a hug." The two briefly embraced and stood at arm's length, holding each other's hands, each looking the other up and down.

"You look marvelous," Alan said, "How is your father?" Alan was very fond that their fathers fought side by side for the IRA. It was said that between Maureen's father and Foy senior they could wreak more havoc than the rest of the IRA soldiers combined.

"He is doing well, still as grumpy as ever," she replied.

Shadow had a clear view of the inside of the apartment and could see Peter Foy and the girlfriend but could not tell who the male visitor was. He saw the visitor embrace the girlfriend and muttered quietly to himself, "You obviously know each other."

He watched as Peter Foy disappeared and returned with a glass, which he handed to the visitor. The man turned to take the glass from Foy, exposing his face to Shadow, he moved towards the window and closed the curtains. Shadow could not believe his eyes, "God almighty, Alan Foy," he said to himself. He could not believe it, one of the IRA's most ruthless soldiers wanted for many murders and bombings. Shadow moved quickly and quietly back to the observation vehicle.

Alan Foy had all of his radar sensors working, as he was never comfortable entering a place that he did not know, even though his brother was there. As he approached the window to close the curtain he thought he saw a movement outside in the alley, but he told himself that he was being paranoid. Alan closed the curtains and walked to the front door of the apartment to make sure that it was securely locked. He walked back into the lounge when he saw that Peter was about to close the window.

"Leave the window open, Peter, but keep the curtains closed, I like the fresh air coming in." He lied; he just wanted to be able to hear any noises outside, especially his beer bottles if anyone got caught in his trap.

"You are safe here," Peter said, "Nobody knows who I am."

"Sorry, little brother, old habits," Alan replied.

Maureen could see that they both had a lot of talking to do and lost time to make up, she excused herself and went to bed.

"Why are you here in England, isn't it dangerous for you?"

As always Peter was worried about his big brother, although he always seemed to be able to get out of any situation. Peter on the other hand had very little experience in getting into trouble, let alone being involved with the IRA. It was his father who, under pressure from his mother, had kept Peter out of the IRA. The thought of possibly losing one son as a result of his activity in the IRA was bad enough for their mother. To have both sons in the IRA was too much for her to bear. The Foys' mother knew that she could never get Alan to leave the IRA, as he was too much like his father.

Shadow got back to the surveillance vehicle where his partner was waiting.

"One, this is Four, over," Shadow said on the radio.

"Go ahead, Four, over," Strain replied.

"We need to meet, over," Shadow had some excitement in his voice.

"OK, take a walk to the park, leave Stan where he is, over," Strain replied.

The park was where vehicle two was located, with team members Jack Kay, known as L.B., short for Lover Boy because of his charm with the opposite sex, and Ian Thomas, nickname Baldy for obvious reasons.

"Bulldog, keep a close eye on things. I will be back in a minute." Strain left the vehicle and walked the two hundred yards to the rendezvous point.

Even though Shadow and Strain knew that vehicle two was only some forty yards away, neither of them acknowledged their presence. This was always the way things were done, as they never really knew if they were under surveillance themselves.

"What is it, Shadow?" Strain asked.

"You're not going to believe this," Shadow was still excited about who he had seen.

"Try me."

"The bloke I just followed that went into Foy's apartment, it's his brother Alan, Alan Foy."

Shadow was watching Strain to see his response, as he knew that this news was going to surprise him.

Strain acted surprised at the news Shadow had given him. "Well, Alan Foy, would you believe it, anyone with him?" Strain asked,

"No, he was alone, the bag he was carrying looked very heavy," replied Shadow.

"Thanks, Shadow, go back to your position and wait for my instructions," Strain was now ready to put the team out of their misery and raid Foy's bed-sit.

Unbeknown to Shadow, Strain was not in the least bit shocked or surprised, as he was the only one who knew that this was the real reason the team was keeping Peter Foy under surveillance. Strain had been waiting for the information from his informant for the last month. The surveillance operation was to keep the team believing that they had effected this result by performing long hours of surveillance and good work. Strain hated deceiving the team this way but it had to be done. This was about to be the biggest job they had pulled off since they had started Mask and he needed to protect his source of information. The capture of Alan Foy was not only going to be a devastating blow to Foy himself but also to the IRA, as he was about to be put back into active service. The mission he was to perform was known to only two members of the Army Council, this was obviously something major and Strain's informant knew it. Alan, as far as he knew, was being recalled back to Northern Ireland to be forgiven for his badly timed actions of the past. He wanted to receive the forgiveness of the Army Council and find out how he could once again serve the cause.

On the walk back to where he had left Bulldog he ran through the plan in his mind just like he had done a thousand times before. Two cars would park close to the apartment in the side street with all four team members going to the front door. This was to be Strain, Bulldog, Andy Hobson ('Screwdriver' was his nickname because of his lack of shape, he was just thin and straight up and down) Terry O'Neil (his nickname was 'Wheels' for his amazing driving skills). The other four team members would go to the rear on foot. Shadow, Stan, L.B. and Thomas. Each group was to leave one member to cover the front and rear of the property. The team members would access the apartment through the front door and cover the rear window, as the rear of the apartment did not have a door.

Strain reached the car with Bulldog eagerly waiting, "OK, Bulldog, we go in five minutes, put your vest on and get the tools out." The tools Strain referred to were a shotgun favored by Bulldog for opening reinforced doors and their Kevlar bulletproof vests. They also had a Sig. P226 9mm handgun, the preferred weapon of each member of the team.

Strain called up the other team members on the radio, "We go in five, you know the drill."

Each member of the team knew exactly what to do, they had gone through the drill at least a dozen times in practice and knew the exact layout of the apartment. All the team members busied themselves putting on their bulletproof vests and double-checking their weapons.

SEPTEMBER 22nd, SPAIN

In the Spanish Pyrenees the canvas-covered truck bounced along the old farm road leading up the mountain track, weaving its way around large boulders and holes in the road. The terrain and the hard wooden floor of the truck were giving the cargo inside a rough ride. The cargo was unusual, a group of four young men aged between eighteen and twenty-one years of age, all of whom were blindfolded sitting on the bed of the truck with their legs crossed. Standing at the back of the truck was a burly unshaven man in peasant clothes holding a shotgun under his right arm and hanging on to the metal canopy frame with the other. The truck eventually stopped outside a deserted farmhouse, three men got out of the front of the truck and walked around to the rear. The canvas flaps on the back of the truck were thrown back and the tailgate lowered. The burly man with the shotgun spat out an order to the young men sitting down, telling them to stand up. Each slowly managed to get to his feet as the two hours in the truck had reduced the circulation of blood in their legs, making it awkward to stand. Each was helped out of the truck and was escorted inside the farmhouse by the three men. Inside the farmhouse the four young men stood in silence, the damp smell of the dilapidated farmhouse creeping into their nostrils, the farmhouse door closed behind them with a loud bang, making a couple of them jump. Orti Ayo was particularly nervous as he thought they had discovered that he was working under cover for the police anti-terrorism squad. It took all of his self-control to stop himself from ripping the blindfold off and trying to escape.

A voice in their darkened world spoke to them, "Remove your blindfolds."

Each young man did as instructed and untied the blindfolds, revealing a light from two kerosene lamps in the room. As each of them adjusted their eyesight to the light in the room they could see that all of the windows were covered with old sacking and the door was closed, giving no view to the outside world, no clue as to where they were.

"Please sit down," the man at the front of the small room said. Without question they all sat on the floor.

One by one they started to recognize the face of the man addressing them, they had seen it on many wanted posters issued by the Spanish government, the great Velasco Basurto, one of the great Basurto brothers, a living legend in the Basque country of Northern Spain. He was nicknamed 'The Crow' by the Spanish police because his name Velasco can also mean 'Crow' in the Basque language. Each one looked at Velasco Basurto like they could not believe their eyes. He was not as tall as they had all been led to believe, but then not many legends are as tall or as big as they are made out to be. Standing around the room were four hardened Basque separatists, all with many years of experience fighting for the Basque cause. As they looked down on the young men in the room they could see fear and anticipation on their faces—the same look they must have had at their age.

Basurto continued, "You have been selected by the group of men in this room to perform a duty for your country. You may ask yourselves why you have been chosen? Because of your dedication to ETA through your actions in the 'Y' group some call the young ETA. The four of you have been instrumental in keeping the cause of ETA in the news over the last two years. Luis and Adame for your bombings of key political offices and government facilities. Mikeldi for your attacks on the tourist leaches that visit our home land and treat us as though we are peasants, holding their drunken orgies in our streets, and eroding away our culture. Finally, Orti, you have helped organize rallies and fund raising for our cause with amazing results. We are most grateful to all of you. We have had a great number of young ETA brothers arrested in the last year, why we do not know, the police have been very lucky."

Orti gave a silent sigh of relief, realizing that they did not suspect somebody was working on the inside.

"We have to train and educate the youth of our homeland so that they can someday take our place in leading the fight for the freedom of our country. There are talks of peace and a continuance of the cease-fire, but the police and government anti-terrorism squads still search for us in the hope to hunt us down like dogs. We have seen our own people demonstrate against us publicly in the streets when we have taken action against the political pawns of the fascist government. We will rise again and become a great nation with our own country, operated and controlled by Basques. This is our homeland, our ancestors have lived here since the beginning of mankind's recorded history, our native tongue is one of the oldest in the world, if not the oldest."

He paused as he paced the floor. He was in one of his political speech modes speaking in his native tongue Euskara, everyone kept quiet as he beat the drum of Euskal Herria, the Basque homeland. He had everyone's attention, even his hardened soldiers around the room. The Crow was preaching the gospel according to him and many Basque separatists before him. He was truly enjoying himself, realizing what a powerful effect he had on people, especially young believers like those in front of him.

He was correct in what he said about Basques occupying the northern regions of Spain and southern areas of France. Basques have lived in the Pyrenees area of Spain and southern France since lower Paleolithic times. The discoveries of some settlements in the region had provided priceless information about Basque history, the most significant dating back to the Magdalenian-Azilian Glaciation. Over 150,000 years of history and culture, with the present-day Basque population exceeding three million. Through their history the Basque people had maintained their identity and to a large degree their independence until 1936, when they took sides with the Republicans against Franco in the Spanish civil war.

It wasn't until 1968 that ETA ('*Euskadi Ta Askatasuna*', which stands for Basque Homeland and Freedom) became active as a true terrorist organization. Since that time they had been responsible for over 800 deaths, many attacks on political, government and business interests throughout Spain and southern France. Like most terrorist organizations they financed their operations by means of extortion and kidnapping. Money extortion from the business community was deemed to be a revolutionary tax by ETA.

"We will not stop our quest until our homeland is independent and that must include Navarre, a region that is truly Basque, the release of our brothers and sisters from Spanish prisons and the removal of the Civil Guard from our homeland. We have certain members of our organization that believe we should put down our weapons and pick up the fight through political means. This is going to lead to the downfall of our organization and the fight for our country."

By now the four young men on the floor and the loyal soldiers standing around the room listening had Basque loyalty and pride pumping through their veins. Velasco could see it in their eyes. Orti even felt like this man could lead them to victory, but he also felt that he was a little insane. He did not have a clue as to what the operation was going to be yet, but he knew that it was going to be huge. At the first opportunity he would pass the information on to his superiors and hopefully he would be a part of history by helping to capture the Great Crow.

"Each of you will be working with one of your brothers in this room. You will accompany him and do whatever he says without question. If any of you feels that he cannot do this then say so now and you will be taken back to where you were picked up today." Each one knew that it would mean certain death if they refused to cooperate. Nobody moved, they sat still and waited for whatever happened next.

"Good, I take it by your silence that you wish to move forward with your roles in the organization. You will all stay here tonight and in the morning you will be told who you will work with and what you are going to do." He paused for a moment, taking in the expressions on the faces of these young men looking up at him, remembering how he had been in their position when he was eighteen years of age, it seemed like it was only yesterday in some ways. Velasco walked past the group of young men and left the farmhouse, almost immediately they heard the engine of the truck outside burst into life, followed by the sound of it being driven away.

"Can we get some fresh air now?" requested Orti.

"You can in an hour when it is dark outside," replied one of the men. "There is water and food in the kitchen for those that are hungry."

Orti stood up and walked through a doorway in the corner of the room into another room, which housed the remains of a kitchen. He was hoping that he would be able to look through the kitchen window to try to see where they were. It would be a huge feather in his cap if he could report where this hideout was. The kitchen only had one small window and like the windows in the other room it was covered with sacking. On the floor by the window was a cardboard box with two large clay pots next to it, the pots obviously contained the water. He bent down to look in the box as if he was looking for food and glanced over his shoulder to see if anyone had followed him into the room, nobody had. He pulled the edge of the sacking from the window but before he could look out he heard the shuffle of shoes on the dusty floor behind him.

"Are you crazy? If they catch you looking out of the window they will kill you," whispered Mikeldi.

"I am sorry, but aren't you curious as to where we are?" replied Orti.

"Not at the risk of losing my life I am not." Mikeldi was sympathetic to his comrade's curiosity and thankfully put it down to just that, idle curiosity.

A voice called from the other room, "You two in there, bring the food and water in here." They obeyed and quickly returned to the other room, food and drink in hand.

"Have your fill and then get some sleep. You will need it, we will have an early start in the morning," one of the men said.

They all did as they were ordered and settled down on the floor for the night. Orti did not make any further requests to go outside.

3

SEPTEMBER 22nd, ENGLAND

Peter was curious as to what his brother had in his bag and Alan saved him the trouble of asking by opening it up, inside was a terrorists toy box. He took out two Heckler and Koch 9mm MP5Ks with full clips of ammunition.

"This is a bad little bastard, it will cut a person in half at close range," he took out two FN 9mm pistols and laid them on the carpet.

"Now these little beauties will blind and disorientate a man long enough for you to either kill him or escape." Alan held out two flashbangs, one in each hand. Peter had never seen these before and was truly amazed at how many weapons his brother had.

"Why have you got all of these weapons, you look like you are going to war," said Peter as he picked up one of the MP5Ks.

"Haven't you heard we are at war, with the British? I know you have never agreed with the way we operate in the IRA, but we have to try to stay one step ahead of the British and one weapon better. Unfortunately we have not really managed to get the full fire power we need to achieve our objective, a United Ireland," Alan replied with some sarcasm.

Peter had heard this same message from his father so many times that he had lost count. He always felt that his father's dark days in the 'H' block prisons in Northern Ireland put him off being involved with the IRA and their cause, so when his father told him he was not going to be involved in the IRA he was relieved.

At the time that his father was incarcerated in the 'H' block prison, it was always in the news with daily updates on prisoners who were on hunger strike. The one thing that really turned Peter's stomach was how the prisoners spread the walls of their cells and themselves with their own feces. He could not find it in his heart to be as strong as these men and felt ashamed for it.

"Listen up," Strain's voice came over the team's earpieces. "Everyone in position in two minutes, nobody enters until I give the go."

Each member in turn replied that they understood. All of the team was now wearing their combat-style pants, shirts and bulletproof vests in all black with the word Police in large white letters on the backs of the vests. On their heads they wore baseball-style caps with a black and white checkered band around and the word Police across the front. On the sleeves of the shirts they had similar checkered armbands, again with the word Police on them.

Strain and Bulldog approached the front of the bed-sit by going through several gardens and keeping close to the front of the building so as not to be seen. O'Neil and Hobson did the same kind of approach from the opposite direction. When all four team members were together Bulldog opened the lock on the front door with his lock pick. The four team members entered the dimly lit hallway, which led to the front doors of two ground floor bed-sits and the stairs going up to the first floor. All four had their weapons drawn, safety disengaged and held in the two-handed position with a flashlight held underneath ready to switch on if the lights went out. Bulldog was the first to make his way quietly and slowly up the stairs, closely followed by the rest of the team. Bulldog and Strain were continually looking up the stairs and scanning for any signs of movement. O'Neil and Hobson were doing the same but looking downstairs behind them. As they reached the top of the stairs Bulldog could see a faint light shining under the bottom of the door from inside Foy's bed-sit. Bulldog pointed out the light under the door to the other team members. As they reached the door Bulldog and Strain stood either side of it with O'Neil covering the stairs and Hobson the door of the other bed-sit and corridor. Although the light in the corridor was dim it was light enough for them to see what they needed to do. The low light was also an advantage when they entered the bed-sit, as their bodies would not show much of a silhouette. Strain waited a further minute, as he knew that the other team would require more time to get into position.

Bulldog saw the light under the door disappear and pointed it out to the other team members. They all instinctively held their flashlights ready alongside their weapons, ready to switch them on a split second before they entered the bed-sit.

Strain pressed the microphone button clipped onto his collar and whispered into the mouthpiece, "One in position." He waited for the reply from two.

At the rear of the building the other team members Shadow, Stan, L.B. and Thomas were making their slow, quiet approach, all weapons and flashlights ready the same as the front team. The six-foot brick walls of the alley giving them good cover until they reached the gate to the yard. Shadow looked up at the bed-sit window from his previous advantage point and indicated to Stan to proceed through the gate. As with Alan Foy the hinges on the gate did not squeak, the only difference was that they knew why, Shadow had oiled the hinges several times over the previous week. All four team members were now in the yard at the rear of the bed-sit with L.B. keeping his weapon trained on the window that the light was illuminating from inside. With the curtains closed and very little light source it was dark in the yard. Even though their eyes had adjusted it was still difficult to see. The three team members moved slowly up the stairs of the metal fire escape towards the open window. Stan was leading the way closely followed by Shadow and Thomas. In the darkness Stan did not see the two beer bottles that Alan Foy had placed on the stairs. As he lifted his foot up to the next step his boot caught the fishing line, causing both bottles to fall off the metal step. It sounded like a brass band playing to the other team members on the stairs as the two small bottles dropped onto the lower step. Everyone froze in the hope that nobody inside heard the noise. Stan and the others heard Strain in their earpieces saying that his team was in position. They dropped into a protective crouched position reducing their target size, their hearts pounding from the sudden noise of the bottles. They were all pointing their weapons at the window only eight feet above their heads, they stared at the light inside.

Peter was holding the MP5K when they heard the noise of bottles falling on the steps outside. Peter went to say something when Alan put his hand to his mouth, indicating to stay quiet. He pointed to the light in the corner and gestured to Peter to turn it off. Peter walked quietly over to the light still holding the MP5K—not that he would know how to use it—and turned the light off. As his brother went to turn the light off Alan picked up the two flash bangs and the second MP5K, knocking off the safety. Alan crouched down by the sofa next to the window and whispered to Peter to keep down. Alan looked outside through a small gap between the curtain and window frame. At first he could not see anything as his eyes were still used to the light in the room. Alan stared into the darkness looking at the fire escape outside straining his eyes to see if anyone was outside, there it was, a movement on the fire escape. He could see at least two men.

Maureen had just finished brushing her teeth and cleaning the make-up off her face in the bathroom. She always took pride in how she looked and was determined that she would continue to pamper herself and apply her favorite age-defying creams at night. She turned the light off in the bathroom and walked towards the bedroom, which was next to the front door, using the light from the lounge to light her way. As she approached the bedroom door the light went off in the lounge, leaving her in complete darkness. She called out loud in the darkness, "Peter what has happened to the lights?" Maureen suddenly felt scared, she never was fond of the dark.

Alan cursed as he heard Maureen shout to Peter, he had no choice now and pulled out the pin on one of the flash bangs and dropped it out of the window onto the fire escape. As he heard the flash bang roll on the metal stairway outside Alan covered his ears with his hands and pushed his face into a cushion on the sofa with his eyes closed. Although most of the disorientating impact of a flash bang exploding would be lost outside, as they were designed for use inside rooms, it would be enough to give Alan an advantage. He heard the flashbang go off outside and the subsequent screams of alarm from the intruders on the fire escape.

As Stan and his team waited in the darkness on the fire escape they saw the light in the bed-sit go out. Realizing that they may have been heard Stan gave the standby signal to the rest of the team. It was their job to cover the rear of the property but not to enter and stay out of the potential line of fire from inside the bed-sit. They all heard Maureen's voice call out in the darkness from within the bed-sit asking Peter what happened to the lights. None of the team members spoke, as they were too close to the window, and Stan could not announce to Strain that they were ready to go, although not quite in the desired position. They waited in the darkness as they heard something make a noise above them on the fire escape outside the window.

Strain and the rest of the team at the front door heard Maureen shout to Peter and immediately realized something was wrong. Two seconds later they heard the flash bang exploding.

Strain immediately shouted, "Go, Go, Go," through the microphone to all team members, he wasn't to know that the rear team could not hear him properly. No time for lock picks, Bulldog blasted the lock and steel reinforcement plate, surrounding it off the front door with the shotgun, Strain immediately kicked the door open.

Peter heard Maureen shouting him and went to the door of the lounge to tell her to keep quiet. As he got to the door of the lounge he heard a deafening sound behind him and a light filled the room for a split second. The blast behind him from the flash bang exploding made him stumble to his knees. As Peter was falling onto his knees he saw Maureen in the brief flash of light, she was standing close to the front door, her arms outstretched, as you would expect to see a person in the dark trying not to bump into things. Peter shook his head and still on his knees looked to where he had seen Maureen. He heard a loud bang and he saw the door spit out a huge flame, which lit up the room and disappeared into Maureen's stomach. Peter jumped to his feet, screaming out her name as the front door burst open.

Alan heard the flash bang go off outside and immediately lifted his face out of the cushion. As he brought his body upright from his bent kneeling position he was facing the lounge door. He heard the distinctive sound of a shotgun blast and saw the flash come through the front door and enter Maureen's body, knocking her backwards. Anger immediately swelled up inside him as the front door burst open, streams of light from the flashlights entered the room. The flashlights revealed the silhouette of a man in the doorway. Alan fired two short bursts from the MP5K in the direction of the front door, bullets peppering the door and walls.

As Strain kicked the door inwards he dropped to his left knee, pointing his weapon into the darkened room. He heard the sounds of Alan's weapon being fired and felt the bullets fly over his head as he was dropping to his kneeling position. Bulldog did not have time to react as two of the bullets fired by Alan hit him squarely in the chest, knocking him down. O'Neil and Hobson did not see Bulldog go down, as they were already entering the bed-sit either side of Strain. Both men fired two shots each into the lounge area of the bed-sit, giving themselves and Strain cover.

Peter stayed on the floor when heard the initial burst of gunfire from his brother's weapon, more out of shock than good sense. He did not stay there for more than a couple of seconds before he stood up to go to the aid of Maureen. As he stood he took a step towards Maureen's body, which was lying like a rag doll on the floor. He was hit in the throat by one of Hobson's bullets. Once it had entered his throat, the bullet traveled upwards deflected by his spinal column and exited out the base of his skull, taking the back of Peter's head with it, killing him instantly.

In the dim light Alan saw the back of his brother's head explode in front of him. He stood up screaming at the top of his voice with the MP5K in his right hand and his Beretta in the left. He pulled the trigger on the MP5K, emptying it in the direction of the front door. He had his left arm out of the window, firing the Beretta blindly in the direction of the fire escape. Strain and O'Neil had taken cover by the bedroom door and Hobson was stranded to the left of the lounge door with no real cover. Hobson lay flat on the floor in a prone position trying to make himself as small a target as possible when the bullets started to fly. Everyone inside and outside could hear Alan's screaming rage and weapons firing. The bullets were tearing up the walls and door in the bed-sit, some exiting the building completely. Strain and O'Neil lay flat on the floor, covering their heads from the rain of bullets.

The rear team was not enjoying Foy's anger either, as bullets ricocheted around them off the metal fire escape. One of the ricocheting bullets found its target hitting L.B. in the left shoulder, missing any bones but leaving a large exit hole in his back. He collapsed to the floor. Stan, Shadow and Thomas kept their heads down waiting for the opportunity to return fire.

Alan pulled the pin on the second flashbang and climbed through the open window, throwing the flashbang back inside. Stan and Shadow both saw Foy climb through the window, both officers shone their flashlights on Foy.

Stan shouted, "Stay where you are, Foy." He ignored the order from Stan and turned towards them as the flashbang exploded inside the bed-sit. They saw Foy pointing the Beretta at them and started to fire at him using the light of their flashlights to see him clearly.

Foy was hit twice, the first bullet went through his right hand, destroying the Beretta it was holding. The second bullet tore into his right hip, smashing into the bone and knocking him down.

Stan and Shadow ran up the few steps covering Foy with their weapons. They could see that he was holding his right wrist supporting the destroyed right hand with his left. Stan told Shadow to cover him.

As he got next to Foy he said, "Roll onto your stomach and put your hands behind your back."

Surprisingly Foy started to do as he was instructed when he pulled a knife from his right sleeve, plunging the six-inch blade into Stan's stomach. Shadow did not hesitate and immediately fired two shots into Foy's upper body from less than four feet. The bullets smashed through his right side and rib cage, one puncturing both lungs, the other went into his heart. Foy rolled onto his back, the life now gone from his body.

Shadow shouted to Thomas, who was below him on the fire escape, "Are you OK?"

"Yes, I am going to check L.B. and call for an ambulance," he replied.

"Hold on, Stan we will have an ambulance and a beer here before you know it," Shadow said.

Stan still had the knife buried in his stomach and was holding on to it, but he did not hear Shadow as he had already passed out. Shadow checked for Stan's vital signs, he still had a good pulse.

Inside the bed-sit Strain, Hobson and O'Neil did not expect the flashbang, and when it exploded it did exactly what it was supposed to do. All three of them were temporarily blinded and completely disoriented by the explosion. The ringing in their ears did not help but they could still hear weapons fire, where it was coming from they could not be sure. In the smoke and dust cloud inside the bed-sit they tried to shake off the effects of the flashbang without much success.

Strain fumbled for the microphone and spoke into it, "Two, this is One, what's happening out there?" Strain could not believe the effect the flashbang had on him.

Shadow replied, "Foy's dead, he stabbed Stan in the stomach, L.B. has been shot, but we are clear here."

Strain replied, "We need you to help us to be sure we are clear inside. We can't tell yet as we are still shaken up by the flashbang."

"Roger, I am coming in through the window," he replied.

Strain sat on the floor with his back to the wall in total disbelief how the operation had turned out. As he looked up he saw Bulldog in a similar seated position in the corridor with his back against the wall, his head drooped forward with his chin resting on his chest.

Shadow cautiously climbed through the window sweeping the room with his eyes and weapon as he walked through. His flashlight was like a beacon in the darkened room. No sense in being dumb at this stage, he told himself. He saw Peter Foy's body on the floor by the door of the lounge. Shadow moved slowly towards the body, still keeping as quiet as possible, checking and double-checking the room as he went. He bent down over the body to check the neck for a pulse, he soon realized that Foy was dead as he could see the back of his head was missing. As he moved into the hallway by the front door he could not believe the devastation.

Strain had managed to get himself to his feet, as had O'Neil. Hobson was still trying to recover his senses and was sitting on the floor. He could feel a wetness in his shirt and on his legs. He looked at his hand as he took it away from his shirt and saw that it was covered in blood. Panic showed in his eyes as he thought that he had been shot. His hands frantically probed around his body and legs, searching his blood-soaked clothing. "No pain, no wounds, where has the blood come from?" he said to himself. His question was quickly answered when he saw that he had been lying on the floor next to Maureen's body, it was her blood.

Shadow came out of the lounge and saw Maureen's body on the floor and Hobson sitting against the wall. O'Neil was on his feet and went into the bathroom to make sure that nobody was in there. "Clear in here," he shouted to Shadow.

Strain was now on his feet, and recovering fast, he looked into the hallway, Bulldog still hadn't moved. "You OK, Bulldog?" Strain inquired as he walked towards him, then he saw the two bullet holes in the chest of Bulldog's clothing.

"Bulldog's been hit," he shouted to the other team members. Shadow and O'Neil came running into the hallway to check on Bulldog.

"Help me get his vest off," Strain said, fear in his voice for he felt sure that his good friend and partner was dead.

Shadow put his hand on Bulldog's neck to check for a pulse when Bulldog's body seemed to burst into life. Bulldog started coughing and shouting, throwing his arms around attempting to get up, unsure what was going on. Strain and Shadow held on to his arms, telling him everything was OK.

"Take it easy, it's only us," said Strain.

"What happened?" Bulldog said.

"We need to take your vest off, you took two rounds in the chest," said Strain.

Bulldog sat still, trying to take in what he had just been told. He looked at his chest and could clearly see the two entry holes in his vest. They carefully removed the bulletproof vest from around Bulldog's upper body, and as they did they could see that the bullets were lodged inside the vest. "You are one lucky bastard," said Shadow as they all looked in disbelief.

"It will take more than a couple of bullets to kill that crazy shit," Hobson said as he walked into the hallway.

"Nice of you to finally join us, Hobson," said Strain.

"Fuck you, boss, with respect," he replied.

Pain surged through Bulldog's chest as he laughed, the bullets may not have gone through the vest but his chest hurt like hell.

They could hear the sounds of sirens in the distance and their thoughts returned to their wounded colleagues and the clean-up job ahead.

"Shadow, secure all the weapons in here. I don't want some nosey rookie cop picking one up and blowing his head off. Hobson, help Bulldog down the stairs to the front and brief the locals before they all come barging in here. Make sure Bulldog is taken care of and send the paramedics around the back."

Strain quickly walked through the apartment towards the window, stepping over young Peter's body. As he climbed through the window he could see Alan Foy's body in the light of one of the flashlights lying on the fire escape.

"What a fine mess you have made," he said to the corpse.

Stan was now groaning and lapsing in and out of consciousness, his hand still on the knife. Strain bent down to look at him and stroked his face, telling him everything was going to be OK.

He called out to the remaining team members on the ground, "L.B., Thomas, you two OK down there?"

Thomas replied, "L.B. has taken a bullet but he will be OK. How is everyone inside?"

"Everyone's fine, Bulldog gave us a scare but he is as ugly as ever. How is L.B., he isn't serious I hope?"

"No problems, just a scratch," said L.B.

The ambulances arrived by the dozen, or that's how it seemed to the team members, paramedics crawling all over the place. The first uniformed police officers arrived on the scene a few minutes after the ambulances. At first most of them just walked around with their mouths open, unable to believe what they were looking at, one officer took a look at Maureen's body and ran outside, leaving the contents of his stomach in the front garden. An inspector arrived and started to take immediate control of the police operation, directing officers around like a conductor. He walked into the bed-sit and saw Strain coming out of the lounge. "Who are you?" he inquired.

"Detective Inspector Strain, special operations unit. Call this number and they will tell you what you need to know. I am going to check on my men to make sure that they are taken to the hospital immediately," he replied.

"You are not going anywhere until I know what has happened here." He turned to the young officer in the doorway and said, "Constable, nobody leaves this property until I say so."

The poor constable did not know what to say, as this was his first night on duty, a true rookie.

The inspector continued with his power kick, looking down his nose at Strain, he said, "We have dead bodies on the floor and I haven't seen any kind of identification from any of the living around here, so where is your ID, Detective Inspector?"

The condescending tone and the way the inspector looked at him did not go down well with Strain; however, he kept calm for the moment.

"Just call that number and they will answer all of your questions. This is a covert group and that is all that I am willing to discuss with you at this time." Strain was really feeling tired now as the adrenaline started to slow down in his body. All he wanted to do was to check that his team were all taken care of and know which hospital they would be going to. As soon as he knew which hospital was going to treat them he would arrange for the security to be upgraded. Protection and medical assistance for the team was now his main priority and this inspector was not helping in that direction. "Inspector, with respect, my men and myself have just gone through a pretty rough experience. I would appreciate it if you would give that a little consideration and call the telephone number that I have given you. I can assure you that you will be satisfied with what they tell you." Strain walked past the inspector towards the door to leave when the inspector caught hold of Strain's arm and stopped him.

"I told you that you were not going to leave until I saw some ID and that goes for you and your men." The inspector was really starting to enjoy his position, thinking that he was intimidating this so-called detective inspector.

Strain pulled his arm free of the inspector's grip; ignoring him, he continued to walk. The inspector was incensed and embarrassed as the young officer was watching everything that had happened. "Officer, stop that man and arrest him," he said.

The rookie was not only totally confused but also terrified at the thought of having to arrest this man in black carrying a weapon. "He is a police officer, sir," he replied.

Strain could see the fear in the rookie's eyes and was about to tell him to move out of the way when the inspector once again got hold of his arm. Strain snatched his arm free and spun around, in one move wrapping his arm around the inspector's. Strain lifted the inspector's arm harshly against the elbow, holding the arm in a locked position. He grabbed the inspector with his right hand by the throat and slammed him against the open front door. The inspector held Strain's right wrist with both hands, trying to relieve the pressure on his windpipe. As he started to choke his startled eyes looked directly at Strain, realizing that this man was going to seriously harm him, he gave a gentle nod of his head. Strain released his grip, his victim immediately gripping his own throat as he gasped for air, Strain walked towards the door. The rookie was still standing in his original place, totally lost as to what to do.

Strain helped him with his dilemma and said, "Get your boss a cup of cold water." Strain looked back at the inspector, who was bent over, still clutching his throat, coughing, trying to clear his breathing passage. "Call the number," Strain said and walked out.

Strain sat in his car and called the telephone number he had given the inspector. The telephone only rang twice when the voice simply said, "Hello."

"Call me on the mobile number." That is all he said and the person answering the phone hung up.

One minute passed and Strain's mobile phone rang, he answered, "Hello."

"You are clear to speak," the voice at the other end said. This meant that the encryption device was activated. Even with the device activated they never said very much and always talked in riddles. Even with encryption you did not know who was listening.

"The party was not a surprise, he had his own gifts for everyone. We have three feeling the worse for the party, none that won't be able to party again. The others partied too much and won't be able to join us next time," he replied. "We are getting some interference from the local police, they are obviously asking a lot of questions."

"I will take care of the locals, call me when you are on a land line." The telephone went dead.

Strain returned to the bed-sit to see the inspector talking to two men in plain clothes, obviously detectives, he thought to himself. He saw the inspector pointing at him, the anger still showing in his face. The two plain-clothes men walked towards him.

"I am Detective Sergeant Powers and this is Detective Constable Sumner of the Regional Crime Squad, you are?" The detective sergeant, sounding his most authoritative, knew that he had more chance of finding out who he was dealing with by catching him off guard. At present this man dressed in all black with the obvious 'Police' markings was an unknown quantity and he did not like that. He was in Powers' district and nobody told him to expect an armed operation to take place.

"I am John Strain. You can call this number and they will answer your questions, until then I will not be discussing anything with you." He handed Powers a white business card with a London telephone number on it, the kind of card that he passed to the unfortunate inspector. "I am not being deliberately awkward, you have to realize that this is a covert unit." He could see that Powers did not like his explanation, but what could he do about it?

Powers handed the card to Sumner and said, "Call that number find out who this John Strain is and I want to know who answers the phone."

The detective walked towards where he had left their car without saying a word. He knew that it was a waste of time to offer any of his advice, as Powers would have bitten his head off and told him to do what he was told. Powers was not known for his patience or subtlety when things were not going the way he liked and this was definitely not going his way. Who did this Strain person think he was to tell him to make a phone call and refuse to answer any questions?

Strain started to walk towards one of the ambulances as he could see Bulldog sitting by the rear doors being attended to by a paramedic.

"Where do you think you are going?" said Powers. Strain ignored him and continued towards the ambulance. Powers knew that he would be wasting his time trying to stop Strain, so he just followed him.

"Is this one of your men?" the sergeant inquired.

"Yes," replied Strain.

"What is your name, Officer?" the sergeant asked.

Bulldog looked up at him and said, "Ask the boss," nodding in Strain's direction.

"I don't suppose you will tell me, will you?"said the sergeant to Strain.

"That's right," he replied. "How are you feeling?" he said to Bulldog.

"I'm OK, just a little pain when I move," he replied.

"How are the others?"

"They will be fine, a few weeks off work maybe." Strain felt like he could do with a few weeks off work.

"Where are the rest of your men?" asked the sergeant.

"Stay away from them until I say so." Strain was in no mood to deal with the sergeant.

A voice called out to Powers, "Boss, it's headquarters, they want to talk to you."

Powers walked to the car and took the radio handset from the detective. "Powers, over." He was really starting to get frustrated with this now and it showed in his face.

The detective stood at the front of the car to try to keep out of his sergeant's way but still within earshot of what was being said on the radio.

"Contact headquarters on a telephone immediately, Sergeant," said the voice over the radio.

"Now we will sort these bastards out. Give me the mobile phone," he said to the detective constable. He dialed the number to headquarters.

Strain and Bulldog were watching the sergeant on the mobile phone. "He is about to get some bad news and he thinks that he was pissed off before," Strain said.

They could not hear what he was saying, but the more the sergeant shouted down the telephone the more he got animated. The sergeant threw the telephone inside the car and walked back towards Strain and Bulldog with renewed aggression in his step.

"Oh dear, he does look upset," said Bulldog.

"You think so?" said Strain. Both men smiling to each other.

The sergeant was definitely not amused and let Strain know. "You smart bastards have not seen or heard the last of me. We will meet again on my terms," he said.

"I look forward to the reunion," Strain replied.

As the sergeant walked away Bulldog could not hold back, he had to say something. "Enjoy making your report, Sergeant." Bulldog knew that the report was going to take a considerable amount of the sergeant's time over the next few days, and all policemen hated making reports.

"Fuck off," he replied.

The paramedic got out of the rear of the ambulance and told Bulldog that they were ready to leave for the hospital.

"I will see you over there," said Strain.

On the way to the hospital Strain stopped to call his contact in London. After a very short conversation he was told to be in London that morning at 11.00am at the Prime Minister's office. It was 4.00 am before Strain left the hospital, and two hours later he was climbing into bed in his hotel in London. Strain lay in the bed looking up at the ceiling, trying to piece together the events of the previous night. The biggest question he kept asking himself was —Why was Foy so heavily armed? Was he expecting them?—Before he knew it he was fast asleep, the trauma of the incident and the previous twenty hours without sleep taking their toll on his body.

SEPTEMBER 23rd, SPAIN

The night was long for the four young men, none of them sleeping very much, the snoring of the older men keeping them awake as much as their anticipation of what the days ahead were to bring. It was six thirty in the morning when they heard the distant noise of a vehicle approaching the farmhouse. Orti was asleep and was totally disoriented when he was woken up by Mikeldi.

"Someone is coming," Mikeldi whispered to Orti.

It took him a minute to remember where he was but not long to see that one of the men was missing. The three remaining men were stretching and groaning as they tried to wake themselves, not an easy task after sleeping on the farmhouse floor. One of the men opened the door and walked outside followed by his two compatriots. It was still very dark outside, a blanket of thick cloud covered the mountain slopes, bringing a cold chill into the farmhouse. Though the blast of mountain air was cold as it rolled into the room the young men welcomed it. Spending the night in a small room with so many men created a very stale environment, not to mention the body odor which two of the men omitted freely. The vehicle was getting very close to the farmhouse and Orti recognized the engine noise as being the same vehicle that had brought them to the farmhouse the previous day. The vehicle stopped and they could hear the door of the vehicle open and close again. Outside the four men knew the driver, Ester Perea, a striking twenty eight-year-old raven-haired woman. Ester had served with ETA since she was fifteen years old, she was put on Spain's most wanted list at the age of nineteen. She was a devout soldier of ETA and girlfriend of Velasco, her love for him was her one and only weakness.

"The mountain is covered in thick cloud all the way down to the valley, light a fire and I will heat the paella I brought with me."

This part of Ester nobody could figure out. Here was a woman who would kill and had killed without a second thought, stand up to any man and fight him until her last breath, but loved to cook and clean up after the men around her. Strange or just the mother coming out in her, who knows? Either way, nobody questioned her about it.

"Keep the others inside for a little longer. I have instructions about our attack from Velasco," she said.

"I will take care of it," said Eneto Urizabal.

Eneto did not like Ester and the less time he had to spend around her the better. His feelings towards women in general were very chauvinistic, their place was in the kitchen or producing children, taking care of a man's needs. Everyone knew his feelings towards Ester, and it always made for a very tense atmosphere when they were around each other. Eneto had another reason to hate Ester, as she was the one who had given him the five-inch scar across the left side of his face. It happened six years previously, they were hiding in the mountains from the police after they had shot and killed a local police chief and politician. They had been there for several days when one night Eneto drank very heavily and tried to have sex with Ester. She put up a hell of a fight during which she pulled out a knife and slashed his face. Eneto was devastated by the cut which ruined his stunning good looks, used so often to charm women into bed. Now his face repelled women. The scar was particularly ugly, due to the fact that they had to field-dress the wound in the mountain hideout and it had gotten infected. It was almost a week before Eneto was seen by a doctor, by which time the infection had spread, eventually leaving a gruesome scar. Eneto swore that he would repay her for what she had done to him, in turn Velasco threatened to kill him if he touched her again.

Eneto was always in a foul mood when she was around and he took it out on whomever he could, this time it would be Mikeldi. He entered the farmhouse to find the four men moving around trying to stay warm, "Stay in here until I tell you to come out," he said.

This is when Mikeldi spoke at the wrong time, "It is dark outside, we cannot see anything, we need to get some fresh air and get away from the stink of the body odor in here."

"You will do as I tell you," Eneto said, stepping forward he slapped Mikeldi across the face.

Mikeldi felt the anger surge through his body, the many years of physical abuse by his father seen in this slap across the face. Mikeldi lunged at Eneto, grabbing him by the throat, screaming at him, "Don't ever hit me."

Both men fell to the floor exchanging blows with their fists as they fell, Orti jumped in to try and separate them. The door of the farmhouse burst open, the other three men and Ester came running in to see what was happening. Orti received a kick in the face from Eneto as he tried to pull Mikeldi off him, knocking him backwards onto the floor.

Ester was now shouting at them, "Eneto, stop, stop."

Esteban lifted Mikeldi off Eneto and threw him to one side of the room like he was a rag doll. Undeterred, Mikeldi was immediately up on his feet again, making a beeline for Eneto, but Orti threw both of his arms around his waist, pulling him down to the floor. Orti hung on to Mikeldi for dear life as he thrashed about trying to knock Orti off him, at the same time trying to scramble to his feet to attack Eneto again. The end of a double-barreled shotgun appeared in Mikeldi's face, pushing him to the ground. Both Mikeldi and Orti froze at the sight of the weapon, they lay on the cold floor, both panting and sweating from the exertion. Neither said anything, they just stared at the barrels of the shotgun facing them.

"What is going on in here?" Ester shouted at Eneto.

"Get out of my way," he said as he barged past her and the other men as he stormed outside.

"Well, you tell me what happened?" she said to Mikeldi.

He was still trying to find his breath and answered her question as he gasped for air. "He hit me and I won't let anyone hit me." The rage was still showing in his eyes.

"Why did he hit you?"

"I don't know, you ask him." Mikeldi was in no mood to talk, he was still incredibly angry and at this point was not scared of anyone or anything.

Orti spoke as usual without being asked, "Mikeldi asked if we could get some fresh air because of the stench in here and he received a slap across the face for it."

"Stay in here, Geraldo, you stay with them." Geraldo nodded his head and moved the shotgun away from their faces and cradled it in his arms like you would a baby.

Ester and the other men knew exactly what happened. Eneto had lost his temper again because of her presence and took it out on Mikeldi. Ester was about to give Eneto a piece of her tongue when she realized that it might only inflame the situation. She asked Geraldo to have a word with him and try to calm him down. The last thing she wanted right now was for the mission ahead to be jeopardized because of some senseless fighting amongst themselves. She still had to brief everybody on the mission, Velasco had entrusted this task to her along with organizing the logistics. Eneto obviously knew that she was to lead the operation and this was not helping the situation, he believed that he should be in charge as he was the oldest and most experienced ETA member. In his mind she was only in charge because of her relationship with Velasco, which was not entirely true, as the woman was deadly and had a reputation to match. She decided to give it half an hour before she briefed everybody, by which time they would all have eaten and hopefully calmed down. She had to rethink the pairings for the mission as originally Mikeldi and Eneto were to be working together.

The heat from the fire was welcomed by all, especially the young men in the farmhouse who were now outside enjoying the fresh air and food that Ester had prepared. Mikeldi was still full of anger and it would not take much for him to attack Eneto again, Ester could see why he had been recruited for the 'Y' group, as he had no fear. Eneto did not join the group to eat, choosing to sit by himself on the tailgate of the truck. She was standing on the opposite side of the fire to the group of young men, the silhouette of her body showing through the flames. The young men watched as the flames appeared to dance around her body.

She looked across at the four of them and said, "You will have to go back inside for a few minutes while I talk to the others."

They reluctantly left the warmth of the fire and slowly made their way back inside the farmhouse, closing the door behind them.

"Geraldo, ask Eneto to join us we need to discuss the mission."

Geraldo walked over to the truck as Ester watched him. She saw him sit down on the tailgate with Eneto and engage him in conversation, she knew that Geraldo was the only one that Eneto would respond to at the moment. She sat on a large boulder, which was warm from the heat of the fire, waiting patiently for Geraldo to work some magic with Eneto.

She did not have to wait long before Geraldo returned. He bent down and picked up a small piece of a tree branch that was fueling the fire, with the burning end of the branch he lit a cigarette. He threw the branch back into the flames.

Without looking at Ester he said, "He will be with us in a few minutes. I think it would be best if he rides in the front of the truck on the way down to Logroño, I will take your place driving, you will have to ride in the back. You know what he is like; when he gets like this there is no reasoning with him. By the time we are ready to leave he will be completely focused. I assume that you will be putting someone else with Eneto?"

"I have been thinking about it since the fight. You take Mikeldi I will switch to Orti, Eneto can go with Luis, and Peli can take Adame."

She felt that she was doing the right thing changing everyone around, she knew that Geraldo would soon tell her if she was wrong. "Do you see any problems with the changes?" she asked. She respected Geraldo's opinion as much as Velasco or Albi Basurto, as he was always calm and calculating, forever trying to think one step ahead. She watched his face as his lips drew on the cigarette. He exhaled the smoke through his nostrils, one jet of smoke from each nostril, making him look like a snorting bull ready to charge.

Geraldo thought for a moment before he replied, conscious that Ester was acting under Velasco's instructions. His many years serving ETA had taught him to be patient and always think things through.

"I do not want you to take what I am about to say the wrong way, but are you sure you want to take Orti, considering what has to be done? He is very strong and may prove to be a challenge even for the strongest amongst us." He did not think that she would be able to handle Orti if things got out of hand, he truly was as strong as an ox and no woman could match his strength.

"I hear what you are saying and I appreciate that you did not insult me believing that I could not carry out the task because I am a woman. I will change the plan slightly because of what has happened. Orti will not suspect anything, especially as he will be with me, he will think that the mission is straightforward. We will wake him up at three in the morning and put him on guard by the camp fire. The others can do two hours each so that he does not suspect anything, this will not give him the opportunity to have a sleep before we leave tomorrow morning. When we get to the bar we will order our drinks as planned, I will tell him to go to the toilet and check that the backdoor is not locked, but to do it quickly, this way he will not have time to make any telephone calls. When he goes to the toilet I will put a strong sleeping powder in his drink, I will give him time to drink all of it. I will then tell him that I am going to the toilet and he is to follow me, I will take him inside the ladies with me. We will go into one of the stalls, where we cannot be seen. By this time a combination of tiredness and the powder will be making him feel weak, the rest you do not need to know, any questions?" She knew that Geraldo would not ask any questions.

"I am glad that I am on the same side as you." He smiled at her, his face lighting up from the glow of the fire.

"Gather everyone around, it is time to discuss their roles in the mission," she said.

4

SEPTEMBER 23RD, NORTHERN IRELAND

Alan Foy Sr. was sitting in his home in Belfast eating his breakfast, which his wife Linda had prepared for him. He always enjoyed this time of the day with his wife as it was so far removed from what he had become used to during his years of incarceration in the prisons of Northern Ireland. He and his wife sat in silence on the sofa with the breakfast trays on their laps watching the start of the early morning BBC news on television.

The newscaster had finished his normal boring introduction of who he was and which channel you were watching. He started his newscast saying, "Police in Birmingham are investigating an incident which took place last night in the Bullring area of the city in which three people died and three police officers were injured. Kevin Harper is our reporter in Birmingham."

The television picture changed to show a reporter standing by a police car next to a row of houses. In the background you could see several policemen in uniform standing around talking. As always whenever there is a police investigation, there were nosey members of the public trying to catch a glimpse of something as they stood next to the cordoned-off scene. The reporter began to speak to the camera, "Police here at the scene of the incident are describing this as a shootout between a Special Armed Police Unit and suspect IRA terrorists." The camera zoomed in towards one-three story building, which had obviously been cordoned off due to the presence of the yellow crime scene ribbon. Two uniformed police officers stood outside the building in their normal television at ease stance, trying to look very official. The reporter continued, "Armed police entered this building at 22, Crescent Avenue a little past midnight last night to arrest an IRA suspect. As they entered the first floor apartment they were met by resistance and a shootout took place between the police and the suspects. It is not clear yet as to the conditions of the police officers involved but three people, two men and a woman, are believed to have been killed in the exchange of fire with police."

Alan's wife jumped up, tipping the tray of food onto the floor, both hands went straight to her face, holding her head in disbelief. They both immediately recognized the address that the reporter had given as the one where their son lived. He put his tray to one side, stood up and put his arm around her shoulder. "Come on, sit down."

She immediately turned on him screaming at him hysterically, "It's all your fault, you should not have gotten them into this bloodshed, they have killed my boys." She began beating him mercilessly about the chest and head, sobbing uncontrollably. Alan pulled her close to him, putting his arms around her in an attempt to control her, she fought him off and ran out of the room. Alan was still staring at the lounge door as he heard his wife run up the stairs. It took several minutes for him to compose himself, at which time he walked to his next door neighbor's house and knocked on the door.

Jean, their neighbor, answered the door, one look at Alan's face told her that there was a problem. "Jean, I need you to sit with Linda, she—"

Jean cut him off in mid sentence. "Alan, tell me that wasn't one of the boys on the news in Birmingham?"

"I don't know, but it doesn't look good," he replied.

Her eyes welled up with tears at what he said. Foy saw her getting upset and said, "Jean, I need some help here, I cannot have you going in to her upset as well." Alan knew that this would compose her. "I will be gone for a short time I need to find out if it is the boys."

Jean thought that he looked pitiful for the first time in the twenty-five years that she had known him. She knew exactly what to do as she had lost her husband, father and a brother to the troubles over the years. Something that she had never really forgiven the police, British soldiers or the IRA for, they were all at fault in her mind. Although Jean blamed the IRA the most for the death of her husband, because they had talked her husband into learning about bomb making, she would never say anything in public. Anyone who publicly went against the IRA was shunned by friends and neighbors or, depending on the severity of the situation, the individual would be punished. Jean was not that stupid to criticize the IRA publicly, she was still a loyal supporter in the eyes of everyone around her.

"Go, leave her to me." She pushed past Alan and took the half a dozen steps to his house.

Alan walked towards the telephone box at the corner of the street, only to find that it had been vandalized. He stood by the telephone for a moment cursing the youth of today for destroying it when he heard his name called.

"Alan, Alan," the voice came from behind him.

He turned to see Stephen Fagan, a good friend and long-time member of the IRA standing in the doorway of his house. Fagan called Alan over to him, he walked across the street knowing that Fagan had most probably watched the news.

"Alan, come into the house," Fagan said.

"I need to make a couple of phone calls, I will see you later," he replied.

Alan Foy was still in control of himself, but realized that it wasn't going to take much for him to break down if the news was about his sons.

"Get in here." Fagan pulled him by the arm into his home. "Is it Peter or Alan they are talking about in the news?" he asked.

"I don't know, but it is Peter's address and I need to find out quickly."

Alan was about to walk out when Fagan said, "You are not going to find a public telephone working that you can use this side of the Antrim Road, use mine, you need to find out if your sons are safe." Alan didn't really care at this point, he just needed to know if his boys were OK and return to his wife.

He was reluctant to use his friends' telephone as he was going to call the London number of his contact. He was desperate to know about his sons and agreed. Fagan told him to wait in the hallway for a moment while he got rid of the children. A minute later he returned after chasing the children out of the lounge into the kitchen. Fagan showed Alan into the lounge and closed the door behind him, leaving him alone in the room.

Alan picked up the telephone and dialed the London number. The telephone only rang twice when a male voice answered, "Hello."

"It's me," Alan replied.

"I knew that was you on my private line, I've been expecting your call. You have obviously been watching the news, this little incident could bring problems."

The man is still as arrogant as ever and never even mentioned my sons, Alan thought. "Was it them on the news this morning?" Alan could feel his pulse increase, realizing that he was about to hear what he already knew in his heart.

"Yes, it was." The man was not quite so arrogant as he confirmed to his hardened IRA contact that his only children were dead.

"What happened?" Alan said.

The man was now becoming nervous as he knew that Foy was either about to explode or he was going to scare him to death with that cold calmness of his.

"I don't have the full story yet," he replied.

"Don't mess me about, tell me exactly what happened to them. I am not going to waste any time with you on this telephone, but believe me I will come to England to find out the truth from you if I have to." Alan could almost hear his contact choking on the on the other end of the telephone, he waited for a reply.

"There is no need for you to threaten me, you know we cannot meet here. You know our agreement, you do not come to London." He was starting to get angry with Alan for suggesting that he would visit him. *How dare he threaten me,* he thought to himself.

Alan calmly made his request again "Tell me what happened and you will not see me at your home."

The contact was now so angry that he was losing his normal cowardice. He hated dealing with Foy, especially when it was not going his way. He lost control of himself and through fear or anger screamed down the telephone at Foy, "How dare you threaten me? If you come to the mainland, to my home, I will have you put in prison for the rest of your life."

Foy was a little taken aback by the sudden outburst but not surprised as fear came in many different ways. He didn't say anything; he remained quiet, waiting for the man to realize what he had just said.

"Are you there? Talk to me, damn you." Foy was correct, he was starting to realize the consequences of what he had said. "Hello, hello, talk to me, you bastard."

The contact continued to shout down the telephone. Foy could feel the panic in his contact and hung up the telephone, he would leave for London the following day, as it was too soon to leave his wife.

SEPTEMBER 23RD, ENGLAND

The man at the other end of the telephone in London was Adrian Bowles, the British Home Secretary. He realized that he had lost his temper as he heard the line disconnect. He knew that Alan meant what he said and was very aware of Foy's past history of carrying out punishments on behalf of the IRA and reputation for fulfilling his promises. He tried to convince himself that Foy would call back, and when he did he would apologize to him for his outburst. Yes, that was the thing to do, apologize and state that he was as horrified and disturbed to hear the news as Foy. The more he talked to himself the more self-assured he became.

He walked over to the filing cabinet in his office where he kept his private supply of Cognac and poured a large drink into a crystal glass. His hand was visibly shaking and he had no control over it, it was as though it had a mind of its own. Walking back to his desk the telephone rang, startling him, causing him to spill some of the Cognac down the front of his jacket. "Blast," he cursed out loud, immediately pulling a cotton handkerchief out of his jacket pocket. As he walked to his desk he wiped the Cognac from his pin-striped suit jacket.

His secretary spoke over the intercom, "Sir, the Prime Minister is on the secure line for you," she paused, waiting for his reply.

He started to talk to himself again, "The PM, what next? He is not going to be very happy about this." He took a couple of deep breaths, trying to calm himself. He leaned over the front of the desk and pressed the reply button on the intercom, "Put him through, would you," he replied.

"Yes, sir," she said.

He walked around his desk to answer the call from the Prime Minister. Still with the glass of Cognac in his hand he sat in his high-backed leather chair as the telephone rang again. He swallowed the contents of the glass in one swift gulp. Picking up the receiver, trying to sound cheery, he said, "Prime Minister, how are you this fine morning?"

The reply was very sharp and business like, "We have nothing to sound cheerful about this morning, have we?" The PM had obviously heard about the incident with the Mask Team. "That bloody operation last night went totally wrong, what happened?" he said.

"I haven't received a full report yet, sir. I expect to hear something within the hour." He almost wished that the caller was Foy, as he was less scared of him than he was of the PM.

"Tell me what you know then." The PM's patience on the matter was very short. His pet security operation had suddenly turned sour. After all the successful operations this, the most important, had gone wrong, why? The opposition party would have a field day if they knew about his involvement with these operations. The questions in the house could be easily answered with the usual, 'It is a matter of National security,' not that this would stop the bloodhounds. The press would pursue it with their normal aggression, as would the rest of the media.

"Apparently the Mask Team received reliable information that Alan Foy was going to visit his brother Peter in Birmingham. They had Peter and his girlfriend under surveillance for a number of weeks, hoping to see Alan Foy. They went to Peter Foy's address in Birmingham last night to continue their observations when they saw Alan Foy. The decision was made by Strain to enter the apartment to arrest Alan Foy, without consulting me, I might add."

The man had no backbone whatsoever, here he was about to turn his back on Strain and his team to protect himself. He was supplying the information to Strain right down to the details of exactly which night Alan Foy would arrive at his brother's apartment. Strain had strict instructions from his superior not to divulge the source of the information to anyone within the Mask group. Strain was told that the PM knew of the information but requested not to be told the details and it was not to be discussed with him further. This was explained to Strain in such a way that it was for the political protection of the PM. Strain accepted this reason as the 'Old Boy Network' protecting itself.

"As you know he has been on the run for some years now, wanted not only in Ireland but here on the mainland." He was stating something that was common knowledge even to the press and public.

"Yes, yes, I know the history," said the PM, somewhat agitated.

"When they entered the apartment there was a gunfight, which resulted in Alan and Peter Foy and Peter's girlfriend dying." He paused for a moment, waiting for the PM to react with shock or surprise to the news. He was in for a disappointment, as the PM never reacted one way or the other, he was very cool and non-committal in his reply.

"Where are the team members now?" he asked.

"I don't know, sir, possibly all at home by now tucked up in bed or at the hospital, Strain is reporting to me at 11 o'clock this morning." *Come on,* he thought, *what is your next question?*

"Good, meet here at number 10 and have the rest of the Mask committee here also, I want a full report." A meeting at Downing Street meant that it would not interfere too much with the PM's other meetings.

"Yes, sir," he replied and before he could say any more the PM hung up on him.

"How I hate this business," he said out loud. He revisited the bottle of Cognac and this time poured a very large drink for himself.

His drinking problem had been a source of embarrassment on a number of occasions in the past, especially at public functions. Adrian Bowles MP had a lavish lifestyle, which reached way beyond what he earned as a Member of Parliament. He had a number of small business interests and was on the board of two London companies, but this was not enough. His favorite overindulgence was expensive Champagne and very expensive ladies of the night, all of which was known by his close friends and the PM. He had learned to keep most of his activities discreet and one in particular secret. The fact that he entertained himself with prostitutes never really bothered anybody because he was so discreet, but his darkest secret was his passion for very young Oriental and Asian girls, preferably between the ages of eleven and thirteen.

The IRA found out about Bowles' activity through one of the prostitutes that worked for them in London. As one would expect the IRA took advantage of the situation. A camera and video recorder were installed in the prostitute's London apartment and the star performer of the recording was of course Bowles. Within five weeks they had several hours of videotape with Bowles and a number of different young girls performing sexual acts. In return for their silence Bowles was required to feed information to the IRA about any Government action targeted towards them.

After a year of passing very weak information to the IRA Bowles made a business proposition to them. He had an old friend in Spain that could supply the IRA with as many weapons as they desired. Bowles was willing to make the introduction, providing that he was allowed to accept an introduction fee from his friend each time a sale was made. The IRA was at first very cautious and checked the contact out with their friends in ETA. He proved to be genuine, even known for supplying ETA and some Islamic groups with weapons. This agreement proved to be very fruitful for Bowles, earning him over a quarter of a million pounds in cash over the next two years. This was a veritable windfall for Bowles, as it gave him the means to pursue his lavish lifestyle and expensive sexual habits, at the same time keeping a normal-looking bank balance. He knew that the PM had the bank balances of several people close to him scrutinized by MI5 and any excessive funds or obviously an account that was in trouble would ring alarm bells. His lavish lifestyle continued with the use of the cash he received from the IRA.

SEPTEMBER 23RD, NORTHERN IRELAND

As soon as Alan Foy left his house Stephen Fagan went into the lounge and removed the screws from the telephone outlet in the wall, he pulled the cover plate out of the wall, revealing a set of wires connected to a mini tape recorder. He opened the recorder and removed the tape inside, replacing it with a blank tape that was also hidden in the cavity, he then replaced everything the way it was before. He was pleased with this little invention of his which he could switch on to record by simply inserting a small needle into a hole next to the plug which pressed against the record button, starting the tape. In his bedroom was a second tape recorder, where he played the telephone conversation to himself.

"My, my, Alan, you do have contacts in high places as if we didn't know. When I play this tape back to our group, things are going to heat up for your contact," he said to himself.

As he left his house he looked at the telephone on the corner and smiled to himself. If they only knew that it was his doing that the local public telephones didn't work, how else was he supposed to get people to use his trusted home phone. He was part of a group of six people in the area that local IRA members came to for the use of a phone that they believed to be safe. He put his coat on and left the house to pass on the information. Fagan walked into the pub where his brother was the landlord and through the bar into the private living quarters on the first floor. The pub wasn't open yet but he could hear his brother downstairs in the basement moving a barrel. He went straight up the stairs to the lounge. The telephone was in the corner of the room on a table, quickly and quietly he checked to see if his brother's wife was around; thankfully, she wasn't. Fagan dialed the number to his associate, the telephone rang twice before it was answered.

"Hello," the male voice answered.

"Can you see me in an hour?" Fagan asked.

"Yes, you know where," was the reply.

SEPTEMBER 23RD, LONDON

The members of the Mask committee; Simon Fletcher, head of MI5; Bryan Harper-Jones, special advisor to the PM on the media; and Gen. Roy Reese, (retired) ex-SAS in charge of the Hereford base, were all patiently waiting for the PM in his backroom at number 10 when Bowles arrived. He graciously shook hands with everybody and took a seat at the table.

Fletcher was the first to speak, "Where is your man Strain?" he asked.

"I should imagine he will be here in a moment," he replied.

"What happened last night?" asked Fletcher.

Bowles knew that one of them would ask before the PM came in and he had guessed correctly, Fletcher could not wait to know. He did not dislike Fletcher, he just did not like the job he did, namely snooping around. This was partly due to the fact that he thought that Fletcher might investigate him more thoroughly one day and find out about his dark habits. Just the thought of that happening made him redden in the face and start to sweat. He did not realize it but he was daydreaming and had not answered Fletcher's question.

"Are you all right, Bowles?" said the General.

Bowles came back from his daydreaming at the sound of his name. "Sorry, must go to the toilet." He jumped up out of his chair and opened the door leading to the hallway where the toilets were located. He almost knocked over Strain as he was leaving, who was rather surprised to see the man move so fast. Bowles continued on towards the toilet without even acknowledging Strain's presence.

"Hello, how are you today, Strain?" he said to himself, mimicking what he thought Bowles would have said to him. He even replied to himself, "I am doing fine, thank you, especially after the shitty night I have just had."

"They will take you away in a straightjacket for talking to yourself." Strain spun around, realizing that he had heard the PM's voice. His ears did not deceive him, there he was walking towards him from the bottom of the stairs.

"Mr Prime Minister, sorry about that, I did not see you there." Strain was feeling like an idiot for mimicking Bowles.

"Don't worry, I do it all the time, but keep it to yourself or I may not get re-elected," the PM replied.

He was in a good mood considering how things had turned out last night, thought Strain.

"Come into my office and tell me what went on last night." Before he could reply the PM was walking in the direction of his office. "Tell the others they can wait there until we have finished," the PM marched on.

Strain stepped into the meeting room where the rest of the Mask committee were sitting. "I guess you heard," he said as he addressed the three men. "Can one of you let Bowles know?" Strain did not wait for a reply and followed the PM to his office.

As he got to the PM's office his secretary waved him in, giving him a big smile and whispered, "Good luck." The PM's secretary Laura had a very soft spot for Strain ever since she met him at the first meeting of the Mask committee. Strike another one up for Strain, as he did not have a clue that she was remotely interested in him. He had a saying, that a woman would have to hit him over the head with a Cricket bat to make him realize that she fancied him. As Strain walked into the PM's office the secretary pressed the button under her desk, which automatically released the door from its open position, closing it quietly behind him. This part Strain was getting used to, as this was his sixth or seventh private session with the PM.

"Please, sit down, John. Would you like a drink of tea or something?" The PM was as cordial as ever, thought Strain.

"No thank you, sir," Strain replied.

"I am beginning to think that you do not like to spend a lot of time with me, John, you never drink tea with me." He did not hesitate any further and called his secretary on the intercom. "Laura, would you bring in a pot of tea for Mr Strain and myself and some shortbread."

"Yes, sir," she replied.

"OK, the door is locked, you can't escape and you have my full attention until Laura brings the tea." The PM settled into his soft leather chair and leaned back slightly, waiting for Strain to start.

"Well, it is a long story, sir, so I will give you the short version from when we entered the house." Holding his hand up with the palm facing Strain, the PM's well-known 'stop talking' move, Strain did exactly that—he stopped talking.

The PM said, "No, I want the full story from when you started the surveillance and where the information was coming from."

This comment rather puzzled Strain, as he was led to believe that the information source was through the PM.

The PM saw the puzzled look on Strain's face and said, "Do you have a problem with passing the information on to me?" The PM looked as though he was going to explode, his face turning red.

"No, sir, I will be more than glad to discuss the whole case with you," Strain replied.

"Good, then why hesitate? You look as though you have a problem with this, why is that?" As always the PM was bang on target in reading people's expressions.

"As I said, Prime Minister, I will be glad to talk to you about the case but you asked where the information came from." Strain was trying to be as diplomatic as the PM in the hope that he did not hear wrong. *After all, we cannot have the Prime Minister losing his memory or has he?* thought Strain.

"Why is that such an unusual question?" said the PM.

"Sir, I was led to believe that the information came from you." Strain could see the surprise at his comments in the PM's face.

"Who led you to believe this?" replied the PM.

Now Strain was definitely feeling uncomfortable and realized that he had been misled by Bowles. "I am sorry, sir, but Mr Bowles intimated on several occasions that the information source was yours and that I was not to let you know that I knew about it."

The PM said nothing and stared at the surface of his desk, deep in thought. What Strain had just said was obviously news to the PM and that brought up many questions in Strain's mind. He sat quietly watching the PM mulling through his thoughts. They both sat in silence for a couple of minutes, it seemed like an hour to Strain, the PM spoke.

"I still want you to go through everything with me and then we will discuss Mr Bowles. I caution you, John, do not leave anything out, I do not want any surprises later." He sat back in his chair again.

"Mr Bowles gave me the information over two months ago that Alan Foy was believed to be returning to the mainland from his hiding place in the Netherlands. It was his understanding that when he did return he would visit his younger brother Peter. The information was so good that Bowles even knew Peter's address and that he had a girlfriend that lived with him. The reason I say the information was so good is that when we checked on the address that Bowles had provided I found out that he had only lived there for five days. I know that this is not that unusual because we generally know where IRA family members live, but when we verified his address with Special Branch records it still showed his old address. A member of the team went to the old address on the SB records and found out that Peter Foy had left suddenly. Even his neighbor who knew Peter well and had a drink at least once a week with him did not know that he had moved. He was very surprised, he thought that he had just gone away for a couple of days with his girlfriend, he did this sometimes. His landlord did not know that he had left either; in fact, Foy was two months ahead with his rent."

There was a knock on the door, "That will be Laura with the tea, come in," the PM shouted. He pressed the door release button under his desk and Laura walked in carrying a tray. "You can put that over here on my desk, Laura, we will help ourselves."

Bowles appeared at the door, his face looking very pale. He knocked gently on the door with his knuckles and said, "You wish to see me, Prime Minister?"

"I will send for you when I do. Close the door behind you as you leave please, Laura," he said.

Laura placed the tray on the PM's desk and turned to leave the two men alone. Bowles still stood in the doorway as Laura said, "Excuse me, Mr Bowles." Laura was a master at ushering people away from the PM's office, even when they stood their ground as Bowles was doing. Laura turned her back to Bowles and walked backwards, closing the door to the PM's office as she did so. Bowles had no option but to move out of the way.

"Why is it the PM is not willing to let me in on the meeting with Mr Strain, Laura?"

"The PM and Mr Strain are obviously enjoying a private conversation before you go in. They were laughing out load about something before I took the tea in. Mr Strain must have been telling one of his jokes, you know how the PM likes to hear jokes." Laura had lied well, as Bowles appeared to be immediately relieved, *but why is he so edgy?* she thought. "The PM did say that he would be in the conference room shortly with Mr Strain." Bowles turned and left Laura's office and walked back to the conference room.

"The Home Secretary didn't look very happy, John. Something is not right here, not only do I feel it, I see it in his face. I also see it in yours, so let us continue, I will pour the tea while you talk."

That's different, thought Strain, *the PM playing mother. Where is the camera when you need it?* "Well, sir, after we verified that Peter Foy was living at the new address in Birmingham I reported back to Mr Bowles with our findings. He wasn't surprised by anything in the briefing; if my memory serves me well he did not want a full report, just the highlights. Mr Bowles then gave me strict instructions not to discuss this with anyone, which at the time did not seem to be too unusual. However, in light of our conversation his instructions do not make sense. Mr Bowles told me that the 'Mask' operation was moving into what he described as a "Critical Phase," what he was about to tell me was for my ears only and it was again a directive from the PM."

"I seem to be doing a lot of that, don't I, John?"

"Yes, sir," he replied.

"Carry on." The PM passed him a cup of tea.

"Here is the interesting part, Mr Bowles told me that information had been received that Alan Foy was about to come out of hiding and go back into active service for the IRA. This really took me by surprise at the time, the thought of Alan Foy on the loose again was something I didn't relish. He stated that Alan Foy was going to return through England to Northern Ireland and stay with his brother Peter on the way. Our remit was to observe Peter Foy and his girlfriend until Alan Foy was seen, at which point we would make the most of the opportunity and arrest Alan before he got back to Northern Ireland. Another condition to Mr Bowles' information was that the rest of the team was not to know about Alan, as far as they were concerned Peter Foy was the target. I asked why and was told in no uncertain terms that I was to follow orders and not question them. At which point Mr Bowles and myself got into a very heated discussion about the Mask Operation and the team. Again, I was reminded of the secrecy of the operation ahead."

"Why do you think that he did not want the rest of the team to know about Alan Foy? It doesn't make sense, does it?"

Strain took the opportunity to drink some tea while the PM talked. Strain welcomed the wetness of the tea on this throat, even if it did taste awful. Too strong and no sugar, Strain liked his tea weak with one sugar.

Strain continued, "I asked the same question during our exchange and Mr Bowles explained that it was a matter of security. The information that was being received was from a top IRA source and the fewer people that knew about it the less chance there was of a leak. He then confided in me that there was already a leak within the government and they did know where it was coming from."

"That part is true and you should not have been told about it. Need I say the obvious, John?" the PM said.

"No, sir," Strain knew too well that Bowles had released information to him that he should not have, but that was his problem. Strain would keep his mouth shut. "As I said, it was a heated exchange of words and I don't believe Mr Bowles meant to tell me."

"Speaking your mind again, John, it does get people a little excited at times, including myself if you remember." The PM was referring to a strong difference of opinion that he had with Strain on only the second occasion they met. They got into a discussion of 'Terrorists and how do we deal with them.' Strain had suggested that the western governments of the world should take stronger action against terrorists and their organizations and play them at their own game. When the PM had asked him what he had meant Strain gave a long explanation, describing how specialized teams would be given an open hand in identifying the whereabouts of known terrorists, locating them and disposing of them in a fashion that they disposed of others. He went on to explain that only terrorists with known atrocities, particularly cold-blooded acts involving death, and the likes of the IRA punishment squads would be targeted. His frankness was not appreciated but he only stated what many were thinking. The PM chose to ignore Strain's remarks and ordered him to keep them to himself. Thankfully, nobody else was in the meeting with Strain and the PM at the time.

The thought of the newly appointed head of the 'Mask Team' suggesting assassination of terrorists did not go down well with the PM and almost had Strain kicked off the team before he really got started.

"Let's move along," the PM said.

"Yes, sir," Strain went silent for a moment, remembering where he was in the briefing. "About a week ago Mr Bowles told me that sometime in the next week or two he expected to receive information of exactly which night Alan Foy would make contact with his brother. I found this to be absolutely incredible, here is a man, a known IRA terrorist with many murders to his name who has been on the run for years, and Mr Bowles is going to tell me exactly when and where I can find him. I was getting very bad vibes about this, but I did not ask any questions, I knew I would be given the secrecy line again. I did ask if he knew whether Alan Foy would be armed, I know that may seem a stupid question but hell, why not, he seemed to know everything else about the man, he told me that he would find out. We kept surveillance on Peter Foy and his girlfriend, nothing unusual, they attended University, went to the pub a couple of times and took food home from the local fish and chip shop most nights."

Strain paused and drank some of the strong tea, fully expecting the PM to say something, but he didn't. "Yesterday morning around 8.30 a.m. I received a call from Mr Bowles telling me to call him at 9 a.m. at his office on the secure line, which I did. He told me that Alan Foy was expected to make an appearance at his brother's apartment that night. He had received further information that Alan was only going to spend one night at his brother's apartment. I told the Home Secretary that this did not give me much time to alert the team and prepare them for the operation ahead."

The PM found it rather amusing to hear Strain refer to Bowles by his title of Home Secretary, he said it as though he had a bad taste in his mouth.

"As soon as I said this he went into orbit, screaming at me over the telephone about how the team should always be ready to move. If I did not feel capable to do the job he would bring in another team leader. I could not understand the outburst; after all I did not say that the team could not do the job, I just stated it did not give us much time. Another odd thing, during his wild outburst he threatened to remove me from the team if I had told any of the team members about Alan Foy. I said that surely it was OK to tell the team at the briefing later in the day, before we continued our surveillance.

"Again, another outburst, he was yelling, 'No, no, no, don't you fucking listen' or 'are you fucking deaf' or something. I could almost feel his blood pressure going up over the telephone. I asked him to listen to something I had to say before he responded. I had to try and get him to calm down enough to listen to a plan I was going to suggest. He told me to wait a moment. He had me on speakerphone and I could hear him moving around, then I heard the sound of crystal and I thought he was pouring himself a drink. I remember thinking that hopefully it would calm him down. Almost immediately I heard him pour himself another, he must have downed the first one in one go, lucky bastard, Oh! sorry about that, sir," he said to the PM, forgetting himself for a moment.

"That's OK, John, a drink sounds like a bloody good idea right now." He got up from his chair and walked over to his bookshelf. He pressed a red bound book and a section of the shelf opened, revealing a small bar with a rather good selection of drinks. The PM took two crystal glasses out and picked up a bottle of Glenturret, 21-year-old single malt whiskey. "Your favorite tipple, if I am not mistaken, John."

"Yes, sir," he replied. *There goes another Kodak moment*, he thought as the PM poured him a drink.

The PM poured a very generous measure for both of them and handed a glass to Strain. "I don't think I will ever forgive you for introducing me to this particular malt whiskey, John. I permitted myself a side trip recently to the distillery in Crieff during a visit to Edinburgh. You were right about the drive to the distillery and the distillery itself, a marvelous place. I can see why you are so fond of it, cheers." He raised his glass, as did Strain, and they gently tapped them together, the glasses giving off that distinctive crystal ring. They sipped gently at the amber liquid, Strain particularly savoring the taste and bouquet, his mind gave him a fleeting visit to the distillery, revisiting fond memories.

He was brought back to No. 10 Downing Street by the sound of the PM's voice. "Yes, John, I will never forgive you, nor do I want to." The PM was holding his glass at eye level and looking through the crystal at the contents. He sat back in his chair holding the glass closely to his chest as if somebody was going to take it from him. "Carry on," he said.

"I told Mr Bowles that I could tell the team that we had instructions to arrest Peter Foy and his girlfriend to bring them in for questioning, that would mentally prepare them. He seemed to accept this part without a problem. I then asked if he had information on whether Alan Foy would be armed. He obviously had not calmed down too much, because he said, 'Of course he's armed—he's a bloody terrorist, what do you think?' I reminded him that he had told me that he would be seeking further information on this. He then stated that not only Alan Foy would be armed but so would Peter and his girlfriend. This was a real surprise, as Peter Foy was known not to carry weapons and was kept out of the terrorist game by his father.

"Maybe Peter was a real sleeper for the IRA and was about to join his brother in some new active unit, who knows? This news obviously gave me a lot to think about, but why was Mr Bowles so aggravated? It kept playing on my mind and still does, Mr Bowles gave me a warning that under no circumstances was I to lose Alan Foy and I was to apprehend him at all cost. He then hung up the phone."

The PM said, "Why would Peter Foy join the IRA after keeping out for so many years, that is a very good question, John. I would have liked to have had an answer to that one, but as he and his brother are dead I won't know, will I, will anyone? The Home Secretary and the rest of the committee will be getting anxious."

"Especially the Home Secretary," said Strain.

"Yes, we need to keep him in the dark about this conversation for now. I want you to dig deeper and find out what you can about the situation with the Foys, what is Bowles' game? Is he just trying to protect my political career and me? So many questions, John." The PM looked truly worried for the first time since Strain had known him.

"Can I make a suggestion, sir?" said Strain.

"By all means, fire away," the PM replied.

"Well, we want to keep Mr Bowles comfortable and make him believe that we did not discuss him or what he had told me about your supposed instruction. If I sit outside by Laura's desk she can call Mr Bowles to the office. When he arrives he will see me sitting there and Laura can ask him to take me to the conference room at the request of the PM. She will apologize for me waiting outside of the PM's office for so long but he really did have to take the telephone call, it was important. She will then tell us both that the PM will be with us shortly. On the way to the conference room he will definitely ask me what we discussed. I will say that we exchanged pleasantries and you asked how the injured team members were doing. Then Laura brought the tea in and a minute later you received a telephone call and you asked me to wait outside. If he asks did we discuss the operation I will say no, we never even started. I can then give you the brief of last night's events with everyone else."

"Excellent idea, John, that should keep him quiet for a while. I want to see you here tomorrow, ask Laura for a good time for us to meet. I don't want it in my diary, tell her it is confidential, she knows what to do." The PM finished his Glenturret as did Strain.

Without saying anything else Strain left the PM's office and spoke to Laura. Everything went according to plan, Bowles was so predictable.

As Strain entered the conference room he could see the rest of the Mask committee all looking very fed up with waiting. They all greeted him in turn, shaking his hand. Strain sat at the table when Fletcher, the head of MI5, asked, "Who was injured?"

The Home Secretary responded immediately, "A full briefing will be given when the PM joins us." That was his polite way of saying no more questions. Only two minutes passed and the PM walked in. The briefing did not take as long as Strain thought it would. The PM asked everyone to leave questions until another time as his schedule was already behind.

At the end of the briefing the PM asked everyone to discuss the operation with Strain and for the Home Secretary to provide a written report by the end of the day, he then left.

After the PM left the Home Secretary asked everyone to keep their questions directed to the actual operation itself, as he would brief the PM on any other issues concerning the buildup to the operation. *Nice move,* thought Strain, *covering your rear end already.* Strain looked at him and could see that he was his smug arrogant self again. *You think you are out of the fire, well, not yet you're not;* Strain was looking forward to the day that Bowles had to explain himself to the PM.

Not many difficult questions to answer, thought Strain as he left No. 10. Laura gave him a note as he left telling him that she had booked him into the Sheraton Park Tower Hotel at the PM's instruction.

SEPTEMBER 23RD, NORTHERN IRELAND

Alan Foy left his home in a very dejected mood. Informing his wife that it was indeed Peter's apartment on television and that they had lost both of their sons was very painful. The news had destroyed his wife.

As Alan stepped out of his front door into the street he could see him, one hundred yards away walking towards him. Maureen's father made an impressive figure, over six feet tall, broad and strong, he always looked intimidating. They walked towards each other at a casual pace as though it was just an ordinary day. The rain started to come down very heavily, adding a wet dismal day to the already sickening start. A British Army Landrover cruised by, adding irony to the situation. The symbol of all that both men hated driving past them like a green hearse adding to their pain and anger, the Army Landrover moved on without pausing.

They stopped almost toe to toe, Donnelly the first to speak, "Alan, I was coming to visit."

"Kevin," Foy replied, he could feel himself choking as he looked at the agony in his friend's face.

"Was it my Maureen that was murdered?" He said murdered because he believed that that is what happened to her and nobody would convince him otherwise. Foy truly hated telling his lifelong friend of his only daughter's death. They had known each other since they were five years old and had moved through the ranks of the IRA together.

"Yes, it was," Foy said.

Kevin was visibly controlling his emotions as the tears welled up in his eyes. "What about your boys?"

My god, Kevin, what a friend you are, Foy thought, you have just had it confirmed that your daughter is dead and your immediate thought is for my sons. "They are both gone," he replied.

Both men stood in the pouring rain, saying nothing to each other. They just steadied themselves as the rain showed no mercy and soaked them both to the skin.

For the first time in their adult life neither man noticed the occupants of the car down the street watching them. The SAS surveillance team was struggling to take decent photographs due to the heavy rainfall. "What do you think those two are talking about?" said Sergeant Bob James.

"Burying their own dead for a change," replied his partner Captain Steve Collingham.

"It is about time they received some misery, they have caused enough in their lifetimes. I don't know who it was that sent them kids to their grave, but good on them." Sergeant James had no remorse at all in his voice and definitely did not feel any pain for either man or their families. He had seen a number of good soldiers go to their graves at a very early age thanks to the IRA.

It was a sudden clap of thunder that seemed to bring both men out of their trance. "We need to talk, Alan," said Kevin.

"I know but not here, let's take a walk," Foy replied. "Do you remember our first hiding place?" Alan Foy referred to the senior school that they both attended. They used the school boiler room to meet and hide when they first started working for the IRA as teenage boys.

"Yes, of course, when do you want to meet?" he asked.

"One hour, give us chance to lose them," Foy was referring to the SAS surveillance team that they had now observed.

"OK, see you there." Both men split up walking in separate directions down the street.

"Where are they going?" said Corporal Collingham.

"If we fucking knew that we wouldn't be sitting here, would we," replied the sergeant very sarcastically. "Follow Foy, he has lost the most here and we are going to bag him. Wouldn't that be something, arresting the legendary Alan Foy just before the peace talks start? Come on, keep after Foy." They stayed some fifty yards behind him.

Alan made his way into the next street, still at a casual pace, the SAS surveillance vehicle was now a hundred yards behind him. As the SAS team turned the corner to regain sight of Foy he was nowhere to be seen.

"Where did he go?" said the corporal. "It's as if he disappeared into thin air."

"Check the alley further down, he must have seen us and run down there," replied the sergeant.

"But that's a hundred yards, away he couldn't have got that far."

"Well, where else do you think he could have gone?" said the sergeant, his frustration coming out.

As they reached the alley they could both see that there was a hundred places he could have hidden. "No point in us going down there, the bastard could be waiting for us, circle back," said the sergeant.

Alan Foy watched through the window as the car went past the house he had sought refuge in. "Thank you, Anne, I appreciate the help."

Anne was an active member of the IRA, mostly helping provide a hiding place for IRA members on the run. She said nothing as Foy stepped outside into the driving rain.

Foy and Donnelly spent the next hour dodging in and out of alleyways and side streets, checking and double-checking that they were not being followed. Foy was the first to arrive at the school, it was deserted due to the fact that it was closed for a week's holiday. As he entered the boiler room the heat inside wrapped around him like a warm blanket on a cold evening. Foy removed his overcoat and jacket and hung them towards the back of the boiler room to dry out. The small window in the room allowed just enough light in to allow him to see what he was doing. He could feel some of the old memories flooding back. He looked to the ceiling in the corner to see if the old hiding place was there. There used to be a ceiling cavity that was just big enough to hold two teenage boys. Not surprisingly the ceiling had been renewed at some time, closing in the secret hide-out. Alan heard the squeak of the hinge on the boiler door and hid himself in the darkness behind the boiler.

Kevin found the same warmth welcoming him and an old familiar smell about the place. Alan could see Kevin as he closed the door behind him. "I'm here, Kevin," said Alan.

"I thought I might have been first for once." He was referring to when they were teenagers. No matter what Kevin did, Alan always seemed to get to the boiler room first. Kevin also removed his coat and hung it up to dry.

"Do you know what happened to our children, Alan?" Kevin was back to business, the one-hour walk in the rain had given them both time to re-group.

"I wish I really knew, but I don't. Apparently the English have some kind of specialist anti-terrorism squad that somehow discovered Alan in Birmingham. When they found out he was at Peter's they went in and killed them all." Alan was not about to tell Kevin how he really knew. "I spoke to a reporter in England and he gave me the information." Alan did not like lying to his friend, but he could not allow him to know who his real informant was.

"The English have always had anti-terrorism units, what is different about this one?" Kevin could sense that Alan was holding back something. "I want the bastards that murdered my little girl. I will be talking to the Army Council about it." Kevin knew that if Alan were holding something back, this would force him into coming clean with him.

Alan knew only too well what his friend was up to so he had to give him something to prevent him from involving the IRA's top brass directly at this time. "OK Kevin, you smart bastard, it wasn't a reporter who gave me the information but I cannot tell you who did, not yet." The 'not yet' was supposed to pacify Kevin.

"They killed my little girl and I will do anything and everything to pay them back. You can help me or stand aside, I will shed the blood of anyone who stands in my way." Kevin was showing his famous temper and quickness to act.

"You are going to have to trust me for a little longer, I cannot tell you who my contact is, not yet. I promise you I want to pay back the people that murdered our children, but I want to make sure that we have all the facts before we move. You notice I said before we move, I will not cut you out of this, Kevin, we have been through a lot together and this is something else we will do together." Alan watched Kevin pacing up and down in the dim light from the windows.

"I thought we already trusted each other, what's with all the cloak and dagger with me? You said it yourself, we have gone through a lot together. Tell me, Alan, or by all that's holy I don't know what I will do." Kevin meant every word.

Alan wasn't scared in the slightest of Kevin, or any man for that matter. How could he get out of this without going to war with his lifelong friend?

"I am going to the mainland tomorrow and I will return the next night all being well. At least give me that much time to put a few things together. When I return I will tell you everything I know right down to names. You have my word." Foy reached into his jacket pocket hanging by the boiler and pulled out a small bottle of Jamesons Irish whiskey. He took the top off the bottle and handed the bottle to Kevin, who at first just looked at it but then snatched it from Foy's hand and took a large drink. Both men stood looking at each other in silence for a few seconds when Kevin handed the bottle back.

"Very well," said Kevin. "But I expect you to call me if you have any information or if I need to do anything here." He picked up his coat and walked out into the rain.

Alan took another drink as his friend walked out and sat on the floor with his back to the wall. Without warning, Alan Foy started to sob uncontrollably as the reality of losing both of his sons hit him. It took thirty minutes for him to calm down, at which point he put his coat on and headed home.

Fagan and Billy met in the old shop that had been partly destroyed by a car bomb a year before. The local youths did not help either, they had set fire to the place on no fewer than three occasions since the bombing.

"I suppose you have heard about Foy's bad news?" Billy Ryan said.

"Yes, I have, but you won't believe what is on this tape," Fagan replied. "Alan tried to use the phone on the corner and of course it wasn't working, so I called him over to use my telephone. This is the conversation that took place." He pressed the play button and both men listened in silence to the recording, any further thoughts for the loss to the Foy family disappeared.

"He didn't waste any time calling him. Eamon is over there now, we had better warn him—this could be dangerous to the new organization." Billy was talking about Eamon Callaghan, the No. 2 in the IRA, whose main role was to raise funds for the cause, he was also a hardened killer. Eamon was the man who came up with the idea of forming a radical left-wing splinter group to kill off any chance of peace in Northern Ireland. He also headed the small group of men who were planning to split from the IRA. His plan was to operate the splinter group without the knowledge or approval of the IRA's Army Council, as he knew that they would not only object but do all they could to stop him.

"I will call Eamon and let you know what he says and what we should do next. Be careful as you leave I will go first, give me two minutes headstart before you go," Billy said.

Although Billy was lower down the ladder in the organization to Fagan, he always contacted Eamon through him. This made it harder for anyone to track who was talking to who and who was in charge.

The rain stopped as quickly as it had started as Alan walked along the side of the school building. Movement across the street caught his eye, he stopped, quickly stepping back against the wall. There was Billy Ryan stepping out of the bombed shop. He immediately turned right as he left the shop and did not see Alan.

Alan's curiosity was aroused, *what are you doing in there?* he thought. He waited a couple of minutes when out walked Stephen Fagan, Foy couldn't believe it, *Fagan with Billy Ryan, they are supposed to be arch enemies.* Billy had a big falling out with the IRA, especially Fagan, over his radical left-wing views. He wanted to increase the bombings and assassinations of members of the British government, right at the time when they were talking about holding peace talks.

Billy walked across the street straight towards the school. Foy turned quickly and ran in the opposite direction out of sight, before Billy reached the building.

As Alan reached the street where his house was he saw a policeman coming out of the front door followed by a second, even though they were in plain clothes he knew that they were the police. Margaret appeared at the door and was saying something to both men, they then got into a car and left. Margaret saw Alan walking towards the house as she was closing the door and she waited for him.

"They came with the news of the boys," she said.

"How is my wife doing?" he asked.

"I called the doctor and he has given her a sedative. She is not asleep yet, you had better go and see her, she has been asking for you."

"Thanks," he replied.

He stood in the doorway of the bedroom looking at his wife sitting up in bed, she looked like she had aged ten years in only a few hours. He walked to the bedside and put his arms around her. She hugged him back as if trying to squeeze the air out of him. They both released each other, his wife stroking his face with her fingers.

"Oh! How we love those boys," she said. "You're going, aren't you?"

Alan nodded his head saying, "Yes, tomorrow."

"Please come back to me and bring our sons home." She was very sleepy now from the sedative her eyes where slowly closing.

"I will, my love," he said. He could not believe how much pain he was feeling, it almost felt as though his heart was actually hurting. He sat on the edge of the bed watching her until he was sure that she was fast asleep.

5

SEPTEMBER 23RD, SPAIN

The ETA meeting took place in a secluded mountain hideout close to the border with France. The hideout was one of the safest that ETA had and was known only to the four ETA leaders. Albi Basurto was the recognized head of ETA and a veteran of some twelve years. He, along with his brother Velasco, had control of the organization. Their cousin Pedro Basurto, the only son of their father's brother, was the explosives specialist. The IRA had trained him when he was a student in Dublin University. He was introduced to the IRA after the untimely death of his father at the hands of the Spanish Guardia in Madrid. His father was a great friend of the IRA, supplying them with weapons for many years. Pedro went to his father's contact in the IRA after he returned to Dublin University from his father's funeral. After a long verbal battle with the IRA member they agreed to train him in the use of explosives in return for which he agreed to continue to supply weapons. The agreement worked well and Pedro proved to be a natural in dealing with explosives. The fourth man was Carlos Blanco, the newest member of the group with only two years experience. He was trusted by the rest of the ETA members even though he was not a family member, except for Pedro that is, he did not like Carlos and could not give a reason why. Carlos had originally come to their notice when they saw him shoot two detectives in cold blood outside a Madrid bank when a bank robbery went horribly wrong.

Apparently the two Basurto brothers were at a café across the street from the Madrid bank enjoying a San Miguel beer. They had arranged to meet at the café the week before, Velasco had talked to his girlfriend and fellow ETA member Ester about the meeting. They made the mistake of discussing the meeting on a telephone that was bugged by the anti-terrorism unit, it was the break the police needed.

The bank was new and it was the day before the grand opening, a perfect opportunity to rob it. The armored truck stopped outside the bank and delivered the money for the vault. The two brothers watched with interest as there were a great number of police and armed security outside the bank. They saw several large bags of what they assumed to be money being removed from the armored truck and taken into the bank. After ten minutes the armored truck left and so did the large contingent of police and private security, leaving only one guard inside the bank. One guard in the lobby of the bank was standard procedure for most banks. A few minutes later the brothers saw two men carrying tools and a small ladder enter the bank.

Carlos was outside the bank in a getaway car ready to drive his fellow bank robbers away, at the same time watching out for the police. There were two undercover detectives sitting at a table outside a café next to the bank. A series of gunshots sounded inside the bank, the two men at the table jumped up and ran to the car where Carlos was and pointed their weapons at him. Carlos did not move, the two detectives were at the car, screaming at him to get out and keep his hands where they could see them. As he opened the car door another gunshot sounded from inside the bank. The two men instinctively ducked, giving Carlos his chance. He drew a 9mm pistol that was tucked into the front of his trousers, firing two shots at each detective, all four bullets hitting the officers, knocking them down. A car was passing the bank, when the driver heard the shots he panicked and the vehicle careered out of control, crashing into the front of Carlos' vehicle.

The Basurto brothers watched in amazement at how fast the man moved, with no hesitation he killed the two plain-clothes policemen. Carlos jumped out of the way of the car that had collided with his and ran across the street. The Basurto brothers almost collided with Carlos as they ran out of the café into the back street. Carlos pointed his gun at them, threatening them with it.

"We are not your enemy," said Albi.

"Then move out of my way." He moved the gun closer at them.

"Follow us if you want to get away from the police." Albi and his brother turned and walked quickly through the narrow back street towards an apartment building. Carlos did not question them, he just followed but made them realize that he was cautious and did not trust these two strangers. From that day he would become a friend and eventually a member of ETA.

The cave entrance was very difficult to find, you had to climb up above the area where the cave was and climb down the cliff face through a series of giant boulders. It was behind one of these giant boulders where the cave entrance was located. From the entrance you could see the whole valley below and a small village some eight miles away, an excellent vantage point.

Albi was sitting by a small fire enjoying the local wine and bread that his brother had brought with him, when Carlos arrived—over an hour late.

"Carlos, if you were much later you would have missed this excellent wine and bread," Albi said. "I thought you were lost."

This was only the third time Carlos had been to the cave. The first time was at night and Velasco brought him but he used a longer route, obviously to confuse Carlos. The second time was also at night, this time Albi brought him by a more direct route, and this was the one he had used today.

The light from the fire lit up the cave, throwing ghostly shadows onto the walls, Albi looked like a demon with the red glow on his face.

"I was delayed on the way of out Madrid, the police had roadblocks everywhere. They are always busy trying to catch ghosts when everybody knows that they could not catch a ball if you threw it to them." They smiled at each other.

"What interesting adventure do you have for us today?" Carlos said to Albi.

"Relax, enjoy the wine." Albi handed the bottle of Rioja to him. "You are always eager to move on to the next job. You must learn to take things slowly, we cannot achieve our goals by rushing into each project."

Carlos took a drink from the bottle. "Albi, you know I do not rush into anything, I am very curious as to why we would come all the way up here to our safest hideout. It must be a very special project, what is it?"

"We are all excited," replied Pedro. "You will have to wait to find out what Albi has in store for us." Pedro was showing his dislike for Carlos and as usual did not hide it. Pedro turned and walked towards the entrance of the cave.

"Take no notice of him, he has been moody all day. He tells you to be patient but he is the most impatient. The fresh air will do him some good," said Velasco, trying to be diplomatic. "Besides, I am the one who has asked everyone to meet, Pedro is to guide us down to the coast."

"I understand what he is like, but this is the first time that we have all been together in one place in over a year." Carlos reached for the wine bottle and took another drink.

Albi called to Pedro, "Pedro, what is the weather like?" Pedro came back into the cave.

"We must leave soon, we only have three hours of daylight left, thanks to Carlos."

"Where are we going?" Carlos said.

"You will soon see," replied Pedro. They all stood, Albi carefully put out the fire and checked that they had left nothing behind.

It was a tough walk, almost at a slight trot in places. Pedro was really enjoying this part, as he was by far the fittest of the group and knew that Carlos would be struggling after thirty minutes, as he really did not have much time to relax after his three-hour walk up to the cave. Carlos was truly thankful that he did not have to walk from the village to the bottom of the mountain range. A local farmer offered him a lift on his tractor for most of the way, at least until they reached the farmer's field, at which point they parted company. As they walked over another ridge facing directly west into the setting sun Pedro picked up the pace, breaking into a slight jog, nobody said anything, especially Carlos. The view from the mountain was magnificent, the colors changing with the moving shadows cast by the setting sun. It was almost like nature was repainting the scenery every few minutes. They could see the coast and the sea in the distance, many miles away. About three miles ahead Carlos could see the lights of a village at the bottom of the gently sloping mountainside, darkness had descended quickly. By the time they reached the village they were all soaked in sweat, their pants and boots wet from crossing two streams.

They arrived at a small stone peasant house on the edge of the village, Pedro was still leading the way and was the first to enter the house.

"Someone start a fire with those logs and I will put some water on the stove to make coffee," he said as he lit the wick of a paraffin lamp that was on an old wooden table in the middle of the room. As the flame grew on the wick it threw out a surprising amount of light. Carlos was picking out some small pieces of wood to start the fire when Pedro and the Basurto brothers went into another room. He was curious as to why they did not include him, and he strained his ears trying to listen to what they were saying. A light shone from the other room, they had lit another lamp. There was another lamp next to a window and Carlos unscrewed the cap on the side to get to the paraffin. He splashed a little of the paraffin on the sticks on the fire and lit them with a match. He added split logs to the fire and had the start of a roaring fire going. He squatted down in front of the fire, still trying to listen to what was being said in the next room. He stared into the bright red and orange flames as the heat increased. The voices in the next room got louder as he heard Albi saying, "This is madness."

What is madness? Carlos was curious. He decided to go into the next room as he thought that it would be suspicious if he did not show that he was curious about the raised voices. He walked into the room, which was a small bedroom, "Is everything all right?" he asked with a deliberate concern in his voice.

"This does not concern you, it is a family matter," replied Pedro.

"Of course it concerns him," replied Albi. "He is a part of ETA and has the right to know what we are planning. I for one would like to know what his opinion is about this proposed madness that you two are arranging."

He could see that Albi was furious, the normal cool and calm exterior had totally disappeared.

Pedro and Velasco started to talk at the same time, telling Albi that Carlos did not need to know anything until the next day. All three of them were now shouting and arguing with each other.

"You are all making enough noise to waken the whole village, don't you think that we should be keeping a little quieter? The people here will already be curious as to who we are." He left the room and went back to the fire.

Albi said, "He is right, we do not need to bring attention to ourselves, we may want to use the house again in the future. We will all go into the other room and talk this over quietly, including Carlos." He was in control of himself again and using his authority as the leader of ETA.

The room was now heated by the log fire, Carlos was taking off his damp shirt as they walked in.

"I hope that the fire will dry our clothes out properly before morning," he said as they came into the room.

The others removed their coats and hung them around the room to dry them.

Pedro was the first to speak, "I want you all to know that I do not agree that Carlos should know anything about the operation until we arrive at the fishing boat tomorrow."

"I agree," said Velasco.

"I disagree with both of you," said Albi. "He has been a very important part of ETA over the last two years and I think that he has a right to know what you two are planning. This madness of yours could mean the end of ETA forever or the start of a very bloody war with the government. I am going to tell him what you have just told me and we shall see what he has to say." He watched both of them as they stood glaring at him.

"Why do we have to tell him now, why can it not wait until tomorrow?" asked Velasco.

"He cannot contribute anything at this time, it does not serve any purpose to tell him now." Pedro was raising his voice again. "We must wait until we get to the boat."

"What if he does not agree and wants no part of this, he has a right to choose just like the rest of us." He turned to Carlos, who was still staring at the flames of the fire, deliberately keeping quiet.

Velasco grabbed his brother by the arm, "I will tell him enough to see if he wishes to continue on with us, if not he can leave in the morning when we get to the boat. If you do not like what I am telling him you can tell him the rest."

"Let us hear what you have to say," Albi replied.

"Pedro and I have been planning an alliance with a Muslim group from outside of Spain. They are going to supply arms to the IRA, arms that they have stolen from various government sources. We have agreed to provide this group with the contact within the IRA and act as the go-between. Tomorrow we will leave with two of the group to deliver the weapons to the IRA in Ireland." He paused as Carlos looked at him.

This wasn't normal operating procedure between terrorist groups, and Carlos knew it. "What does ETA get out of this?" Carlos was very careful to say *ETA* and not *us*, as he still wanted to show allegiance to the organization.

"One million US dollars in cash," said Velasco.

"Why US dollars?" he asked.

"Because that is how they are being paid, you dumb bastard," shouted Pedro.

Velasco raised his hand to Pedro and said, "There is no need for us to get worked up about this again." He continued talking to Carlos, "Do you want to be a part of this or not?"

Carlos knew that if he said that he did not then he would be a dead man, "Of course I want to be a part, I am a member of ETA the same as the rest of you. A million dollars is a lot of money, it will be a great boost to our finances. Why has this Muslim group come to us for assistance, why did they not go to the IRA directly?"

"That is a good question," said Albi.

Pedro was quick to answer, "They came to me because I have the contacts and the trust of certain members of the IRA. I agreed, in principle, to help them if they agreed to pay us a share in return for the help."

"What assistance did you agree to give?" asked Carlos.

"It is none of your concern," Velasco replied.

"It is if you want him to understand everything that is going on here," said Albi.

"We don't want him to understand what is going on, that is our objection," said Pedro.

"We agreed to arrange for the sale of the weapons and the boat to transport them to Ireland. That is all that I am willing to tell him," he said to Albi.

"Tell him what you intend to do with the money that you gain from this arrangement. Try to explain to him that this is not madness and could mean the end of ETA." Albi stood up and walked to the window, trying to keep himself calm.

Carlos watched the three of them and realized that he must not take sides, he decided to give Velasco and Pedro a way out without upsetting Albi.

"I will go to the boat with you tomorrow, I have a suggestion. Once the money is handed over to you in Ireland you return to Spain and we will all discuss how the money is spent. If there is not a majority vote on the plans that you have for the money then it will be frozen until such time that we can all agree on what to do." He looked at them, hoping that he had managed to give each of them a way out of the disagreement.

"I do not like what you are up to, my brother, or you, Pedro, but Carlos has a point, it should go to a vote, the money will be a good boost to our finances." Albi sat down again, waiting to hear what their response was.

"I do not like the idea of him knowing what we are doing, but what he says makes sense," said Pedro. "We need to talk about this," he said to Velasco and stood up, "Come." Velasco got up and followed him into the other room.

"He gave up very easily, I don't like it," said Albi.

"We are a little tense at the moment. A rest and a good sleep will help us all see things clearer in the morning." Carlos lay down on the hard floor next to the fire and closed his eyes.

Albi wasn't as sure as Carlos, he knew how dangerous his brother and cousin could be.

"We do not need their help, they think that we are coming straight back to Spain. We agree to talk about this as suggested by Carlos when we return, they do not know that we are stopping in England first to start our new campaign. We are just agreeing to talk as they suggest, it will be too late for that by the time we get back, they will have to take part or stand aside," Pedro said.

"You are right again, my cousin, and as shrewd as ever, we will be making history in England and in Spain on our return. I have another idea. I will talk about it in the morning. Let us get some sleep, we have a long day ahead tomorrow." He smiled. They both settled down to a short, restless night.

Eneto joined the group around the campfire a little calmer and ready to listen to what Ester had to say.

"Before we bring the young ETA members out to join us I want to let you know who you will be working with tomorrow."

Each man knew the reason for being there, they just did not know who their partners were going to be, nor did they know anything about the plans for Orti. Velasco had only trusted this part of the operation with Ester and Geraldo. When Ester concluded nobody questioned whom they were working with, including Eneto, they just wanted to proceed with the plan.

"What we are about to do is going to be a great surprise to everyone. This will have a great effect on the Spanish government, it is the start of a very intensive campaign against them. We must not fail tomorrow, the future of the new ETA is in our hands. It will show those soft hearts and minds within the organization that we can still be a strong power and fight for what is rightly ours, our own country."

Although she was only five feet four inches tall and weighed ninety-five pounds, she had, through her short speech, built herself up to feel like she was six feet tall and indestructible. This was another thing she had in common with her boyfriend, the ability to give pep talks to ETA members, believing every word that they preached. The men around the campfire had heard it all before but her words still aroused them.

"Geraldo, would you bring them out?"

Inside the farmhouse they could hear Ester in the distance but could not make out what she was saying. "When are they going to tell us what is going on?" asked Orti.

"You cannot keep quiet for long, can you?" said Luis. "We will be told when they are ready and not a minute sooner, so sit still and keep quiet."

The tension was starting to show in all four of the young men.

"Shhh!" said Mikeldi. "Someone is coming."

They all listened intently and could hear footsteps approaching the farmhouse door. The door swung open and in stepped Geraldo.

"OK, all of you outside by the fire, come on, quickly," he said, waving his hands.

Walking towards the fire seemed to take forever to Orti as he tried to do so casually, not showing that he was overeager to learn about what was going to happen.

"Come, sit down," said Ester.

All four did as they were told, getting close to the fire to feel its warmth once again.

Ester started to tell them the details of the mission, "Tomorrow, you will all go to the town of Logroño, where we will strike a great blow, making the dogs in the Spanish government pay attention. Mikeldi, you will be with Geraldo, Luis with Eneto, Adame with Peli, and Orti, you will be with me. Today you will all be given instructions and training by your partner. In these instructions you will get to know what role you are to play, but you will not be told which location you are going to attack. The basics of the operation are to be the same for each team. We will go to a restaurant or bar that has already been chosen, there you will plant a bomb and leave. Each device will be set to explode one hour after you leave the bar, this will give us time to telephone the police. We tell the police what time the bombs are to explode, where they are located and that there are several devices in each location. This will give them time to evacuate the civilians but not time to investigate and search for the bombs. The damage to each location will be devastating, the properties will be completely destroyed. These restaurants and bars have been chosen because they refuse to pay war taxes to ETA or they are supporters of the government. As you all know, it is the second day of the wine festival tomorrow and we will shock the world with our message. The streets will be full of people, it will be a nightmare for the police to try to get everyone to safety, but they will have time. Each of you are to become members of the new ETA when you are successful tomorrow, go with your comrade and listen well to their instructions, your life will depend on it."

The young men rose to their feet as Ester stood up, keeping the shock and surprise of the news they had been given to themselves. Each followed the man that they had been chosen to partner except for Orti, who walked over to Ester. He noticed that each man was taking his fellow 'Y' members to a different part of the camp, not surprising really, as they all had different locations to discuss.

"Come, Orti," Ester said and waved at him to follow her.

His mind was jumping from one thing to another, what was his part in this? How was he going to pass on the information to his superiors? Could he do it in time to stop them from planting the bombs? As he followed Ester he could not help but notice what a stunning body she had, very firm and slim, with a beautiful face. He could not believe his luck, he was to work with the woman who was the third most wanted person in Spain and he would be instrumental in her downfall, or so he thought.

Ester noticed how he was looking at her and was going to use his interest in her to her advantage. Ester deliberately walked away from the camp and found a secluded spot for her to educate young Orti on the events ahead. She did not waste any time in distracting him and keeping his young hormones working overtime, lusting after her. Ester opened her jacket, revealing a very thin crème blouse tightly fitted to her large breasts. Orti immediately took the bait. Staring straight at her breasts, she had him exactly where she wanted. The teasing would go on all day, with the ultimate tease to be just before dark, keeping his mind on her all night.

"Orti, why don't you get us one of those pots of coffee on the fire?"

He obligingly turned and ran back down the slope to the camp without saying a word, eager to please. At the fire Eneto called him over to the truck, "Orti, come over here."

He did not like Eneto and was looking forward to seeing him arrested and put in jail for the rest of his life. Eneto was taking out two large canvas backpacks out of the truck, they were very heavy-looking.

"Here, take these with you and give them to Ester."

"Yes," he replied.

Orti slung a backpack over each shoulder and picked up the pot of coffee on the way back to Ester.

She saw him walking back up the hill and continued the game of keeping his mind on her body, she bent over, giving him a good view of her cleavage, again he was bitten.

"Eneto asked me to give these to you." He put the backpacks down at her feet.

"Ah! We will need these later." She could see that he was curious about their contents. "Don't worry, you will find out soon what they contain, pour a coffee out for us, would you?"

Orti did as he was told, he did not think of saying that he did not want any coffee. He was totally under Ester's control and he didn't even know it.

"Orti, we all have the same job to do, the only difference is that we are doing it in separate locations. You and I will be attacking a bar in the main square, the owner is a supporter of the local political party. He has continually refused our appeals to stop supporting the government and has recently held a party to show his support for the local mayor. He owns three other bars and restaurants in Logroño and we will put him out of business tomorrow. We will show all of the other business owners in Logroño and other towns and cities that they will pay the tax that we request or they will have the same fate. It is a huge statement that we are making and the first step in the future growth of ETA. It is exciting to me to be involved in this new beginning, how do you feel about it?"

Orti wasn't going to say anything to show that he disagreed. "I do not know what to say, I am just privileged to be involved."

"Good, let us discuss what we are going to do." She started to draw a floor plan of the bar in the dirt. "When we go into the bar we will walk to the back of the room close to the restaurant and around the corner from the toilets." She was pointing with a stick to the plan in the dirt. "Come, sit next to me."

She patted the rock that she was sitting on. Orti did not need telling twice; he almost stumbled in his haste to accept her invitation.

She continued, "We will meet two people sitting in the booth, as we approach they will finish their drinks and they will offer us their seat, we will accept and they will leave. You will place your backpack on the seat next to you like this."

She pulled one of the backpacks next to her and placed it so that the pockets were facing towards her. "Like this, nobody can see you lift this flap revealing the timing device for the bomb."

Ester opened the top most flap on the backpack, Orti could see the red digital numbers of a clock. The sight of the red numbers brought chills to Orti's skin, making him shiver.

"The clock is no different to one that you would have at home, you set the alarm like this, one hour ahead of the time when you want it to detonate." She pressed the alarm set button on the front of the clock and the fast forward button at the same time. Orti watched as the numbers advanced on the clock face, the numbers stopped. "When you have the alarm at the correct time, press this set button and close the flap to conceal the digital display. Under the seat that you will be sitting on there will be a loose panel, I will slide the panel to one side and you will place the backpack under the seat, I will then replace the panel." Ester was being very deliberate, she did not want Orti to make any mistakes.

"Is the bomb already wired to the clock or do we have to wire it ourselves?" Orti asked.

"The bomb is pre-wired." His reaction was predictable, Orti sat back in surprise. "Don't worry, I did not press the set button." She smiled at him as he gave a nervous laugh.

"What do we do with the second backpack?"

"A good question." She patted him on the back to show her approval, achieving the desired effect, he sat up with pride. "I will take it into the toilet with me, there is a metal panel in the ceiling. I will set the timer and place it above the ceiling behind the panel. I may need your help with this part as the ceiling is seven feet high."

"How big is the bomb?"

"Big enough," was all she said.

"What happens next?" Orti was very concerned about how much time he would have to warn his police contacts of the intended bombing.

"We will quietly leave the bar via the backdoor and call the police from a public telephone. We will then disappear, you will make your way back to San Sebastián. Now, go through everything that I have told you, including how to set the alarm." She smiled at him, giving him false security.

As the morning wore on they ran through the plan at least a dozen times, wearing down Orti mentally. They returned to the camp to eat lunch, which Ester cooked. The afternoon was just as tiring, as Orti had to go through the whole plan again and again, but this time with Geraldo. He was told that this was in case something happened to Ester; that way they would have a backup for Orti. The rest of the group members went through a similar routine, just not as rigorous as Orti's, as this was designed to exhaust him in preparation for the following day. It was an hour before sunset and Ester asked Orti to go through the plan with her one more time, as they walked. She was making her way back to the spot where they had been sitting that morning, a good quarter of a mile from the camp. Orti was exact in his final presentation of the plan, he should have been—he had gone through it at least twenty times. As soon as they arrived at the morning location Ester put the final hook in his flesh.

"Orti, I want to bathe in the stream over there." She pointed over the ridge behind them. "Would you mind watching to make sure nobody comes up from the camp? I don't trust Eneto." She looked at him with those deep dark eyes and he melted on the spot.

"Of course," he replied, swallowing hard, his mind already had her naked in the stream; besides, he felt flattered that she would trust him over Eneto.

She walked over the rocks behind them and made her way down to the mountain stream. Orti could not resist, he wanted to see her naked, he circled around the rocks and hid behind a tree. He was just in time to see her entering the water totally naked, it was one of the most fabulous sights he had ever seen. Down in the mountain stream Ester was enjoying the cold water as it washed over her body, taking the dirt with it. She could not see Orti but she knew that he would be watching.

Orti heard someone calling Ester's name in the distance behind him, quickly he scrambled back down the rocks towards the place where he had been sitting with Ester. He could still hear Ester's name being called and looked down the path they had taken from the camp and could see Geraldo walking in his direction. Orti stood where Geraldo could see him, he called out to him, "Geraldo, up here." He waved his arms to attract his attention.

"Come down to the camp," Geraldo shouted.

Orti gave a thumbs up signal to show that he understood, Geraldo turned around and walked back towards the camp.

"What did he want?" the sound of Ester's voice behind him made Orti jump.

"You surprised me, he wants us to go down to the camp."

Ester was continuing her mind games with Orti, she had not fastened the buttons on her blouse or jacket, her blouse was wet, revealing just enough of her breasts to keep Orti eager.

"We had better go down, it is getting dark." She walked past him, fastening her blouse.

Everyone was gathered around the campfire as they walked into the camp. It wasn't until he felt the heat from the fire that Orti realized how cold it was getting, Ester had done well playing with his mind.

Geraldo stood up, “After we eat you four will take turns keeping watch tonight.”

He was pointing at the four young men. “Luis, you go first, then Mikeldi, Adame and Orti last, one and a half hours each, you will stand half a mile down the track by the old gate. You can sleep here by the fire or inside the farmhouse.”

SEPTEMBER 23rd, LONDON

The Home Secretary was at No. 10 Downing Street prompt at 5 p.m. with his completed report on the Mask Team’s previous night’s work. The police constable on duty outside recognized the Home Secretary’s car and then Mr Bowles himself as he got out.

“Evening Constable,” said the Home Secretary

“Evening sir,” replied the police officer.

The Home Secretary went straight to the PM’s outer office. As protocol dictated he reported his presence to Laura for his meeting with the PM.

“Good evening Laura.” He was in a much better mood than in the morning, but not for long.

“I’m sorry, Mr Bowles, but the Prime Minister is not back yet, his schedule has been behind all day. He asks that you leave the report with me.” Laura could see the immediate change in the Home Secretary’s face.

“I will wait for the PM to return, as you know this is a very important document.” Bowles was trying to sound calm, but assertive at the same time. He should have known better, as Laura could not be swayed by anyone, especially when she had a specific order from the PM himself.

“I realize the importance, sir, but you can leave it with me. I do not know when the PM will return, if in fact he does.” Laura was enjoying herself, twice in one day putting Mr Bowles in his place. She was looking the Home Secretary squarely in the face and held her hand out for him to give her the envelope. She knew that the Home Secretary was not enjoying this, when she noticed something very odd, he was starting to perspire. She could see little beads of sweat appearing on his forehead.

“Very well,” he said and left the office.

Laura looked at the envelope and noticed that it was very crumpled on the side where Mr Bowles had been holding it. There was also a damp patch from his hand. Laura did not think that the office was warm and checked the wall thermostat, 68 degrees, the same as always, slightly chilly for most visitors to No. 10. Laura pressed the intercom button to the PM’s office. “He has left, sir,” she said.

“Thank you, Laura, please bring in the report,” the PM replied.

She let herself into his office and placed the envelope on his desk. The PM looked up from the document he was reading and saw the look on Laura's face.

"What is bothering you, Laura?" the PM knew that look on her face, after ten years he had seen them all.

"Something rather odd, sir, Mr Bowles was understandably agitated to know you were not here, but look at the envelope." She watched him pick up the envelope and saw that he had noticed the way in which it was crumpled. "It is most odd that the Home Secretary would hand in an envelope of any description in that condition. He is something of a neat freak." She could have cut her tongue out for saying that, but it was too late. "It also has a sweat mark from his hand."

"Yes, that is rather odd for him. Did you notice anything else out of character?" he asked.

"Yes, he was perspiring for no apparent reason. It seemed to come on all of a sudden after I told him that you were possibly not coming back. I checked the temperature of my office and it was the normal 68 degrees." Laura did not like the man but she felt as though she was telling tales after school. This was one thing that would not change, and the PM found it admirable.

"Was he wearing a heavy duty coat perhaps?" he asked.

"No, sir, just a suit jacket, maybe he is coming down with a cold or something."

Good old Laura, thought the PM, *she does not like the man but is trying to offer an excuse for him.* "Thank you, Laura, I am sorry about all the cloak and dagger business. Can you contact Mr Strain and ask him to meet me here tonight at 8 p.m.? Tell him that we will be eating here. Have something light brought in for us, Laura, sandwiches, you know the sort of thing." The PM was anxious to move things forward, the Home Secretary's actions were becoming troublesome.

"Yes, sir, can I make a menu suggestion?" She was as efficient as ever back into her secretarial role.

"Please do," he replied.

"Smoked salmon and capers with caviar and chicken salad as a main course. If you wish to have a dessert perhaps a light crème brulee." Laura was describing some of Strain's favorite food, particularly the smoked salmon and caviar.

"Yes, excellent choice. I was forgetting that you know Strain's expensive taste in food and whiskey." He gave her a smile.

"And yours, Prime Minister," she replied, knowing that this was also one of his favorite selections.

"Touché, Laura," the PM said, laughing.

Laura blushed brightly and excused herself to make the arrangements.

As the Home Secretary left Laura's office he tried to compose himself once more, something he was doing more and more of lately. He stood on the step of No. 10 looking at the rain coming down. He took two steps forward and stood next to the police officer that he had exchanged pleasantries with on the way in. "Wet night again," he said to the policeman.

"Yes, sir," he replied.

"Must be going, by the way, has the Prime Minister returned yet?" Hopefully this would give him an answer to some of his questions, thought the Home Secretary.

"I am sorry, sir, but you know I cannot comment on the PM's whereabouts." The policeman looked at him and smiled.

"Yes, quite right," he replied and walked to his waiting car.

Strain arrived at No. 10 Downing Street at shortly before 8.00 p.m. "Evening Laura, seeing me twice in one day, you are having a bad day." He smiled.

"The PM is waiting and asked that you go straight in. I will be leaving shortly but some supper is ready for you both in his office." Laura wished that it was her that was sharing dinner with him and not the PM.

"Thank you, Laura, you are on the ball as usual." Strain then did something that shocked and pleased Laura, he squeezed her hand.

As Strain walked into the PM's office Laura could feel herself shaking and covered in goosebumps. *John Strain, you have no idea what you have just done to me,* she thought.

Strain and the PM ate their meal as they discussed the report that the Home Secretary had handed in. After an hour and a half the PM again opened the drinks cabinet for the second time that day and poured two large Glenturret whiskeys.

"John, what the hell is going on here? There is nothing in the report to suggest where the information on Alan Foy came from. He does not say why the surveillance was started. I look at your report and his and apart from the actual incident last night they are completely different." The PM was truly perplexed. Here were two men that he trusted implicitly but it was quite obvious that his long-time friend and Home Secretary was hiding something. "What do you suggest I do about this, John? I am at a loss, I do not understand what is happening here."

"May I speak freely, sir?" Strain asked.

"I thought you already were, for Christ's sake, man, you haven't held back before, why start now?" The PM paused. "Sorry, John, but this is really starting to get me. You're a good man, of course speak freely." The PM slumped back into his chair and took a drink of his whiskey.

"Sir, I understand that this is not pleasant for you, especially as the Home Secretary is a long and trusted friend. I will ask that you hear me out and then we can discuss what I am suggesting," Strain looked at the PM for approval but never received any, verbal or otherwise, so he continued. "I agree that there is something wrong with what the Home Secretary is telling both of us. I would not be sitting here if you thought that I was the problem. I am recommending that the Home Secretary be put under surveillance and his telephone calls monitored. He has one telephone line that as you know is restricted to the 'Mask' operation, I would like to look at that log.

"What do I hope we achieve by keeping him under surveillance, answers to both of our questions, hopefully happy ones. I think that the 'Mask' team should perform the surveillance, as we do not know if other members of the 'Mask' committee are at risk here. If accepted I will bring the team members that are fit for duty here tomorrow and set up the surveillance. The worst part of my recommendation is that I truly believe that we must perform counter-measures on his office and home. If we do not find any bugs, I believe we must then perform an electronic surveillance of his telephones at least. I would bring in trusted specialists for this part. You, sir, would have to ensure the MI5 do not do any counter-measures or sweeps during this time. Sir, I do not particularly like the man, but I will not do anything that you would not approve of, he is innocent of things at present." Strain watched the PM for several minutes, he just sat quietly sipping his whiskey.

The PM finally spoke, "Supposing we do this, John, what happens if we do not find anything as a result of the surveillance. What do we do then?"

"Other than bring him to your office and confront him, I do not know," Strain replied.

"Why don't we do that now? What have we got to lose? We have nothing to suggest that anything is wrong other than some peculiar behavior on his behalf." The PM was trying to justify to himself why he should do this to a friend and colleague.

"As I said, sir, we do not know what is behind the odd behavior, but at least we can try to clear up the situation," he replied.

"OK, proceed, but I want to be briefed at the end of each day on any developments." The PM really hated doing this but realized that Strain was right. "Speak to Laura in the morning, she will arrange the expenses to be given to you. Don't screw this up, John. I don't want him to find out what we are doing. If he is only guilty of stupidity or being overzealous then I do not want him to be dirtied by what we are doing." The PM stood up. "Thank you, John."

Strain knew this was his cue to leave. His mind was running wild as he left No. 10. He looked at his watch; it was 10.30 p.m. Too late to call the team members, they needed their rest, the call could wait until tomorrow morning. On his way back to the hotel the realization of what he and his team were about to do struck home. Surveillance on the Home Secretary, this was most unusual, but most certainly not the first time. As he thought this he dismissed it, *first time no chance this has happened before but how many times? Now there is a statistic that would shock the Houses of Parliament.* Strain smiled to himself as he visualized half of the pompous windbags coughing in disbelief if the statistics were ever read to them.

6

SEPTEMBER 24TH, SPAIN

The morning was a long time coming for Orti, he did not sleep before his turn on guard at the gate, he could not get Ester out of his mind. He heard the truck coming down the track and saw the faint glow of the headlights as he turned around. As the truck got closer he could see Ester standing on the step next to the driver's door.

"Good morning Orti," she said. "Come, you are in the back with the rest of us."

They both climbed into the rear of the truck helped by Peli. Ester went to the front, where she had placed a thermos of hot coffee, she poured the last of the coffee into a metal mug and handed it to Orti.

"Here, Orti, take this, it is the last of the coffee."

The coffee was laced with a sleeping powder. He accepted it gladly, as he needed something to warm his insides.

It took two hours for the truck to reach the outskirts of Logroño, where they split into two groups. They left the truck and continued on into the town in two cars, both of which had been stolen and the number plates changed. They were still at least a half a mile from the town center when they left the cars in two different parking lots. The four groups with their deadly backpacks walked the rest of the way to the target locations. Orti could not believe how many people there were in the streets, many of them were tourists, some wearing backpacks of varying shapes, sizes and colors. He now realized why they were carrying backpacks.

The city of Logroño in Northern Spain is the capital of La Rioja region, known for its wine and part of the Basque heartland, with over one hundred and twenty thousand residents. Famous not only for the ancient parts of the city but for its Vendimia Riojana festival held in September to celebrate the grape harvest. All of the local hotels, bars and restaurants scattered around the city's squares and side streets bursting at the seams during the festival, this was when the city was at its busiest.

Velasco had chosen this time of year for his attack because the city was so busy. Orti could feel the sweat running down his back as the walked up to the bar in one of the town squares. Each time he let go of the shoulder straps of the backpack he felt his hands shaking, the thought of what they were about to do terrified him. He kept looking at Ester to see how she was reacting, she was as cool as ever, not even a hair out of place. He started to look at her in a different light for the first time, she was smiling at people as they entered the bar, like an angel of death with the bomb on her back. The bar was reasonably quiet, for it was only mid morning. They walked through to the back of the bar, and exactly as Ester had described there was a man and woman sitting on the bench seat. As they approached the table that they were sitting at they stood up and walked past Ester and Orti without a sign of recognition. Ester sat down and placed her backpack on the floor by her feet, Orti sat next to her, placing his on the seat next to him.

"I will buy us both a glass of wine, you like red, don't you?"

She wasn't going to take no for an answer and headed towards the bar. At the bar she added a sleeping powder to his wine, quite surprisingly it did not cloud the wine very much, not that he would see it under the dim lights. This would weaken him even more and help her complete her task.

Orti did not really feel like having wine, as he already felt incredibly tired, he thought that it was from being awake all night. She returned to the table and engaged him in small talk to keep his mind off the drink. Twenty minutes passed and Ester requested another glass of wine, insisting that Orti have one also, she stated that it would calm his nerves. Unbeknown to Orti, the sleeping powder was starting to work and he felt as though he just wanted to leave and go to sleep.

They had been in the bar for forty minutes when Ester asked him to check the rear doors. He suddenly realized that they were actually going to go through with the plan, his stomach turned over and he felt like he was going to throw up. Ester could see how pale he had gone, a combination of no sleep, no food, wine, the drug and fear, she smiled at him.

"I think I will go to the toilet," he said.

"OK, why don't you rinse your face, you will feel better."

"Good idea," he said and left her with his backpack.

The minute he left Ester looked at her watch, the time was 11.15 a.m. She pulled Orti's backpack over to her and lifted the flap, revealing the digital display, it showed the correct time. Ester set the alarm for 12.30 p.m., pressed the set button and closed the flap to hide the clock. Just below the seat cushion she could feel the loose panel that she had described to Orti. Slowly and quietly she moved the panel to one side, she then lifted the backpack onto the floor and with her feet maneuvered it into place under the seat. The darkness of the room made it very difficult for anyone to see what she was doing. With the backpack safely in place she slid the panel back in place, making sure that it was not going to be dislodged easily.

In the toilet Orti was vomiting, he could not stop himself, thankfully there wasn't anyone in there to see him. He went to the sink to wash his hands and face and looked at his reflection in the mirror. He normally did not talk to himself but this time he did. "What are you doing? This is madness," he told himself.

He could not believe how pale-looking he had gone, most probably from the vomiting, he thought. He cleaned himself up as best he could, he did not want Ester to see that he was weak. On the way into the toilet he noticed a public payphone on the wall, this may be his opportunity to contact the police and warn them. He could feel himself coming back to life again at the thought of the police arriving to help. He wanted to check on Ester to make sure that she was still sitting at the table before he made the telephone call. He looked around the corner to where she was sitting, she was not there and both backpacks were missing. His skin went cold. *Where is she? Where are the backpacks?* His mind was going into a panic when someone put their hand on his back, he jumped with surprise, quickly turning to see who it was, it was Ester.

"Relax, you are so tense, follow me," she said as she walked to the ladies' restroom.

Ester held the door open and pushed Orti inside, his natural instinct was that he should not be in a ladies' room. He could not help but notice how dirty the toilets were, for some reason he always thought that the ladies' toilets would be much cleaner than the men's, not so.

"Quickly, into the cubicle."

Orti followed her inside as she closed the tall wooden door behind them. The space was a little cramped and Ester sat on the toilet seat with Orti stood facing her. She passed him the backpack.

"Here, put this on the floor by the door and open the flap so that you can check that the time is correct on the clock."

Again his stomach gave a turn, he took the backpack from her, turned around and placed it on the floor.

"Orti, you are going to have to kneel down, you are sticking that tight little bottom of yours in my face and it is distracting me."

He felt a little embarrassed at the thought of her looking at him that way. He knelt down on the wet floor with his back to Ester, he could hardly move, the space was so tight.

"Check the time," she said, keeping him distracted.

Ester opened her shoulder bag and took out a small brown bottle and a man's handkerchief. She unscrewed the top on the bottle and poured the contents of the bottle onto the handkerchief. The fumes almost got to her as she poured out the chloroform.

Orti started to say something, "The time—"

That was all he said as she quickly put the handkerchief over his nose and mouth. She hung on with all of her might, pulling his head to her chest. Orti panicked as the handkerchief hit his face, he grasped Ester by the wrists to try and pull the cloth from his face. He pushed back against Ester, using her as support as he tried to get off his knees. The more he struggled and thrashed out with his feet as he tried to stand, the more his boots slipped on the wet floor, the more he gasped for air the quicker the chloroform worked. It seemed as though he was struggling forever, but it was only about ten seconds before the chloroform did its job and he slumped to the floor.

Ester was surprised at how strong he was as he held on to her wrists, knocking her against the sides of the toilet walls in his effort to break free. She could feel his feet slipping on the wet floor, thankful that she had the foresight to wet it first for that exact reason. He started to weaken and passed out. Ester felt briefly winded from the brief struggle. She immediately dropped the handkerchief into the toilet and flushed it before the fumes affected her. Getting Orti onto the toilet seat was not an easy task for Ester, as moving an unconscious body was never easy. Through sheer determination she eventually managed to sit him on the toilet seat. From the side pocket of her backpack she removed a role of duct tape. She first placed a piece of tape over his mouth in case he regained consciousness and then taped his head to a water pipe on the wall. She was taking no chances that he could call out for help or try to break free, she systematically wrapped duct tape around his whole body, attaching it to the toilet bowl and water pipe. Finally his legs were lifted off the floor, with his knees bent she taped his legs behind him, giving him no chance of using his legs for leverage. Ester tried to push his torso from one side to the other, but it was not going to move, she had done a good job.

"Now you realize why people do not try to infiltrate ETA," she said to him. She hung the backpack on the coat hook on the back of the toilet door, after lifting the flap she set the alarm to time the bomb to detonate at 12.30 p.m. Now came the totally vicious part of her plan, she removed a bottle of smelling salts from her shoulder bag, after taking the top off she waved the bottle under Orti's nose. It took several seconds before he started to wake up and several more waves of the bottle under his nose before he began to realize where he was. As he came around the first thing he saw was Ester's face smiling at him. He tried to get up, only to find that he was firmly tied down and could only breathe through his nose. His eyes were now wide open, mostly with fear. Staring into Ester's evil eyes, he tried to scream something at her, but she could hardly hear even a muffled sound.

"Nice of you to join me, Juan Rodríguez. Yes, I know your real name and everything else about you. As you can see I am going to leave you a gift." She leaned to one side, revealing the red digits of the clock. "To answer your question, yes, I have set the alarm, it will explode at twelve thirty, just under one hour. You are going to die for your treacherous acts against ETA, you are responsible for many good ETA recruits going to jail, and for that you will pay by watching your life tick away in front of you."

She pointed to the clock, as if he didn't know what she meant, she stared at him with an obsessed look in her eyes. He could see that she was most definitely insane, he could also see why she was called the angel of death. He tried to speak, muffled sounds coming from behind the duct tape, his eyes pleading with her for mercy.

"We have to teach you, the police and everyone else that you cannot stop us from gaining our homeland and dogs like you will be exterminated. I told you that I know all about you, well, I do. I know, for instance, that it is your birthday tomorrow and that you were going to have a party with your family. Do not worry, you are still going to have a party with your family. We have invited them here for a surprise party for you, your parents, brothers, sisters and whoever they bring along. They will all arrive as planned at twelve noon, ready to surprise you at twelve thirty when you are supposed to arrive, but you will already be here."

Orti was totally frantic, every ounce of his being fighting and screaming at the bonds around his body to let him go.

"You are wasting your time, here, watch the clock."

She taped the flap open on the backpack, kissed him on the forehead and left him on his own to watch his life tick away. Once outside the cubicle she used a knife to force the lock on the door back into place, locking the door to prevent anyone discovering him. As she left the bar, she smiled to herself, pleased with the job she had done, especially the lie about his family coming to the bar, that was particularly enjoyable to her.

The early morning call of a rooster outside the house startled Albi and Carlos out of their sleep. "Damn you, bird, my heart nearly jumped out of my chest," said Carlos.

Albi started to laugh. "He did the same to me, perhaps we should eat him for breakfast so he cannot do that again." They both laughed at the thought of a chicken scaring two hardened terrorists.

"I will make some coffee for us all." Carlos picked up the water bucket to fill the cast iron kettle. The fire still had some burning embers, with the addition of some thin dry wood he soon had the flames licking at the bottom of the kettle.

Albi stretched his arms towards the ceiling as he got up, trying to shake the sleep out of his bones and muscles. He moved the sacking on the window to one side and looked outside, he could see the first signs of light as the sun started to rise, it was 7.30 a.m. on his watch. The sleepy village had one or two lights showing through the windows of the houses, signs of people getting up out of bed and preparing themselves for the days work ahead.

"They have closed the bedroom door," said Carlos, pointing at the door.

"They must have closed it last night after we went to sleep. They are really angry about involving you in their new venture, I don't understand them at times. I will wake them up when you have the coffee ready. I am starving, is there any bread left from yesterday?" he asked.

"No, we ate it all, but I am sure that we can pick up some fresh bread and cheese on the way. A village like this will have a baker's and a butcher's, we can buy food for the journey. Talking about the journey, how are we going to make our way to the coast?" said Carlos.

"There is a bus that goes to San Sebastián, it leaves at around 8.30. We will be able to take that. We will be getting off before it reaches the city. I will wake the others," he said.

Albi opened the door to the bedroom, the faint light from the kerosene lamp slightly illuminating the bedroom. "It is time to get up, you lazy hogs," he said, there was nobody in the bedroom, they were gone. "They have gone, those bastards are gone," he said.

Carlos ran to the bedroom door in disbelief, he looked inside the room—they had gone.

Albi was standing at one of the windows, "They climbed through this window, we have to catch up to them." He pushed past Carlos and started to dress, "Come on, Carlos, we don't know what time they left or how far they have gotten."

Both of them got dressed quickly and put their coats on.

"I will put the fire out," said Carlos as Albi opened the door.

Velasco and Pedro walked through the village looking for a car or any kind of vehicle that would get them to the coast. They scanned the side streets as they walked through the village, "There," said Pedro. He pointed to a Peugeot car outside a house on the corner of the main road.

"That looks good, can you get it started?" Velasco asked Pedro.

"Yes, we will have to get into it first and push it down the street a little so that the person in the house does not hear the engine start."

They walked over to the car, making sure that nobody could see them. Pedro took out his penknife and forced open the small quarter light at the front of the driver's door. He opened the door and released the handbrake and both men pushed the car about thirty yards. Pedro cut the ignition wires with his penknife and touched two of them together, starting the engine.

"We have a good head start on the others, they will never catch us now," said Pedro.

"I hope that you are right, cousin, my brother will be in no mood to talk to us if he does catch up to us," he replied.

"I must admit it was a stroke of genius to think of leaving through the window while they were asleep. We will reach the dock a little earlier than the rest of the group but it doesn't matter. Mohammed and his people will be there early anyway, he always is, cautious bastard." He hoped that the rest of the journey to Ireland went easier than the first part.

"We are going to have to watch Mohammed and his cronies, they cannot be trusted. He has double-crossed a number of people in the past and killed several of his business partners. He has arranged for a safehouse for us in England after we set off our first wave of bombs. We will lay low overnight and drive back to the port early the next morning ahead of schedule. Mohammed expects us to be in the safehouse for several days and I get the feeling that he may call the police after the bomb goes off. If the police catch us it will give him time to escape from England before he calls the police to lay claim to his campaign of bombs. Watch your back with this one, cousin, he is a true snake and will slit your throat if it saved his own," Velasco said.

They dressed quickly and left the house hoping to catch up to the others. As they started to walk at a fast pace through the town Carlos said, "We are not going to catch them on foot, we have to find some wheels." As he spoke a police car turned out of one of the streets ahead of them, they both slowed down to a casual walk. They watched the police car as it made its way towards them.

"We are on a hiking holiday if they ask, heading towards Logroño for the festival." Albi knew that they were going to be stopped by the police.

"Yes, where are we from, Madrid?" he replied.

"Yes, that's a good idea, we have spent a few days camping before we go to the festival." He watched as the police car came closer.

They could see that there were two policemen in the vehicle as it stopped on the opposite side of the street. They continued walking and gave a casual wave to the policemen as they walked. They could not look back as they knew that this would bring attention to themselves. They heard the police car drive away as they continued down the road. "They have gone," said Carlos.

"For now," he replied.

They had walked about two blocks when they saw the bus stop ahead of them, "We have twenty-five minutes before the bus comes. We really need to get a lift from someone or steal a car, what do you think?" He was about to step into the road when another police car screeched to a halt in front of them, blocking their way.

The policeman was leaning out of the window, "Where are you two going?" he asked.

"To the bus stop to get the bus to San Sebastián," said Carlos.

"Why are you going there?"

"We are not staying there, we a going to get the train to Logroño for the wine festival."

"Have you got any ID on you?"

"Yes," replied Albi as they both produced false IDs.

The policeman and his partner looked at the IDs and then handed them back. "You are free to go, at least you are getting a bus instead of stealing a car as someone did this morning. They most probably knew that the bus service has been cancelled today, good-bye," he said and they drove away.

Both men gave the policemen a slight wave of the hand as they drove off.

"They stole a car, that puts them even further ahead. We have got to catch up to them. No bus service, we will have to try to hitch a lift from somebody," said Albi.

They had been walking almost five hours when a truck drove towards them, closely followed by a car. Carlos stuck his thumb out to try and get a lift, the truck drove by as though he did not exist. He started to sit down when the car behind the truck stopped just past them. They looked at each other as the driver beeped his horn gently to attract their attention. Albi walked over to the driver and talked to him, Carlos was watching when Albi called him over as he got into the backseat of the car.

The old man driving the car was on his way to visit his sister in Tarnos, a small town on the coast, and wanted to have some company for the journey. The radio was playing in the old man's car and he kept jumping from one station to the next. They were thankful for the ride, but the old man never stopped talking the whole journey. Albi offered to drive as the old man never exceeded thirty-five miles an hour, much to the annoyance of other drivers on busy sections of the road, he politely declined the offer. They had been driving for two hours when they came to the junction of a main road.

"It must be an accident, there are a lot of police," said the old man.

"That's all we need," said Carlos.

"I know another way around." The old man was turning the car around in the narrow road.

"We are going back the way we came," said Carlos.

"Not for long," replied the old man as he turned down a narrow farm road. They complained no more as the old man drove through a farm and followed a well-worn path along the edge of a field. Ten minutes later they stopped at a gate at the edge of the farmer's field, which fed them out onto the main road.

"You see, we have passed the police and the accident," he chuckled. "One of you open the gate and close it behind me when I drive through."

Carlos got out of the car and did what the old man requested.

"I will have to drop you off in about fifteen or twenty minutes, as I will be visiting a friend on the way."

"Thank you," Albi replied.

The old man changed channels again when they heard an announcement coming over the radio. "This is a news update on the series of bombs that exploded two hours ago in the center of Logroño. We are still receiving police reports of extensive property damage and many wounded but no deaths so far. An individual claiming to be from the Basque separatist group ETA called the police with a warning that the bombs had been planted. We will notify you with an update soon." The old man turned the radio off.

"They are crazy people that do this kind of thing, why kill innocent people? I do not understand it." The old man was shaking his head.

Albi and Carlos said nothing, they just looked at each other.

Velasco drove down to the harbor where the fishing boat was waiting and as expected he saw that someone was already on board. As always he proceeded with caution as he boarded the vessel, who was on board? Hopefully the other ETA members or Mohammed. He and Pedro both stepped on board the boat, weapons at the ready inside their coats if they needed them. The galley door opened as they got to it, startling both men. It was Mohammed.

"Ah! Welcome, welcome, it is about time that you arrived." He stepped out onto the deck and kissed Velasco on both sides of his face in the traditional Arab greeting.

"Mohammed, on time as usual, how are you?" He didn't really care how he was doing, he just went through the motions of making him think that he was pleased to see him. "This is my cousin, Pedro," he said.

"I have heard a lot about you, Mohammed."

"Whatever this scoundrel has told you, he lies. I am really a horrible person." He laughed, slapping Pedro on the back. "I have good coffee inside your boat." He stepped down into the galley from where he had come.

Inside the galley was one of Mohammed's soldiers, "This is Adel my trusted friend and brother, where is your brother? You said that he will be coming?" He was suspicious that something was wrong.

"He has decided that he is leaving everything to me and Pedro. We will take care of things. I expect some of my men to join us here soon, one of them will captain the boat. He has made this journey before and knows the waters well." He sat down and sipped at the hot coffee that Adel had given him.

"You could make clay out of this coffee," said Pedro with a big smile on his face.

"You Europeans do not know how to make good coffee," he replied with a grin that showed a mouth full of decaying teeth.

As Ester came out of the bar she saw Geraldo standing across the street, they walked towards each other and hugged as old friends do. This was done for effect in case they were being watched.

He smiled at Ester and said, "I take it that you did not have any problems?"

"Everything went fine, what about the other groups?" she asked.

"Everything is in place, Peli has taken the 'Y' members back to San Sebastián. We must make the telephone call to the police and tell them where the bombs are, I will make the call when we get close to the car."

"I will make the call, Geraldo, it will sound more threatening coming from a woman, especially when I say who it is calling, I will meet you by the car."

Ester walked towards a bus stop where he could see a public telephone. She had instructions from Velasco that she would offer to make the call, however, she would not actually call. He wanted to make this the most memorable and bloody event of ETA's history, with more to follow. Albi Basurto, his brother, had no knowledge of the operation and if he did, he would not sanction it. This treachery was going to split ETA down the middle, with Albi Basurto fighting for a cease-fire and peace talks and Velasco Basurto going completely the opposite way by creating havoc.

Geraldo did not know why but there was something wrong, why would she make the call? In the past he or Peli made the call. As Geraldo walked around the corner to the parking lot where the car was parked he realized that they had chosen this parking lot because it had a public telephone. Now he was convinced that Ester was up to no good, he ran back to the corner of the street to see if Ester was using the telephone. Carefully, he looked around the corner of the building across the street from the bus stop and could see Ester sitting on a bench smoking a cigarette. It suddenly hit him, *she is not going to warn the police, it will be a bloodbath.* Geraldo ran as fast as he could to the telephone by the car and dialed the number of the anti-terrorism squad in Barcelona. This was the number that he always called to warn of bombs that he had planted. When the telephone was answered he quickly gave his warning message, identifying the four bomb locations, he hung up the telephone, happy that they knew the call was genuine.

Ester was watching from the corner of the parking lot, curious as to why he was using the phone and who was he talking too? Could he be calling the police after she said that she would do it? The worst thought of all then hit her, *he is an informer!* Geraldo, someone she had known for so many years, worked together on many terrorist attacks. Her well-known paranoia was starting, she would deal with Geraldo, he would regret being a traitor. Ester already had him guilty, as usual she was acting as judge, jury and would be the executioner. She watched him until he put the telephone down, then kept out of sight.

Geraldo watched Ester walk across the parking lot towards him, she smiled at him as she got to the car.

"We can go," she said and got into the car.

"Were the police convinced that the call was genuine?" asked Geraldo.

"Yes, they kept me talking, most probably trying to trace where the call was coming from. They are such idiots to think that they can stop us, they will never catch me, not alive anyway." She meant what she said.

"I bet they transferred you to the terrorism unit, they always try to keep you talking." Geraldo kept the conversation going, he wasn't sure why.

As Geraldo drove out of the parking lot a young policeman was standing on the side of the road. Geraldo ignored him but not Ester, she had to play the game by waving at him, giving him a big smile.

As he drove down the street to the junction of the main highway Geraldo could not hold his temper any longer, "You had to push our luck, didn't you, what were you thinking of? Damn you, Ester."

She said nothing, just laughed out loud.

They were on the way to meet the rest of the ETA members at the coast. Geraldo had been driving for exactly an hour when Ester leaned forward and switched the radio on.

"Music?" Geraldo said with curiosity in his voice.

"No, the bombs will have detonated ten minutes ago, I want to hear what the press are going to say about our greatest victory. There will be panic and mayhem in Logroño as we speak, it will be broadcast all over the world."

She looked at Geraldo with a crazed look in her eyes. They listened to the radio for almost fifteen minutes before the news flash was announced. Ester turned the volume up, she did not want to miss a single word.

"We are receiving breaking news from the police in Logroño. There have been a number of explosions in the city. Police are reporting several buildings have been severely damaged, but thanks to a warning from someone claiming to be from the Basque separatist group ETA there have been no fatalities reported at this point in time. We will give you further news on this breaking story as we receive it."

Ester was leaning forward in the seat, holding her head between her knees, she never said anything.

Geraldo knew to keep quiet as he had seen her respond like this before. *It won't be long before she loses total control,* he thought.

It was almost another forty minutes before the radio station gave an update on the bombings. The radio station announced that there had been many people with minor injuries and still no fatalities reported. An extensive search was under way for survivors by rescue crews.

"Stop the car, stop the car," screamed Ester.

Geraldo slowly pulled the car over to the side of the road. He was thankful that they had left the main highway and were on a quiet country road, if she was going to go berserk a quiet country road was as good a place as any. They were only twenty kilometers from the fishing port where they were meeting the rest of the ETA members, including Velasco Basurto.

Ester got out of the car and was stomping around in amongst the trees at the side of the road. Geraldo watched her as she kicked out at the ground in temper. It was what happened next that put him on alert. She stopped her temper tantrum as fast as it had started and looked in his direction with death in her eyes. As she started to walk towards him, Geraldo slowly pulled the 9mm out of the waistband of his trousers. Ester came closer as he hid the weapon under his jacket and aimed it at the door, ready to shoot if necessary.

As she got closer to the car he thought that she seemed to be calming down, he was wrong. As she got level with the driver's door Ester pulled out her 9mm Browning and pointed it at him. She stood there, the weapon in both hands, a perfect stance with knees slightly bent, feet at shoulder width.

Geraldo looked at her and said, "What are you doing, are you losing your mind?"

She did not say anything at first and he contemplated shooting her, he should not have hesitated. He slowly raised the weapon under his jacket, pointing it at the door, where he thought it would be in line with her body.

Ester finally spoke, "You are a traitor, you informed the police, don't deny it. I saw you on the telephone in Logroño."

"I called the police, yes, but that was what we were supposed to do. You did not even try to warn them, why?" His finger tightened on the trigger.

"It was supposed to be our greatest hour, we were going to shock the world, and you spoilt it."

He did not wait any longer, Geraldo pulled the trigger as fast as he could, at the same time he dropped down on the front seat. He was too slow, his gun going off startled Ester and she pulled the trigger on her weapon, releasing a deadly bullet which hit Geraldo in the side of the head, killing him instantly.

Ester fell backwards, one of Geraldo's bullets hitting her in the lower abdomen. She writhed in pain on the ground, her stomach felt like it was on fire as the blood started to soak her clothes. She tried to compose herself, telling herself to stay calm and control her breathing. She stood up and went over to the car, pointing her weapon into the window, she could see that he was dead and spat on him. In an attempt to stop the bleeding she ripped the shirt off Geraldo's dead body and placed it on her wound. She tried to pull Geraldo's body out of the car but she was too weak, all she managed to do was to sit him up in the seat. In the distance she heard a vehicle approaching and stood in the road to flag it down. An old farm truck came around the bend at a very modest pace and slowed down as the driver saw her. The driver was an elderly farmer from the local village and thought that there had been an accident when he saw blood on her clothes. He pulled over about fifteen feet from their vehicle and got out. As he walked towards Ester he saw the weapon in her hand and started to run back to his vehicle, she shot him three times in the back. She returned to the car with Geraldo in it, she leaned across his body and started the engine. It took all of her energy to turn the steering wheel to point the wheels towards the trees at the side of the road. She jammed Geraldo's foot against the accelerator, causing the engine to race, she rammed the car into gear and it shot forward, knocking her out of the way. She lay in the grass screaming in pain from the fall, but had achieved her goal, the car ran into the trees and was hidden.

She somehow managed to get to her feet again and staggered towards the old man's truck, she saw that he had fallen into the long grass and could not be seen from the road, she left him where he lay.

The ETA members had all arrived at the dock except for Ester and Geraldo. They were starting to get concerned, as they were almost an hour late. Velasco stood on the deck of the old fishing trawler pacing up and down, waiting for his beloved Ester. He saw an old truck come careering along the wharf in the direction of the trawler, he called out to the other ETA members. He had his hand under his waistcoat, holding on to his sidearm, unsure what he was about to face. The other members joined him, they all recognized Ester at the same time, the truck lurched to a halt. They all ran to the truck, Velasco reaching the driver's door first, as he opened it Ester fell out into his arms. The group members helped lift her out of the truck and quickly took her on board the trawler before anybody saw them. Velasco held her blood-soaked body in his arms as she looked at him.

"What happened, where is Geraldo?" he said.

He watched her face as her eyes closed and she died without saying anything. Velasco pulled her dead body to his chest and cried like he had never cried before, they all got off the boat, leaving him alone to grieve.

Velasco had calmed down and started to throw the orders around, "Eneto, Peli, Pedro, come on board. I want to talk to you."

They walked to the boat and joined him in the galley. On the way they could see that he had covered Ester's body with a dirty sheet.

Mohammed and Adel stayed on the quayside, as they knew that they would not be welcome at the meeting.

"We are going to continue as planned, Pedro and I will go to Ireland with Peli. Eneto, you will get rid of that truck that Ester drove here and the other vehicles we drove here from Logroño. I do not want anyone to connect them with the dock or give them ideas that we have left on a boat. Take them somewhere away from the port and leave them in different locations." Eneto hated the way Velasco was talking to him, like some mindless recruit that had just started. "Return to your home and wait for me to call you from England. We will not stay in England as long as we originally planned, maybe three or four days. When I return I want to move quickly with our bombing campaign here and in France, I will talk to Mohammed, he will want to be a part of the French operation." He was ready to show the world a new ETA, and anyone that stood in his way would pay with their life.

Eneto left the boat and told Mohammed that they were getting ready to leave. Both he and Adel boarded the boat as Peli started the engine.

Velasco came up out of the galley, Mohammed went to him and threw his arms around his shoulders like a great bear. He took a step back and said, "I am sorry for your loss, but you will have your revenge on those that caused your pain. I will help you in this quest, you have my word as a Muslim and a brother." He meant what he said, but his words were wasted on his friend.

"We will leave as soon as Peli is ready, I want to get to Ireland early. It will keep our IRA friends on their guard." He stepped off the boat and picked up a length of old anchor chain that was rusting on the dockside.

"What is that for?" asked Adel.

"For her," he replied as he dropped the chain next to the covered body of Ester. "We will bury her at sea in deep water."

Eneto watched him with hate in his heart and pleasure in his loss of Ester, "I hope you go to your death," he said as he wiped the blood from the seat of the truck.

A few minutes later the fishing boat was leaving, Eneto totally ignored the vessel and the people on board. He did not clean the vehicle properly and covered the seat with a piece of old tarpaulin that he found on the dock. He drove the truck six miles to a small town inland from the coast and dumped it next to a local market. It would be some time before it would be discovered. He took the local bus back to the coast and only had a mile and a half to walk to where the other two vehicles where. He moved one of the vehicles to another area of the docks where there were a number of cars and trucks parked, it looked very odd on the quayside by itself. He would eventually drive it to the train station in San Sebastián, where he would leave it and catch a train home. He walked back to the last vehicle, anxious to be done with his part and go home.

The old man dropped off Albi and Carlos, they were much the wiser about the old man's family life and medical condition, as well as his views on ETA.

The minute they were out of the car they talked about the news bulletin on the radio.

"I don't believe it, it has to be the work of Velasco," said Albi.

"Why would he do such a thing without your knowledge or approval?" Carlos replied.

"He wants to move ETA into a full-blown war with the Spanish government. He has grand ideas of completely overthrowing the government and of killing King Juan Carlos. I did not believe that he would go this far. I realize now that he is serious about doing business with the IRA and Muslim fundamentalists from Algeria." He started to walk faster as he spoke.

"Why is he involving the IRA and Muslims?" he asked.

"Because he wants to raise money to support a costly program of attacks against the Spanish government. By organizing an arms deal between the Muslims and the IRA he will receive a third of the money for the weapons supplied to the IRA. He and Pedro acted as the go-between with the IRA and supplied the boat to transport the weapons. I made him tell me where the boat was and who we were meeting. I specifically forbade his involvement with the IRA or Muslims until I had time to talk to them and review my brother's plans." He added the last part because he, like Carlos, had only found out about the arms deal the night before.

"If he is responsible for the attack in Logroño, why would he not include you in the organization?" he asked.

"I think that my brother is trying to form a splinter group. He has many people that would support him in this effort, mostly out of fear. It has to be his work, nobody else within ETA has the capability." He hoped that he could get to the boat before it had left.

"I don't know if it is Velasco or not, but I am here to help." He knew that this would be gratefully accepted by Albi.

"Thank you, let's hope that we can reach him in time." They both picked up the pace with an urgency in each step.

It took them another hour to reach the dock where the boat was supposed to be moored. As they walked through the dock they saw Eneto heading towards a car, his back toward them.

Eneto was getting into the car when he was forcibly dragged out and held up against the vehicle. He was surprised to see Velasco and Carlos, "What are you doing? Let go of me," he said as he knocked Albi's hands off his jacket.

"Where is Velasco?" Albi asked.

"What do you mean, where is he? You know where he is, he left on the fishing boat." He was genuinely surprised to hear Albi ask where his brother was.

Albi slammed his fist on the roof of the car, "Damn, we missed him," he said.

"What is going on here?" Eneto asked.

Carlos and Albi realized that Eneto did not know that they were not involved in Velasco's deal. "Did he say which port they where to stop at in Ireland?" asked Carlos.

"Don't you know?" He was now very curious as to why they didn't know.

"No, he forgot to tell us before he left." Carlos was trying to cover for Albi as he could see that he was not listening to Eneto.

"Is this your car?" asked Albi.

"It is a car that we have been using." He did not get chance to finish what he was saying.

"I need it, get in, Carlos," said Albi.

Carlos got in the passenger side and they drove off, leaving a bewildered Eneto standing on the dock.

"You crazy bastards can all go to hell, I have another car that I can use," he said as they drove away.

"Where are we going?" asked Carlos.

"We are going to Vitoria. I know someone there that will fly me to Ireland and I will try to find my brother and the boat," he replied.

"I want to come along, you may need my help."

"I am not forcing you, it may get nasty in Ireland. I do not know what the IRA will do when I ask them to help me. They will not be very pleased if I ask them not to accept the weapons; in fact, they will most probably want to kill me. I need to think of something before reaching Vitoria, I will call my IRA contact from there and ask him to meet me in Dublin," he replied.

Albi was trying to drive to the speed limit but was finding it very difficult, the last thing they needed at the moment was to be stopped for speeding. Unknowingly they drove back along the same route that Ester had taken only a few hours earlier.

They were making good progress when they came across a traffic jam, they could not see what was causing it as they were on a bend in the road. They crawled along in the line of traffic and eventually saw a wrecker pulling a vehicle out from a line of trees.

"Someone must have been going too fast," said Carlos.

"Yes, there are a lot of police cars there, it must be a bad accident," he replied.

As they got within a hundred yards they could see police officers checking the ID of the motorists ahead of them.

"They never miss an opportunity, do they? Look at them checking IDs in the middle of a traffic accident." Carlos thought that this was no ordinary traffic accident, something was wrong.

As the line of vehicles moved along a policeman approached them in the car.

"Do you have identification?" This was just another checkpoint duty that he did not want to do and it showed in his voice and mannerism.

They both passed their false IDs, hoping that they would fool the police once more. He was looking at them when they heard the sound of a collision. The policeman walked down the line as did several others to look at two cars, one had run into the back of the other.

Albi was watching a policeman sitting on a motorcycle at the side of the road. He was paying a lot of attention to them and he was talking on his radio to somebody. He turned to Carlos and said, "What do you think the policeman on the motorcycle is up to?"

Carlos gave the policeman a passing glance, "He is most probably checking out the license plate on the vehicle. I just hope that it is not stolen, we did not ask Eneto who it belonged to."

The officer walked back to them with their identification. He was almost to the vehicle when the motorcycle policeman called him over. They stood talking for a minute and inspected the IDs once more. The motorcycle policeman was on the radio again when they noticed a number of policemen turn and look in their direction.

"Something is wrong," said Albi.

"Stay calm, it may be nothing," Carlos replied.

The policemen by the motorcycle started to draw their weapons out of the holsters.

"They are drawing their weapons, get out of here," said Carlos.

The engine was still running and Albi quietly slid the car into gear and accelerated as hard as he could. He swung the car around the line of vehicles and sped along the grass at the side of the road. The police officers were all shouting instructions at each other, particularly those at the front of the line of cars. A policeman stepped out in front of them, pointing his revolver at the car. Albi didn't hesitate, he drove straight at him, causing the policeman to dive for safety. They passed the front of the line of cars, still accelerating as fast as the car would go. The police officers now had a clear line of fire at the car and it sounded as though they all fired at once. A hail of bullets flew into and past the car. Carlos lay as low as he could in the front seat, as did Albi, trying to hide from the bullets, and their fate was sealed. Two tires burst and Albi lost control as a bullet hit him in the shoulder, the steering wheel spun out of his hands. The car lurched violently to the right, rolled several times before coming to rest on the roof in a cloud of dust and steam. A swarm of police officers descended on the vehicle, ready to shoot anyone that tried to get out. They did not have to worry, as both occupants were unconscious inside.

Carlos felt the car going out of control and tried to brace himself for the inevitable but to no avail. As the vehicle rolled down the road he and Albi were bounced around like rag dolls. His chest and head were pounded against the dashboard and roof. He felt a searing pain, he was not to know a broken rib had pierced his lung. Albi was much more fortunate, receiving a broken wrist and severe bruising as well as the gunshot wound.

The police officers dragged the bodies out of the car with no regard for the individuals and their injuries. A sergeant stood over them and immediately recognized Albi as the most wanted man in Spain.

"Call for an ambulance." He barked at the group of police officers who were standing around. "I want this one to stay alive." He pointed at Albi.

By the time the ambulance arrived at the hospital in Vitoria the counter terrorism unit was on its way. Albi was still unconscious when they put him in the private room. The doctors had done a good job of removing the bullet from his shoulder and resetting his broken wrist. He had received a number of blows to his head, causing trauma to the brain and a concussion, X rays showed no permanent damage. As a result his body went into a coma that would last for several days.

Carlos was not as lucky; he underwent two hours of surgery to repair the damage to his ribs and lungs. Along with a fractured skull and severe bruising to the brain the doctors gave him a fifty-fifty chance of surviving.

A week later Albi slowly came out of the coma, it took him some time to realize where he was. He looked around the room to discover that he was in a private hospital room on his own with a uniformed police officer outside. A man in a suit was talking to him, a detective, thought Albi. The detective was explaining to the policeman that the man in the next room was an undercover police officer and he was in critical condition. Albi looked through the glass dividing the two rooms and saw Carlos. He could not believe it—Carlos a policeman, a traitor. Albi did not let anyone see that he had regained consciousness and spent the next twenty-four hours recovering some of his strength. Although he was still very weak he would escape from the hospital the following evening.

7

SEPTEMBER 24th, ENGLAND

Strain knew exactly who he was going to call for the electronic surveillance of the Home Secretary. George Barton was an absolute genius in this highly specialized field. George was working for Government Communication Headquarters (GCHQ) based in Cheltenham, their role was a very basic one, monitor and intercept communications worldwide for the government. In the Cold War days this was a relatively simple process and normally involved electronic communications of one kind or another and of course bugging people and property. Nowadays the situation was totally different, with the advancement of technology came more sophisticated encryption methods, mobile telephones and the Internet. GCHQ had approximately 4000 employees, a far cry from the 7000 plus in the Cold War days. As a support group GCHQ had proven itself invaluable over the years, providing information and resources to government agencies, their primary function.

GCHQ also worked closely with their US counterpart, the National Security Agency (NSA). GCHQ utilized the NSA spy satellites, so sometimes they really did not have any choice but to work with the NSA.

Strain telephoned GCHQ and was put through to Barton. "George, John Strain here." It had been almost a year since he had spoken to George.

"John Strain, my, my, to what do I owe this honor, or are we just after a favor again?" George was used to Strain asking for favors, borrowing equipment from him to perform surveillance work was the normal request, unofficially of course.

"No, George, the government is going to make YOU earn your money this time," he replied.

"Sounds interesting, John, what do I have to do, listen in on the House of Commons and tell you what those bloated old bastards are saying?" Whatever it was he was definitely interested, as he knew that if Strain was involved it was going to be juicy.

"Meet me at the Hog in the Pound pub on Oxford Street at twelve noon tomorrow. We will discuss the basics of the job. George, you are going to need all of your best equipment and skills on this one, it is highly sensitive.

I will have to get you reassigned for a short time to another group, you cannot be connected to me, don't worry, it is legal. You will need to have another technician to assist with the surveillance. I do not know how long this will last, but it will be twenty-four hours a day split between two of you, any questions will be answered tomorrow. Do you have anyone in mind that you can trust one hundred percent?" This was Strain's biggest worry—confidentiality. A leak at this stage of the operation would be devastating.

"Typical, questions will be answered tomorrow," he replied.

"Do you have someone you can trust at this level?" Strain asked again.

"Yes, yes, remember Chalky White? He was on that job with us last year tracing the Neo-Nazi gang. He is working with MI5 at the moment and they are driving him insane with bureaucratic bullshit. He would like nothing more than to be given a job with some meat and excitement." George really enjoyed being around Chalky, as he was about the best counter-surveillance man he had ever worked with, hence the reason MI5 had him.

"That may be a problem, George, I cannot afford for MI5 to get wind of this job. Is there anyone else you can use?" That was all Strain needed, if Fletcher, the head of MI5 and Mask committee member, found out what he was doing it could blow the whole operation.

"Sorry, John, it is him or nobody, I do not trust anyone else if this is as sensitive as you are making out." He paused for a moment and said, "I have a suggestion, how about Chalky goes sick for a week or two, you would have to clear his record afterwards, but it would be worth it. If not I don't know what to suggest unless we can use one of your lads." He really did not want anyone else working with him on this job as he had the feeling that he would need a true technician.

"No, that won't work, I need all of the team members, we are already shorthanded and will be for a week or two. Tell Chalky to meet us tomorrow, he can report sick in the morning. Do you still have the same mobile phone?"

"Yes, same number," he replied.

"See you tomorrow." Strain hung up. *That was a good suggestion by George,* thought Strain, *report sick for work, I wonder how many times they had done that before to cover another job.* It didn't make any difference they were needed. Thank goodness that they both worked for the good guys, they would be worth their weight in gold to anyone in the criminal or espionage world.

Strain telephoned the hospital at 5.30 a.m. the following morning to check on L.B., Stan and Bulldog. Bulldog had already been released with nothing more than severe bruising to the chest, which would keep him out of commission for a few days. The condition of L.B. and Stan was not so good, but they would be hospitalized for a couple of days; better that than dead, thought Strain. He contacted the other team members that were fit for duty and told them to meet him at his hotel in London at 2 p.m. Bulldog was not pleased about being left out and cursed his luck and his bruised chest.

George and Chalky arrived at the pub the next day at about the same time. They did not wait outside and walked downstairs to the basement restaurant. "What is Strain up to?" asked Chalky.

"I don't know yet, but it is going to be very interesting, you know he always seems to get the best jobs," George replied.

"The best or the worst, it all depends on how you look at it. Whatever it is I don't care, it will get me out of Thames House for a while." Thames House was the headquarters of MI5 located at Millbank on the River Thames.

"You must be in the know these days at MI5, was Strain involved in that job in Birmingham where the IRA members were killed? Some kind of special operations group, I understand?" George had not heard anything at all about the operation, which only made him all the more curious.

"No, I haven't heard a thing. I know that it is the talk of the shop, but nobody seems to know anything. I do not believe for a minute a police operation, certainly not a standard firearms support unit." Chalky was being completely honest, the Mask Team members had not been identified. Even when they had worked with the team the previous year they did not know the true nature of their business. It was just another regional crime squad group as far as they knew.

The waitress came over and took their drink order. Chalky was watching a man and woman who had just walked into the restaurant, the woman was pointing to a table in the opposite corner of the restaurant to them. Both George and Chalky watched them make their way to the table. They were really watching her.

"She is good-looking," said George.

"No kidding, I bet you that is his secretary, if it is he is definitely doing her. Lucky bastard," Chalky replied.

The mobile phone in George's pocket burst into life with a low ring, he took the phone out and pressed the receive button. "Hello."

The voice on the other end was instantly recognizable, Strain. "Go to the toilet, I will call you back."

George knew something was wrong immediately and said, "Hello, hello" into the telephone. "I guess they don't want to talk to me," he said to Chalky, making out that there wasn't anyone on the other end.

"I don't blame them, I don't like talking to you either." Both men laughed, mostly for the benefit of anyone listening.

"I am going to the toilet," he said to Chalky.

In the toilet he turned the ringer off on his telephone and put it on vibration and locked himself in one of the toilet stalls. He did not have to wait long in the stall when the telephone started to vibrate. He pressed the receive button and held the telephone to his ear.

He could hear Strain's voice again, "Leave the restaurant, turn right out of the door and about twenty yards on your left is a café with tables outside. Go into the café and through the kitchen at the rear there is a backdoor leading into an alley, I will see you there. You are being followed, so don't waste time once you leave the pub." The line disconnected. *Here we go, I knew this was going to be juicy.* He really enjoyed working with Strain. George tore off a piece of toilet paper and wrote on it, 'Follow me' and put the paper in his shirt pocket.

George flushed the toilet and opened the door to let himself out of the stall. Standing at one of the urinals was the man from the restaurant that was with the attractive woman. George went to the sink and washed his hands, all the time he could feel the man's eyes watching him. *It may not be him,* he told himself, *it could be anyone*. He dried his hands on the towel and returned to the restaurant. At the table he pulled out the tissue from his shirt pocket and made it look like he was wiping his nose with it. At the table Chalky was as cool as ever, waiting for the news. George put his hand on the table and gently revealed the paper napkin with the message. Chalky picked up his drink, at the same time reading the message. George screwed up the napkin in his hand and both men made their way to the stairs leading out of the restaurant to the street above. At the bottom of the stairs was one of many mirrors on the walls advertising a local beer, in the reflection of the restaurant behind him he could see the man and woman standing up from the table. *So it is you,* he thought, *you should have finished lunch.* At the top of the stairs they gently pushed past two young women entering the pub. They turned right out of the pub door as instructed by Strain. George took off at a run, closely followed by Chalky. Both men entering the café before the man and woman following them had time to see which way they had gone. They walked towards the kitchen door and a man dressed in what looked like a cheap chef's outfit waved them in, he pointed to the rear door that they were to use.

Halfway up the stairs the man and woman met the same two young women that George and Chalky pushed past as they left the pub, the man and woman wasted valuable seconds trying to politely negotiate their way past them. When they reached the street outside the pub the man and woman were looking around to see where the two men had gone. "Where the fuck did they go?" said the man out loud.

A group of young skinheads sitting at a table near the door were watching them when one of them said, "Hey! Are you looking for two fellas that just came out of there?"

"Yes," the woman, said, "Did you see which way they went?" She was using her most pleasant of voices, trying to charm the group of men at the table.

"Yeah, darlin', they went across Oxford Street towards Selfridge's. Why don't you let ugly go after them and you can stay here with us, we will show you a good time." He then stuck out his tongue, waving it up and down at her in a suggestive oral act. The group of men started to laugh as the man and woman headed towards Selfridge's.

"Fucking pigs, look at them run," he said to his friends. "I hope they enjoy shopping in Selfridge's."

This was said for the benefit of the rest of his friends at the table. It was also the codeword to let Strain know that the coast was clear. Strain was listening in his earpiece to the conversation the skinhead was having through a hidden microphone worn by the skinhead on his jacket. The skinhead was really Detective Constable Marvin Gould, an undercover officer working with a task force who were trying to infiltrate soccer hooligans. These gangs were responsible for murders, armed robberies and numerous serious assaults. They roamed from soccer game to soccer game causing violent fights to break out before, during and after the games. Interpol had recently been involved as they were now attending European soccer matches outside of the UK involving British teams. A network had been developed between the UK hooligans and European gangs, extending their activities across Europe. More recently there was strong information being developed that they were involved in the drug trade. Gould and the other task force members knew exactly how dangerous it was for him to be involved, one wrong move, a slip of the tongue, and his cover would be broken, which would most certainly mean his death.

Strain was waiting at the backdoor of another shop in the alley as George and Chalky came out of the kitchen.

"Come on, you two, what took you so long, you couldn't tear yourselves away from her, could you? Follow me." Strain led both men through a maze of shops and side streets until they came to a grey van with 'London Construction' on the side. As they approached the vehicle Strain pressed a remote control locking device he was carrying and they could hear the doors unlock. Strain opened the backdoors and all three men climbed into the rear of the vehicle.

"What the fuck is going on, John?" said George.

"I will explain on the way. Stay in the back, nobody can see you there, let's see if we have lost our friends." He slid a wooden panel open in the front of the van, which gave access to the front seats. Strain got into the driver's seat and started the engine; as he drove the vehicle out of the side street he noticed a parking ticket stuck to the windshield of the van. He smiled to himself and thought, *Try and collect that fine.*

He had been driving for at least ten minutes when he told both men to get closer to the front where they could hear him.

"It's about bloody time," said Chalky.

"OK, you know me by now, I had to take precautions and you will understand why in a little while. We have a very delicate surveillance to perform, most probably the most delicate that you will ever perform. I was afraid that you might be followed, that is why I did not meet you. I need you both to be invisible for however long it takes to get this job done. I am going to take you to a house from where you will run the surveillance. You will stay there until further notice, no contact with anyone from this point." Strain knew that they would not like this and they didn't.

George's frustration showed through. "Hang about, John, you expect us to stay put in one house for an unknown length of time with no clothes or personal cleaning gear, no contact with anyone? How do you expect us to do the job, we have no equipment. Don't tell me that you have it, because we don't know what we need yet until we know what the job is or see the premise."

"Come on, John, you need to be more open with us," said Chalky.

"Boy, you two are touchy today, I told you that I was going to brief you. I need a commitment from you before I go any further. I have got to have your assurance that you are in on the job before I can tell you anything else." *Here they go again,* he thought.

"Look, I know that this is a lot to ask but I need to know that you are in, you will understand why as soon as I tell you who the surveillance is on. Trust me, you know the individual and you really will want to be involved." *That will hook you,* he thought.

Both men looked at each other. George nodded his head to Chalky and he said, "What the hell, this has got to be better than the office. OK, we are in," said Chalky.

"Good, we are going to keep surveillance on the Home Secretary." Strain could feel the gasp from both men.

"Bowler?" said George.

"Well, do you know any other Home Secretary?" asked Strain.

"I hate that obnoxious prick. I am really going to enjoy this one. What about our equipment?" As always George was concerned about his electronics.

"I have brought some equipment with me that we have used in the past. I was hoping that we can plant the listening devices in his residence later today. You will find the equipment in the boxes in the back along with British Telecom outfits. Have a look and see if there is enough to get us going." Strain looked in the rearview mirror and could see both men rummaging around in the back of the van going through the boxes of equipment. He just hoped that neither of them would be too mad at him when they saw what he had back there.

"You bastard," said George. "You told me that this equipment was lost in the boat that sank on Lake Windermere fifteen months ago."

"He gave me a similar story about some of my stuff, look at what is in here. You have almost enough equipment to supply the government," said Chalky. "You are a prick at times, Strain, is all this equipment reported lost?"

"Yes, lost or damaged beyond repair. It has all been accounted for with the various police authorities or GCHQ, wherever the equipment originated from." Ironically the Home Secretary covered the equipment losses through the Chief Constables, so Strain did not have to answer any questions.

"I don't see any camera or camcorder equipment in here, John, are your lads taking care of that?" said George.

"Yes, they will be delivered soon, some will have infrared capability, you will also have night vision binoculars, the usual stuff."

The van pulled up at the rear of a building that was once a large luxury home for an upper-class family. As with many properties of this kind in London, this had been re-designed and made into private apartments. The three men unloaded the boxes from the van and took them to an elevator. The apartment that they were to use was located on the top floor. It was a loft conversion that had recently been completely re-decorated.

"This explains the construction van," said George, as they walked around the apartment.

"The neighbors won't suspect anything if they hear you moving around, they have seen and heard the decorators for the last two weeks. There are used painters pants and shirts in the white box in the corner. As you can see there are various decorators' tools and equipment scattered around, almost looks like you are working for a change. Not bad accommodation for a couple of slobs like you," said Strain. "Go through the equipment, I will be back in an hour or so and you can tell me what else you will need. Be ready to go into Bowles' place when I return if we have enough to get the job started."

"Where is his place?" asked Chalky.

"Look out the front window, it is the building across the street with a black door and white window frames."

"Doesn't he have a policeman on security duty outside, I don't see one?" said Chalky.

"He has continually refused to have a police security detail, he is a privacy freak. I will see you later." Strain left them to sort out the equipment.

SEPTEMBER 24TH, IRELAND

Billy finally managed to contact Eamon in London. "Christ, I've been trying to contact you all day," said Billy.

"What's got you so excited?" he replied.

Billy told him about the conversation that Fagan had taped between Foy and Bowles.

"Well, I guess I will be going back to his house to visit him, we can't have Alan talking to him. Has Alan left yet?" he inquired.

"I don't know for sure, but he may have been on the two o'clock flight."

"Tell Brian to bring the plane into the private airfield by Heathrow. He is in Dublin, you know the number. Tell him to come over straight away and wait for me." He put down the phone.

Eamon knew that it wouldn't be hard to convince Bowles to meet him; he had the ultimate bait, the promise of a new twelve-year-old Asian girl. He explained to Bowles that he knew he had gone through a bad time lately and the IRA wanted to reward him for his loyalty. He fell for it, hook line and sinker, the twelve-year-old clouding his mind. They arranged to meet at his home that evening.

SEPTEMBER 24TH, ENGLAND

By the time Strain had driven back to his hotel the team members were waiting for him in his room.

"Nice to see that you have made yourselves at home," he said. The team were sitting eating food that had obviously been ordered from room service. "I hope that you paid for that, or is that too much to expect?"

"No, we put it on your room bill, you need to have your mini bar restocked as well," said Thomas.

"As long as you have left me a beer," he said.

O'Neill threw a can of beer to him. Strain sat down with the team and explained what had transpired at the Prime Minister's office. He again left out the part that he knew Alan Foy was going to show up in Birmingham. He explained that the Home Secretary appeared to have a personal agenda, that was enough to get their interest.

"What exactly is he up to?" asked O'Neill

"We are not sure, but it could have a connection to the IRA. I have George Barton and Chalky located at a residence across the street from Bowles' home, this will be the listening post. When we go over there we will gain access to Bowles' home by using the old telephone repairman scam and they can go to work planting their devices." This still did not seem right to Strain, bugging the Home Secretary's house, but he was going to enjoy it. "Let's get going, we are running short of time. What cars have you got?"

"Four cars we have never used before, they have only just been delivered. They are scheduled to be used as traffic patrol cars. They haven't even been registered as received by the local police garage yet. We brought along the camcorders and other gear you asked for," said Thomas.

"Good, let's go." Strain was anxious to get the surveillance under way, especially the bugging of the Bowles household. This was going to be the most risky part of the operation, if they were caught in Bowles' apartment there was no story or excuse that they could give that would justify them being there, not without involving the PM, and they could not do that.

The team arrived at the apartment, ready to perform their individual tasks as a part of the surveillance operation, everyone shook hands and exchanged insults. The team members had a great deal of respect and admiration for George and Chalky, as they had shown their skills to the team on more than one occasion, particularly when they had to track a vehicle or individual. George and Chalky had wasted no time in setting up the surveillance and recording equipment. It looked as though they had been there for a couple of days—not just over an hour. Two sets of tape recorders were being used, mainly as a precaution in case one failed for some reason. Next to the tape recorders was a 12-inch television screen and VCR. They would be recording the clandestine interception of any telephone conversations as well as any recordings from the hidden microphones in the premise. Next to each window were two sets of binoculars, standard and night vision models.

"How does it all look, lads?" said Strain as he passed the camera equipment to Chalky.

"You have kept the equipment in good condition and we should not have a problem with starting the surveillance. Ideally we would have liked to get some additional Harmonica bugs to go inside the telephones and maybe a couple of additional leaches, we have plenty of series radio taps and Vox to activate the transmitters," replied George.

"What is a Leach and a Vox? I have never heard you use those words before." Strain found their work fascinating but boring at the same time.

"You would know them if you saw them, we always use them on a job like this. A leach is a parasitic device, it's a series radio frequency device that often uses the telephone line for an antenna. A Vox is a voice-operated switch used to activate a transmitter, recorder or some other device in a room. You have seen us use them before. I would like a directional microphone, but there isn't one in the kit you provided." George was starting to enjoy himself now, he loved to get new equipment, as did Chalky.

"OK, write the specifications down and we will get them for you. Are you ready to go over to his home?" Strain already had the Telecom van ready at the back of the building.

"Ready when you are, Chalky will stay here. I will need at least one of you with me." George thought that Strain would join him.

"I won't be able to do it. Bowles knows me. Shadow, you have done this before, you go in with George. All the Telecom paperwork is in the vehicle if he should come home early. A call to Telecom maintenance has already been made to register a problem in the street with the telephone lines. Good luck, George, we will see you back here with the other equipment in a few hours." Strain wasn't sure where he was going to get the directional microphone at this late stage, it may have to wait until tomorrow. "Just so you know, the rest of the team will be parked up in vehicles to watch for Bowles coming home. He uses the same route every time, much to the annoyance of his driver. If we see him we will call, you will have approximately four minutes from the first call and two minutes from the second. Get the important wiretaps done first, George, and the rest is gravy. OK, let's do it, we will be in the observation positions in about five minutes, by then you should be inside, good luck."

"It may seem like a dumb question, but how do we get into his house, and is there likely to be anyone at home?" said George.

"I have a key that will get us in," said Shadow.

"Yeah! What kind of key is that, I wonder," replied George.

"Bowles lives alone, he has a maid that comes in Monday through Friday to clean house and do his laundry. She arrives at 10 a.m. each day and leaves at 4 p.m. Bowles does not allow her to visit at any other time, he is adamant about her hours. When she first started working for him some two years ago she stayed late to finish off her work one afternoon. Bowles came home at 5 p.m. and she was still there, he went ballistic with her, she has never done it since. He is something of a privacy freak." He was a total freak as far as Strain was concerned. "No more questions, let's get started."

George and Shadow stopped the Telecom van outside Bowles' home and walked straight up to the front door. They knocked on the door and waited to see if anyone answered, nobody did. Shadow went to work on the lock, opening it within five seconds.

George was amazed at how fast Shadow opened the door. "Remind me to change the locks on my house, will you, I don't like the speed at which you opened that lock."

"It won't do you any good." Shadow smiled.

Once inside they quickly located the living areas and master bedroom. They were both very impressed by the luxury and style of the furniture and fittings. Bowles surrounded himself with only the best furniture, mostly very expensive antiques and artwork.

"He really lives well does our Home Secretary," said George as he looked around the home. "OK, you go ahead and start unscrewing the transmitters on his telephone handsets and replace them with these. Thankfully he is a tight bastard and still has the standard crème-colored BT phones." The transmitters he was referring to were the microphones in the handset. "I will concentrate on the leaches first and tapping into his lines to see how many he has. We can do it all in about forty minutes if everything goes right."

Before they knew it they had been in the house twenty-five minutes, George testing reception of the bugs with Chalky. Shadow had been busy unscrewing cover plates on light switches and electrical outlets and replacing them after George had concealed his bugs. George was about to start placing some additional bugs in the study or library, he did not know what to call it, when Shadow came running in from the lounge.

"We have four minutes, he has left his office already. We need to pack everything and go," he said.

"I haven't had time to place any bugs around the room yet, they need to stall him," replied George.

"They can't do that, pack up and let's get out of here." Shadow knew that they could not screw up now and destroy the operation before it got started.

"OK, you put everything away. I will tidy up here." George was furious, why did the lazy bastard choose tonight to finish work early?

"Time to go, he will be here in two minutes," Shadow said.

"One second," George said. He was removing a rivet in the top of a large leather chair by the drink cabinet, one of many that formed a line of rivets that decorated the edge of the leather on the chair.

"Christ all bloody mighty, George, what are you doing? We don't have time." George quickly pulled out a rivet from his pocket that looked just like the one he had removed from the chair and placed it in the vacant space. Now Shadow was physically pushing George out of the study towards the door. Both men tried to walk casually out of the house and got into the British

Telecom vehicle they had left outside. As the van turned the corner and disappeared out of sight, Bowles' vehicle entered the street from the opposite end.

Once he heard the four-minute call Chalky was making a note of the time, when the two-minute call came he started to mutter to himself. "Come on, where are you? get out, forty seconds and still no sign of them. What is going on? Get out, get out." With that he saw both men appear at the door and walk to the van. Chalky kept looking up the street to see if Bowles' vehicle would show, as the van disappeared around the corner Bowles' vehicle appeared at the end of the street. "That was too close for comfort, boys," he said to himself.

Inside the van, Shadow was going nuts at George, "You crazy bastard, you almost had us caught, what the hell were you thinking? You nearly gave me a heart attack." The sweat was starting to appear on the foreheads of both men. George did not say anything, he just smiled. They slowly worked their way through the heavy traffic returning to the rear of the building that was their base.

By the time they returned to the surveillance apartment Chalky already had the tapes rolling and was recording something.

"What have you got, Chalky?" asked George.

"Nothing, just a telephone call to his secretary to arrange lunch for him tomorrow at the Connaught Hotel. Sounds as though he is pouring himself a drink. Come to think of it, what are we going to do for food and drink?" Chalky was really hungry; after all, their lunch was cut short by Strain.

"There is a refrigerator in the kitchen, we filled it up when we arrived. Sorry, forgot to tell you," said Hobson "I must leave you to it, I am returning the van and meeting the rest of the team. Keep radio silence. John will call you on this mobile phone." He handed a mobile phone to George.

"See you later," George said.

Strain gave Laura a call at the PM's office. "Laura, John Strain here." He didn't have to tell her who it was but he did anyway. "Can you do me a favor?"

"Yes, no problem, what is it?" She would walk on broken glass for him if he asked her.

"I need you to call the Home Secretary's car phone, his driver will answer. Mr Bowles will not be in the car, but I need you to ask for him. When you are told that he has already dropped him off at home, I need to know if he has dismissed the driver for the evening, or if he is to pick him up later. I know this is asking a lot, but it is important." He thought to himself, *she knows that it is important, you idiot, otherwise you would not be asking her to do it.*

"Do you wish to stay on the line while I try, Mr Strain?" she replied.

"Yes please, Laura."

A minute later she was back on the line. "Mr Strain?"

"I do wish you wouldn't call me Mr Strain, Laura, you make me sound like my father, call me John." *Always good to keep the PM's secretary sweet,* he thought.

"Why of course, John." She was being humorously sarcastic now. "The Home Secretary had indeed been dropped off at home and he did dismiss his driver for the night. Stated that he was going to have a quiet evening with his feet up, as it had been a very hectic day. Is there anything else I can do for you?" she inquired.

"No thanks, Laura, you're a real gem, thanks a lot. Bye." The news of Bowler staying home helped John and his team tremendously. This would give them the opportunity to gather their thoughts and plan the next day's events. A few blocks from the Home Secretary's house was a small quiet Italian restaurant. Strain told the rest of the team to meet him there. When they arrived at the restaurant it was deserted, much too early for the dinner crowd. This suited them as they could eat and discuss the plan without worrying about who was listening. They all ordered garlic bread and pasta dishes of one description or another and washed the food down with a couple of bottles of Chianti Classico Gold between them. Strain checked in with George for the third time since they had arrived at the restaurant. All quiet, nothing doing, he was told.

It was just after 6.45 p.m. when Eamon arrived at the basement entrance next to Bowles' home. He let himself in with the key as always and locked the door behind him. This was the entrance that Bowles had the prostitutes use when visiting him so that nobody knew that it was his home they were entering. Bowles rented the one-bedroom basement apartment in someone else's name and always sent his rent, which was a cashier's check made out to the owner, by mail. Once inside there was a door in the wall that Bowles had installed not long after the IRA recorded him. He no longer trusted the prostitutes and they always had to come to him now, the new entrance gave access to his home without anyone knowing about it.

Eamon pressed the bell button by the door to let Bowles know that he was there. The door had a one-way viewer installed in it to allow Bowles to see who was on the other side. The only locks on the door were on his side of the door, giving him complete control of the access.

Bowles was sitting in his study reading the newspaper when he heard the bell ring. He was expecting Eamon to visit and didn't even check through the viewer if it was indeed him, he was too excited about the young Asian that he had been promised. Eamon could hear the door being unlocked from the other side and as the door opened there was Bowles to greet him.

"Come in," said Bowles as he was looking past him for the young lady.

"Don't worry, she will be here in thirty minutes. We have something to discuss first," Eamon said.

Both men moved to the rear of the house where Bowles had his study.

"Drink?" Bowles asked.

"No thank you, but you have one please." The last thing he wanted was two used glasses to be seen by the police.

Bowles sat in his favorite leather chair and turned on the television with the remote control. The news came on the screen, the local news always got his attention, he took a sip of his drink.

"You know, that looks good, I think I will have a drink." Eamon stood up, "Stay there, I can help myself," he said.

Eamon opened the drawer on the drinks cabinet behind Bowles chair, inside as always was the Smith and Wesson .38 that Bowles kept loaded. He checked the weapon. Bowles had his back to him, without hesitation Eamon turned around with the gun in his hand. He placed the barrel against Bowles' right temple and pulled the trigger once.

Bowles did not have a chance, the bullet entered his right temple and exited just above the left ear, taking the left side of his head with it. The glass in his right hand dropped to the floor from the lifeless fingers and rolled behind his feet. Eamon wiped the handle and trigger of the weapon clean and placed it in his victim's right hand. Again he held the weapon to Bowles' head and let the arm drop, the gun falling to the chair. *That should convince the police and everyone else that you committed suicide, perfect,* thought Eamon.

Talking to the dead body, he said, "Now, me old son, this is why you committed suicide. The shame was finally too much for you." He took out three videotapes from his coat. He placed one in the VCR and pressed play at the same time turning the television on. The tape began to play to its dead audience, it was showing Bowles having sex with a twelve-year-old oriental girl. The other two tapes Eamon hid, not very well, behind some books on a shelf. "There, you should find those," he said to himself. He cleaned everything he had touched before he left the apartment, standing in the hallway, he gave one quick last look to satisfy himself that he had not forgotten anything.

Eamon quietly closed the basement door behind him, leaving it unlocked. He walked a couple of blocks until he reached Piccadilly Road and caught a passing taxi. The taxi did a quick U-turn in the road and drove off with Eamon comfortably in the rear.

George was watching the street outside Bowles' home, wearing his headphones, ready to listen to anything that went on inside the house. He did not have to worry about pressing any buttons to record anything, as it was all activated automatically. Noises like the telephone ringing, somebody talking or noises over a certain level kicked off the recording; however, you always wore the headphones to listen for other unusual sounds, it also cut out any noise in the room you were in when you were listening to the surveillance sounds. He saw a man in a black raincoat with the collar turned up walking towards the house. George started the camcorder and ran off a few shots of him with the camera. The man passed the entrance to Bowles' home and went down the steps to the basement apartment next door.

Chalky stood looking over his shoulder eating a sandwich. "Mmm, wasted a few shots there, George," he chortled.

"Here, you watch for a while. I am going to make a sandwich, not the size of that one you have though." Chalky could only just about hold his sandwich with both hands, it was so big.

He sat in the chair enjoying his sandwich watching the street as George had. Several minutes had passed, Chalky had almost finished his giant sandwich when he heard George behind him.

George screamed at him, "Chalky, the tapes are revolving, where are your headphones?"

Chalky nearly fell off the chair in his haste to get to the headphones, "Oh fuck, George, I forgot to put them on." He quickly put them on his head and immediately could hear somebody talking. George turned up the volume on the tape so he could hear what was being said.

"That sounds like an Irish accent," said Chalky. "How did he get in there? Nobody went in the door."

George was furious at Chalky and he could see it, "How did you miss him? He must have gone in when you were eating."

"No, no, I didn't take my eyes off the street, he must have gone in through a backdoor," he replied.

"Strain said that there isn't a backdoor and the first-floor windows are eight feet off the ground," George replied.

They both listened to what was being said. They could hear the Irish man talking to Bowles, or at least that is who they thought he was talking to, for all they knew there could be a dozen people in there.

Chalky instinctively had both of his hands pressed on the headphones holding them closer to his ears. This did not help him hear any better, it just felt like it did. There was a very loud bang and Chalky ripped the headphones off his ears and covered his ears with his hands. "What the fuck was that? Oh! My ears." All he could hear was a loud continuous high-pitched noise in his ears.

George heard the same noise over the tape recorder, at the same time he saw Chalky pull the headphones off his ears, he was obviously in pain as the microphone that picked up the bang amplified the noise to the headphones.

George picked up the mobile phone and dialed Strain's number, it was ringing. "Come on, John, answer the phone," he said to himself. "You OK, Chalky?" George asked.

He only just about heard George through the ringing in his ears, "Yeah, just can't hear properly, that sounded like a gunshot, George. What do you think?"

"Yes, it most definitely was a gunshot," he replied.

Strain answered the telephone, "Hello."

"John, we just recorded a gunshot at the residence, you need to get over here," George said.

"On the way." That was all Strain said.

"I wish for once that he would sound like he is going to panic," said George, talking to the telephone. "Chalky, start the camcorder, let it record the front of the building, you photograph anyone that enters, leaves or just walks past the place. Wait, I can hear something else on the tape." He picked up the headphones and held one side to his right ear. "It sounds like he is listening to something on the television, what is going on in there?"

The team members saw the expression on Strain's face when he answered the telephone, 'something's wrong' written all over his face.

Strain stood up from the table and leaned forward to talk to the team; as he did this they all leaned forward to listen. "George thinks they heard a gunshot at the residence." Strain threw more than enough money on the table to cover the cost of the meal.

Everybody headed towards the cars outside at double quick pace. At the cars they all went into a well-rehearsed routine. Open the trunk of the vehicle, take out the bulletproof vests and weapons. On the way to the house Strain contacted George on the mobile.

"George, are you sure about what you heard?" He knew that George would not be wrong.

"Yes, definitely a gunshot, only one. No signs of anyone entering the premise, but we heard him talking to someone else just before the gunshot. Now it sounds like he is watching television. Wait a minute, John," he said.

Chalky was pulling at his shirtsleeve and pointing to the street. "The man in the raincoat that went into next door's basement is leaving." Chalky was clicking away with the camera, trying to get some close-up facial shots.

"John, this may be something or nothing but a white male, approx. 5'10" tall, slim build, wearing a dark-colored raincoat, just left the neighboring basement apartment. He turned right on the street and took the first right into the side street. He is not hanging about, John, he is really walking fast, something is wrong here." George knew that the man coming and going so quickly out of the neighboring building was not a good sign.

"We are one minute away, keep me posted, stay on the phone," Strain replied. *No concerns about radio silence at the moment,* thought Strain. "Hobson, over."

"Go ahead, over," came the reply.

"White male, 5'10" tall, slim build, wearing a dark raincoat, has just left the neighbors' property. He turned right into the first side street, find out who he is, over." *Maybe it is just the neighbor, what if this is nothing and we go barging into his place, we will blow the whole deal.* He was on the radio again, "O'Neill and Thomas, you cover the rear of the property, we will go in the front. Everyone be careful, we don't know if there is anything wrong, let's not blow the job." Strain was frantically thinking of what excuse he could use if Bowles answered the door. Strain's car calmly pulled up outside the house. He and Shadow got out of the car, bulletproof vests concealed by their sports coats. Everything looked fine from the outside, a dim light showing inside from a room at the rear. Strain indicated for Shadow to check the neighbors' basement door. Strain stood by the window next to the front door and looked inside, no movement, all quiet, he thought.

"John, get down here," whispered Shadow from the steps of the neighbors' basement.

Strain looked over the metal railing next to Bowles' front door and saw Shadow looking up at him, waving for him to come down.

As he walked down the steps leading to the neighbors' basement door he could see that Shadow had gone inside, Strain followed him. Shadow covered a door in the wall to the left of the front door. Strain quickly and professionally checked that the basement was clear, the basement was empty. Only one door was left, that was the one that Shadow was covering in the wall close to the front door, but it did not look like a door, it had no handle or lock. The only reason that it looked like a door was that it was open by about half an inch. Both men approached the door, Strain indicating to Shadow to open it quickly. He opened the door as instructed and Strain stepped into position to check the inside of the room, using his gun for protection. They were momentarily startled as they thought that they saw someone inside, it was only a coat on a hook. The room was only two feet deep with another door on the inside, both men immediately realized that it was a closet. George nor Shadow went into the hall closet and did not see the door. This was one area where they did not have time to plant any bugs.

Again they went through the process of opening the inner closet door as if there were bad guys waiting to shoot them on the other side. To their amazement they found themselves in the hallway of Bowles' home. They could hear voices coming from the rear of the home and the familiar flicker of light from a television screen reflecting off the walls.

Shadow covered the stairs while Strain approached the room at the rear. After a quick check of the two side rooms and kitchen he looked into the study, where he could see Bowles sitting in his leather chair with only the light from the television illuminating the room. He could see the television screen and immediately recognized Bowles receiving oral sex from what appeared to be a very young Asian girl. This sickened Strain, but he could still not let Bowles know that he was there. Strain knew something was wrong here and there was the faint smell of burnt gunpowder as though a gun had been fired in the room. It looked as though George and Chalky had heard correctly. Strain approached the chair slowly, trying not to wake him when he saw something on the side of Bowles face. He did not need to go any closer, on the drinks cabinet to the far side of his chair was blood splattered all over it. Strain stood up from his crouched position and immediately saw that part of Bowles' head was missing. He was stunned for a moment, then suddenly snapped out of it as he realized either he had committed suicide or he had been murdered, if it was the latter the murderer could still be in the home. He quickly made his way back into the hall and proceeded up the stairs without saying anything, they checked all rooms but found nobody.

Strain broke the silence, "Bowles is dead, he is in the study."

"How?" he replied.

"He blew his head off, or it certainly looks that way."

"Suicide, that doesn't seem like something he would do, John; besides, he was a weasel, I wouldn't have thought he would have had the balls to take his own life," Shadow replied.

"Find out if Hobson caught up with the raincoat that left next door and get the rest of the team in here." Strain went straight back down the stairs to the study. He could hear the coded conversation on the radio between the team members as he entered the study. The television was still showing the video of Bowles and the young Asian girl, this time in a full sexual act. He turned on the lights and turned off the television, removing the tape from the VCR.

"I knew I didn't like you for a reason, you child abusing sicko. Christ, Bowles, that child in the video could not have been more than twelve years old. You deserve to die just for that." Strain never gave it a thought that he was talking to a corpse. As he did a visual inspection of the body he saw that Bowles had a TV remote control still held in his left hand, which was resting on the arm of the chair, explaining why it did not fall out of his hand when he shot himself. A Smith and Wesson thirty-eight caliber revolver resting between his right leg and the side of the chair, his right hand partly covering it. "Well, it really does look like you shot yourself," he said to himself, but there was something not right about it, Shadows, words sticking in his head, *he was right, you don't have the balls to kill yourself.* He carefully scanned the room without walking around, as he did not want to accidentally destroy any evidence. Everything perfectly in its place, nice and tidy, except for a drawer behind Bowles' chair which was partly open. On the bookshelf he saw that two books were not pushed back in line like all the others, they really stood out compared to the rest, which were in regimented lines. He heard someone in the hallway and turned to see O'Neill and Thomas walking towards the study.

"Sorry, John, the raincoat was well gone, he could have disappeared in any one of a dozen places. Well, looks like he did a good job," he said as he pointed at Bowles.

"Yes, certainly looks that way."

Thomas accidentally dropped his radio on the carpet and bent down to pick it up, as he did so he something caught his eye under the chair behind Bowles feet. "Did you see that glass on the floor behind his feet, John," he asked.

Strain bent down and saw a crystal glass on its side resting against the heels of Bowles' shoes. "No, I didn't, well spotted, how did it get there?"

"He must have been having a last drink for courage and dropped it when he shot himself," replied O'Neill.

All three men were now standing over the body, checking it out, as well as the chair and carpet, looking for any other clues. "There is a slight wet patch on the side of his trousers just above the right knee, it could be blood." He bent down to take a closer look and said, "No, it's not blood, it smells like whiskey." He bent down and carefully lifted the glass into an upright position with a pen out of his pocket and gently slid it out from under the legs of

Bowles. One sniff of the small amount of liquid in the glass confirmed that it was indeed whiskey. "Yes, it's whiskey, John," he said.

"Now that makes it a murder in my books, very suspicious," Strain replied.

"What makes you say that, John?" asked O'Neill

"Well, you haven't had time to inspect the body as I have, look at what we have here. A TV remote control in his left hand, a gun on his lap next to his right hand. Yes, so far suicide, so where does the glass come into play? Bowles is right handed and could not have held a glass and gun in his right hand at the same time and pulled the trigger to kill himself. I think that he was sitting here enjoying a drink with his mysterious visitor when he was shot in the head and the gun was placed to make it look like a suicide." Strain was totally convinced that this was a murder, as the other two now were. "Give George and Chalky a bump on the radio tell them to have everything ready for us to review in, say, twenty minutes. Get the rest of the team in here. I want to go through this place with a fine toothcomb, have another look upstairs, see if there is anything suspicious." Strain knew that they would not find anything, he just wanted both men to leave the room long enough for him to have a look at the misplaced books on the shelf.

Both team members left the room and Strain wasted no time checking out the books. As he tried to push the books back into place they were being blocked by something on the shelf behind them. Strain moved the books aside and saw two videotapes at the back of the shelf. He removed both tapes from the shelf and saw that they were exactly the same as the one that he had taken out of the VCR. He concealed them inside his vest and left the room.

It only took Alan Foy eight minutes to walk from his hotel in New Bond Street, an upscale area of London, to the street where Bowles lived. As he walked into the street he saw four men outside Bowles' home talking, they all appeared to be wearing jackets that were very bulky. He knew from his days in Northern Ireland that they had bulletproof vests underneath the jackets. He stepped behind a large builder's skip that was in the road and watched what was going on. He saw one of the men talking into a handheld radio, at the same time looking upwards towards a block of apartments across the street. At the top of the building Foy could see a dim light on the inside, apart from a ground floor window it was the only light showing in the whole building. *This smells like the police, that was very careless of you looking up there,* he thought to himself. *What are you boys up to, I wonder.* He saw the men go into the apartment.

There was only one way for him to find out and that was to find a vantagepoint, and it looked as though somebody already had the best one across the street. He counted the number of doors along the street and figured out the number of the apartment block that he had to enter.

Foy casually walked across the street and down an alley about a block from Bowles' apartment. Working his way along the alley at the rear of the buildings, he noticed that every back entrance had the number of the building on the rear doors. He soon found the one he needed and to his amazement found the door to be unlocked, he entered. Inside was a corridor and set of stairs leading up to the top floor and an old elevator that looked like it was still in working order. He opted for the stairs, gradually making his way to the top floor. When he got to the top of the stairs he could not see any way of accessing the roof. There was only one door on the top floor, which obviously gave access to an apartment. He could not see any light shining underneath the door, he put his ear to the door and could hear somebody talking inside, it sounded like somebody on a two-way radio.

"So I have the right place, but no roof access, so I have to get inside." He had the element of surprise so far and wanted to keep it that way, he tried the door handle, turning it very slowly—no luck, it was locked. The sound of a door closing downstairs echoed up the stairwell, a second later the elevator motors started, sending the elevator to the ground floor. Someone was calling the elevator down. Foy looked around for somewhere to hide in case it was one of the policemen from outside, he looked across to the elevator doors and saw a hatch in the wall. Foy quietly made his way to the hatch, the elevator was now making its way up. The hatch was fitted with a lock and he did not have any way of opening it, at the side of the elevator was a small space just big enough to conceal him. He just managed to squeeze into the recess when the elevator stopped at the top floor. The metal gate on the elevator was slid open and he heard someone step out and walk towards the apartment. He could not risk looking around the corner of the alcove as he was sure to be seen. Foy heard the man knock twice on the door, pause and knock twice again. After a very short wait he heard the door being unlocked.

"What the hell is going on down there?" he heard one man say, obviously one of the occupants of the apartment.

"Bowles is dead, someone tried to make it look like suicide. Do you have everything on tape?" He heard the visitor reply and then the sound of the door being closed.

Foy could not believe his ears, Bowles dead, someone tried to make it look like suicide, Who? He did not have to think long, Eamon, but that was impossible, what would he be doing with Bowles, what would he have to gain? He waited for three minutes when he heard the door open again, this time someone left, taking the elevator down. Foy slid out of his hiding space and carefully looked down the stairwell to see who had left, it was one of the men he saw standing in the street. If Eamon was involved, then there was an IRA connection and that stunk because he was supposed to be the only contact with Bowles. If these people were bugging Bowles' apartment then the evidence of who had committed the murder would be inside the apartment. He had to get in and find out without being recognized. He pulled a handkerchief out of his pocket and placed it around his face, tying it in a knot at the back of his head.

Foy approached the apartment door and gave the same knock as the previous visitor, at the same time removing his gun, a Walther PPK, out of his pocket. He heard someone approaching the door inside, as the door was being unlocked he heard the man inside talking, "What did you forget?" the man said as the door swung open.

Foy was in like a flash, knocking the man to the floor as he entered, he pointed the gun straight at the man's head and put a finger to his lips to tell him to stay quiet. Foy checked him for weapons but he was not carrying any, he waved the man to his feet and pushed him towards the backroom, where there was a light. George had his back to Chalky when he walked in the room with Foy but he could see their reflection in the television monitor in front of him. George was thinking quickly on his feet, he thought that this must be the person who killed Bowles.

"Come on, we haven't got all day, we need to make a copy of this tape they will be up here in a minute to listen to it." With that he swung around in the swivel chair to face Chalky and the unwelcome guest. "What the fuck is going on here, who are you?" George said in his best surprise voice.

"Never mind who I am, give me the tape and I will tie you up and leave you alone," Foy replied.

"Irish voice, you must be the bastard that killed the Home Secretary, if you want the tape you can take it off the machine yourself." George was hoping that this would distract the Irishman and he would not notice the tape on the floor by the window. This was the first reel that he took off the machine, he hadn't got around to taking the second one off.

"How about you rewind the tape for me and let me have a little listen to what you have recorded," Foy said, pointing the gun at George.

"Don't you worry, we got everything you and Bowles said on tape," George replied.

Foy pushed Chalky violently towards the tape player and said, "Play the tape or I will shoot you and then I will play it anyway, your choice." He pointed the gun at Chalky's legs.

"Play the tape for him," George said.

Chalky rewound the tape and pressed play. Bowles' voice was remarkably clear, thought Foy and then he heard another voice, it was Eamon. He was confused and didn't not know what to think now, but it confirmed that his fellow IRA members were involved in something with Bowles. *If they are involved in the deaths of my boys they will regret it,* thought Foy.

"Stop the tape and give it to me," he said.

Chalky did as he was told, his nerves totally shattered at this point. He looked at George and he could see that he was also not handling this situation very well, the fear was in his eyes. Chalky turned to give Foy the tape, at which point Foy took his eyes off George for a second. Whether through fear or courage or a combination of both nobody knew, George lunged at Foy, unfortunately Foy was more than up to the challenge, sidestepping George smashing the butt of his weapon into the back of his skull, George collapsed to the floor unconscious. Foy swung the weapon up into Chalky's face, "Now, do you want to be a hero?" he said. Chalky just shook his head, indicating that he didn't.

"Drag your friend over to that closet in the wall and you get in there with him." Foy knew that someone could come back at any time.

Chalky did as he was told and got into the cramped space with George. Foy closed the door on them, placing a chair under the handle, preventing them from getting out easily. He picked up the tape with the voice recording on it and noticed the camcorder on the table. Without checking the tape in the camcorder he removed it and placed it in his pocket, as he did so he looked out of the window and saw someone walking across the street from Bowles' home.

"You will be too late to catch me," he said to the figure as he walked away from the window. Once downstairs Foy left by the backdoor and soon disappeared into the night.

By the time George and Chalky were rescued from the closet Foy was back at his hotel.

George regained consciousness just as Chalky and Hobson were lifting him out of the closet. A small pool of blood had formed on the floor where he had been lying. Chalky pulled him into a sitting position and checked the wound on the back of his head. "You are going to need a few stitches in that thick skull of yours, George. If it had been anyone else they would have had a fractured skull."

"I suppose he got away?" George said.

"Yes, he did, but we will find him, George," said Hobson. "Strain is going to make a phone call, then he will be on his way up. Run through what happened and what you remember about this bloke that slugged you."

They both went through the evening's events systematically, including how George made the intruder believe that he had the only voice tape.

Chalky noticed that he had taken the camcorder tape but not the VCR copy. "He has taken the camcorder tape but he missed the VCR tape." Chalky was still a little shaken.

Strain went to a public phone box to make his call to the Prime Minister. "Sir, this is John, sorry to bother you at home."

"What is it, John?" he replied.

"Have you got us on scramble, sir?" he asked.

"Yes, go ahead."

"Mr Bowles is dead, sir, he was murdered at his home this evening." *That was the only way I could tell you,* he thought.

The PM was totally shocked at the news, "What happened, how?"

Strain went through everything with the PM, including how they had only set up the surveillance a couple of hours before.

"Made to look like suicide but it wasn't, who do you think could have done this, John? You mentioned an Irishman, is it the IRA?" He was hoping that it wasn't the IRA, because they were to start discussions about possible peace talks, to kill the Home Secretary at this time would not make sense.

"Yes, I do think it was the IRA, but the reason why is what I don't know. It may be to destabilize the potential for peace or it could be something completely different." He was just guessing as he did not really have any idea as to why this had happened.

"I do not want anyone to find out about this, gather what evidence you have and have his body collected by Fletcher and his MI5 clean-up crew. I want to keep this under wraps for a day or so to give us time to figure out what the hell is going on. Come to the house when you are done. I will be waiting for you. Not a word to a soul, John," the PM said

"I don't think that we should involve MI5 at the moment, sir. We do not know how deep this is going to be or who is involved. I may be a little paranoid, but I think that it is safer that way." Strain really did not want Fletcher involved. MI5 had a way of taking over an operation and not telling anyone what was happening, including the PM.

"It's your game. Play it as you see fit. Come and see me when you have sorted things out, I will not be going to bed until late," he replied.

"Yes, sir." John hung up the phone and made his way back to the surveillance location.

After a quick briefing, he had the team standby in Bowles' home and in the surveillance apartment and left for his meeting with the PM. He knew that the PM was not going to like what he was going to say, so he took Bowles' porno tapes with him as well as the surveillance tapes.

Eamon got a taxi to Heathrow airport and paid the driver, including a standard tip so as not to bring attention to himself. He walked inside the terminal, located a pay phone and called for a taxi to take him to the private airfield where his plane was waiting. Twenty minutes later he arrived at the private airfield. Inside the small terminal building the night shift staff had just come on duty and were busy running in and out of the building. He had to call his contact to let him know about the evening's events, he picked up the telephone at the reception desk and made the call.

His contact answered, "Hello."

"It is done," was all that Eamon said.

"What are you doing? Don't call me here, call my mobile." He was furious at Eamon for calling him on his home phone.

Eamon put the phone down and picked it up again, he dialed the mobile number.

"What is wrong with you calling me at my home?"

Eamon did not care about the man's ranting, "Do you want to know or not?"

"Of course I do." He was calming down.

"As I said, it is done."

"Straightforward, I trust."

"Yes, no problems," Eamon replied.

The telephone in the study rang, "I have got to go, give me the number where you are, I will call you back in ten minutes." He wrote down the number on the back of one of his business cards. After answering the call he used his mobile phone to call Eamon back on the number he had given him. As he waited for Eamon to answer he started to get a bad feeling about Strain's involvement, Eamon answered the telephone.

"This deal is not working out. We have to close the contract, the head of the Birmingham operation is becoming a problem." He was referring to Strain and his team.

"I agree, this is starting to get complicated, do you wish to terminate their contract?" The conversation, as always, stayed very vague and anyone listening in would not have a clue what they were talking about, it would sound like two businessmen discussing a deal.

"Yes, the sooner the better, do you have something in mind?" He knew he most probably had a thousand ways of terminating Strain and his team.

"I have a few ideas but I will need to know who the board members are, names, addresses. I think I will use the—" he was stopped by his contact.

"I do not want to know how or when. I will e-mail the details, they will be waiting at your office for you when you get back, goodnight."

Eamon walked outside, where the plane was waiting to take him to Ireland.

When he arrived at the PM's residence Strain could see that the news of Bowles' death had a deeper effect on the PM than he would have admitted. The butler took Strain to the PM, who was sitting in his study with a very large malt whiskey in his hand.

"Come in, John, and close the door behind you, there is a drink on the table. I did not think that you would refuse one after what you have been through this evening, even though you must be somewhat used to dead bodies. Don't take that wrong, that was not a dig at you, John, I just don't know how you can function properly after finding a body in such a bloody mess."

The PM was visibly holding back his emotions as he had a drink of his whiskey. Strain sat in the chair and picked up the drink on the table, saying nothing, just letting the man speak. "He and I went back a long way, John, and I appreciate your kind thoughts about protecting him and his dignity from the bloodhounds. I know that the policeman in you also wants the truth hidden for your own purpose, it was a kind thought all the same. Do I need to see the tapes? I can see that you have them with you." Strain had the tapes in a plastic bag and had placed them on the floor.

"That is entirely up to you, sir, all I can tell you is that they look genuine, not fake, and it is most definitely Mr Bowles taking part." Strain did not say any more, leaving it up to the PM to make his decision.

"If you are convinced that it is him and they are not fakes, I do not see any reason why I would want to see them. I would, however, like to listen to the recordings that you made of the conversation before he was murdered." Strain felt the venom in the PM's voice when he said murdered. This was almost personal and very close to home, too close for comfort. They sat and listened to the whole conversation between Bowles and the Irishman, the PM jumped at the sound of the gunshot as it took away his friend's life.

"Any ideas, John, as to who would do this and why?" the PM said.

"Not yet, sir, but we will get answers." Strain made that a mental promise to himself as well as the PM.

"It is a pity that Bowles did not mention the Irishman's name. What do you suggest we do now, John?" said the PM.

"Someone wants us and everyone else to believe that the Home Secretary committed suicide, why? Was he being blackmailed and refused to pay? I don't think so, because he was rather relaxed in the presence of the Irishman. That brought up another question after debriefing the team, especially George and Chalky, they do not believe, and nor do I, that the man in Bowles' home and the one that attacked George and Chalky are the same person. George is convinced that the Irishman that slugged him over the head is a different person to the one that they video'ed going into and coming out of the apartment next to the Bowles residence. Why, because he was wearing completely different clothes, he was slimmer and has a slightly different accent."

"Plus, if he had murdered Bowles there is no way that he was going to hang around. I don't think that the second Irishman even knew that Bowles was dead. I think that we should give whoever faked Bowles' death their wish and announce his death but withhold the true cause of death." Strain was already building a plan in his mind but had a slight change of heart about including MI5.

"What have you got in mind, John?" the PM replied.

"As you suggested, we can have the Home Secretary collected by an MI5 team. Mr Fletcher can be told, by yourself, that he is responsible for keeping the condition of the body a secret, when he sees the body he will believe that the Home Secretary took his own life. He will be instructed to keep the body somewhere safe out of public view and that you will take care of the announcement that he died of a heart attack. For obvious reasons, both personal to Mr Bowles and politically to you and the party, you do not want the suicide story to get out to the press and public, Fletcher will understand. Mr Harper-Jones would be trusted with this task of keeping the press hounds at bay." The PM cut in at this comment of the press.

"I know perfectly well how to deal with the announcement and the press, John." A quick reminder for Strain to understand who was in charge.

"Yes, sir, my apologies." Strain did not take it personally, he knew the PM was under tremendous emotional stress as a result of his friend's death. "Mr Bowles' coffin will be sealed and the body given the appropriate service and cremation befitting his position. This will be seen by anyone watching that knows what truly happened to Bowles as the'old boy network' covering for him. Hopefully this will put them into a relaxed position thinking that the fake suicide worked, giving myself and the team time to dig around quietly to find his killer."

Strain was confident that this would work, but he did not have a clue how he was going to find the person or persons responsible for Bowles' death, or the reason why he was murdered.

"It sounds as though you have got it all figured out, John. Make what calls you need to get the thing rolling, my only concern is how do we say we found him and how do we explain the hidden door in the closet?" the PM said.

"I will say that I had a meeting arranged with Mr Bowles at his home to discuss the Birmingham operation, when I arrived at his home I found the door unlocked and let myself in. The rest is an act of discovery. I will have the door in the closet screwed into place to make it look like it could not be used and place a couple of his coats etc. in the closet in such a way that it hides the door. Even if the door is found nobody will think anything of it," Strain replied.

"Very well, John, you can contact Harper-Jones and I presume that you will tell him that I have been informed and will expect a briefing first thing in the morning," he said.

"I have one final request, sir, I do not want to be bumping into other police agencies or MI5, as they will all want to investigate the suicide. If possible I would like the police commissioner and MI5 to be told to leave the investigation to myself. If they start to snoop around too much it may spook the villains. If the directive came from you they would not question it." Strain held his breath at this point, waiting for another icy blast from the PM.

The PM was tired and in no mood to play political games; besides, he knew that Strain was right. "OK, John, but find the bastards I want them brought to justice for what they have done to Adrian. You talked to me a long time ago about forming a special group to deal with terrorists to hunt them down and erase them from the face of the earth. It is times like this that I wish that I had approved your plan. It is time that we did something about animals that take a life like Adrian's and the lives of innocent women and children. Damn those people to hell, damn them."

Strain stayed quiet, allowing the PM to vent. "I am not going to allow anyone to interfere with your investigation, as far as anyone else is concerned outside of your group and MI5 he died of natural causes. I will make it clear to the police and MI5 that this case is closed. If I find anyone performing any kind of investigation on Adrian it will be the end of their career.

"Do what you have to, John, I don't care how you get the information, but find out who did this. If I am going to tell everyone else that this case is closed you and your team had better lay low for a couple of days. Fletcher will be watching to see if anyone is doing anything to investigate the suicide, especially you. Thank you." He finished talking as quickly as he had started.

Strain excused himself and left. Outside he called Bulldog and told the team to stand down and go to the hotel once the body was picked up. Next he called George, "George, you and Chalky call it a day and leave. Tomorrow I want you to check all of the local private airports and obtain details of all flights that left after five o'clock tonight. Let's see if you can find out anything interesting. See you in the morning."

"You don't want much, do you? Goodnight."

Chalky was listening to the one-sided conversation and watched George put the phone down. "What does he want now?"

"You know what he is like, he wants information on all of the flights that left all of the local private airfields after five p.m. tonight."

"When does he want this information?" Chalky just wanted to go to bed.

"We start tomorrow."

"Well, that's very generous of him."

"Let's get a good night's sleep. I get the feeling we are going to need it."

Foy left the hotel and walked two blocks to a public telephone box, he was not happy using the hotel phone system, electronic records were made of all calls made by guests. He stepped inside the phone booth, closing the door behind him, he did not want anyone hearing his conversation. As he dialed the number to Donnelly's home in Belfast he could not help but smile as his eyes scanned the endless number of cards attached to the inside of the phone booth displaying scantily clad ladies and their telephone numbers. He heard the telephone ringing on the line, it rang several times before it was answered.

"Hello," was the simple answer Donnelly gave when he answered the telephone.

"Michael, is that you?" Foy said in his strongest Belfast accent.

"You got the wrong number," he replied and hung up the telephone.

Donnelly knew this was the code to contact Foy at the call box in London, he had thirty minutes before he had to call him back. After waiting ten minutes he put on his heavy overcoat and left the house. As he walked out of the front door of his home he noticed the car at the end of the street but paid no attention to it, if it was a surveillance team he would soon lose them. As he made his way through the many side streets and alleyways he did not see anyone following him. He removed a cell phone from his coat pocket and pressed the numbers on the keypad.

As Foy left the telephone box he took one of the cards with him, to anyone watching he had just arranged to meet a lady for entertainment. Foy now performed his counter surveillance routine, which included going back to his hotel and sneaking out again through a rear door used by employees. After a brisk fifteen-minute walk he arrived at the telephone box, thankfully nobody was using it. The telephone box was in complete darkness, Foy had damaged the light fitting earlier in the day. He stood inside the box and picked up the telephone, resting his elbow on the receiver, and held the handset to his ear as though he was using the telephone. As soon as the telephone phone rang he lifted his elbow, connecting the call.

"What have you got?" Donnelly said at the other end.

"I need you to find out where Eamon Callaghan is, I believe that he is in London but I need to know for sure. Also, find out how he got here, I have a feeling that he may have come over on a private plane, if he did, where did it drop him off and when?

"Please don't ask too much, as we do not have enough time, I will tell you everything when we meet." Alan knew that his old friend would be chomping at the bit to get going, he wanted to deal with the bastards responsible for his daughter's death, but he had to wait a little longer.

"If he has traveled by private plane I know who he would use. When will we meet?" he replied.

"Hopefully tomorrow, call me back in an hour, is that enough time?" He did not want to push his friend too hard, but time was against both of them.

"One hour," he replied and turned off the mobile phone.

Foy needed time to try and figure out what was going on and the best way to think was with an Irish whiskey in his hand. Not far from the telephone box was O'Neill's bar, an old hangout from when he was running bombing campaigns in England.

The time dragged by as he sipped on his whiskey, the more he tried to figure out what was happening the cloudier it got. He walked back to the telephone box, anxious to hear what Donnelly had found out. The telephone rang as he got to it, *perfect timing for a change,* he thought. "Hello," he said, answering the call.

"You were correct, he has a plane waiting for him at a private airfield outside of London, could be any one of three that we know to be safe to fly in and out of. Apparently he was over there for a few days just visiting London, if you believe that. I am going to meet someone in the morning who may be able to throw some light on the reason for his trip. Have you any more information?" he asked.

"No, what time is your meeting in the morning?"

"I am not sure about a time, how about you call me at eight, I should know something by then. You know which number to call." Donnelly wasn't going to say who he was meeting over the open telephone line and knew that his friend would understand.

"Tomorrow then," Foy said.

Foy returned to his hotel to try to get some rest, life promised to be busy over the next few days.

8

SEPTEMBER 25TH, IRELAND

The plane carrying Eamon landed at a small airstrip just south of the border, only an hour and a half drive from his home. As he crossed the border he was stopped by a Royal Ulster Constabulary (RUC) patrol. They asked him the usual routine questions about who owned the car, where had he been, all the questions were answered promptly and he moved on without any further delay.

He switched on his computer at the house, entered the passwords, which were all encrypted, and checked his e-mails. Four messages, but only one of interest, the one from his associate in London. He printed the list of names, one of which was in bold print, *John Strain*, with an address next to his name. He was obviously the number one target or the head of the team, either way he was a dead man in Eamon's eyes.

How to get to these men was something that he had thought about all the way back from the mainland. He realized that it was easier to let someone else figure out how to eliminate this group of men. Who better than Foy and Donnelly, they had a vested interest in seeing them dead.

It was five thirty in the morning when Eamon arrived at the street where Donnelly lived. He stood in an alleyway at the end of the street for ten minutes, watching to make sure that nobody was around. All he had to do was slip the list of names through his mailbox. He had added to the list of names a typed line at the bottom, which read, 'These are the people responsible for your daughter's death.' He knew that Donnelly would not be able to control himself and would kill them within a matter of days. He was about to move out of the alleyway when he heard the familiar sound of the milk truck coming around the corner. As he stood in the shadows the truck stopped about six feet away from him. He watched as the milk deliveryman went to the back of the truck, he was putting milk bottles into a small carrying crate to deliver them. Not one to expose himself to unnecessary danger, Eamon thought that he could use the milkman to deliver the list for him. Without a second thought he stepped out of the alleyway and stood behind the milkman. He pressed up against the milkman's back and stuck the end of his revolver in his back. The milkman froze thinking that he was about to be killed.

"Don't move, just listen to what I have to say," said Eamon.

The man was totally at his mercy, he knew that he was going to do exactly as he said.

"Go to number twelve and put this through his letter box, that is all you have to do. If I see you turn around or if you don't deliver the letter I will shoot you in the knees, now go."

The milkman did not hesitate, he swiftly walked over to Donnelly's house and delivered the letter. By the time he turned around to go back to his truck Eamon was well gone.

Inside the house Donnelly was sitting in his front room in the dark, he had been awake for almost an hour and decided to go downstairs. He heard the noise of the letterbox and looked through the curtain. He saw the milkman walking away and wondered what he was up to, nothing much, he was sure, he had known him for twenty years. He walked into his hallway and saw the paper on the floor. As he read the list of names and the note at the bottom he could feel his temper starting to rage. He heard the sound of milk bottles banging against each other outside as the milkman approached his house. He heard a gentle tapping on the door and pulled it open with anger. The milkman was bent over putting milk bottles on the step, he stood up, looked Donnelly straight in the eyes and said, "Drag me in the house." He did not have to ask a second time. Donnelly pulled him into the house with such force that he tore the collar off his jacket.

Donnelly was holding him against the wall and said, "What is this note about, where did you get it from?"

"That is why I asked you to pull me into the house, he might still be watching," he replied.

"Who might be watching, come on, speak up." Donnelly was getting angrier by the second.

"Kevin, calm down I have come here to tell you, why do you think that I came over and tapped on your door? Someone approached me when I was standing by the milk truck, he came up behind me, stuck a gun in my back and told me to deliver that letter that you have in your hand. He told me that if I looked around he would shoot me in the legs. What else could I do, Kevin, the man was going to shoot me."

"You don't know who it was then?" He trusted his friend and knew that he would not do anything against him or his family. The man had stored weapons and explosives for Kevin for almost as long as he had known him.

"No, I am sorry, I don't." He genuinely was sorry.

"I appreciate your help, now I will throw you out as roughly as I brought you in, you are right, he may still be watching." Kevin opened the door and pushed him out into the street.

He waited for some time before he left to meet with his contact to get the information on Eamon Callaghan's movements. The fact that someone had arranged for the letter to be dropped off at his home and the peculiar activity of Callaghan made him even more cautious. His contact did not have much else to add to what he had already told him, but offered to continue to see what he could find out.

SEPTEMBER 25TH, ENGLAND

Although he did get a little sleep Foy was restless and unable to get the death of his sons out of his mind. The hot shower and brisk walk in the cool morning air seemed to help freshen him up. It was a little before eight o'clock when he arrived at the payphone, he dialed the number to call Donnelly.

"How are you this morning?" asked Donnelly.

"I have had better nights and you?"

"The same, we have an interesting development. I will not be able to tell you about it over the phone, I suggest that we meet today. I am going to make some arrangements for a party and we can discuss who to invite when we get together. Meet me at the airfield where Colin keeps his glider, can you make it there by four o'clock?"

"Yes, we have a lot to discuss, I will see you there." Foy was really concerned that his friend would go off the deep end, but it looked as though he had his emotions under control for the moment. He headed back to the hotel and collected his change of clothes and bag. He checked the times of the trains for Liverpool and had plenty of time to catch the next one heading north.

As the train departed Euston Station in London for Liverpool Foy fell asleep and did not wake up until the train stopped at Crewe. He looked at his watch and realized that he had been asleep for almost two hours. The guard made an announcement that the train would be delayed for up to an hour due to a problem on the track. He could not wait an hour and left the train, he received directions from a railway employee to the local car hire office. He hired a car with a false driving license and credit card and drove to the rendezvous point at Southport airport north of Liverpool. Southport was a local municipal airport that received very little or no attention from the police or customs.

Donnelly flew the twin engine Piper from southern Ireland himself. He was an accomplished pilot with many flying hours experience, most of which was totally illegal. He had flown in and out of the UK on numerous occasions, dodging detection from radar by flying extremely low. He liked to use an airfield that did not have a control tower, that way there were very few questions to answer.

Foy saw Donnelly standing outside a hangar as he drove through the airport gates, Donnelly pointed to the inside of the hangar. Foy drove the car straight inside the hangar and parked it next to an aircraft. They gave each other a hug when Foy got out of the car.

"Come on, let's talk inside the hangar office, I have some surprising news for you." They both had surprising news for each other.

They brought each other up to date on what had happened in the previous twenty-four hours. When Foy told Donnelly that he had seen Billy Ryan and Stephen Fagan coming out of the derelict house by the school he did not seem at all surprised.

"Why are you not surprised about Fagan and Ryan? They are supposed to hate each other." He realized that his good friend knew a lot more about these two than he wished to admit.

"There have been rumors floating around for about a month now about a new splinter group being formed. I have asked a number of people about it and everyone gives the same answers, heard rumors, know nothing. Those two together does add some credibility to the rumors as many felt that they were really still friends. I am trying to find out who delivered this to my house this morning."

He produced the letter that had been put through his letterbox. "As I told you, it lists the names of the Police Special Operations group that murdered our children. I don't know why I was given the list but I intend to avenge my daughter's death. The only thing that struck me was that this was delivered the morning after Callaghan got back from the mainland. Either he is trying to be a good friend and give us the killers, or there is something else going on. What do you think?"

Foy was silent for a minute as he looked over the list.

"I agree with you, I think that there is more to this. I think the people that I crossed in London could be the same ones that are on this list. Callaghan is not that kind to give something like this without wanting something in return. Something is not right here, I can feel it in my gut. This is too simple, we are given a list of names in order to kill the individuals who have killed our children. The police team involved must be a highly kept secret, but their names and the address of what we assume is the head of their group are given to us on a plate. Why do I feel like we are doing someone else's dirty work here?"

"I am still going to get the bastards for killing my little girl, I don't care why we got this list, they are dead men. The one listed with the address is obviously in charge or he was the one that pulled the trigger. I am setting something up for tomorrow night, you can join me if you want to." It was obvious that he had thought this through and had a plan of action, which Foy was not going to interfere with.

"I am with you, but I think after we do whatever you have in mind we need to return home. We are being used and I don't like it, Fagan or Ryan will be the ones to tell us. Callaghan is behind it, but I do not want to go to him yet."

Foy also knew that Callaghan would not talk to them even if they tried to beat it out of him. "Before we go ahead with your plan to attack this police team there are a few things that we need to clear up. I think that you should go back to Belfast." Donnelly responded to this suggestion with immediate anger, not allowing Foy to finish what he was saying.

"I am not going anywhere until I finish what I have come here to do."

Foy interrupted him, "I am not suggesting that you cancel what you are here for, listen to me. You have agreed that things are not right here and I think that we should try to find out what is going on before we move against the police. I am only talking about putting things off for a couple of days. Let's suppose you go back to Belfast and try to find out what Stephen Fagan and Billy Ryan know about this whole affair, if they know anything. We also need to know what Callaghan has to do with all of this. I don't care how you get the information. Depending on what you find out from them will possibly depend on how we proceed against the police team. I am only suggesting that you go back because you can fly that infernal machine in and out without anyone knowing."

Foy hated to fly, especially on a small plane like the one Donnelly was using. "We can talk to each other over the next day or so and then make our minds up how to work the plan. If you find out that this is much bigger than we thought and you need me to help in Belfast then I will return immediately."

"Supposing I agree to this, what are you going to do here?" he asked.

"I will go to the address on the list to see if the man called Strain really lives there. I will also re-establish contact with some of our mainland supporters and set things up for us to carry out our attack on the police team. We will need vehicles, weapons, explosives and possibly a place to hide out if something goes wrong." He could see that Donnelly was agreeing with him.

"OK, but I don't think that Fagan will talk to me, even if I was to try to beat the information out of him. Billy is different, with enough pain he will crack, the man is a total coward without the IRA muscle to support him. I will take care of him, he will give us what we want." Foy did not doubt for a second that he would extract the information out of Billy, but he did wonder what would be left of him when he had finished.

"I will buy a mobile phone, one of those use as you go deals. I can buy the phone cards to slot in the telephone, that way nobody will know who purchased it or who was using it. I will call you with the telephone number but I will use the one-short system that we have used in the past."

The one-short system was something that they had devised when they wanted to leave a telephone number for each other. They would give the number over the telephone but would reduce the numbers given by one to get the correct number, for example 262 would really be 151. "Call me on the mobile phone as soon as you have the information and we will arrange our next move."

"I will have the information by noon tomorrow, I'll fly back now." Donnelly never was one to hang around.

"Be careful when you go back, they may be expecting you." *God help them if they are,* thought Foy.

They shook hands, Foy headed to the car and Donnelly to the plane.

SEPTEMBER 25TH, IRELAND

The flight back to Ireland was uneventful for a change. Donnelly had experienced many bad crossings over the Irish Sea. Thankfully the storm predicted by the weatherman was a little late arriving. He landed the plane at the airfield some fifty miles south of the border with Northern Ireland. It was a safe location and different to the one from which he had left. The stolen car was there waiting for him as planned, driven to the airfield by one of his brothers, he did not trust anyone else. The number plates on the vehicle had been changed to correspond to a similar vehicle that was not stolen. By the time he arrived back in Belfast it was time for the local pubs to close, he went straight to Billy's favorite watering hole.

The storm had finally arrived, just in time to give him a good soaking as he stood in the shadows across the street from the pub. He watched as a number of people slowly left the pub, the familiar sounds of people merry with drink reaching his ears. He could hear the landlord inside asking people to drink up and go home. The rain was driving down the street blown along by the strong winds. A huge clap of thunder caught Donnelly off guard, making him jump, it was what he needed to keep him sharp.

There he was at last. Billy was shouting goodnight to someone inside and not being very quiet about it. Donnelly watched him as he walked down the street, he had a half mile walk to his house and Donnelly knew exactly where he was going to cut him off. He ran through to the next street where he had left his car. He drove down the street parallel to where Billy was walking and parked the car next to an alleyway. Donnelly got out of the car and unlocked the trunk, leaving it partly open. He then hid in the alley, where he could not be seen but had a clear view of the street where Billy would appear. Billy came down the street on cue, the collar on his coat turned up to protect him from the rain. He was walking quickly but looking at the ground, not paying attention to what was ahead of him. He got level to where Donnelly was waiting and saw the car trunk open. He slowed down his pace slightly as he looked at the trunk, his curiosity aroused.

Donnelly was on him in a flash, clubbing him on the back of the neck, knocking him unconscious. As Billy started to fall Donnelly swiftly and expertly put his arm around his waist and tossed him into the trunk of the car. Donnelly closed the trunk of the car when he heard the familiar sound of a British Army Landrover approaching, he looked around and could see the beam from the headlights shining across the junction of the two roads. He darted back into the alley as the Landrover slowly crawled across the junction and disappeared out of sight.

"Just like old times," he said to himself.

He drove off with the unconscious body of Billy in the car, he just hoped that he stayed unconscious.

Donnelly headed west once he was outside the city, dodging the known police and military checkpoints. It only took thirty-five minutes for him to reach the old water pumping station on the shores of Lough Neagh. Donnelly enjoyed visiting Lough Neagh, as it always felt so calm and peaceful, even in a storm like tonight's.

The Lough was a huge inland sea extending over one hundred and fifty square miles, with County Antrim covering the length of the east shoreline. The eels in the Lough had been harvested by the local fisherman for generations, a great delicacy in Ireland, many hundreds of tons being exported every year. The Lough dominated the scenery and was the source of many local tales and folklore.

As he got to a bend in the narrow country lane he slowed the car down as he looked for the gate that would give him access to the track that would lead down to the pump house. There it was, rather the worse for wear, but still in place, blocking the track. He turned the lights off on the car and took out a large flashlight from under the driver's seat and switched it on. He got out of the car to open the gate as the rain started to ease. The gate had a broken hinge on the bottom and was sitting in the mud, making it impossible to just swing open. He used his strength to lift the end of the gate out of the mud and swung it open on the surviving hinge. He looked at the mud at the entrance to the track as he went back to the car, hoping that it would not get bogged down. In the car Donnelly wedged the flashlight on the dashboard, pointing it forward so that he could see where he was going. The mist coming off the Lough was not helping him, he could put his headlights on but decided against it as he did not want anyone to see the car.

The half-mile drive down the track was slow going as he avoided the worst of the mud.

As he drove down the trail in the darkness towards the pumping station, he heard Billy shouting in the trunk of the car, "Let me out of here, let me out."

"You will be out soon enough," Donnelly said out loud.

He parked the car in a gap in the trees next to the brick building. The beam of light from the flashlight looked like a giant searchlight in the dark as he walked to the back of the car. He put the key in the lock and turned it very quickly, expecting Billy to do something.

Billy felt the car come to a halt and lay quietly in the trunk, wondering what was happening. He knew that he was in trouble but with who and for what? He heard someone outside the car walking towards the trunk. He braced himself in the trunk, lying on his back with his knees bent to his chest. As soon as they open the trunk he was going to kick whoever it was with both feet and try to escape. The trunk opened, Billy was ready to attack when a blinding light hit him straight in the eyes, he instinctively covered his eyes with his arms. He could not see anything, the sudden blast of light took him by surprise.

Donnelly stood by the trunk, shining the flashlight inside as the lid opened. He saw Billy throw his arms over his face to hide his eyes from the light. He took out a 9mm Browning from his jacket and pushed the muzzle into Billy's face.

"Get out," he said.

Billy froze at the feel of the gun in his face, now was not the time to try to escape, he thought.

"OK, take it easy, I am getting out." He could feel the weapon being moved to the back of his head as he climbed out of the car.

"Walk over to the building," Donnelly said and pointed the flashlight where he was to walk.

"What is all this about, why am I here?" Billy asked.

"You will find out soon enough," he replied.

Billy spun around quickly, bringing his right arm up, trying to knock the weapon out of his abductor's hand. He did not surprise Donnelly in the slightest, he took a step back and hit Billy in the side of the head with the butt of the flashlight. Billy crumpled to the rain-sodden ground, screaming in pain.

"You bastard, I am going to get you for this, do you realize who I am?" he continued to complain about the pain.

Donnelly kicked him in the buttock, "Get up and behave yourself and you won't get hurt."

Billy stood up slowly, holding the side of his head as he walked to the building that was being illuminated by the flashlight.

As he walked through the open doorway he could smell cow dung and rotting wood. The place was obviously deserted.

Billy could not make out what the building was as it was so dark. Donnelly pushed him in the back, "Move into the next room, over there." He shone the flashlight towards a door.

He had learned not to try anything funny and did as he was told. He could feel himself walking through cow dung in the darkness, the pungent aroma rising to his nostrils. He pushed open the wooden door and walked into the room, helped by a slight prod in the back from Donnelly. The room was very small, measuring about six feet by five feet, the light from the flashlight let him see that there were no windows in the room. In the center of the room was a large piece of pipe coming out of the ground with an old broken gauge attached that was obviously no longer in use. Across the top of the pipe was a long inch-thick piece of rounded steel that looked like a giant handle, Billy realized that this was used to lower the pipe into place when it was originally installed.

"Get a hold of that metal bar in the top of the pipe with both hands."

Billy did as he was told, grabbing the bar with both hands. As he did he felt the gun being pushed harder into the back of his head.

"Move your feet back," he said as he kicked one of Billy's shins.

"What are you going to do to me?" he asked.

Donnelly did not reply, he just pressed the gun harder into his skin, Billy moved his feet. In this position he could not move quickly, as he was leaning forward onto the pipe.

Donnelly moved around to the opposite side of the pipe, keeping the flashlight shining in Billy's eyes. The fact that he had not seen his abductor's face yet only added to his concern. He tried to look past the light but could not see anything, he dropped his head slightly to give his eyes a rest from the light.

Donnelly pulled out a piece of rope from his jacket pocket and tied it to one of Billy's wrists. He then wrapped the rope around the metal bar and tied the other wrist to the bar.

"Now then, let's you and I have a talk," he said to Billy.

"What about, who are you?"

"You don't need to know who I am, you just have to answer my questions and you and I will get along fine." He didn't believe for a minute that Billy was going to cooperate easily, at least not at the start.

"What is it you want to know?"

"Why was Eamon Callaghan in London yesterday?"

"You can go and fuck yourself if you think that I am going to tell you anything about Eamon; besides, he would kill me," Billy replied.

"Well now, that does leave you with a problem, because if you don't tell me, I will kill you. It is up to you die now or die later, what is it to be?" he asked.

"I don't know why Eamon was in London, I didn't even know that he was in London. I am not his keeper, why would he tell me the reason for him going over there?" Billy thought that he might be able to convince whoever this was that he really did not know anything about Eamon's trip.

"We are running out of time, Billy, it's talk or pain." He did not have time to play the game, he had to move things along.

"What do you mean pain? I have told you everything I know, I can't help you. Untie my hands and let me go. I won't tell anyone, let me go."

He was shouting at the top of his voice, fear starting to build. He heard his abductor walk out of the room, leaving him in the darkness.

"Hey! where are you going? Come on, I have had enough of this, you can't leave me here, you bastard." He could not see anything or hear anything, where had he gone? He heard him walking back into the room. "Let me out of here and I will try to find out what you want know."

The room lit up again with the light from the flashlight as the man walked in front of him. He let out a scream as the man grabbed him by the hair, pushing his head back. He felt something being shoved into his mouth, he recognized the smell—it was cow dung. He was choking as the man kept his hand pressed on his mouth, forcing the foul matter into his throat. He could not take any more and started to vomit, the man moved his hand. His throat cleared immediately as the force of the vomit pushed everything out of his mouth.

Donnelly was standing to one side, watching Billy vomit and choke as he threw up.

"Not very pleasant, is it, Billy my boy. Let us try again, shall we, why was

Eamon in London?"

Billy was spitting the vomit and cow dung out of his mouth, all the time coughing and choking. "I have told you I don't know anything, but I will find out if you release me."

"You know that I cannot do that, I have to have answers to my questions and I have to have them now."

He brought down a tire iron onto Billy's right hand, smashing the fingers. Billy gave an unmerciful scream as the pain surged through his hand and arm. The tire iron struck again, this time on the left hand with the same result, Billy passed out. He wasn't unconscious for long, thanks to the water thrown on his face by Donnelly. He immediately wished that he was unconscious again as the pain returned. Tears welled up in his eyes, he was becoming very angry with his assailant, the pain momentarily taking over his fear.

"Are you ready to continue?" Donnelly asked.

"I am not telling you a fucking thing."

Donnelly did not wait for him to finish what he had to say, he bent the fingers backwards on Billy's right hand, again he screamed with pain. He leaned over and did the same to the left hand, the screams again filling the room and vibrating into the walls.

"Please, please, no more, I will tell you what you want to know, I can't take any more." He was pleading and begging, the fear of more pain taking over.

"I am listening."

"He has a contact in London who he gets information from, he is in the government. I don't know why he went to see him."

The tire iron slammed into the metal pipe, making him jump, his fingers made an involuntary action to grab the metal bar that his hands were tied to, fresh waves of pain visited his hands.

"I want everything that you know about this contact and any others that he has in London. I do not have a great deal of patience and even less time." He tapped the pipe with the tire iron.

Billy did not want any more pain, he could not deal with it. "He is the Home Secretary, Adrian Bowles."

"Why would he visit him?"

"We received information from a prostitute that works for us in London that he enjoyed sex with children. Eamon set him up and video'ed him with a number of young girls before he broke the news to him. He was terrified of the news going public and agreed to cooperate with Eamon, he passed information on about the anti-terrorism units operating in the mainland. We also paid him a substantial amount of money over the years for passing information on to MI5 about our activity. The information he passed on was nearly always false, it gave us time to carry out some of our bombing campaigns. Even though most of the information was false we had to give some good information on arms caches and supporters." He was getting thirsty. "Can I have a drink? I am thirsty." He did not realize it but shock was starting to set in.

Donnelly did not object to this, as he did not want him to pass out again as he was starting to get the information he wanted. He went outside and fetched some rainwater from an old metal container.

Billy found the water like nectar, it helped wash out some of the taste of the cow dung from his mouth.

"Carry on, Billy, you are doing well, what about his other contacts over there?" He took a drink of the rainwater himself.

"I don't know anything about his other contacts, he doesn't tell anyone who it is." He heard the man's feet move on the floor. "Please, you have got to believe me, I don't know who it is, I don't." He braced himself, waiting for his fingers to be bent or hit again.

Donnelly knew that he didn't know, he was in no mood for more pain.

"What do you know about the special terrorism unit that is operating in the mainland, how did they find out about Alan Foy's sons?"

"I don't know anything about them, I was told that they were put together to locate and arrest terrorists of any kind, not just us." He could feel himself starting to shiver. "I don't know what happened to the Foy brothers, I was shocked when I heard about their deaths; honestly, I don't know anything." He could not understand why he was shivering, he wasn't feeling cold.

"OK, you can tell me about your friend Stephen Fagan, what is his role in all of this?"

"He is no friend of mine, we are enemies, everyone knows that." He tried his best to sound convincing, hoping to make this man believe him.

Once more he struck the pipe with the tire iron, "Billy, you were doing so well, why would you lie to me now? I know that you and Fagan are friends and planning activity outside of the IRA. I know where you both meet, shall I say a burnt-out building by St. Patrick's school. So you know that I am better informed than you realize, this is the last time that I will ask this question, what is Fagan's involvement?" He hoped that his bluff would work as he had told Billy everything that he knew about him and Fagan.

"You can't tell him that I told you anything, he is nuts, you have got to promise me." He waited for a reply but did not get one. "Fagan and I were asked by Eamon to join him and several others. They were starting another group to escalate the bombings and assassinations on the mainland. As you know the peace talks are scheduled to start in a month, the idea was to destabilize the talks. We are starting to earn a small fortune through our increased extortion activity and drug sales, they said that all we had to do was keep the peace talks unbalanced for two years and we would all retire rich men. Once we were rich it didn't really matter if they achieved peace or not, we wouldn't care."

Donnelly could not believe what he was hearing, these animals were going to continue the pain and suffering for personal gain. Financial gain for the IRA was fine, but this was something new. He did not care about the British on the mainland, but he did not want to see any more pain and suffering in Ireland.

"You bastards are willing to see our families, our children, suffer for money." He was losing control of his temper. "I have a good mind to kill you right here," he said.

Billy knew that he should not have said anything but it was too late, the fear came back to him. He had to try to do something to calm this man down, he could feel his anger.

"There is something I can tell you about Fagan, but he mustn't know that I have said anything about it, you have got to promise me not to say that I told you."

"He won't harm you," he replied.

"Fagan has a recorder somewhere in his house, when people use his phone he records the conversation, sometimes the information is valuable and he passes it on to me, I then pass it on to Eamon. The information always went through me to Eamon because he and Fagan did not want anyone knowing that they were working together. He called me when Foy made a call from his house the day after his sons were killed. Foy called Bowles for information, he wanted to know what happened to his sons. Fagan called me and I passed on the information to Eamon. During the telephone conversation Foy told Bowles that he was going to visit him in London, we could not afford for Foy to know about our involvement with Bowles." He tried to look past the light again to see who the mystery man was.

"What was Eamon going to do to Bowles?"

"I don't know, who cares, anyway?"

Donnelly looked at Billy with the light shining on him, his body was visibly shaking, he wasn't going to take much more. He knew that he was still withholding something and he had to move things along quickly.

Much to Billy's surprise, Donnelly started to untie his hands. "What are you going to do now?" he asked.

"Get up," he replied and walked out of the room, carrying the flashlight with him.

Billy did not hesitate, he scurried after him into the fresh air and the torrential rain. Donnelly walked over to the car and put the flashlight on the roof, the light shone directly on him. Billy looked over to the car and could now see who it was that had abducted him.

"Donnelly, it's you." He was truly shocked to see that it was Donnelly.

Donnelly held a gun in his right hand, he raised the weapon, pointing it at Billy.

"Wait, don't shoot me, I can tell you more, I didn't know that this was going to involve your daughter, you have to believe me. Eamon set it all up with the help of Fagan, they put the plan together to bring young Alan Foy back to Ireland. Eamon suggested that Bowles should arrange for Alan's return through his father on the belief that young Alan would receive amnesty as part of the peace talks. Eamon was the contact with Alan, he was the one who arranged for Alan to assassinate the policeman and his wife before he went into hiding. That was also a deliberate act to keep the troubles going. Eamon has been in touch with Alan the whole time that he was in hiding."

Donnelly was surprised by this, "Alan's father didn't know that Eamon was talking to his son."

"Eamon convinced Alan not to tell his father, he told him that his father was trying to retire from active service with the IRA. Fagan can tell you more, he and Eamon had some other plan for Alan, I don't know what it was about, that's all I know, honestly."

He looked a pathetic wretch standing there in the driving rain, his arms cradling his damaged hands to his chest, his hair so wet that it was matted to his head. He continued to plead for his life, dropping to his knees in the mud.

"We are going back to Belfast, get in the car," said Donnelly.

"Thank you, thank you," he replied with relief in his voice.

Billy got up and walked to the car as Donnelly went to the trunk and threw the rope inside. Billy was only three feet from him when he raised the weapon again, he pulled the trigger three times, all three bullets devastating Billy's head. The body fell to the ground and lay in the mud with Donnelly standing over it, no emotion in his eyes, no regret in his heart. He lifted Billy's lifeless body and for the second time that night dropped it into the trunk. He drove back to Belfast, where he abandoned the stolen car, with the body still in the trunk.

9

SEPTEMBER 26TH, ENGLAND

Strain was enjoying a deep sleep when he was wakened by a telephone call from Shadow.

"John, I have got a problem and I need a couple of days off, I hope that's OK?" Shadow did not sound himself, something was very wrong.

"I will put a pot of tea on, come and see me," Strain replied.

It only took Shadow five minutes to explain to his boss what was going on, but not until Strain gave him some gentle persuasion. Strain called the rest of the team members in the hotel and asked them to meet him in his room. They all assembled with reluctance, as they wanted to go back to sleep.

"I think we all know Shadow's sister, Susan, and the useless bastard that she married."

Terry interrupted Strain. "What has he done now?" he asked.

"Well, he hasn't been beating her, if that's what you are thinking, he has really gotten into deep shit this time. He stole a van in South London that was being loaded with boxes at a warehouse, the driver left the keys in the ignition while he worked. After the work was finished the driver apparently went into the warehouse to get something and Danny, being the thieving opportunist that he is, stole it. Well, one of the workers at the warehouse recognized Danny but didn't say anything at the time. He had a change of heart when he found out that a reward was being offered for information leading him to the thief. The worker must have gotten greedy or something, and the information was extracted from him for free by the warehouse manager's bullyboys. That is the good news, now the really bad news. The boxes that were being loaded into the van not only contained men's shirts, they had several thousand pounds worth of cocaine hidden in them." The noise of disbelief and anger from the team members was predictable. Strain continued, "The news does not get any better, the warehouse manager and owner is the head of the local 'Yardie' gang."

"That little fuck doesn't do anything in halves, does he, what are we supposed to do, John, catch the little bastard?" Terry said.

"I am getting to that, again, I wish it was that simple. The body of the warehouse informant was found floating in one of the local docks minus several fingers. The Yardies, as you know, are totally ruthless and will kill or maim anyone who crosses them. Once they extracted the information from the employee they went around to Susan's house. Susan answered the door, she did not know anything about the drugs or the van. As soon as she opened the door one of the gang members punched her in the face, knocking her down. Four men then entered the house, one of them grabbed Susan by the hair and dragged her into the lounge. Danny was upstairs when he heard her answer the knock at the door. He was in the bedroom at the time and went to the top of the stairs and saw who it was. He saw her open the door and watched as they barged into the house. He ran into one of the back bedrooms, quickly pursued by the gang members. He barricaded the bedroom door with the chest of drawers, giving him enough time to jump out of the bedroom window and escape. He later called the house to see how Susan was doing and one of the gang members answered the phone. They put Susan on the phone and she pleaded with him to give them the van back. As usual he wanted something out of the deal and thought that he was too smart for the Yardies. He tried to cut a deal on the telephone and their response was to beat Susan as he listened. They then told him that if he did not bring the van back to the warehouse by midnight they would have their fun with Susan, then peel the skin off her body, but not kill her. That was in the early hours of this morning, that was when he called Shadow."

"What are we going to do, boss?" asked Terry.

"First of all I want to find out where they have got Susan, then try to figure a way of either getting her out or negotiating her release in exchange for the drugs. None of you have to get involved with this, as you know, anything that we do is strictly off the record and any screw-ups could cost us our jobs." It did not surprise him that they all volunteered to participate. "Right, let's head to Tower Bridge, Danny is going to be waiting for us in a café across the street from the vinegar warehouses."

The 'Yardies' is a name given to Jamaican-born gang members, they operate in a number of countries around the world, particularly England. The name 'Yardies' comes from Jamaica and refers to the criminals that live and operate in the backyards of the poorer areas of Kingston. There are many different Yardie gangs in the same cities with no affiliation or loyalty to each other. It is not unusual for the different gangs to fight with each other, or to have fighting and conflict within their own gang. Conflicts, whether between gangs or within a gang, is normally sorted out very quickly, usually by execution. This reputation for committing extremely violent acts and cold-blooded murders is known and feared wherever they operate in the world. It has been said that they have a philosophy of live for today and to hell with tomorrow, this could be due to the fact that nobody stays on top in a Yardie gang for long. Like most gangs they obtain funds by trafficking drugs and committing armed robberies. The difference between their gang members and most other gangs is that they often participate in drug abuse themselves, an act that is normally frowned upon by organized crime gangs. They are also involved in arms deals and they have been somewhat successful at this. Again, they do not have any affiliation or conscience as to whom they sell drugs or arms to, if you have the money they will accommodate your needs.

Yardies think nothing of showing off their wealth, displaying in public their expensive designer clothes, jewelry and flashy cars. They live by their image and will not tolerate anyone or anything that tarnishes that image. Their love for guns is another part of the image that they portray, especially around young males and female gang members. As a result of the image portrayed by the Yardies, there are many copycat type gangs springing up in inner cities started by young black males. No doubt their hunt for glory, respect, image, wealth or whatever it may be will result in the same fate as most Yardies, an early grave.

Many law enforcement agencies around the world have set up special task forces to try to combat the Yardie gangs with very little success. Even London's Metropolitan police set up an operation called Trident in an effort to gather and collate information on the gangs, with very little success.

The Mask Team members parked their cars in a side street away from the café.

"Terry, stay here with the car, I will take Andy with me and leave Ian with Shadow to keep him away from Danny. If he gets near Danny at the moment he will tear his throat out the minute he sees him," Strain said.

"I wouldn't blame him if he did, the bastard has deserved it several times over the past two years." Terry had a soft spot for Susan and wanted to take care of Danny himself.

"Well, we all feel like that at the moment. I don't know what we are getting into here, so I need everyone to stay focused. Danny will have his punishment coming very soon, I have a good mind to feed him to the Yardies myself."

"I thought that we were staying focused?" Terry said with a grin.

"Touché, Terry, touché. I will be back soon." He got out of the car and walked over to the other vehicle.

"Andy, you come with me; Ian, stay here with Shadow, don't argue,

Shadow." Strain used his most forceful voice to try to keep Shadow from getting out of the car.

They both headed towards the café closely watched by the other team members. The café was very small, only ten tables, frequented by the locals and some warehouse workers from across the street. The smell of bacon, sausage and eggs cooking and fat burning always took Strain back to the dockland cafes in Liverpool. His favorite was always Franks on the Dock Road, the best mixed grill on toast in the world, he always told everyone. Every table had the obligatory bottle of tomato ketchup, vinegar, glass sugar pourer and salt and pepper, with a slight grease film on the wooden tabletop. For such a small place it was very busy, with all the tables occupied. They walked past the counter, where the fat cook was standing talking to a customer.

"Can I get you lads started with a hot cup of tea?" the cook said.

"Yes, and eight sausage on toast to take with us, we won't be staying long," said Andy.

The cook didn't reply, he just went to work on pouring the tea out and cooking the order, it was the biggest order of the day.

"Nice of you to buy breakfast for us all," Strain said, patting him on the back as Andy walked back to the counter.

Danny stood up from the table as Strain walked towards him.

"Sit down," Strain said. Danny did as he was told.

"I can explain everything, John."

Strain told him to shut up and listen to what he had to say. "I am not going to waste any time, Shadow has told us everything that has gone on since you stole the van. Did you miss anything out when you discussed it with him?" Strain said.

"No, I—"

Strain interrupted him. "Do you know where they are keeping Susan?" Strain asked.

Danny answered, his voice trembling with fear as he did so. "I talked to a couple of people and I think I know where she is."

"Where is she?" Strain replied.

"I think she is in a massage parlor that Justin Barti owns. He is the bloke that owns the warehouse that I took the van from. You have got to believe me, I didn't know that they were Yardies, otherwise I wouldn't have touched the van." Andy arrived at the table with the two mugs of tea.

"You are a lying little fucker, you would steal your mother's teeth if you could get away with it." Andy put the mugs on the table as he rebuked Danny. To his surprise Danny actually reached for one of the mugs, for which he got a slap on the head from Andy. "You cheeky bastard, get your own tea," said Andy.

"Where is this massage parlor?" Strain asked.

"In Brixton," he replied.

"Marvelous, sticking our heads in the lion's mouth was bad enough, but now we have to go into his lair to do it. Have you been in this place before?"

"No, not many white people go in that place," Danny replied. "Are we going to get her out?"

"What is this we? You are going to stay away from the place, when we leave here you will stay with Shadow."

Danny immediately panicked. "Please don't let him near me, he will kill me, please John, don't."

"Keep your voice down," said Andy.

"Let's get the food and leave," said Strain

They left the café, sandwiches in hand, ready to feed the rest of the team, it was going to be a very long day and the food may have to sustain them.

As they approached the cars Shadow saw them, he was out of the car like a greyhound out of the traps at a race. He made a beeline for Danny and got to him as he turned to run. Shadow punched him mercilessly, the team members giving him a little time to get his frustration out before they stepped in and stopped him.

"That's enough, Shadow," said Ian as he pulled him off.

"Put Danny in the car, Terry," said Ian.

Danny was hurting and bloody but glad to be away from Shadow.

Strain knew that he had to keep Shadow occupied, "Shadow, you and Ian go to Scotland Yard, get what information you can on the Yardies, especially Justin Barti. We will meet you at the Bow Bells safehouse in about two hours. We will go to the massage parlor location to see what we are up against and try to find out if Susan is in there."

"John, I think I should go with you to the massage parlor, she is my sister."

"Shadow, I know that you are going through hell right now worrying about Susan, but we cannot afford for you to go kicking doors down, not yet anyway. Go on, do yourself and the rest of us a favor, find out the information we need." Strain was pleased to see him nod his head in agreement.

"I will take Danny with us and drop him off at a safe location, don't worry, Shadow won't touch him," said Ian.

"Where are you going to take him?" asked Strain.

"Somewhere safe, I will think about it on the way," he replied.

The team members knew by the expression on his face that Ian already had a place in mind, nobody asked where it was, let's face it, they didn't care what happened to Danny at the moment.

SEPTEMBER 26TH, IRELAND

It was mid morning when Donnelly woke up to the sound of a telephone ringing. He reached across to the phone at the side of the bed when he realized that it was his mobile phone. He climbed out of bed and took the mobile phone out of the jacket that was lying on a chair in the corner of the room. "Hello," he said.

"Have you got a pen handy," came the reply from Foy at the other end.

"Yes," he replied, as he picked up a pen on the bedside table, he took down the number that Foy gave to him.

"How did things go for you?" asked Foy.

"Very well, and you?"

"Yes, good, I will be there in about an hour, I left early this morning. Keep the number in case you have a problem before we meet. Can you meet me in an hour at the canoe builder's?" He really meant the warehouse at the old ship building dock.

"Yes, see you there," he replied and switched his telephone off.

Donnelly drove onto the dock, giving the security guard a casual wave, and he waved back as though he saw him every day. The guard did not have a clue who he was waving at, he just assumed that because the man in the car waved at him he must be one of the local workers. As he drove past the warehouses and old dry docks it saddened him to think how barren it all looked.

Only twenty years previous the docks were a hive of ship building activity, this dock in particular was one of the most prolific. Harland and Wolff ship builders employed thousands of men, many for over twenty and thirty years. The closing of many areas of the ship building industry in Ireland had brought mass unemployment, particularly to the Belfast area.

He drove into one of the warehouses and saw another vehicle parked in the back. He proceeded cautiously, he did not recognize the car. He didn't have to worry—Foy stepped out of the vehicle and watched Donnelly drive towards him. Foy got into the car and started to pass on the information that he had found out about the address on Strain. Donnelly took a lot longer to explain what had taken place since he returned, especially the information that he had extracted out of Billy. Needless to say Foy was furious as well as curious as to what Eamon was up to, did he cause the death of his sons? What is his involvement? His head was spinning with questions.

"Do we know where Eamon is?" Foy wanted to talk to him personally.

"No, but I believe that he may have traveled down to Dublin or crossed over to London again. I have someone working on finding him and find him they will."

"We have only just started to untangle this mess Kevin, we have to find out what is going on between Fagan, Eamon and the British," he said.

"I think that there is a connection between the British, Eamon and the team that killed our children. It is not just a coincidence that Eamon was in Bowles' place just before you arrived, as I told you he was given the information after Fagan recorded your call to him. I have been thinking about the recording that Fagan does, perhaps there is a way that we can use that to our benefit, that is until I kill him."

"There you go wanting to kill someone else already." He smiled at his friend, trying to lighten his mood. "Do you think that you could get into Fagan's house and use his telephone to call me?" Foy said.

"I can, what have you got in mind?"

"I have a plan. If it works, I think it will tell us if Fagan and Eamon are working with the British, it will also help us set up the police unit that killed our children. If you get inside his house, at his invitation, you could call me on the mobile phone, I want them to think that I am still on the mainland. Arrange to meet me tomorrow night at the pub where we organized the blue mission, suggest that we meet an hour before the pub closes. Only Eamon and a handful of other people, other than us two, would know where we first arranged that mission. We will keep observations on the pub, if this Strain and his team show up we will know that Eamon is passing the information on to the British. I have already made some arrangements to repay Mr Strain and his team, we can take care of them." Foy was not looking for revenge, to him it was justice for the death of his sons and his friend's daughter.

"If Bowles was Eamon's contact and he is now dead, who would he contact on the mainland? Do you think that his other contact could be that high up in the government that they could arrange for this Strain and his men to be there?"

"I don't know, he may have another contact, it could be this Strain fellow or someone else, or Bowles may have been his only contact. It will be a lot clearer if they take the bait from the phone call. If Strain and his team show up we will have more work to do, we will have to get the information out of Fagan or Eamon as to who their other contact is. How are we going to get you into Fagan's house?"

They discussed several different potential strategies before they agreed on the one most likely to succeed.

Donnelly was looking agitated about something. "I want to be there when you go to Liverpool, I want to see how this thing plays out."

"I told you before that I am not going to do this by myself. If you are successful in getting into Fagan's house and making the phone call to me, we can meet at the airfield where you left the plane and we will fly back to Liverpool tonight."

"I'll be off then, wish me luck," Donnelly said.

"You don't need luck, you cunning old bastard," he replied.

Foy made a telephone call to the police on the mainland to ask about his sons and when they would release their bodies. As always they were totally non-committal and stated that it would be several days before they could release the bodies to him. He found it harder and harder to control his anger, being away from his loving wife at this time did not help either. He telephoned her to check on how she was doing, his neighbor answered the phone and told him that she was heavily sedated. He told her that he would be back in a day or two, as soon as he found out when he could bring the boys home. His neighbor knew that he was not just checking on when he could bring his boys home, he was up to something else. She had been around the IRA enough to realize that this was only just starting.

SEPTEMBER 26TH, ENGLAND

The massage parlor was above a row of shops in a fairly busy shopping area. The building had four floors with a butcher shop occupying the ground floor, *kind of ironic,* thought Strain, *that this group of bloodthirsty bastards should be above a butcher.* They individually walked past the butcher's shop a couple of times to see what the entrance was like. Next to the butcher's shop was a single wooden door with a sign on it saying, 'BRIXTON MASSAGE'. Andy went around the back of the building and found that it had a narrow six-foot alley between the rear of the shops and a two-story storage unit. The alley was full of trashcans and cardboard boxes. Each rear door to the shops was steel clad, with metal bars on all of the ground and first-floor windows. *You can see that you have all suffered from burglary in the past*, thought Andy. For the same reason the rear wall of the storage unit was made of solid concrete. On the opposite side he could see a six-story apartment block, *a good observation point,* thought Andy. He rejoined Strain at the car.

"Where is Terry?" Strain asked.

"I don't know, he went to look at the shops on the opposite side of the street, I thought that he would be back by now."

As Strain said it Terry appeared at the end of the street where they had parked. Strain drove towards him and picked him up.

"What kept you?" Strain asked.

"I think I have a way of distracting those bastards if Susan is in there, if we can find a way in," Terry replied.

"There is an apartment block at the back of the shops on the other side of a storage building. If we can get a good vantage point we might be able to see inside the rooms of the massage parlor," Andy said.

"Well, we will not be able to see anything at the front because all of the windows are blacked out," Terry replied.

"Let's take a look at the building," Strain said.

There were plenty of vacant apartments in the building, most probably due to the fact that the place was like a slum. The caretaker was very helpful, especially when they told him that they were the police. They gave him a story that the building at the front of his property was being used as a pornographic film studio. This was bound to keep him occupied looking out of his window to try and get a cheap glimpse of something, when in fact the property they were interested in was on the opposite side of the building.

He gave them a vacant apartment on the fourth floor that he said they could use for as long as they wanted. They set all the surveillance equipment up by the window in the hope that they may see something.

"You said that you had a way of distracting the people inside, Terry, what is it?" Strain asked.

"When I went to look at the shops on the opposite side of the street I could hear music coming from a room above one of the shops. I noticed a 'For Rent' sign on the window so I went inside and sure enough there was a group of kids singing and playing guitars and drums. They wanted to know what I wanted so I told them that I was looking for a place to rent. I spent some time talking to them about the local shops and asked questions about what the area was like. They said that they all lived in the area and it was great except for the Jamaicans across the street. I asked them what was wrong with them and they said that nobody liked them because they think they own the place. The Jamaicans had even threatened them three days ago for playing their music too loud. One of the groups, the lead singer, stood up to the thugs and received a beating for his cheek. They were told to be out by the end of the week or the Yardies were going to break their legs. I asked them if they were for hire, of course they said yes, I told them that I would go back to see them this afternoon."

He could see that they were wondering if he had lost his mind.

"What has all of this got to do with Susan?" asked Andy.

Strain was looking through the high-powered lens on one of the surveillance cameras as he listened to Terry, he suddenly burst into life, "She's there, she's there," he said.

Terry and Andy stopped talking, "Where is she, John?" said Terry.

"Top floor, I just saw her walk past the window, I don't see her now, but it looked like she was on her own. If we could get on the roof of that storage place opposite we would have a much better view. Have a look, lads, tell me what you think."

Both of them spent time trying to see her but neither of them did.

"OK Terry, she is in there, what is your plan?" Strain said.

"Well, as I said I have a way of distracting them, but not a plan of how to get in," he replied.

"I have a plan to get us in but we will need an edge." Strain wasn't sure what that edge was, maybe Terry had it.

"What is your plan to get in, boss?" said Andy.

"If we get onto the roof of the storage place we could put a ladder across to the window of the room where Susan is being held. There is a small ledge that we could rest the end of the ladder on, we would then scramble across, open the window get her out and retreat the same way. Not the best plan in the world, but the only one I can come up with."

Strain knew that the plan depended on nobody being in the room with Susan and required a lot of luck.

"What if I can get those kids to play their music as loud as possible, it may catch the attention of the Yardies inside the massage parlor and distract them long enough to buy us some time. The building they play in has a flat roof, if they set their equipment up on the roof the noise will be much louder and will be directly in line with the top floor of the Yardies' building. The front door to the floor where they practice has a steel door fitted, they can secure the door from the inside and the Yardies will not be able to get to them. I will offer the kids a hundred and they will play their hearts out for that kind of money." Terry knew it was a little thin, but they didn't have anything else at the moment.

"I like it, you know, it might just work," said Strain.

"You two are definitely crazy," said Andy.

"We have got a lot of work to do. Andy, will you stay here on surveillance?"

It seemed strange to Andy for Strain to ask him if he would do something, he was so used to him giving orders, but this showed what kind of a boss he was; after all, they were all volunteering to do this and Strain recognized the fact. Strain needed Terry to visit the group to make sure that they would not disappear. "We will go and get the rest of the team and set things up for about nine o'clock. The Yardies are not going to expect anyone to try to rescue Susan, especially now that they know what a weasel she has married. We will get Danny to contact them and tell them that he will meet them as planned at midnight, but he wants to meet in a public place. They will argue with him but he still has the upper hand because the drugs are more important to them than Susan. We need to think of somewhere that they will feel comfortable meeting him."

Andy spoke, "We passed a fairground on the way here, one of those roving gypsy types. It will be packed with locals tonight, it was only half a mile up the road. If we can get Danny to convince them to meet him at the fairground there is a good chance that they will keep Susan at the massage parlor."

"Bloody hell, Andy, you had better go lay down after that thought, your brain will need the rest. I hate to admit it but that is rather clever, old sport." Terry was being as sarcastic as possible, putting on his best public school accent.

"He is right, Andy, that is a smart idea, he is right about one other thing as well," said Strain with a serious-looking face.

"What's that?" Andy replied.

"You had better lay down, I think you burst a blood vessel on that one." Strain and Terry both headed for the door as Andy jumped at them, beating them about the shoulders as they ran out of the apartment laughing. It was a tonic for the three of them to laugh after all that had happened.

SEPTEMBER 26TH, IRELAND

As Donnelly walked along the street towards Foy's home he could not believe his luck, there was Fagan, and his wife stood outside their front door talking to a neighbor. He had to walk right past them to go to Foy's house, a perfect opportunity to talk to Fagan.

Fagan watched him as he walked down the street, he looked like a tormented man, he thought, not surprising really.

"Kevin, I am sorry to hear about your daughter," he said. His wife and neighbor both nodding their agreement and sympathy.

"Thank you, it is a very tough time my family is going through at the moment," he replied.

"You look like you could do with a cup of tea, come into the house," Fagan's wife said.

"I could do with one, but I am going to visit Alan's wife to pass on my condolences."

"You are wasting your time at the moment, Kevin, the doctor has given her something to keep her sedated, she won't even know you are there. Come in for a cup of tea," she insisted.

"I will just make a quick telephone call and I will be right in." He pointed to the phone box on the corner as he spoke.

"You won't be able to, the kids have broken it, you are more than welcome to use our telephone," she was persistent.

"I don't want to put you out, I have to phone Alan on the mainland, he is checking when we can have the children brought home."

"I will put the kettle on." Fagan said, as he quickly stepped into the house.

"Nonsense, you are not putting anyone out, you can use our phone." Fagan's wife was not going to take no for an answer.

Donnelly stalled for a moment to give Fagan time to set up his tape recorder.

"You're a lovely woman so you are," he said.

As he went into the house he saw Fagan coming out of the lounge and head towards the kitchen.

"Here, go in the lounge and make your phone call." She ushered him into the lounge.

They left him alone for several minutes, during which time he made his prearranged call to Foy. He talked very deliberately and clearly so that if the call was being recorded it would be clear.

When he finished his tea he excused himself and stated that he was going over to Alan's house, he felt that it was the right thing to do. Fagan did not suspect anything from his visit, and it could not have gone better.

Foy and Donnelley met as planned at the airport south of the border in Southern Ireland and within a few minutes they were airborne, en route to England.

SEPTEMBER 26TH, ENGLAND

The safehouse was a four-bedroom luxury apartment in Canary Wharf, an area that had been reclaimed from the Docklands and redeveloped with luxury accommodation and expensive shops. The rent on the apartment was more than most of the team members earned in salary, it was the 'in' place to live or own a property with movie stars and entertainers. You never found the team members complaining about staying at this safehouse as the furnishings and surroundings were luxurious.

The apartment was on the top floor of the old warehouse building, commanding an incredible view of the redeveloped Docklands and Yacht basins on one side and the River Thames on the other. The security at the apartment building was excellent with all entrances and exits monitored by close circuit television. Access to the apartment was via an elevator, which was controlled by a security system, if you did not have the correct access code the elevator would not work. The apartment itself had the highest grade of security possible, with solid steel doors and steel-lined walls capable of withstanding an attack by a small army. Inside the apartment was an inner sanctum with equally strong security, this was designed to be used as a fall-back or holding position to give the occupants time to wait for backup or escape via a hidden hatch leading to the roof. The windows were triple glazed, each pane made with bullet-resistant glass. The security at the apartment was designed by Strain a year previously at the request of the Prime Minister. The intention was that the apartment would be used by the PM when he retired and he wanted to feel safe from potential attack by the likes of the IRA. Strain tried to tell the PM that if they were going to attack him it would be at street level or at some public function where they could not guarantee the normal high level of security. Strain always stated that there was no such thing as 100% security, the attack on the Grand Hotel in Brighton at the Conservative party conference in 1984 by the IRA had proven that point.

Strain ran through what they had found at the massage parlor and described the buildings at the rear, indicating where everything was on a plan he had drawn. He then described his thoughts on the possible entry and Terry talked about his distraction plan.

"Andy has a good observation point and will call on the cell phone if he sees anything of interest. What do you all think of the point of entry and distraction, let's hear your thoughts."

He knew that they would all have something to say about how they should extract Susan, they always did speak their minds, which was one reason why they were so successful.

The all agreed that Shadow was the one to cross on the ladder, because as soon as Susan saw him she would keep quiet and do anything that he said without question. After they had discussed the extraction, Strain went through the plan that they had all agreed to.

"Terry, you get your rock and roll group set up on the roof as it gets dark, at about eight o'clock, make sure that they are safe on the roof and have an escape route. Tell them that they can collect their equipment tomorrow afternoon, if anything happens to it we will find a way to compensate them. Terry, Andy and myself will make our way onto the roof of the storage building, if there are any lights out there we will have to extinguish them. Ian can stay with Danny and ensure that he makes the call and sticks to the script. By the way, where did you take Danny?" he said to Ian.

"I locked him in the storage room at the garage."

They smiled, because the storage room he was referring to was only just about big enough for someone to sit down. The garage was where they kept the spare surveillance vehicles.

"John, do we really need Danny? I don't think this Yardie bloke knows him, if he doesn't he wouldn't know what his voice sounds like, not from the couple of calls he has made," said Shadow.

"He's right, John, I can make the call, I can make my voice sound like his," said Ian.

"OK, let's do that, but keep Danny locked up until we get Susan out. Any final thoughts?" he asked.

"What are we going to do about the van full of drugs, Danny told me where he had hidden it, should we pass it on to the drug squad? The little bastard has hidden it in a lockup at the back of that café we met him at this morning," Ian said.

"How about we tell them where it is when Susan is safe and have the drug squad waiting for them?"

Terry liked the idea of getting something over on the Yardies twice in one day.

"Good idea, what do we do about Danny, Shadow?" Strain said.

"Susan isn't going to care, she has been trying to build up the courage for six months to leave him. She spoke to me about helping her to move back to Liverpool. She hates the man but has been too scared to leave him in case he beat her again. I promised her that he would not get near her. I say that we let Danny out in the morning, it will give me time to pack Susan's belongings and move her out of the house," Shadow replied.

"I think we should let him out tonight and tell him that the Yardies have got his house staked out, he won't go near the place. If he asks about Susan tell him to mind his own business. We have two hours of daylight left, let's go down there and set ourselves up." Strain wanted to get this over as much as the rest of them.

When Terry offered the rock group a hundred pounds to set up on the roof and play for him they jumped at the chance. He had a special request for them, three songs that he liked, which they knew, but they had to play them in a certain order, they agreed for an extra twenty pounds.

Darkness fell as they all readied themselves for the job ahead. Andy joined the rest of the team at the storage building, he was to cover the alleyway between the buildings and watch their backs as they got on and off the roof. The remainder of the team used the ladder to get onto the roof and pulled it up after them so that they could use it to get across to Susan.

Thankfully there weren't any lights at the back of the building; in fact, it was almost too dark as they made their way to the back of the roof. From this vantagepoint they could see inside the room where Susan was being held. There was a dim light shining from a table lamp inside the room, sitting next to it was Susan.

"Nobody in the room with her," whispered Ian.

"Five minutes to go, maintain silence until we hear from Terry, we don't want to miss his cue," said Strain.

Each man lay still on the roof in their all black coveralls, listening to the silence in their headsets, eyes scanning the building where Susan was being held. Waiting for the GO, GO, GO, signal was always the worst part of an operation.

Terry was having a hard time keeping the group members quiet, as they were excited at the thought of getting back at the people in the massage parlor. They had all of the speakers, amplifiers and equipment connected ready to go, volume levels set at maximum—or at least as high as they would go without blowing the speakers. A few lights were spread around them ready to switch on when they began to play.

"OK, let's move the speakers to the edge of the roof, we want them to enjoy your music, don't we?" he said to the band members.

They were now ready to play and Terry gave them the signal. The lights came on and the music blasted out from the rooftop, the bass tones instantly vibrating through the walls of the massage parlor.

Inside the massage parlor the Yardie gang members were startled by the sudden blast of sound. One of them went to the window and looked through a gap in the blackened glass, there they were for the whole world to see, playing music on the roof of the building opposite.

"What the fuck is going on out there?" said Justin Barti, the sudden blast of music made him jump, spilling the hot coffee he was holding into his lap.

"It's those kids that we told to get out of the building across the street, the stupid bastards have set up their equipment on the roof," replied the Yardie looking out of the window.

The music was so loud that they were shouting to each other in order to be heard.

"Come on, we are going to shut them up for good," said Justin.

They made their way down the flights of stairs to the street below without giving a second thought to Susan. Outside the girls from the massage parlor were standing on the sidewalk as were a number of other people all looking up at the band. Some of the girls were dancing to the music.

"What are you doing?" Justin said to the girls.

One of them replied, "This is one of my favorite songs, 'Here comes trouble' by Bad Company."

"Well, they got that fuckin' right. I am going to throw them off that fuckin' roof," Justin said as he crossed the road, closely followed by the rest of the gang.

On the roof of the storage building they could hear the music loud and clear, over the headsets, they could also hear each other laughing even though it was muffled. Shadow broke the silence, "You crazy bastard, Terry." They all looked at each other for a second, smiling as they all recognized the song that was being played.

Terry was at the far end of the roof when he saw the gang members start to cross the street, he gave the signal, "GO, GO, GO."

The team were focused again on the room as they saw Susan stand up and walk to the window, they heard Terry give the signal to go.

Strain and Ian lifted the ladder up and quietly laid it on the window ledge of Susan's temporary prison room. Susan did not see anything until the ladder actually rested on the ledge, but she could not see anyone or where it came from, she knew who it would be, she unlocked the window and opened it. She then saw Shadow scurrying across the ladder like a scalded cat. He climbed in through the window and they both hugged each other.

"I knew that you would come," she said.

"Come on, sis, we have got to go." They heard the music outside change, this time it was 'The Boys are back in Town' by Thin Lizzy.

"What's that music?" she said.

"I will tell you later." Shadow guided her to the window. She did not hesitate climbing out of the window onto the ladder. She knew it was a long drop to the ground as she had opened the window when her captors first put her in the room to see if she could escape, but there was no way she could get down.

Strain and Ian had their feet firmly pressed against the bottom of the ladder, keeping it locked against the window frame. They watched as she slowly crawled across the ladder, hoping that she did not slip. Shadow watched her as he held on to the ladder, wishing her to go faster. As she got to the other side Strain and Ian grabbed her by the arms and pulled her across the rest of the way.

They immediately turned around to hold the ladder in place for Shadow, but he was already making his way over. The ladder twisted as they grabbed at it, throwing Shadow off, as he fell he reached out with his right hand, grabbing one of the rungs on the ladder. Strain and Ian hung on to the ladder trying to keep it on the window ledge. With the ladder on its side there was little they could do to help Shadow. Susan screamed out his name as she saw him fall, she quickly covered her mouth so she would not be heard. Shadow had a firm grip on the rung but knew that he could not hold on for long. He started to swing his body, as he gained momentum he grabbed out with his left hand grasping another rung on the ladder. He hung there for a few seconds, adjusting his grip on the rungs and made his way hand over hand towards his waiting team members and sister.

"This is like being back at Hereford," he said out loud, reassuring everyone on the roof.

He made it safely to the edge of the roof and swung a leg up, hooking it over the edge. That was when he felt himself being lifted into the air, it was Strain's powerful arms and upper body hauling him onto the roof. Shadow landed on top of Strain, at which point Strain kissed him on the forehead and said, "Welcome home, dear."

Shadow jumped to his feet, helping Strain to get up, when they heard Ian, "When you two have finished, Susan and I would like to go for a drink."

They all made their way across the roof, Ian carrying the ladder. As they put the ladder over the side Strain gave Terry the all clear. Susan started down the ladder as the music changed, it was another Thin Lizzy song, appropriately called 'Jailbreak'.

They all heard Terry's voice over the headsets, "How do you like this song, it's one of my favorites, I know that it's one of yours, boss," at which point they all could not help but laugh out loud.

The Yardies could not get inside the building to stop the music.

"I am going to shoot those little fuckers," said Justin. He walked back across the road and in front of the crowd gathered in the street, he started to pull out the gun he had in his coat pocket when one of his gang members put his hand on Justin's arm.

"The police are coming, man."

Justin stopped and saw the police car coming down the street. The music changed again, this time Justin hearing the lyrics turned to his gang members and said, "Check on the woman, quick."

They all ran inside to the room where Susan was being held. They were too late—she was gone.

Terry got the call from Strain, "We are all safe, no thanks to you, you crazy bastard, but the music was pretty good." Strain and the rest of the team made their way to the safehouse.

Terry stopped the group from playing and told them to get off the roof. They were all ecstatic to get one over on the Yardies.

On the way to the safehouse Ian made a quick detour and released Danny, telling him that the Yardies were waiting for him at his house. He didn't even ask if his wife was safe, he thought only about himself and took off running.

Shadow rang the telephone number for the massage parlor to talk to Justin.

The telephone rang several times before somebody answered, it was a man's voice. "Hello."

"Is that Justin?" Shadow asked.

"Who wants him?"

"Tell him I have his van." Shadow could hear muffled voices over the phone.

A different voice spoke to him. "Who is this?"

"Are you Justin?" he asked.

"Yes, who is this?" he replied.

"I believe that you are looking for some merchandise that belongs to you?"

"Who is this?" Justin asked again.

"You don't need to know who I am. However, you do need to know that I can tell you where your van and contents are located."

"I don't know what van you are talking about?" Justin was not claiming ownership of the van, as he did not know if this was the police trying to set him up.

"I think you do know what van I am talking about, we have our property back, now you can have yours." Shadow was referring to Susan.

"I will find out who you are and you will regret the day you were born." He meant every word.

Shadow wasn't bothered in the slightest by Justin's threat and told him where he could find his van and hung up the phone.

Justin was much smarter than the men that worked for him, he knew something was wrong and sent two of his junior gang members for the van. They found the garage where the van was hidden and followed Justin's instructions, driving past it several times to make sure that there wasn't anyone watching them. They eventually felt that the area was safe and forced open the garage doors. Inside they could see the van described to them by Justin, they quickly went to work on checking the contents, everything was in place. As they drove the van out of the garage a swarm of police officers and vehicles surrounded them. Both men were shocked, they couldn't understand where they all came from. Both of them were arrested and taken to the local police station, where they would be interviewed. The interviews would take several days but neither man would tell the detectives who really owned the drugs, they preferred life in prison to death at the hands of Justin.

10

SEPTEMBER 27TH, IRELAND

Pedro stood on the deck of the fishing boat and called the IRA contact on his Iridium satellite telephone (SATCOM). The SATCOM phone is a portable telephone that communicates directly with one of several satellites that continually orbit the earth. By picking up a signal from the satellite the telephone signal could be transmitted back to earth to call anywhere in the world. The call was very short, "Your delivery will be four hours early." That was all he said.

The person at the other end said nothing.

Under the shadow of darkness and a welcome overcast sky Peli guided the old fishing boat into the harbor of a quiet coastal town in Eire—or southern Ireland, as it is commonly known. There was no harbormaster on duty and the night security man was sent home with some extra money in his pocket.

Watching from the quay was Eamon Callaghan and two other IRA members.

"Here they come," said Eamon. "Watch them, they are sneaky bastards." He did not trust any of them, including Pedro, who he had known for many years.

They let them dock and secure the boat before they revealed themselves.

"Roy, go to the boat and tell them that I am here. I will be in that portable office over there." He pointed at a rusting old container that had been converted into an office.

"I will be right back," he said.

Mohammed was on deck, as were Pedro and Velasco as Roy approached.

"I trust that you had a good trip, Mr Callaghan is waiting, follow me." He turned and walked back along the quay.

Velasco did not say anything, he stepped onto the quay, followed closely by Mohammed and Pedro.

"Adel, stay here," Mohammed shouted into the galley.

This was the part that none of them liked. They could be walking into a trap and end up with no money, or even worse, end up dead. Peli and Adel stood on guard, weapons hidden but ready to repel any unwanted boarders.

Roy opened the door to the office and there was Eamon sitting on an old, worn-out sofa.

"Come in, gentlemen, sit down," he said.

"We do not have time for small talk," Velasco replied.

"What is your hurry? Relax for a few minutes, I have something to discuss."

"Make it quick," said Mohammed.

"I have another business proposition for you, if this one is successful," he replied.

"What do you mean if this one is successful, we are here with your merchandise as promised," Pedro said.

"Ah! Pedro, I wondered when you would speak up. I have another order for you, but it has to be delivered in four weeks no less. My sources tell me that you, or I should say your friend Mohammed here, has access to a number of MP5Ks and some nice grenade launchers like the M79 and M203s. I have a need for such weapons and have the money to pay for them." He was surprised that they showed no signs of interest in his new business offer.

"We want to conclude our present business with you before we start to talk about new business. You send your man over to the boat and they will show him the merchandise. You show us the money and we will transfer the weapons to you then and only then will we discuss further business."

"Very well, have it your way, Roy, go check the merchandise, see that it is all there."

"Pedro will go with him and we will stay here and count the money," said Velasco.

"Trusting soul, aren't you," he replied.

"Trust is for fools and not for business, where is the money?" Velasco was getting very impatient and Callaghan could see it.

Callaghan got up off the sofa and moved it away from the wall. He bent down behind the sofa and produced a large suitcase.

"There is half of your money, the other half will be given to you when all of the weapons are unloaded."

He opened the case, revealing neat stacks of one-hundred dollar bills, he closed the suitcase.

"What are you talking about? We want to see all of the money, just like you want to see all of the weapons," said Mohammed.

"If you think that you can play games with us you are making a big mistake." Velasco did not like surprises, all of the money was supposed to be waiting for them.

"Don't be getting excited, my Spanish friend, you will get your money."

"I am not your friend and I am not Spanish. I am a Basque." The anger was building in him and he was having a problem controlling it, he just wanted to shoot this man and take the money.

"You are easily agitated, that is not a good sign." Callaghan lifted the suitcase and bent over, placing it back behind the sofa. Callaghan suddenly turned around, holding a sawn-off shotgun, he pointed it at Velasco and Mohammed. The other IRA man standing close to them also produced a shotgun from under his coat.

Neither of them moved, they both stayed very calm, Mohammed was the first to speak, "Does this mean that our agreement is canceled?" he asked.

"On the contrary, it is to show you both that I mean business. I haven't got all night to fuck around with you two and this is my way of letting you know that if something goes wrong before I get my weapons then you will die. Now sit down both of you, we will wait until Roy comes back."

The next fifteen minutes were very tense with nobody saying anything. The door to the temporary office opened to the sound of grinding and crunching of rusted steal. Roy stuck his head inside.

"It is all there and some very nice equipment it is, shall we unload?" he asked.

"You take the Arab with you and show him the other half of the money, stay with him until you get the word to pass the money over, then drive him back here. Mr Spanish and myself will organize the unloading," he replied.

"Come on then, Mr Arab, let's take you to your money," Roy said.

Mohammed got up out of the chair, he glared at Callaghan for his disrespect.

"Go on then, off you go," he said to Mohammed.

"Divide and conquer, is that your strategy?" asked Velasco.

"Ah! What a doubting soul you are, I have told you that you will get your money and you will. Let us take a walk, you and I can help unload the weapons," he replied.

They finished putting the weapons into the two trucks that the IRA members had with them. Much to Velasco's surprise the unloading was uneventful and the suitcase was turned over with the money in it.

"Start you boat engine, Pedro, and cast off, ready to leave," said Callaghan.

"What about Mohammed?" he asked.

"He will be along shortly, don't you fret none." The strong Belfast accent was confusing Velasco and he did not understand some of the things he said.

"What did you say about Mohammed?"

"He is coming," Callaghan replied in a very slow, deliberate voice.

"I hope he is for your sake," he replied.

They waited for twenty minutes before the car showed up with Mohammed. He got out carrying a suitcase.

"There, you see, he is here with your money, safe and sound," Callaghan said.

Velasco turned to Pedro onboard the boat and spoke in his native Basque tongue. "Watch them," was what he said.

"What did you say to him?" asked Callaghan.

"I told him to kill you if anything happens." He smiled at him, Callaghan roared with laughter.

"What is funny about that?" he asked.

"I told Roy to do the same to you."

Roy smiled at Velasco and for the first time a slight grin appeared on his sullen face.

Mohammed joined them, "I will take this on board, goodbye Irish Pig," he said to Callaghan.

"Not very friendly the Arabs," he whispered to Velasco.

"You mentioned another deal, what are the details?" he asked.

"I will contact Pedro in the usual manner if you are interested."

"We are interested." He boarded the boat and Peli slowly steered the vessel away from the dock.

Velasco did not take his eyes off Callaghan until they were beyond the harbor wall, and he did not take his off the boat.

SEPTEMBER 27TH, ENGLAND

Strain and the team members had worked together getting Shadow's sister relocated back to Liverpool. The team arranged to meet for lunch in the Ring O'Bells pub about twenty-five miles outside of Liverpool in the small village of Daresbury, Cheshire. It was a long time since he had enjoyed a quiet lunch, he was looking forward to it. The pub served excellent meals, Strain's favorite was the steak pie, it was always served piping hot, which frustrated him as he was normally too impatient to wait for it to cool down.

During the lunch Strain told the team that they were to be in London the following day to continue the investigation into Bowles' death. The team was sitting around, quietly discussing the previous night's events in London and enjoying a good laugh about the music. The relaxing lunch did not last long. Strain's pager started to vibrate on his belt, he hated the thing. He checked the display and it showed the telephone number—it was his Chief Constable's direct line. He knew that it must be important. The rest of the team watched him as he checked the message on the pager. He excused himself and made his way out of the pub to make the call to the Chief on his mobile phone.

"Here we go again," said Shadow.

"Maybe not, we have to be in London tomorrow, I cannot see them pulling us off the other job," Terry replied. They carried on eating their lunch in silence.

Outside Strain dialed the number on his mobile phone, the Chief Constable answered the call immediately, "Yes."

Strain could feel the tension in his voice. "You paged me?" he said.

"Yes, I have to talk to you straight away, where are you?"

"Daresbury, where do you want to meet?"

"The Wheatsheaf on the A56, is your team available?"

"Five of them, the others you know about, they are all here, we are having lunch." Strain was definitely curious as to what the Chief had going.

"Put them on standby, you will need them, I will explain when I see you, say thirty minutes." He put down the telephone.

When he returned to the pub the team inside could see by the expression on his face that lunch was over.

"We have to leave, finish your food and meet me outside," he said and left again.

Strain sat in the car outside and switched on the car engine. He placed a cassette in the player in the dashboard and turned the volume down slightly, 'Che Gelida Manina' from Puccini's opera *La Bohème* played. He called Bulldog on his mobile phone to see how he was doing.

"It's John, how are the ribs?" he asked.

"Fine, I am ready to come back to work, but the bloody doctor won't declare me fit for duty until he sees me tomorrow. You have been having some fun without me, Shadow told me about his sister. I would have given anything to see your faces when you heard the music that the group was playing." He also would have given anything to be part of the action instead of sitting at home.

"We will have to pay him back, soon hopefully."

"Don't leave me out of that one, John, I want to join in the fun." Bulldog was always ready to play a prank on his fellow team members, or anyone else if the truth was known.

"Call me when you get the all clear, enjoy the rest, you will need it," Strain replied.

"I will call you as soon as the doc finishes with me." After he put the telephone down he thought about the conversation and realized that opera was playing in the background. He cursed his luck, as he knew that they must be on another critical job. Thankfully he was recovering quickly and would soon be back in the thick of the action.

The team members came out of the pub, as they approached Strain's car they could hear the opera playing.

"Looks as though we have trouble on our hands, he is playing opera," said Terry.

"Yes, he looks pretty tense," replied Andy. "What have we got, boss?"

"I don't know but I have got to meet the Chief Constable in twenty-five minutes at the Wheatsheaf on the A56 the other side of Helsby. I want you all to follow me and wait for me in the parking lot at the B.I.C.C. Social Club in Helsby. I don't know any more at the moment, keep your radios on, see you later." He drove away, turning the volume up on the cassette player.

Strain pulled into the parking lot at the Wheatsheaf pub, he slowly looked for a parking place that was not too close to all the other cars. He saw a dark green van to his right drive onto the parking lot from the second entrance. He chose a parking spot close to the main entrance where the Chief would see him. He sat watching people come and go from the parking lot for several minutes, people watching was something of a habit.

The music had him in a totally relaxed state, his mind running through the events in London. Two attractive young women in short skirts got out of a car by the main entrance to the pub. He looked at them as they made their way into the pub, his eyes suddenly refocusing on the green van as they walked past it. He realized that he had not seen anyone get out of the van, or had he missed them getting out? He was sure that he hadn't. As he studied the van a little closer he noticed that the windows were heavily tinted and it appeared to be sitting a little low on the suspension. His curiosity was increased as he thought that he saw the van sway slightly, as if someone was moving around inside. His sensors went on alert, something was not right about the vehicle and he knew it. He was too far away to see the number plate and too close to use his binoculars without someone seeing him. He turned slightly in the seat so that the occupants of the van could not see his face.

He pressed the talk button on the radio that was on the front passenger seat, "This is One, come in, Two, over."

The team members were all standing next to their vehicles when they heard Strain's voice on the radio in Terry's car.

Terry responded, "This is Two, over."

"Make your way over here A.S.A.P. I am under observation from a dark green Ford van with tinted windows. It is in the parking lot on the right side as you drive in, get the second car to park down the road from the pub, over and out." He turned back in his seat to face the entrance to the parking lot.

About five minutes later the Chief's car rolled into the parking lot, he saw Strain and pulled alongside his car so that their driver's windows were next to each other. They both rolled down the windows, Strain made the first move putting his index finger to his lips to let the Chief know that he should not say anything. The Chief was curious but did not question Strain, as he knew him well enough to realize that something was wrong, he handed Strain a brown envelope, which he took. He watched as Strain scribbled a message on the outside of the envelope and showed it to the Chief. 'Green van, far side of parking lot watching us, team will arrive in two minutes, follow me when I drive away'. Now the Chief was really curious, he deliberately paid no attention to the van. Strain watched the surprise in the Chief's face as he read the note. He thought that it was most probably twenty years since he was in a street situation, he did not want him involved. He watched as the Chief put the sun visor down on his side of the car. Strain smiled to himself, the Chief was obviously trying to hide his face from the people in the van.

The van started to move towards the exit of the parking lot. "Two, this is One, the van is leaving turning right towards Chester, over." Strain stayed where he was, waiting for the reply.

Terry was a quarter of a mile from the pub when he heard the call on the radio. In the distance he saw the van. "Roger, I have him in view, over," he replied.

The van drove off at a normal pace, no signs of being in a hurry.

The Chief was getting anxious. "Shouldn't we follow them?" he asked.

"No need, the rest of the team arrived as he was leaving." He wondered if he was being paranoid, the van did not do anything unusual as it left.

They could hear Terry talking on the radio, "I have the subject traveling at forty miles an hour towards Chester."

Strain let the other two cars follow the van and he would stay about two minutes behind them.

"I am three cars behind you," replied Thomas.

The Chief looked at Strain, he was visibly nervous, it had been a long time since he had been in the hunt. "I will follow them if you head back to Chester. I will let you know what develops, sir." He did not want him involved in the surveillance.

Before he could reply Terry spoke on the radio again, "Subject now turning left, left, left at traffic light, cancel, he is turning around in the middle of the road, accelerating at high speed back towards the Wheatsheaf and Helsby." Terry could not turn around due to oncoming traffic and was shouting at the traffic to hurry up. A gap appeared and he turned the vehicle in the opposite direction. He saw Thomas doing the same thing, almost colliding with an oncoming car, the driver of which had his hand hard on the horn.

"I will turn my car around to face the road," said the Chief, Strain just nodded slightly.

The van was accelerating at an amazing pace as it flew past the Wheatsheaf pub doing eighty miles an hour and accelerating. Strain started his engine to join in the pursuit and was driving away when the Chief's car crashed into the front of his car. He could not believe what was happening, he looked across at the Chief sitting in his car, he was blabbering on about being sorry.

"Reverse your car out of the fucking way," he screamed at his boss.

As his boss tried to reverse his car, which only moved a couple of feet, Strain tried to drive forward but the car did not move, something was wrong. He jumped out of his car, only to see that the front wing had been embedded into the tire by the collision. He kicked the front of his car as he heard the two team cars racing past the parking lot. He looked at the Chief's car and saw that his front tire was flat punctured by the impact.

"Sorry about that, John, I guess I got a little excited about being involved in the pursuit."

Terry could see the van again as he went past the pub, he looked at the speedometer briefly and saw that he was doing ninety-five miles an hour. Thomas was close behind him as they sped along the winding road with its high hedges and fields on either side flashing past them. The van was about two hundred yards ahead of them when they saw it braking, Grey smoke pouring from the tires. All commentary between the two pursuit cars had stopped momentarily as they could both see what was going on ahead of them, they needed to concentrate on the pursuit.

Shadow was in the passenger seat of Terry's vehicle when he heard Strain's voice. "One is out of commission, let me know what is happening, over." Strain immediately went to work on changing the wheel and putting the wing in a position where he could drive the car.

"Roger that, over," Shadow responded. "I wonder what happened to him," he said to Terry.

"I don't know, but he won't be happy about missing this," Terry replied as he threw the car into a sharp left turn to follow the van, his hands expertly maneuvering the steering wheel. He narrowly missed a black Ford that was coming from the opposite direction as it turned into the same side road. Thomas was not so lucky, the front of his car ploughing into the Ford, causing his car to go out of control and fly through the hedgerow, crashing into a muddy field.

Shadow heard the collision behind them and looked into his rearview mirror just in time to see the car Thomas was driving disappear into a hedge. "Are you OK, Thomas?" he called on the radio.

Thomas and Hobson were both trying to get their bearings as they lay in the wreckage of the car. "Are you two OK?" Shadow tried again.

Thomas was the first to realize where he was and answered the call, "Yes, we're fine," he replied groggily.

Strain could not stand it, he felt totally useless. As his team gave pursuit, he worked furiously to fix his car.

Terry was gaining on the van down the narrow country lane, as it could not negotiate the bends as well as his car. "I have got you now, you bastard," he said as he tried to clip the rear of the van, trying to force it to crash. Shadow looked at Terry as he drove the car, he was so calm and yet the car was sliding and bouncing front side to side.

The driver in the van felt the bump from the car behind him and braked very quickly but lightly, this caused Terry to brake a lot harder out of instinct. The van gained a little ground but not for long as Terry was accelerating again behind him. The van scraped the hedgerow as it forced its way around the next curve, almost losing control as the back end fishtailed from side to side, mud and grass from the side of the road was being thrown up into the pursuing car.

"Come on, Terry, catch him, I want to know who this is," said Shadow.

"Trust me, so do I, he can drive that fuckin' van that's for sure." He continued to fight with the car as it tried to spin out at almost every bend.

"Someone is hanging out of the passenger window," shouted Shadow.

The passenger was now sitting part way out of the passenger side window. The van slid around the next bend, the centrifugal force causing the passenger to slide back into the front seat, but not before he threw something at the pursuing vehicle.

"He has dropped something, it looks like." Something peppered the front of the car and windshield, Shadow instinctively ducked. "Christ, the bastard is throwing star nails at us."

Star nails were pieces of steel that looked like nails that were specially designed to form a pyramid, not matter which way they landed they had sharp points sticking up ready to burst the tires of a vehicle.

"We're fucked if he gets them on the road in front of us," Terry replied.

The passenger was bringing his upper body out of the window again, trying to get into a position where he could throw more nails onto the road in front of Terry's vehicle.

Terry accelerated closer and moved his car over to the driver's side of the road in an effort to reduce the amount of road between them. They hit another bend which was tighter than the last, the passenger was being battered by the thick hedging, he tried to get back into the van but couldn't. The van and passenger's body smashed into the hedge, throwing twigs and branches into the air.

"Ha! Ha! that will teach you, the hedge is chewing him up, Terry," Shadow said.

As the bend sharpened, the speed of the vehicle and the centrifugal force pushed the passenger deeper into the hedge. Suddenly his body was sucked out of the van, it bounced off the hedge and flew into the path of Terry's car. The body smashed into the windshield and roof, causing Terry to brake and Shadow duck down into the front of the car. The body continued on over the car, landing in the road as Terry fought to control his vehicle. He could not see anything through the smashed windshield and the car hit the hedge, causing it to spin wildly out of control, bouncing it off one side of the road to the other until it eventually came to rest by a farmhouse. Both men slowly got out of the mangled wreckage of the car, steam blowing out from under the hood from the ruptured radiator.

They could hear Strain on the radio, "Come on, lads, tell me what's going on."

"He's not going to be happy," said Shadow, he leaned into the car and called him back on the radio. "Sorry, we lost the van but we have a passenger."

The driver of the van could see the car spinning out of control in his rearview mirror, he reduced his speed knowing that the chase was over.

They both walked over to the body in the road and could tell immediately that he was dead. Terry went through his clothing looking for ID but could not find any, "Unusual that, not even a wallet on him," he said.

They heard Hobson talking to Strain on the radio, giving him directions to where they were. Strain managed to get his vehicle into working order as did the Chief, the followed the directions and picked up the team members. They could not miss the turning described by Hobson as there were several cars stopped, the occupants all offering advise and assistance.

"Whose is that car?" Strain said to Hobson, pointing at the black Ford.

"Don't know, he collided with us and the next thing we know he is getting into another black Ford and taking off, this stinks, John, there is more going on here than we know." Strain had to agree.

To the amazement of the other drivers standing around the men involved in the accident got into the car and left.

As they drove down the country lane followed by the Chief Constable

Strain relayed the story to both men of how the Chief had crashed into his car. They could see the hedge damage as they drove along the road and called Terry on the radio. He warned them about the star nails, Hobson got out of the car and started walking, they proceeded with caution, slowly driving behind Hobson as he walked along, picking up the nails. By the time they had reached Terry and Shadow they were standing by the farmhouse drinking something out of a mug. The farmer's wife had made them tea while the farmer helped them tow the car off the road. Fortunately the farmer did not see them put the body in the trunk of the vehicle.

"You both look like you have found yourselves a new home," said Hobson as he approached them.

"Yes, nice place." He lowered his voice, "Typical farmer's wife, just wants to feed and water us. She could most probably arm-wrestle any of us."

Strain parked the car next to the wreck at the side of the road. "Not like you to let one get away, Terry," Strain said, knowing that this would aggravate him.

"He did not play fair, John, throwing those fucking star nails out of the window. The driver escaped in the van but the passenger didn't." He opened the trunk of the car wide enough for Strain to look inside.

"Christ almighty, did you do that to him?" he asked.

"No, he was hanging out of the passenger window and was dragged out by the hedge. His body hit our car, smashing the windshield, causing me to crash. We have checked the body for identification but he had none, not even a wallet." He closed the trunk.

"What do you suggest we do about the body?" asked the Chief.

"We can call the Constabulary wrecker and have the vehicle taken to a private garage and we will transfer the body to the morgue later. In the meantime we can run a trace on the vehicle, not that I expect us to find an owner. We can fingerprint the body to see if we can identify our mystery man. Hobson, arrange for the wrecker and stay with the car until we meet later. Does anyone have a place in mind where we can take the car?" said Strain.

The Chief cleared his throat and gave a slight grunt, "I know a place, my daughter is in the process of renting her house in Waverton just outside of Chester. Her house is empty, she moved out a couple of days ago to work in London. I have offered to put it in the hands of a real estate agent and take care of the rental. I haven't had time to get in touch with an agent yet, the house is secluded and has no neighbors overlooking the property."

"That sounds like the perfect place, can you give Hobson the directions, boss, and we will meet him there in a couple of hours. The rest of us will go to the carpool and pick up a couple of new vehicles. I will need you to call ahead, sir, and arrange for the cars to be released to us," Strain said to the Chief Constable.

"Yes, yes, of course, I will call right away, here is the address, I will see you at the house," he replied, passing a piece of paper to Strain with the address written on it.

Strain and the others left Hobson with the wreck and headed towards Cheshire police Headquarters to collect the new cars.

Strain arrived at the Chief Constable's daughter's house followed closely by the rest of the team in their two new vehicles. The Chief's car was already in the drive and Hobson was stood outside by the front door.

"Where is he?" asked Strain.

"Inside pacing up and down, he has been here for an hour and hasn't said a word other than hello," he replied.

"Stay out here, lads I will go talk to him and find out why he called me." Strain walked inside the house. He wandered through the lounge and into the kitchen before he saw the Chief standing in a glass conservatory attached to the kitchen.

"Hello boss," he said as he walked into the conservatory.

The Chief Constable spun around on his heels at the sound of Strain's voice, "Where the bloody hell have you been? You were supposed to be here forty minutes ago." He was visibly sweating and bright red in the face.

"Sorry, sir, they were slow in releasing the two cars to us, you know how protective the garage is about giving cars out." He could not help but wonder what was wrong with the boss as he had never seen him like this before.

He gathered himself together and bowed his head slightly as he stepped forward towards Strain, "Sorry about that, John, it has been a rather hectic day, what with me ramming your car and the chase. I guess I was a little more shaken up about the incident than I realized."

"That's OK, we all have bad days, you want to tell me what is going on, sir?" He was being deliberately polite as he did not want to embarrass his boss any further. "Your telephone call sounded quite urgent."

"Yes, I have received information that two IRA members are going to meet in a pub in Liverpool tonight. They are apparently going to plan a revenge attack for the death of the Foy brothers. It is supposed to be a bombing or series of bombings to take place here on the mainland." He was staring out of the window, looking into the garden outside as he talked to Strain.

"Do we know who is going to be at this meeting or which pub they are going to be in?" he replied.

"The pub is called the Castle on the corner of Chapel Street and The Strand by the Atlantic Tower Hotel. I don't know who is attending the meeting, I only know that it is supposed to be two men. I know that it is not very much to go on, but it is better than nothing, I want you and your team to go to Liverpool and find out who they are and what they are up to."

"I will have to take a reduced team, as some are still unfit for duty. Can I ask where you got the information from and when did you receive it?" Strain was starting to wonder if there was a connection between this information and the people that they had chased that afternoon.

"You know better than to ask someone where they receive their information from, John, it has always been good information in the past." This was true, as the Chief had given his team information on four different occasions in the past that had led to them arresting several IRA members.

"Do you have any thoughts on who could have been following us today? It's very odd that the body did not have any ID. They certainly seemed to be well organized, the way they rammed Hobson's car and another vehicle picked up the occupants. Whoever it is, they certainly know their business." He watched as the Chief paced back and forth, deep in thought.

"I don't have a clue as to who it could be, but I do think that it was you they were following and not me. I mean, why would anybody follow me, there is no reason to." He continued pacing up and down, it was driving Strain mad.

"Why, sir? he asked.

"I don't know, you do have a lot of people pissed off at you at the moment, especially after the Birmingham fiasco. Perhaps it is the IRA or someone else that has got it in for you." He was becoming agitated by the questions that Strain was asking. "I will ask around but I don't expect anyone to be jumping up and volunteering that they attacked you."

"I guess you are right, I will let you know when we get the results from the fingerprints that we took from the body. You never know, we might get lucky and find out who he is. I have made arrangements for the car to be removed from the house tomorrow morning, in the meantime I am having a forensic specialist look at the car that rammed Hobson as well as the boot of our car where the body was hidden from the farmer. If you don't need me any further I will leave, sir." He waited for a reply but did not get one, the Chief just stared out of the window, Strain left the room and drove off with the team members.

11

SEPTEMBER 28TH, ENGLAND

The bus service between towns and cities in England was excellent and Velasco was advised to use the bus service to get them to the train station at Exeter in the southwest of England. A lot of tourists used the bus service, and they would be able to travel relatively unnoticed. At Exeter they boarded the train bound for London. Velasco was excited about the operation, Pedro and Peli, however, were a little nervous.

"You both look worried about something, what is it?" he asked.

"Nothing," said Pedro.

"I know you too well, my cousin, what is the problem?" Velasco was going to find out and they knew it.

"We are worried about the job, we are not used to being away from the safety of our homes and the mountains," replied Peli.

"Worried, I would be concerned if you were not worried, it is natural to feel this way. In a week you will be back home, drinking wine and celebrating. Hell, don't you think that I am worried, of course I am." He had to keep them reassured and confident, they had several difficult and dangerous days ahead of them.

"Where are we going to stay, Velasco?" asked Peli.

"It is somewhere in London, I don't know the address, we are being met by Sebastián at the station." He hoped that there would not be any complications and he would be there to meet them. He was genuinely concerned because he failed to get the address from Sebastián.

As the train pulled into the station in London it was as though somebody had rung a bell and everyone stood up at once. The three of them watched the other passengers as they impatiently pushed their way towards the doors. Velasco looked out of the window—there was Sebastián, leaning against a wall by the escalators. "He is here," he said as he turned to the others.

They left the train to be met by the embracing arms of Sebastián. "It is good to see you again," he said to Velasco. He greeted Peli and Pedro and said, "This way."

They all followed him as he took the lead, weaving his way through the mass of passengers that were trying to exit the station platform. People were running and walking in all directions in what seemed to be total confusion to the Spanish visitors, but it was a common feature of any major London railway station. They followed the signs for the underground trains. At the entrance to the underground station Sebastián stopped and handed each of them a ticket. "These tickets are to get you onto the underground train, follow me."

The underground train system was one of the quickest ways of getting around London. The train system, as its name suggested, was built underground throughout the city of London

He walked away at an increased pace down some steps into the underground station. They watched as he placed his ticket into a small slot in the front of a steel box with a turnstile attached to it. The steel box sucked the ticket out of his fingers, magically making it reappear in the top of the machine. They saw him retrieve his ticket from the top of the machine as he moved through the turnstile. They all followed his example and one by one made their way through the turnstile towards the escalator. Sebastián was the only one of the group who had ever been in an underground station, they found it to be totally confusing but fascinating.

The escalator took them down into the depths of the station, a hundred feet below ground. They saw other people being transported from the bottom of the shaft on another escalator; like their escalator some were standing still while others forced their way past. There were posters advertising all manner of things along the walls by the escalator, local budding artists had changed some faces on the posters by adding beards, moustaches and glasses. They were all very impressed with Sebastián, as he seemed to know exactly where he was going. Sebastián took them around a number of corners, down another escalator, and eventually arrived at the platform. The air on the platform had a damp, stale smell to it. A sign above the platform showed that the next train was due in two minutes.

The air around the platform started to move like a gentle breeze and picked up to a powerful rush. The three newcomers to London and underground travel found this rather alarming.

"The air gets pushed out of the tunnel as the train approaches," said Sebastián, reassuring them.

They nodded in unison as they heard the train approaching. They looked to the tunnel entrance with curiosity as the noise got louder and the wind got faster. The saw the two headlights on the train as it shot out of the tunnel like some kind of angry two-eyed demon. It slowly rumbled to a stop, as the doors of the train slid open a group of passengers got off and they all boarded.

Twenty minutes and one train change later they were at their destination. The house that they were staying at was only a five-minute walk from the station and they wasted no time in getting there.

They were glad to arrive at the house, as they felt like everyone that looked at them knew exactly who they were and what they were going to do. The four of them sat around a small table in the kitchen sipping on strong black coffee that Sebastián had made.

"Here are the maps that you requested," Sebastián said to Velasco.

"Good, have you already marked them to show where we are going?" he asked.

"Yes, each tells you who is going where. The first bombs are already in place at the Olympia Exhibition Center. The Spanish Trade Exhibition starts at 10.00 a.m. tomorrow. The bombs are set to explode at 10.05 a.m. Victor will be here soon, he will drive Pedro and Peli tomorrow to the Spanish ambassador's home. We will go to the Spanish Embassy. The cars we are going to use tomorrow will have the weapons in them tonight. US made 66mm Light Anti-tank Weapons (LAW) will be supplied as you requested. Both vehicles will have sunroofs large enough to put the upper part of your body through to fire the LAW. There will be two launchers in each car, in addition I have these for everyone," he pulled out a cardboard box from under the table. He opened the box and revealed an assortment of handguns, "Choose your own," he said. They all picked a weapon each, mostly 9mm semi-automatics.

Victor's latest girlfriend, a beautiful blonde, twenty-nine years of age with plenty of money, dropped him off outside the house. He had met her two months previously at a party and was enjoying the challenge of trying to bed her, she was not proving to be as easy as his previous girlfriends. The night before he had tried to seduce her at one of the houses his boss allowed him to live in, unfortunately she resisted his advances. But he was confident that she would submit like all of the others with time.

The front doorbell rang. "That will be Victor," said Sebastián. Before he opened the door he looked out of the window at the side of the door, he could see Victor. "Come in, Victor, they are here," he said.

Victor was surprised to see them all standing when he walked into the room. They all had guns in their hands and looked as if they where ready to use them.

He put his hands in the air and smiled, saying, "Easy, I am only a poor peasant boy." He smiled and saw them all immediately relax.

With the introductions over Victor had a suggestion. "It would be good if we could all go out and look at tomorrow's targets. This way you will see the targets and what you are going to aim at and hopefully what you will blow up."

"Yes, that would be a good idea," said Velasco.

Mohammed and Adel also traveled by train to London, where the remainder of the fundamentalist group was waiting. They took a separate route to the ETA members and were a little better organized. They had spent a number of months planning the various attacks that would take place the next day. Mohammed was keen to learn how the plans were progressing and was there to ensure that the operation went smoothly. The fact that he was there was a tremendous boost to the morale and confidence of the others. He was seen as the man that was going to lead them into a new era, where the Algerian government would recognize them and the power that they had. Some even believed that he would one day rule Algeria as the elected head of state.

They all gathered in one room in a house just off the Edgware Road in central London. Everyone was anxious to make their own presentation on how their part of the operation was going to take place. Tarek was the leader of the group in Mohammed's absence, he was the first to speak.

"We have gone over our plans together many times over the last three months. We have rehearsed our parts in the plan so much that if something happened to one of us, we would all know what to do to take that man's place. We have not left any trace of who we are or where we have been during this time. I think that you will be very impressed with what we have to tell you today. All of the bombs are made with Semtex plastic explosive attached to a simple travel alarm clock. They will all be timed to explode at exactly 9 a.m."

Mohammed stopped him. "How much Semtex have you used in the bombs?" he asked.

"That varies according to the individual bombs. They all have two to four pounds of Semtex with standard detonators, except for the train bombs, they have ten pounds of explosive each, the intention is that the train will be derailed. We used our complete supply of Semtex for these attacks. I have asked each man to keep his briefing short, as I know that you would not want to hear the full details of each plan. Mustafa will be the first to give his presentation." He sat down.

Mustafa was a very pale-skinned individual compared to the rest of the group, this was due to his having severe jaundice when he was a baby. He was the most feared by the other members, he had been involved in the murders of many people back in Algeria. His favorite weapon was the knife, which he used with great effect on anyone who crossed him.

"I have a very simple task to perform compared to my brothers." He was having a slight dig at Tarek, as he did not agree that he should be given this lowly job. "There is a house in a town called Wilmslow that the French ambassador owns, he thinks that nobody knows about it. I will go to the house and place a bomb in the bushes next to the front door. The ambassador's brother and his family are using the house for the next two weeks, they are on vacation. I will then go to the city of Manchester, where there is an Air France office. The original plan was to leave a parcel in the doorway, but the police patrol all of the time and they would find it. There is a shop next door to the Air France office that is empty, it has not been used for at least four months. I found a way into the empty shop through a first-floor window. The shop has an alarm system but it does not cover the first floor. I plan to return tonight and place the bomb in the empty shop against the wall next to the Air France office. That is all that I have to do." He sat down, visibly agitated by his lack of participation.

Another man stood up. This was one of his most loyal soldiers; he bore the same name of Mohammed.

"My brother, Hassan and I will go to Birmingham to New Street railway station, where we will purchase two platform tickets. These tickets will allow us onto the platform, they are what people buy to meet passengers on the trains as they arrive. We will place two bombs on the train that leaves for London at 8.00 a.m. and one bomb on the platform. We will leave the railway station and drive back to London by car."

Next came Magreb. He had been with the group for only a year, he was a first cousin of Tarek. He had never met Mohammed before and was particularly excited.

"I am Magreb, I am proud to be of service to you." The others smiled at his introduction. "I will go to Gatwick Airport to the Air France cargo depot. They have a very big warehouse that ships cargo in and out of England. There is an office where the people go to collect parcels and packages, you can even walk into the warehouse sometimes. I have found a place outside where they throw all of their empty boxes and trash. This is where I will place my bomb. I will then take the Gatwick shuttle train to Victoria Station and return here."

The last to stand was Sami, another devout and long-serving soldier.

"I have three bombs to place, all are distraction devices as you requested, Mohammed. The first bomb will be placed against an oil storage tank that is located in an area of London called Wapping, it is next to the railway shunting yards. The next one will be placed underneath a propane storage tank, it is in the yard of a large propane supply company on the A43, just outside the city. The final bomb will be attached to an eighteen-wheel petrol delivery vehicle. The vehicle is already in place at a truck stop in the dock area of London. These bombs will create a tremendous amount of chaos and will stretch the police and fire services to their limit." He sat down with the others.

When they had finished he realized that they had a total of nine bombs planned in different locations, all minor in size compared to his, but combined they would have a devastating effect. He did not reveal the two major attacks that he had planned, nor the ETA attacks that would take place at the same time. The two groups would create more fear and chaos in one day than at any other time in the history of terrorism in England.

"You have done well, my brothers. Our attacks will make the French government wake up and listen to us. The English will not appreciate our actions and will try to hunt each one of us down. You must stay in hiding for at least two weeks and then slowly through the different planned routes leave this country and return to Algeria. The French are going to realize that we are not to be ignored, that we will attack them in any country we choose. They cannot escape our vengeance and that of the Algerian people as long as they support those that run our country. This is the start of our liberation from the political chains that our enemy has wrapped us in. It is time that we are heard and feared by all those that stand against us. It is time for our dead brothers and sisters to be avenged. Allah be with you." They all stood embracing him in turn. "We must leave," he said to Tarek.

"Yes, Mohammed," he said as they walked out together.

"I want to see the van you have prepared."

"It is only a short drive from here," he replied.

The van he was referring to was going to contain a huge six-hundred-pound bomb.

As they left the house Tarek saw a parking ticket on the windshield of his car, he took the ticket and cursed out loud.

"This is one thing I hate about this country, you cannot park anywhere without getting a parking ticket." He got into the car and put the ticket into the glove box with several others that he had received in the previous months.

They arrived at a petrol station that was also an auto repair shop, at the back of which was a row of garages. These garages were used by the local residents to park their cars at night, as there was no parking in the street. Tarek stopped the car next to the petrol pumps and got out, he filled the fuel tank with two gallons of petrol and went into the garage to pay. At the cash register was the owner of the garage. "That is ten pounds please," he said.

Tarek handed him a twenty-pound note and he received a ten-pound note in return. Wrapped in the five-pound note was a key to a padlock. Tarek did not say anything and walked back to the car.

He drove away, turning right out of the petrol station and right again into a courtyard immediately at the back of the petrol station. There were several garages, all in a neat row.

"This is the place," he said to Mohammed.

They both got out of the car, Tarek used the key that was given to him to unlock the padlock on the garage door. He opened the door slightly and they both entered, closing the doors behind them.

"This is the van, it is ready to go as soon as you need it."

In front of them was a dirty, rusting white Ford Transit van with a sign on the side, 'Exterior Paint Specialists'. He opened the two rear doors, revealing six large metal drums inside. On top of the drums were two sets of painter's clothes with old paint stains all over them.

"How long ago did you make the bomb mixture?" He knew that the fertilizer mix used to make the bomb was very unstable.

"Last night, we have not primed anything yet or prepared the explosive charge to detonate the bomb. I knew that you wanted to leave that until the last minute," he replied.

"Let me see the timing device."

Tarek went to the front of the vehicle and took out a travel clock that was in a box on the front seat. "This is the timing and detonation device."

Mohammed checked and double-checked the device, everything looked in order. "Good, where are the anti-tank weapons?"

"They are here."

He reached under a wooden bench and slid out a long heavy-duty cardboard box with a cloth over it. "This is exactly the same as the ones that we provided to the man from ETA." He pulled back the cloth, inside the box were two anti-tank weapons.

"You have done well, Tarek. Where is the car that I am to use?"

"It is in the garage next to this one, do you want to see it?"

"No, bring it to the house at seven o'clock in the morning, make sure that the fuel tank is full. Where are the other weapons I asked for?" He wanted to see everything that he was supposed to be supplied with.

"They are in the trunk of the car that you will use, we can look at them if you wish." He did not want to see the car but the weapons were something else.

"Let me see them."

They left the garage and replaced the padlock. The other garage that Tarek referred to was directly next door, he used the same key to open the padlock on this garage door. The weapons were like new, when Mohammed inspected them there was an Uzi with four magazines and a Browning 9mm pistol with two clips. Mohammed tucked the Browning into the back of his pants in the middle of his back.

"We can leave, have this vehicle brought to the house at the same time as the van."

On the way back in the car Mohammed surprised Tarek with something, "Tarek, I want you to take care of the van tomorrow. You know where it is to be left outside the French Embassy in Knightsbridge at 8.55 a.m. You park the van outside and walk up to the front of the Embassy dressed in your painter's outfit. If anyone stops you tell them you have been requested by Monsieur La Roche to estimate how much it will cost to paint the window frames and doors. La Roche is in France this week and they will not be able to speak to him. Make sure that you have a pen and writing pad in your hand, make it look as though you are taking notes. The sign on the side of the van will buy you time. You will only be a few yards from the corner of the building, slowly walk around the corner and quietly disappear. Set the timer for exactly nine a.m. like the rest and meet me back here." He could see that Tarek was taken aback by the request.

"I thought that I was to go with you to kill the French Foreign minister?" He was also very scared that there wasn't much time for him to get away from the van.

"The plan has changed. Adel will be my driver, you do not have a problem with your duties, do you?" He knew that these words would scare him.

"No, Adel is a good man." He wasn't happy about the situation, but what could he do?

12

SEPTEMBER 28TH, ENGLAND

It was 6.30 p.m. when Donnelly drove the car down Vauxhall Road in Liverpool, closely followed by Alan Foy on a motorcycle. He turned the car into a side-street and parked it close to the Castle Pub. Donnelly locked the car and walked through a narrow alley to the next street, where Foy was waiting on the motorcycle. They rode the motorcycle back to the garage on Vauxhall Road, where they had a second vehicle hidden.

They left the motorcycle in the garage and they both made their way back towards the pub in the car. Keeping observations on the Castle Pub was not a problem as there were a dozen places to observe from. Foy, as always, chose to be in the middle of it all and entered the pub. He ordered a whiskey and sat at a table by the window overlooking the street outside. He wore a scruffy-looking false beard and glasses, which changed his appearance dramatically. The heavy brown coat, dirty shoes and trousers made him look as though he had just walked off the dock after a hard day's work.

Donnelly waited at a bus stop at the junction with the main road. He hardly recognized his friend as he walked into the pub, a master at work, he thought to himself. He waited as arranged for thirty minutes and then walked to the parking lot by the entrance to the Birkenhead tunnel.

As the evening wore on Foy had ordered about nine whiskeys, but only drank one, disposing of most of the whiskey down the back of the bench seat he was sitting on. He wanted to give the appearance to the bar staff and clientele that he was drunk, without actually being drunk.

Ian Thomas and Andy Hobson won the toss to go into the pub, much to the aggravation of the other team members, as any one of them would have welcomed a beer. They gave the other team members a little ribbing about going to enjoy a pint of beer before they left for the Castle.

At 9 p.m. two men walked in the pub, Foy watched them as they ordered beer at the bar. One man slowly looked around the room, he was taking note of who was in there. The barman served them two pints of beer, each man took a small drink from the glass.

Foy listened carefully to their conversation and heard one of them say. “Do you want a game of pool?

His friend replied, “Yes.”

They picked up their drinks from the bar and walked towards the pool table. Foy stood up as they approached and staggered into one of them, making it look like he was drunk.

“Be careful, mate, you nearly spilt my beer,” the man said, as he gently moved Foy to one side.

Foy did not say anything, he just waved his hands at him as if to say go away.

“Christ, he is shit faced,” said his partner.

Foy staggered through the bar, finding his way out into the street. He had found out what he needed to know, the man he bumped into was wearing a shoulder holster. As he staggered up the street he went past a car parked in a side street that had two men sitting in it. Neither man paid much attention to him as he staggered by, he knew that this had to be the Strain group. When he was convinced that he was not being followed he called Donnelly on his mobile phone and asked him to pick him up. They went back to the garage on Vauxhall road and relaxed for an hour.

Tony Williams helped himself to another cup of tea, *this is going to be another long evening*, he thought to himself. He went to his desk in the center of the reporters' floor in the *Liverpool Echo* offices. As a junior reporter he did not have his own office. This was where he would sit and wait for the scoop of the year to come through on the telephone. He had been with the newspaper for eighteen months, starting straight from school. He was assigned to Kevin Parker, the oldest and longest-serving reporter with the newspaper, he was also the designated drunk, which Tony disliked with a passion.

Parker burst into the office in his normal bad-tempered way, this was due to the fact that he had not had his evening drink at the Castle public house, which was close to the office. Parker was a large man of some 300 lbs with a beer gut the size of a walrus that hung over his belt.

Tony often wondered how the belt managed not to break under the strain of all that fat. Parker's cheap suit had cigarette burns and beer stains in various places. Tony had witnessed the most recent burn the night before when Parker had returned from the pub at 9.30 p.m. The worse for drink, he had fallen asleep at his desk, with a cigarette in his mouth. Tony found it rather amusing as he watched Parker try to stay awake, seeing his head bob backwards and forwards with the lit cigarette delicately balanced between his lips. On this occasion Parker was unable to stop the cigarette from falling from his mouth and landing in his lap. Tony's immediate reaction was to rescue the cigarette before it burnt his mentor's trousers, for some unknown reason he didn't and watched as it slowly burnt through the material of Parker's trousers and reached the flesh of his leg. It was at this point that Parker woke with a screaming fit, frantically beating at his trousers, wondering in his drunken stupor what was attacking his crotch. Tony found this very funny, even more so when Parker fell backwards into his trashcan.

"Good evening Mr Parker," said Tony.

"Haven't you got some work to do?" Parker screamed at Tony.

"Yes," he replied.

"I'm going to the Castle for a drink, come and get me if anything breaks."

How many times had he heard that line in the last eighteen months? It never really bothered him, as nothing much happened. The boredom and the fact he had already worked ten hours eventually got to Tony and he drifted off to sleep at his desk. He was only asleep for a few minutes when the telephone rang, "Bloody hell," he shouted out loud as the phone startled him, something for which his mother would have given him a clip around the ear. Tony picked up the telephone and answered in the prescribed manner, "Hello, *Echo* night desk."

There was silence at first and then the strong Irish accent said, "Listen carefully to what I have to say."

Another bloody hoax bomb call, he thought. "Yes, I'm listening," he said with boredom.

The voice started again and spoke with a very deliberate tone and again repeated that he listen very carefully. This time something told him that this was different from the other hoax bomb calls he had received in the past.

"I represent the Provisional Irish Republican Army, codeword, Emerald."

Tony knew that this was a pre-arranged password for the press used by the IRA to filter out hoax callers. He immediately felt his heart start to race and his palms get sweaty, he pulled his notepad and pen across the desk and waited for the voice to start again.

"There is a bomb outside the Liver buildings set to go off in thirty minutes." The line went dead as the terrorist hung up the telephone. The Liver buildings were a historic landmark that overlooked the River Mersey next to the local ferry crossing.

Panic set in with Tony as his hands began to visibly shake. *What do I do*, he thought to himself, *go for Parker then call the police?* Parker always said, "Call the police last so that we can get to the scene of the story before them."

He ran through the office, grabbing the camera bag on the way, and headed down the two flights of stairs towards the main entrance of the building. As he passed reception the security guard at the desk went to say hello but only managed to open his mouth before realizing the young trainee reporter was already heading out of the front door.

"He'll have a heart attack running around like that," he mumbled to himself.

It was 11 p.m. when they left the garage, Foy rode the motorcycle and parked it half a mile from the pub, Donnelly was just across the street from him in the car. Foy was the first to move; at 11.15 p.m. he drove past the pub and could see the same car parked in the side street, still with two occupants. Through the pub window he saw one of the men that he believed to be the policeman standing by the pool table. He returned to his original parking spot and flashed Donnelly with his headlight. This was the signal that the surveillance team was still in place and Donnelly was to proceed with the planned detonation of the car bomb. Donnelly followed the same route as Foy, past the pub, and turned left a couple of blocks further down the street. As he turned into the street he took the remote control out of his jacket pocket, extended the aerial and pressed a red button. The explosion was instantaneous, he could almost feel the shock wave as he accelerated down the side street. He was too far away and in the wrong direction to be impacted by the explosion, he drove away quickly to rejoin Foy. He was waiting on the motorcycle a mile away and followed him to the town of Crosby just north of the city. This was where they would dump the car and transfer to the motorcycle.

Thankfully the Castle pub was only two hundred yards down the street from the newspaper offices. Tony got to the front door and pulled on the handle, they were locked. He banged on the doors, startling everyone inside who was drinking illegally after the licensed closing time. This was not unusual, as most of the public houses in Liverpool serve drinks after hours to the locals, something the police turned a blind eye to as they themselves enjoyed a sly pint of beer on duty, especially the detectives. He heard someone inside shout, "We are closed." He realized that it was past closing time and he would have to go in through the backdoor. He made his way around to the rear of the pub. Once inside he made his way to the bar, where he knew Parker would be, the stench of stale beer and cigarette smoke hitting him. The landlord, 'Fat Harry', was almost knocked over by Tony as he ran into the bar. Fat Harry shouted obscenities at him, which he did not hear as he ran to the end of the bar where he knew Parker sat. Parker was fast asleep with his face on the bar, snoring and snorting like the bloated hog he was.

Fat Harry shouted, "You won't wake him up tonight, lad, he's had enough beer to keep me in profit for the rest of the week." Everyone in the bar laughed.

Tony shook Parker violently in an attempt to wake him but he knew it was useless trying. He ran out through the backdoor and headed towards the Liver buildings, which were only two hundred yards away, in direct line of sight of the Castle pub. He thought to himself how many times had he done this, received information on a story and had to cover it himself because Parker was too drunk to do it. Parker had Tony to thank on numerous occasions in the last year for covering stories for him and of course he received all the credit.

Back inside the pub his entrance got the attention of the two team members. "He seemed a bit excited about something," said Hobson.

"Yeah, his friend is too drunk to care."

"Talking about being excited, I think we are wasting our time in here, I will be back in a minute."

"OK." Thomas knew that he was going to call Strain to see if they could call it off for the evening.

Hobson walked out the backdoor of the pub and called Strain on his mobile phone, "John, it is all quiet in here. Nobody but locals with Liverpool accents, not a sign of an Irishman. It is past closing time, I don't think that anyone will come now, should we call it a day?"

"Yes, I think you're right, make your way to the car and call me on the radio."

"Roger," he replied and made his way back inside the pub.

As Tony came out of the pub he realized that he had not telephoned the police. He looked at his watch and saw that ten minutes had already passed since he took the telephone call from the terrorist. He stepped into the telephone box on the opposite side of the street and placed a twenty-pence coin in the slot and dialed the number for the police. Tony knew the number of Merseyside police headquarters by heart, as he called it at least three times a night.

The operator answered, "Merseyside police."

Tony announced who he was and requested to speak to the duty sergeant.

"What is it in connection with?" the operator said.

"Who is the duty sergeant?" he shouted.

"Sergeant Howard," came the reply.

"Put me through to him immediately, tell him it is Tony from the *Liverpool Echo* and I have received a telephone call, code Emerald." The operator casually told him to hold, which only frustrated him even more.

"Tony, Sergeant Howard, what can I do for you?"

Tony relayed all the details of the conversation with the terrorist to the sergeant, but not before being told to calm down several times.

"Where are you now?" the sergeant said.

"In the telephone box by the Castle Pub on the Strand," he replied,

Before the sergeant could say anything else he heard a loud noise on the telephone and the line went dead. At the same time that the telephone went dead the sergeant heard the explosion outside, the building vibrated slightly from the effects of the bomb. *It must be close,* he thought.

Young Tony didn't know what happened. The car was only thirty feet from him when it exploded, practically vaporizing him. The force of the combination of homemade and plastic explosive completely destroyed the car in a fraction of a second, the engine block flew a hundred feet into the air landing a block away from its original position. The shock wave from the blast blew out all of the windows on the North and East sides of the Liver buildings. A passing taxi with its contents of nighttime revelers being transported to the local nightclub was blown apart. The bodies of the driver and passengers where destroyed beyond recognition, with body parts being spread over a large area.

Fat Harry and the after-hours drinkers in the castle pub heard the explosion and within a split second felt the immediate effects of the explosives and shock wave as it hit the pub. Shrapnel from the car, brick, glass and wood from the front of the building sprayed the occupants of the pub, tearing into flesh and bone as if it were shredding paper. Fat Harry was carried backwards through the rear door by the metal pub sign, which a second previously was hanging outside, killing him instantly. Nobody was left alive inside the pub, sixteen dead friends and patrons, including the alcoholic Parker, whose obese body was now just a red and yellow decoration to the carnage.

Thomas was bent over the pool table taking a shot, like Fat Harry and the rest of the people in the pub he was killed instantly.

Hobson went into the toilet after he had called Strain and was walking back towards the bar when the wall disintegrated in front of him.

The Atlantic Hotel was designed to look like the bow of a ship to blend with the history of shipping in this part of Liverpool. Being only a very short distance from where the bomb exploded, the hotel took a very severe hit. It now looked more like a ship that had run aground onto rocks at full steam than a hotel. Windows were blasted inwards, concrete reinforced floors collapsed one on top of the other killing and trapping people inside. The bomb had destroyed a third of the front of the hotel building.

Strain and Bulldog were discussing what time to start the surveillance of the pub the next day when the car exploded. Slate roof tiles from the building they were parked next to showered down onto the car severely denting the bodywork and smashing the rear windshield.

"No, please no," said Strain as he got out of the car, quickly followed by Bulldog.

As they came out of the side street all they could see was a cloud of dust where the pub used to be, they ran towards the cloud of dust and debris of what used to be the pub.

Shadow and Terry were parked by the Liver buildings when they received the call from Strain to stand down and wait for them by the entrance to Albert Dock. Terry started the car and drove around the back of the building following the road that would bring him out onto the Strand. Luck was with them, as they were on the blind side of the building when the bomb exploded. The shock wave from the bomb carried glass and debris into the road as they approached the bend in the road. The explosion took them by surprise, "Christ, that sounded like a bomb," said Terry.

"It was a huge explosion of some kind," replied Shadow.

"There's glass everywhere." Terry maneuvered the car as best he could around the larger pieces of debris. As they came around the building they could see the smoke and dust rising from the area of the pub and hotel.

"Oh! Fuck, the lads were in the pub." Terry put his foot to the floor, causing the rear wheels on the car to spin as they tried to grip the road surface. He swung the car around the mangled wreck of what looked like a taxicab. There was what appeared to be part of a body next to it in the road, there was blood all around the cab wreckage. As he drove the car along the wrong side of the road they both saw that the pub was demolished. He stopped the car fifty yards from the pub as he could not get any closer because of the amount of debris in the road. They ran towards the pub, as they got closer they could see Bulldog with his arms wrapped around Strain's body.

Strain could not believe it, his men were underneath the rubble, he climbed onto the mound of bricks and wood screaming out their names, "Ian, Andy."

He was clawing at the debris trying to find his colleagues. A section of the pub wall that was still standing collapsed as Bulldog pulled Strain away from the rubble.

"We have got to get them out, come on," he shouted at Bulldog.

Bulldog held on to Strain as he fought with him to let go. "John, wait, we cannot help, the building is still collapsing." He wanted to get them out as much as Strain but not at the risk of losing more team members' lives.

Terry and Shadow arrived and helped Bulldog restrain their boss. They all knew that their friends were dead.

When the clean-up was completed the record would show that thirty-two were killed and one hundred and sixty-eight injured. Mostly people attending a function in the hotel ballroom.

Foy and Donnelly arrived at the parking lot of the Blundell Sands Hotel just fifteen minutes after they had left Liverpool City center. Donnelly locked the car and walked over to Foy, who stood by the motorcycle taking his crash helmet off.

"What are you doing, Alan? We have to get to the airport before the police start getting organized and check all of the points of exit from the country," he said.

"I am going to stay here, I want to see if we managed to get them all." He passed the helmet to his friend.

"I think that is madness, we can check that out from Belfast, unless you have some other reason to stay?" He was sure that there was another reason.

"I don't know why, but I get the feeling that this is not over yet. When you get back to Belfast I think that you should catch up with Stephen Fagan and ask him what his part in all of this was, and what are he and Eamon up to? You know that Fagan won't volunteer the information and torturing him won't work either. You will have to be inventive to get the information out of him."

"I will get the information out of him, rest assured, but I don't understand why you should stay here. Have you got something else up your sleeve?" he asked.

"I want to snoop around a little bit more in London, try to find out what Eamon's game is. You know that he is up to something and it has got to be more complicated that what we have seen so far. You can contact me on my mobile telephone, I will keep it switched on, but be careful, we don't want someone to overhear what we are discussing." He regretted saying that the minute that he opened his mouth, as he knew that Donnelly did not need to be told to be cautious.

"Oh! I wouldn't have thought of being careful," he replied very sarcastically but with humor in his voice, as he knew that Alan did not mean it to come out the way it did.

"Call me soon," Foy said as he turned towards the car and left Donnelly to put his crash helmet on.

13

SEPTEMBER 29TH, IRELAND

Donnelly did not waste any time when he returned to Ireland. He started putting his plan together to get Fagan to talk about his involvement with Callaghan. He contacted three of the local IRA supporters that he trusted, all of whom had worked with him for about ten years on various projects. They all leapt at the chance to be involved, and when they learned that they were going to inflict grief on Fagan it was a bonus to them.

Fagan did not have a very good reputation with some IRA members, especially as he used to throw his weight around a lot, to them it was payback time. He had a bully mentality with recruits and liked to show them how tough he was, mainly by teaching unarmed combat to those much smaller and less capable than himself. One of his favorite jobs was terrorizing young teenagers that had fallen foul of the rules and regulations of the IRA. Some had a relationship with a Protestant girl, some stole property from the IRA and others committed crimes that were not tolerated by the IRA. In some cases stealing property from the IRA, especially weapons, earned the thieves a knee capping, this is where they would have a gun placed behind the knee and the knee cap would be blown off, or they would be killed. For some of these breaches in the rules and regulations they would be banished from Northern Ireland, never to return to see their families or homes again. The banished normally ended up on the mainland of Britain, living with relatives or on the streets. The street dwellers were the most vulnerable as they had not only been thrown out of the country they grew up in, they had lost the love and comfort of their family and had a very grim future. To return to Northern Ireland was almost certain death. Most of them would end up committing street crimes or abusing drugs and/or alcohol, a very difficult situation for any of them to survive.

Donnelly arranged to meet the three volunteers at the shipyard, they all showed up on time. "We have a very interesting but difficult job to do today, it doesn't help that the job involves Stephen Fagan. I want you three to abduct his wife this afternoon and take her somewhere safe for a few hours. Have you any suggestions as to where you could take her?" he asked.

Kevin O'Hara was the first to speak, "Before we talk about where we are going to take her, I presume that you have a way of us abducting her?"

"Yes." He realized how tired he was from having very little sleep since his daughter's murder. "I will go over the plan and you can be thinking of where you are going to hold her until I tell you to release her. She goes out every day to the local bingo hall at around six thirty p.m. The bingo hall is only around the corner from her house, about three streets away, she cuts through the back streets to a friend's house and they walk to the bingo hall together. Before she gets to her friend's house you can snatch her just after she crosses the children's playground on Bannion Street. There should not be too many people around and nobody will see anything even if they are asked. I want all of you to wear the normal black woolen hoods and wave around a shotgun in case we have any potential heroes. I want this to look like an IRA abduction, the word will filter back to Fagan and he will realize that this is a serious business," he paused.

"What if she does not go her normal route, what should we do?" asked O'Hara.

"She will, she has done this for as long as anyone can remember, I think that it is the only time that she gives her old man any peace. If for some reason she doesn't you use your judgment, but don't try it if Fagan is in view, the crazy bastard will have a go at you, guns or no guns. He absolutely idolizes her and won't think of his own safety," he replied.

"When we get her why don't we just bring her here? She will not know where she is anyway because we will immediately blindfold her," said David Barr.

"Yes, that's not a bad idea. It is very quiet down here, we could use the old loft space above the container base office on the next dock," said O'Hara.

"That sounds good, let me know as soon as you have her safe. David, you still work for the telephone company, don't you?" he asked.

"Yes, I am supposed to be at work now," he replied.

"Good. I have a job for you once she is safely tucked away at the dock. You will need your telephone equipment and van of course," Donnelly said.

"Yes, no problem at all, just let me know what you want me to do," he replied.

"I will go through that with you later. Is there anything else that we should know?" asked Sean, who was always the designated driver in these situations.

"No, just keep all four wheels on the road and don't bring attention to yourself once you have her," Donnelly replied.

"Don't you worry about my driving, I will take care of my end." Sean never did like anyone telling him how to drive.

"That's all, do it right, lads. This one is important, we cannot afford any mistakes. It is not official IRA business so if you are asked you know nothing."

It did not take Sean long to find a van that he could use for the abduction, it was from a butcher's store two miles away from the intended abduction point. The butcher parked it at the rear of his shop and for some unknown reason never locked it. Sean climbed into the driver's seat and inserted the threaded end of a T-shaped metal bar into the ignition key barrel, over the shaft of the bar was a metal tube. Once the thread was firmly screwed into the barrel he slid the metal tube up the shaft of the bar as it smashed against the T shape at the end, it ripped out the ignition barrel. He then inserted a flat-ended screwdriver into the vacant barrel space and turned it, starting the engine. The whole thing from getting into the vehicle to driving away only took him fifteen seconds.

He drove the van to the corner and picked up Barr and O'Hara.

"What took you so long?" O'Hara said, joking.

"Maybe you can do it next time if you think that you could do better. Mind you, I would imagine that you could try to start the ignition with your dick, after all it is most probably small enough to pick the lock." He grinned as he poked fun back at O'Hara.

"Well, you wouldn't like it as a wart on the end of your nose," he replied.

"All right girls, settle down, we have a job to do," said Barr.

They drove past the park twice to make sure that they were not going to run into any road works or police patrols, everything was very quiet. Sean parked the van with the rear end facing the direction that she was supposed to be walking from. They had only been parked for ten minutes when they saw her walking towards them. Barr was already sitting in the rear of the van with the doors unlocked ready to throw them open. O'Hara got out of the van and stood by the corner of the wall, positioning himself where she could not see him and where she would walk between him and the van. Within a minute she was almost level with O'Hara, he slipped on his woolen hood and watched her walk just past him. He grabbed her from behind by throwing his arms around her waist and lifting her off her feet. She immediately started to scream, lashing out with her arms and legs, trying to fight off her attacker. The van doors burst open and Barr grabbed her by the arms as he tried to drag her into the van. She continued to fight, lashing out with her feet, catching O'Hara squarely in the crotch, he fell to the floor. Barr lost his grip on one of her arms and she swung around at him with her bag. Fortunately the bag hit the door of the van and Barr grabbed her by the hair and dragged her into the van. O'Hara was back up on his feet and was climbing into the van when two men came running towards them. Barr did not wait for them to back off, he fired the sawn-off shotgun into the air, both men retreated. Fagan was still fighting like a wildcat and Barr punched her in the face, knocking her out. Sean was already driving away as both men in the back of the van struggled to close the rear doors.

"Jesus Christ, she almost got away from us, she can fight, that's for sure," said Barr.

O'Hara still had one of his hands nursing his crotch and was complaining about the pain, "The fucking bitch kicked me right on the balls, the pain is unbelievable."

"She must be a bloody good shot to find those two grapes, you have still got them, haven't you?" He and Barr both burst out laughing at their friend's misfortune.

"Is she OK? She doesn't seem to be moving," said O'Hara.

"She is unconscious, what do you expect her to be doing—an Irish jig? Come to think of it, we had better tie her hands and feet together before the witch wakes up," Barr replied.

The two men watched as the van drove away, the shotgun blast was enough to scare them. "That was Ann Fagan," said one man.

"It was, I think we had better give the news to Stephen, because if we don't and someone saw us here he might think that we are involved," said the other man.

Fagan was sitting in the kitchen when he heard the doorbell being rung continuously. He was curious as well as cautious, as he did not know who was at the front door. He walked into the front room and looked through the net curtains and could see the two men standing on his step. He recognized both of them from the local pub that he drank in, he went to the front door.

"What is all this noise about?" he said to the two men outside.

"It's your wife, Stephen, she has been taken," the man said as he tried to catch his breath.

Fagan went cold. "What do you mean she has been taken, what do you mean?" He went into a fit of rage, grabbing the man by the arm and shaking him.

"Stephen, wait a minute, let us explain," said the other man.

"Where is she?" he shouted.

"We don't know, two men grabbed her down by the children's park and pushed her into a van. We ran to help her, but they fired a shotgun at us. We have no weapons, we couldn't do anything else, they drove off with her in the back." He looked at Fagan, his eyes were wild with anger.

"Did you see who took her?" he asked.

"No, they wore black hoods, I am sorry, we could not tell who it was, we came right here to tell you."

Fagan turned and went back into the house, slamming the front door shut, leaving the two terrified men on the doorstep.

He sat by the telephone and waited, knowing that whoever it was would call soon, what he could not figure out was why had they taken his wife. Maybe an old score to settle, someone out for revenge, he had no clue as to who it might be, he had to be patient and wait for the call.

As they pulled into the old shipyard Ann Fagan started to wake up, they had tied her hands and feet and blindfolded her.

"Now then, if you behave yourself we will untie your feet and let you walk out of the van, if you don't behave I will knock you out again," said Barr as he whispered in her ear. "Are you going to cooperate?" he asked.

She nodded her head and Barr untied her feet as they drove into the warehouse. With her feet untied it was easier for them to get her into the loft space as she could walk instead of being carried. Sean left them to deal with Fagan's wife and drove back out of the shipyard to dispose of the van.

O'Hara called Donnelly. "We have what you need, let us know what you want to do next," he said.

Donnelly was sitting at home watching a video which he had hired, about the Mafia. The scene showed that a woman was about to be tortured to make her tell her captors where her husband was hiding. He jumped up out of his chair and ran into the kitchen. He frantically rummaged through the kitchen drawers searching for his pocket-sized tape recorder, he found it and ran back into the lounge. He checked to see that it had a tape loaded, which it did, but the batteries were flat. No problem, he took the batteries out of the TV remote. The scene in the movie showed the woman tied down on a bed and the Mafia villain was holding the burning end of a cigarette over her face. He pressed record on the machine just as the cigarette was placed onto the woman's skin, she screamed in agony. The villain repeated the process two or three times, with her screaming and sobbing at the same time, Donnelly stopped recording. A minute later the telephone rang, he answered, it was O'Hara. He listened to what he said and replied, "I will be there in thirty minutes." He put down the telephone.

On his way to the docks he stopped at a store and bought another miniature tape recorder. He arrived at the docks and sat down with the three

IRA members and talked about what he intended to do with Fagan.

"You all know that my daughter and Alan Foy's sons were murdered in England." They nodded there heads. "Well, Foy and myself have reason to believe that Fagan might have had something to do with it, we don't know what yet. You can see now why I asked you to get his wife."

"Kill the fucker and be done with him." said Sean.

"All in due time, I have to get some information out of Fagan before I kill him. I want you to get a taxi, Sean, and pick up Fagan outside his house in two hours. I will be keeping him busy until then. When you see him walking to his house call him over to the cab and tell him to get in the back. If he argues or tries to ask any questions just tell him that you have been told not to wait, he will get in the taxi. Once he is in the taxi take him to Quarry Farm, you know the place, drop him off at the gate and tell him to go inside the barn, where I will be waiting for him. Call me on the mobile phone when you drop him off and let me know if you think someone is following you. You two stay here with her and be ready to receive a telephone call from me, here is a mobile phone that I will call you on." He handed the phone to O'Hara. "Fagan at some point will want to talk to his wife, David, take this tape recorder and get her to say that she is OK. I want a clear recording of her voice," David took the tape recorder and climbed up the stairs to the loft.

"I will call you and give you the number of a phone box where Fagan will be waiting, when he answers tell him to wait. I want you to put her on the telephone. Tell her to say that she wants to go home. As soon as she says it, grab her by the hair or do something to make her give a bit of a squeal. This is really going to get Fagan to play into our hands and tell us what we want. He will most probably want to know that she is safe before he tells us much, I want to fool him into believing that she is at home. That is where the tape recording will come into play. When he has told me what I want to know I will call you and you can take her home, drop her off a few streets away."

"What do you want me to do when I have dropped him off?" asked Sean.

"Hide the taxi down the road in the sheep pens and get yourself into a position where you can see the barn and the road leading up to the farm, he may try to have someone follow the taxi. You may want to take your sniper rifle with you, just in case we get company you can pick them off. I will see you all later for a celebration drink."

David came down the stairs with the tape recorder in his hand.

"Any problems?" asked Donnelly.

"No, I told her that I had a mobile phone and that her husband wanted to know if she was OK. I held the recorder to her face so that she thought it was the phone and this is what she said."

He pressed the play button. Her voice said, "Stephen, I am all right." The recording stopped. "I stopped it there, I didn't think that you would want her to say anything else."

"Good, Sean will call you when he has Fagan in the taxi I want you to go to the street where Fagan lives and access the telephone junction box that his phone line goes through. When I meet Fagan I will tell him that he can talk to his wife at home. I will give him my mobile phone so that he can dial the number to his house himself. When he calls I want you to intercept the call, he will assume that his wife will answer the phone. As soon as he speaks play the recording that you just made of his wife's voice, then cut him off as she stops talking. I will tell him that someone is with her and he has fifteen minutes to tell me everything or she dies. He will talk. If there are no questions I am leaving, I will call you later." He got up and walked to his car, as he left the warehouse he called Fagan on his mobile phone.

The telephone in the lounge of Fagan's home rang twice, he answered, "Hello." He tried to sound calm.

Donnelly disguised his voice, "You have twenty minutes to get to the public telephone next to Jury's Belfast Inn on Fisherwick Place, walk there and make sure that you do not have anyone with you. We don't want any surprises, Mr Fagan."

"What have you done with my wife, you bastard?" Fagan shouted down the telephone. It was no use—the line was dead.

He knew that he could make it to the telephone in twenty minutes easily, he called one of his trusted friends and IRA soldiers, Colin Flaherty, at the garage where he worked as a mechanic.

"Colin, I have a problem and I need your help, someone has abducted Ann, can you meet me in the lobby of the Jury's Inn on Fisherwick Place in twenty minutes? I need you to bring one of those location devices of yours." He knew that Colin would not let him down.

"I won't ask any questions now, see you soon," he replied.

Fagan grabbed his coat and left the house.

Donnelly was going to give Fagan a little run around before he actually met him face to face, he did not want to give him much time to organize help from anyone else. He wanted him totally unbalanced, worrying about the safety of his wife.

Fagan walked at a faster pace than normal, even though he was continuously trying to slow the pace down. He watched everyone around him as he walked, wondering who was involved. Who was watching him?

Everyone he looked at became a suspect to him, the paranoia was setting in. He listened to the Gaelic music spilling out of the pubs as he passed them and some of that new popular music that did not make sense to him. All of these people going about their lives, and his world felt as though it was falling apart. His family had never experienced the misery or pain of the conflict with the British, he had never lost a family member to the troubles. He had served time in the 'H' block prison system for a few years but that was as close as he had come to the pain, now the shoe was on the other foot. He arrived at the telephone box just as it started to ring, he pulled open the door and lifted the receiver, he answered, "Yes."

"You have ten minutes to get to the telephone outside of the City Hall." That was all Donnelly said as he watched him from across the street. Ten minutes was more than enough time and it would give Fagan the opportunity to meet Flaherty, he walked into the Lobby of the Jury's Inn. Donnelly moved to the inside of a shop and watched the front of the hotel to see if Fagan came out with anyone.

Inside the hotel lobby Colin sat in a seat facing the reception desk when he saw Fagan walk in. He walked past Colin and headed towards the restrooms, making no attempt to acknowledge Colin's presence. Colin waited a minute and followed him into the restroom.

Fagan checked the stalls to make sure that nobody was inside and stood by the wash basins.

Colin walked in, "There is nobody here," said Fagan.

"What the hell is going on, Stephen?" he asked.

"I don't really know, but someone snatched Ann when she was on the way to the bingo hall and they told me to be at that telephone box outside. I have got to get going, I have to be at the City Hall in four minutes. Did you bring the locator?" he replied.

"Yes, it has range of about five miles. It is not very sophisticated, I am afraid, press this button when you want to activate it. What have you got in mind?"

"I am going to do whatever they say, but you are going to have to back me up with a couple of guns. I don't know what they have in store for me but whatever it is just make sure that Ann is OK. I don't care what they do to me. If you manage to find my signal from this device of yours follow us, but be careful, I have got to go." He left the hotel with only three minutes to go before he had to be at the next phone box.

Donnelly watched Fagan as he ran out of the hotel entrance, he waited to see if anyone came out after him. About two minutes behind Fagan appeared

Colin, looking very suspicious as he hailed a taxi. "Naughty boy," Donnelly said quietly.

He walked outside again and called the phone box by the City Hall. It rang several times when a woman answered the call. "Hello," she said in a curious voice.

Donnelly heard a slight scuffling sound on the telephone and Fagan's familiar voice sounded, "It's me, I'm here," he said with panic in his voice.

"Go back to the other phone," he said and hung up.

Fagan cursed and slammed the phone down, this time he did not waste any time getting to the phone.

Donnelly could see Fagan walking towards the telephone box at the same time as two young ladies opened the door. Fagan did not stand on ceremony and pulled the girls away from the door as they protested. He waited a minute as he watched him standing there waiting for the call. "That's right, you bastard, you worry about your wife and I will think of how I will kill you when this is over," he said to himself. He dialed the number to the telephone box, it rang.

"Yeah," Fagan said.

"I suppose you will want to talk to your lovely wife," he said.

"If you have so much as touched her I will—" Donnelly hung up the telephone. He watched Fagan, realizing that he had been cut off he stood in the phone box, beating the walls in anger. He let him lose his temper for a moment and then called back.

"I do hope that you will be more civil this time, Mr Fagan," said Donnelly.

"What is it you want? Where is my wife?" he replied.

"Information is what I want, information about you, Eamon Callaghan and what you are up to in London," he said.

"I don't know what you are talking about, why would I know what Eamon Callaghan was up to?" he tried to bluff.

"It is a shame that you are trying to lie to me, your friend Billy tried the same thing," he replied.

"Billy who?"

"You know who, I will leave you now, Mr Fagan, as you obviously do not want to discuss this further."

"I will not tell you anything, you can go fuck yourself," he replied.

"I am sorry you feel that way, here is your wife." He turned on the tape recorder loud enough for Fagan to hear faint sounds of someone screaming in pain.

He could hear Fagan on the telephone yelling at the top of his voice,

"Leave her alone, you bastard, I will kill you, stop hurting her, stop it."

"I think that you are ready to talk to me, go back to the other telephone, I will call you in ten minutes." He hung up again. He watched Fagan in the telephone box, he was leaning on the door, his head in his hands.

Fagan was losing control of himself, they were torturing his wife, the only person or thing that he had ever truly loved in his life. He promised himself that no matter what he would pay back whoever had done this, in blood. He eventually gathered himself together and made his way back to the other telephone by the City Hall. On his way back to the City Hall telephone he realized that he had the locator in his pocket, he did not want anyone to find it if he was searched for a weapon, so he forced the stitching in the lining of the pocket to burst open. He pressed the button to activate it and pushed the locator through the hole so that it dropped into the lining of his coat. He tried to look around him as he walked, convinced that he was under surveillance, but he could not see anyone.

Colin arrived back at the garage that he worked at and told his boss, who was also the owner of the garage, that he had to take the rest of the day off. As usual he never questioned Colin, as he knew that he was involved with the IRA. The owner turned a blind eye to the activity of his employee for selfish reasons, as well as fear for what the IRA would do to him if he did not cooperate. His selfish reason was that he did not have to pay any extortion money to the IRA for protection, unlike the rest of the local business owners.

Colin took a black metal box out of his locker and carried it to his pickup, the box contained the tracking device that he was going to use to watch where Fagan was going. He had done this on several occasions for the IRA to track informants in their cars. The system was rather antiquated but operational, he wished that he could get his hands on some of the new tracking devices that operated through satellite communication. Inside the box was a tray, underneath this was a false bottom containing a .38 caliber Smith and Wesson. He checked the weapon to make sure that it was loaded, something he did out of habit even though he was the only one to use it. The spare bullets were in a speed loader in the tray, he removed the bullets and reloaded them again, an unusual routine that he went through. He turned on the tracker and set it on the floor next to him, it made the usual bleep noise as it came to life. He drove out of the garage and headed back towards the hotel where he had met Fagan. He had only traveled a mile when the tracker picked up the signal. The screen showed a rough road-map of the City of Belfast and he could see that the signal showed a yellow flashing light traveling south on Dublin Road towards the City Hall.

"There you are, you will have me watching your back now. We will have Ann home safe and sound before you know it, Stephen," he said, talking to the screen.

Within four minutes he was parked in a side-road off East Bridge Street watching the screen.

Fagan waited inside the telephone box outside the City Hall, he kept looking at it, wishing for it to ring. He looked at his watch—fifteen minutes had passed, he was getting even more worried.

Donnelly watched him from a safe distance. He called O'Hara. "Here is the number I want you to call, Fagan will answer. Tell him to stay on the line and put his wife on the telephone, don't forget what she has to say. When she has said her piece tell Fagan to walk home and he will be contacted."

"No problem," he replied.

Donnelly could see Fagan answer the phone. It didn't take thirty seconds and he was out of the phone box making his way home. He called Sean and let him know that Fagan was on his way, it would take him about fifteen minutes. Donnelly went back to his car and drove to Quarry Farm, trying to figure out on the way what Colin's part in this was. He knew Colin from his work in the IRA as an enforcer. He would normally be part of a group of men that would be a punishment squad for anyone suspected of informing on the IRA or committing crimes against them.

Sean received the call from Donnelly and drove to Fagan's home. He disguised himself by wearing a false moustache, dark glasses and a flat cap. He did not like the idea of sitting outside Fagan's house in the taxi cab so he parked in the road across the junction from his house. It wasn't long before he saw Fagan, he let him walk into the street where he lived. As he got close to his home Sean drove across the junction and pulled up alongside Fagan. He rolled down the window of the taxi as Fagan looked at him and said, "Get in if you want to see your wife." Sean took no chances and had his gun ready to shoot if necessary.

Fagan stopped and glared at the driver of the taxi, he knew that he had no choice when he was told to get in, he did as he was told. As expected he did not say anything all the way to the farm, Sean kept watching him through the rearview mirror. As they drove down the country lanes Sean thought that he saw a car in the distance that may be following him, he slowed down. A dark blue car was about a half a mile behind them driving at a slow pace. Sean pulled over to the side of the road and watched as the car got closer. He tried to watch Fagan in the rearview mirror as well as the car behind him.

"Why have we stopped?" asked Fagan.

Sean ignored him, as the car got closer he pulled a shotgun out from under the seat and rested it on his lap. The blue car came around the bend and slowly drove past the taxi, Sean counted three male occupants. He waited for a couple of minutes before he continued. He was only three miles from the farm but drove with caution, watching for the blue car, but he never saw it again.

They arrived at the farm and Sean stopped at the gate, "In the barn," he said to Fagan and pointed down the farm path. Fagan got out without a word and started to walk down the path, it was approximately three hundred yards to the barn.

Sean drove away and called Donnelly on the mobile phone. Donnelly was watching from inside the barn when he saw the taxi stop and Fagan got out. He had the mobile phone in his hand when it rang, "Hello," he said.

"I think that we may have company but I don't know who," Sean said.

"It could be someone called Colin, I don't remember his last name, he was an enforcer worked at the garage on Park Road. I saw him come out of the hotel today after Fagan left. Do you know who I am talking about?" He looked through the gap in the wooden slats in the barn door, keeping an eye on Fagan.

"Yes, he is pretty handy to have around, quite a good boxer. Wait a minute, he was also into the electronic surveillance game. If it was him in the car he has two others with him, be careful, he is a nasty piece of work that one," he replied.

"Don't worry about me, I am safe in the barn. Watch out for yourself, got to go." He hid in the corner of the barn in one of the empty horse stalls.

Fagan tried to survey the building as he walked towards it, taking in everything around it. He felt totally vulnerable walking down the farm path, nowhere to run or hide, whoever this was he knew what he was doing.

Sean turned the taxi around and drove back past the farm entrance the way he had come. He did not like the idea of continuing on in the direction that the blue car went. He drove a half a mile and parked the taxi next to the entrance to a field. He took out his rifle case and walked behind the hedge in the field making his way towards the farm. About two hundred and fifty yards from the barn was a small copse of trees in the middle of the field. He was about a hundred yards from it with nothing but open fields all around, he had no way to get to the trees without being seen. He saw Fagan going into the barn as he continued to backtrack along the hedgerow. About fifty yards to the left of where he had gone into the field he came across a shallow stream. It was only four feet wide and about a foot deep, as his eye followed the line of the stream he could see that it led to the copse of trees.

Colin and his two companions drove past the taxi parked at the side of the road and saw Fagan sitting in the backseat.

"There he is, boys," Colin said.

They all tried to ignore the taxi like it wasn't there.

They drove on further down the lane when they came across a field with a number of sheep pens in it. Colin stopped the car and got out to see if the taxi was in sight, the tracker was not much use anymore, as it did not show the minor roads, just the direction of travel. He climbed onto a fence to get a better view when he saw the taxi appear around one of the bends about a half a mile away. The taxi stopped and he saw Fagan get out and walk towards a barn in the field. The taxi drove a short distance and turned around, going back the way it came. He continued to watch to see if Fagan would go into the barn, which he eventually did. There was no way of them getting to the barn without being seen. The sun would set in approximately thirty minutes, he decided to wait.

Fagan pulled on one of the barn doors and struggled to open it, the bottom was dragging in the dirt. He opened it enough to squeeze his way inside into the semi-darkness. He allowed his eyes to adjust to the dim light inside, the interior looked striped from the light shining in through the gaps in the wooden walls. Old straw was scattered here and there around the barn floor with a couple of hay bales set to one side, a pitchfork still embedded in one of them. He looked into the corners of the barn and up into the hay loft area, he couldn't see anyone but he knew that someone was there. He noticed three or four horse stalls at the far end of the barn.

"OK, I am here, let's get this over with," he said.

A voice came out of the darkness, "Take your jacket off and throw it away from you."

"What are we doing, playing games again, like you did in town running me from one phone box to the next?" he replied.

"Just do as I tell you and we will get along," the voice replied.

He took off his coat and threw it to one side. "There, what now?" he asked.

"Lift up your shirt and then your trouser legs, let us see if you have any weapons with you, shall we?"

Fagan lifted his shirt up, "Turn all the way around," the voice said. Fagan did as he was told. “Now the trousers,” the requests continued.

Fagan slowly raised his trouser legs one at a time, the right leg had an ankle holster strapped to it.

“That isn’t very friendly, now is it?” Donnelly said. “Slowly take the gun out of the holster with your left hand and toss it away from you, no tricks, I don’t want to have to kill you,” Donnelly knew that he would not try anything until he knew his wife was safe.

Fagan slowly bent down and took the gun out of the holster and threw it towards the hay bales. He watched the gun as it landed on the floor of the barn, he wanted to make sure he knew exactly where it was in case he had the opportunity to use it.

“Turn around,” the voice said.

He did as he was told, as he turned a blinding light came on, shining straight into his eyes. Fagan put his arms up in front of his face, shielding his eyes from the light.

“Sit on the floor.” This time he did not complain as he knew that it would be useless to argue; besides, he could not see a thing.

“Put your feet through this loop and pull it tight.” A rope was thrown to him, he could see a crude-looking noose at the end. He put his feet through the loop as instructed and pulled it tight. The rope was pulled hard quickly raising his feet off the floor of the barn, forcing him to lose his balance. He put his hands down behind his body to stop himself from falling flat on his back, he could hear the rope being tied on to something.

The light went out and Fagan tried to see who was there, “What is all this about?” he asked.

“I told you, I want to know what you and Eamon are up to in London.” He waited for Fagan to get his vision back to where he could see again.

He blinked his eyes, trying to get them to re-adjust after the blinding light, he played for time, hoping that Colin would find him. “Why should I tell you anything?”

The voice sounded familiar to him. “That is not a serious question, you know it and I know it. Billy tells me that you and Eamon are real close these days, you even have made a friend of the British Home Secretary, Adrian Bowles. You see by me telling you this little piece of information you should know that I have spoken to Billy.” He moved closer to let Fagan see whom he was talking to.

Someone moved out of the shadows from the back of the barn, Fagan could not make out who it was.

David unlocked the gates at the local telephone exchange and drove the van into the yard. He took his toolbox out of the van and punched in the security code to open the door, allowing him into the building. Inside the exchange looked like any other, a mass of wires that were connected to some kind of grid. He looked along the grid, which had thousands of codes and numbers, he found the section he was looking for and there was the connection for Fagan's telephone. He quickly connected the test telephone by crocodile clips to the wires on the Fagan line, he had a dial tone. When a call came in on the Fagan's line the caller would still hear the normal telephone ringing sound. Next he took out the tape recorder and played the recording into the mouthpiece of the test phone, and listened to how it sounded in the earpiece, it sounded perfect. He disconnected the line to the house and waited for the call to come through his test phone.

Donnelly stopped so that a beam of sunlight that was shining into the barn from outside caught his face. The expression on Fagan's face was priceless, now he could get down to some serious work. "Tell me what I want to know and your wife will not be harmed," he said.

"Donnelly, of all people I would not have believed that you could be involved in all of this." He was caught totally off guard when he saw his face.

"Don't start to preach to me about why I should be involved, I have not only reason but just cause. How about my daughter's death and the death of two of my best friends' children." He remained surprisingly calm.

"It wasn't supposed to turn out that way," he replied.

"So you do know what is going on, give me the full story." He moved to the hay bales and sat down.

"Where is my wife?" he asked.

"She is safe," he replied.

"What do you intend to do with her?" Surely they would not hurt her anymore if he talked, he knew that he had to strike a bargain. Donnelly just stared at him, saying nothing. "I am willing to make a deal with you, my wife goes free and you do not harm her and I will cooperate. I want to talk to her to make sure that she is safe first, I want her to be taken home." The sound of his wife's request to go home still rang in his ears.

"I thought that you would say that, she is there now." He threw the mobile phone onto the ground next to Fagan. "Call home and see for yourself," he said.

Fagan picked up the mobile phone and lay on his back as he dialed the number to his house, he heard the phone ringing then the sound of the phone being answered. "Hello, Ann, is that you?" he said.

Ann's voice spoke to him, "Stephen, I am all right I—" The phone line went dead.

"What the fuck are you playing at, Donnelly?" Fagan said.

He stepped forward and snatched the phone out of his hand.

At the telephone exchange the indicator light on David's test phone flashed, showing him that a call was coming in, he hoped that it was Donnelly. He let it ring a few times first, then made the connection, he heard Donnelly on the other end of the phone and pressed play on the recorder. Before he left the telephone exchange he reconnected the Fagan line but made it a loose connection, so that it would not work properly. They would have to make a call to the telephone company to have the line tested for them to find the fault. It would not be unusual to find a loose connection at the exchange. He secured everything and left.

"She is safe for now, someone is with her, it is up to you if she is to stay that way," said Donnelly.

"You're a bastard, Donnelly," he said.

"That may be, but I am also a father without a daughter. You have fifteen minutes to tell me everything. If I do not call your home in that time your wife will be killed. What is it to be? You are down to fourteen minutes." He leaned forward, looking Fagan squarely in the eyes.

"How do I know that you are not going to kill her even if I do tell you what you want to know?" he asked.

"I have no quarrel with your wife, only you and Eamon, she will be left alone if you tell me what I need to know." He knew that he was going to talk now.

"Billy was right, we had the Home Secretary working for us, he was a piece of shit anyway. He gave us some good information on the government's actions against the IRA and we used that to our advantage. Likewise we gave him information, which he passed on to the security forces, some of it was good information and some bad. Arms shipments coming in by boat were the best ones, we used him to give the name of some innocent fishing boat to government intelligence. Our boat carrying the arms shipment would travel slightly ahead of the fishing boat, this way the government vessel would not hit our boat for fear of giving the game away to the boat that they thought was the real weapons carrier."

"I am not interested in Bowles. What about Alan Foy?" Donnelly asked.

"You should be interested, Alan was different. As you know a couple of years ago Alan killed that policeman and his wife just when it looked like we were leaning towards peace talks. Eamon told Alan that the Army Council wanted him to kill the policeman and his wife. He also told him that he was to become a leader of the Army Council in the future and this would guarantee his position. It was a total lie, he just wanted to upset the potential for peace and Alan was a pawn. The crazy thing was that Alan didn't give a fuck about being on the Army Council, he just believed in the Irish cause. Alan had been in hiding for a long time and things were changing in the IRA during his exile.

"There were genuine concerns of the development of peace talks between our political wing and the British Government. Eamon came to me with a plan to disrupt the potential for peace talks. When I asked him why he would want to stop any chance of peace he said it would only be for two or three years. He wanted to build up enough cash so that he and the rest of us could retire millionaires. We have a lot of money coming in from North America from fund raisings in the Irish community and from our extortion and drug action here in Northern Ireland. Anyway, Eamon and I started a splinter group on our own, obviously without the knowledge of the Army Council. We were doing great, really pulling in some serious money, when the peace talks started to take place. We only need another year and we will have enough money to retire." He sat up again, supporting himself with his arms behind his body.

In the field outside Sean took his shoes and socks off, rolled up his pants and stepped into the stream, the water was freezing. He waded through the water his bare feet sinking into the mud on the bottom. The stench from the mud started to rise out of the water, "God Almighty, that stinks," he said. He pushed on through the shallow water.

Inside the barn the questions continued. "What was the deal with Alan coming back to Belfast?" he asked.

"Oh! That was Eamon again. I don't think that he was very happy with the way things were going, the peace talks really moved along and it got to the point where Eamon thought that peace may really come to Northern Ireland. He made a deal with Bowles, for money of course, Bowles had to convince Alan Foy to contact his son and bring him out of hiding."

"Why was Alan chosen to do this?"

"As you know, Alan and Bowles know each other from the past when Alan was selected by the Army Council to be the official voice of the IRA. What Alan didn't know was that Bowles was on our payroll, therefore anything they discussed was passed straight to Eamon. The idea was Alan would arrange for his son to be captured and arrested on his way to Belfast through the UK. As part of the peace negotiations the government was agreeing to have an early release program for all convicted IRA members. After Alan was arrested he would be sentenced and imprisoned, only to serve about a year, when he would be released with the chance of a new life. His father was very suspicious of the whole deal. Bowles told him that it was important to the peace process that all wanted IRA members were located and imprisoned before peace was agreed, his son was not the only one that was going to get this opportunity. When Alan talked to his wife about it she convinced him that it was the only way their son was going to have a chance of a normal life. Foy agreed to contact his son and told him that he was to meet him in Anglesey to talk about something. This wasn't unusual, as they had met there several times during his time on the run.

"Eamon had a different plan, he contacted young Alan when he knew that his father had been in touch with him and gave him a warning about his trip to England to meet his father. He told Alan that he had information that his father was going to be double-crossed by the government. He asked Alan not to say anything to his father until he could confirm how he was going to be double-crossed. He also told Alan to keep in touch with him so that he knew where to contact him in the UK."

"So that was how the police knew that he was at his brother's apartment," said Donnelly.

"We have been almost fifteen minutes by now, I want to talk to my wife," he replied.

Donnelly did not think of him asking to speak to his wife again, he had to bluff. He made it look like he was making a call on the mobile phone, he put the phone to his ear. After a few seconds he spoke into the phone, "Fifteen more minutes." He put the phone back in his pocket.

"What are you doing? I want to talk to my wife, you didn't even dial the number." He was furious with Donnelly.

"You don't have to dial to call the last number that you called, you just press send and it automatically dials the number. You have fifteen more minutes and no more." He grinned at Fagan.

"How do I know that you spoke to anyone?" he asked.

"You don't," he replied.

"I am not saying anything else until I speak to my wife again." His temper was getting the better of him and Donnelly could see it.

"Your funeral or should I say your wife's?" he replied.

Fagan screamed like some caged animal and reached for the rope on his feet. Donnelly was up like a flash and kicked him in the chest, knocking him on his back. Fagan lay on the floor, the wind knocked out of him by the kick, breathing heavily as his lungs gasped for air.

Outside the light was fading fast as the sun set, Colin was getting very impatient and decided that it was time to make a move towards the barn. "We will work our way across the field to the barn, keep as low as you can," he said to the others as he slung the shotgun across his back and took out his revolver. His two colleagues checked their weapons and all three started a slow stooped stop and start like scurry across the field. Each time a car came down the country lane they lay flat to keep out of any light that shone on the field. It was going to take some time to reach the barn.

Sean had found himself a comfortable spot under a low bush at the edge of the line of trees. His feet began to warm up again with his shoes and socks on. He had smeared some dirt on his face to take away the whiteness of his skin to help camouflage him a little. His rifle was in the rested position with the bipod under the end of the barrel giving it stability, as with other parts of the weapon he had converted the bipod so that the end of the barrel would swivel, horizontally and vertically. He hadn't been under the bush for long when he saw the three men making their way across the field from the direction of the sheep pens.

"Good job you didn't go up there to park the taxi, Sean," he said to himself. He was always talking to himself in this way. Sean had to warn Donnelly that they were coming. He reached into his pocket for the mobile phone, it was gone. He rolled onto his back and frantically searched his other pockets, it wasn't to be found. He realized that he must have dropped it. He cursed his stupidity and rolled back on his stomach and regained sight of the three men.

The men were about fifty yards from the barn and had not been seen, "Nobody must be watching the outside," whispered one of the men. Colin indicated for them to go to the side of the barn and he would go to the front, they both nodded. Both men stood up and started to slowly creep towards the side of the barn, Colin made his way to the front.

Sean watched the two men as they started towards the side of the barn and chose them as his first targets before they were out of sight. Three hundred and forty-one yards, his range finder had told him; an easy distance for him, and no wind. He did not have much adjustment to make for the drop or movement of the bullet en route to the target. He had all of the range estimation formulas in his head for working out how much he had to allow a bullet to drop or move to the side for shooting at targets.

When it came to shooting at a person he had to take into account height, whether they were sitting, kneeling or standing, terrain and of course how much light was available. All of these factors had to be taken into consideration. The rifle he used was a Parker-Hale Model 82, which took a 7.62mm round, he had a four-round box that was magazine fed. His telescope was nothing exceptional—a variable power V2S4 x 10mm with a ballistic cam.

He took careful aim at the first figure, controlling his breathing. He liked to exhale and then hold his breath before he took a shot, he could hold his breath and be rock solid like this for at least two shots, sometimes three or four. He practiced it all the time when he would dry fire, getting used to the trigger pressure. The first target stood almost upright, he squeezed the trigger very gently, a bullet was sent on its way to the target. A second was fired within two seconds.

Colin and the two men heard the first shot, by which time it was too late. Colin threw himself to the ground when he saw one of his colleagues fall. The first bullet hit the man in the side of his rib cage, spinning him around. He crashed to the ground, dead. The second man caught the bullet squarely in the chest, throwing him onto his back, his body landing in a crucifix position in the dirt.

Sean moved the butt of his rifle slightly to take aim at the third man. He saw him firing a handgun at the barn, he was up and running. He took aim and fired a quick shot. The man fell behind a small mound of dirt, he could not tell if he hit him or not. He focused carefully on the mound of dirt that the man had fallen behind, he waited for his opportunity to shoot again.

Colin did not have a clue where the shots had come from, he started to shoot at the barn, thinking that they had come from there. He was up on his feet running from side to side in a zigzag pattern, trying to make himself a harder target to hit. His bullets tore through the wooden structure of the barn as he emptied his revolver. He headed towards a mound of dirt about fifteen yards from him. He lifted the shotgun off his back, ready to use if needed. As he ran he did not hear the shot that was fired at him, he just felt something slam into his leg. It felt like he had been kicked, this was followed by a fiery pain. He lay behind the mound of soil screaming in pain, he held on to his left leg. Blood was pumping through the leg of his jeans, soaking them from the knee down. He took his belt off and made a tourniquet, fastening it around the middle of his leg, he knew that he had to stop the bleeding.

Fagan hadn't said anything for almost five minutes and Donnelly was starting to get concerned that he just may not talk anymore. He walked over to the rope that was tied to Fagan's feet and pulled on it. He had the rope over a beam in the barn, which allowed him to keep the tension on the legs of Fagan. "Well, it looks as though you are finished talking to me, so you won't mind if I suspend you upside down by this rope." He started to pull harder on the rope when Fagan spoke.

"What about my wife," he said.

"I told you before, her life is in your hands and you haven't told me everything I need to know yet," he pulled on the rope.

"Wait, wait, I will tell you the rest." He was supporting his whole body now with his hands on the floor, the rope slackened slightly, allowing him to resume a seated position.

"Be quick, you only have ten minutes left." He sat down on the bale of hay again.

"Alan called Eamon and told him when he would arrive at his brother's apartment, he even gave him the address and phone number. Eamon told him he had found out that the police were going to try to kill him before he got to Anglesey to meet his father. He advised Alan to be well armed just in case the police showed up. Eamon said that he was going to arrange for two active service unit members to meet him at his brother's apartment the morning after he arrived to escort him to the meeting with his father. Alan trusted Eamon and never questioned his advice or judgement once." He noticed that Donnelly was very agitated by his last comment as he saw him stand up and start to pace up and down.

"He is responsible for the death of my daughter," Donnelly said.

Fagan continued, "Eamon called Bowles, who set the wheels in motion for the police to raid the apartment after Alan arrived. The idea was that Alan would be killed in the raid but not his brother or your daughter, that's the truth."

Truth? He wouldn't know the truth if it ran him over, thought Donnelly.

"His father would then want to kill the police responsible for his sons' death and knowing Alan he would stop at nothing to repay them. He would wreak havoc on the mainland, it would be disastrous for the peace negotiators. It would take a long time for them to recover from Alan's actions, long enough for us to be wealthy and retire. We did not expect Alan to move so quickly, the idea was that he would mourn the death of his sons and go to the funeral. After the funeral Eamon was going to visit him and give him the information on who had killed his son. Unfortunately he got onto Bowles immediately and threatened him, we did not expect him to do that. Bowles was a coward and would have told Alan everything, including our deals with him, we could not afford that."

"So you killed him," said Donnelly.

"Well, Eamon did," he replied.

"Who is the other contact you have in London that Eamon works with?" he asked.

"That I do not know, Eamon would never share that information with me, he is very protective of that source." He was telling the truth, but Donnelly did not believe him.

"You said deals, what other deals did you have going with Bowles?" he asked.

"It wasn't so much Bowles as—" He stopped talking at the sound of a powerful gunshot outside quickly followed by a second.

Donnelly pulled out his 9mm and bent down to look through the gaps in the wooden walls of the barn. He heard more shots being fired as bullets tore through the walls, causing splinters of wood to fly. He dove onto the floor behind the hay bale to avoid being hit.

Fagan took the distraction of the gunfire as his opportunity to try to escape, he scooted himself forward on his hands to slacken the rope and quickly loosened the noose slipping his feet out. He rolled over and over on the floor to the opposite side of the barn to Donnelly. He lay in the dark shadows of the barn trying to see where his gun was on the floor, he saw it. Fagan did not hesitate, he only had one chance and this was it, he was up on his feet running across the barn towards the weapon.

Donnelly dropped his gun as he dove behind the bale of hay, he pushed his hands through the straw on the floor trying to find it, he couldn't. He heard Fagan moving and looked up to see him running towards him, he was trying to get to the gun. He was up on his feet with amazing agility, he leapt over the bale of hay, pulling out the pitchfork as he tried to cut off Fagan.

He saw that Donnelly was on his feet and heading towards him. *Too late, I will get to it first,* he thought as he dove to the floor in a rolling fashion. He picked up the gun as he rolled on the floor and brought himself up on one knee, raising the weapon all in one action.

Donnelly gave a blood-curdling yell as he ran at Fagan with the pitchfork. He saw him coming up onto one knee and was bringing the gun to bear on him. He hit Fagan with it so hard that he raised him to his feet, at the same time a round was discharged from the gun. He pushed him back three feet with the prongs of the pitchfork buried in his stomach. They both stopped with a sudden thump as Fagan's back slammed into one of the barn support posts. His body hit the post with such force that the prongs of the pitchfork went clean through his body and embedded in the wooden post. He looked at Donnelly, the shock in his eyes as he struggled to try and pull the fork out of his body.

Donnelly stood watching him for a few seconds as blood trickled out of his victim's mouth. "That is for my daughter," he said and spat in his face. He realized that someone may still be outside and picked up the gun that Fagan had dropped. He bent down by the barn door and scanned the field outside to see if he could see anyone, he couldn't. He had to go out or try to draw their fire so that he knew where they were. He lay flat on the floor and slowly pushed open the door enough to get out. If anyone was out there they would shoot at the door as it moved or at him as he came out. No shots were fired, so far so good, he crawled out on his hands and knees when he heard Colin.

"I wouldn't move any more if I were you. Roll on your right side so I can see who you are." Colin could not tell from his position who had come out, the light was poor and they were face down, if it was Donnelly he would blast him with the shotgun. He saw the man slowly roll onto his side, he raised his head further over the mound to get a clear look, it was Donnelly. That was the last thing he ever saw as the bullet sent by Sean exploded into his face.

Donnelly saw Colin's head ripped backwards by the impact of the bullet. He got to his feet and walked over to where Colin lay, covering him with his gun to make sure that he was dead. He did not have to worry, he was well and truly dead. He heard the faint sounds of Sean shouting in the distance, "Are you OK?"

"I am thanks to you, bring the taxi down here," he replied. He could not see Sean but he knew from the sound of his voice that he was somewhere in the small copse of trees.

Sean and Donnelly drove up to the sheep pens in the taxi and brought the car down and loaded the four bodies inside. The car was later dumped three miles away in a quiet country lane, Donnelly and Sean returned to their homes. As planned Ann was released close to her home and would eventually be told by the police of her husband's death.

14

SEPTEMBER 29TH, LONDON

The Spanish Trade Conference and exhibition was only two minutes from opening its doors. The general manager of the exhibition center, Fred Watts, was inside the exhibition hall checking with his employees and security that they were all ready before he gave the signal to open. One of the employees was wheeling a plastic container full of ice past the doors heading towards the refreshment area. Fred was trying to get his attention and in doing so distracted the employee. He ran into one of the steel support columns, which knocked over his ice container. Fred was quick to move as usual and called his cleaning crew on the radio. The ice-carrying employee was already going to work on picking up the ice.

"Are you OK? You're not hurt are you?" asked Fred.

"No, sir, sorry about that. I will have it cleaned up in a minute."

"A cleaning crew is on its way to help." He called security on his radio. "Please be advised that we will not open the doors, there will be a slight delay of four or five minutes." The security control room acknowledged his call and advised the door security.

Fred did not want the other entrance doors open until this entrance was clear to open.

Six minutes later the spill was cleaned up and the floor mopped dry, Fred gave the signal to open the doors, it was 9.04 am. The attendees immediately flooded into the exhibition hall spreading out like ants between the rows of exhibits. The attendees had not traveled more than twenty feet into the aisles when the bombs exploded.

The bombs had been placed in two locations, one at an exhibition booth that was selling coach tours in Spain and the other in a booth displaying signs for wine traders. Both booths had been paid for in cash and looked totally professional, neither was manned by anyone.

The timing device attached to the explosives reached the pre-set time and detonated the explosives. The blast had a devastating effect, sending a shock wave through the hall. Exhibit booths and display items were turned into flying shrapnel as they flew through the air. Some of the exhibitors were torn to shreds by the shrapnel along with their exhibits as the explosives did their evil deed.

A black and gray cloud of smoke filled the hall as the debris settled to the floor. The fire sprinkler system had activated, raining water down on the hall, adding to the chaos of those beneath it. People were screaming, some were moaning in pain and shock as the water from above was extinguishing the small fires that had broken out around the hall.

Eighteen people lay dead, over forty severely wounded or maimed, and more than a hundred more had cuts and bruises. Thanks to the ice being spilt at the entrance the delay in opening the doors had saved many lives.

Outside the exhibit hall the attendees heard the explosion and felt the shock wave as it forced its way through the entrance doors. Panic filled many of them as they turned to run towards the main exit. Very few had regard for their fellow man as they pushed each other out of the way in an effort to escape. Some were knocked down and trampled underfoot, causing others to trip over them in a chaotic scramble for safety.

The Spanish ambassador had already left home when Victor, Pedro and Peli drove up to the gate at the entrance to the drive. The security guard on duty stood at the gate, watching the car as it stopped outside.

Pedro got out of the car with an envelope in his hand. "Good morning," he said to the guard.

"Good morning," the guard replied.

Pedro extended his left hand with the envelope in it. The guard instinctively reached for the envelope and said, "What is that?"

"It is for the ambassador," Pedro replied.

As the guard's eyes focused on the envelope Pedro raised his right hand, which was holding a gun, he shot the guard twice.

Peli was out of the car as soon as the guard was shot. He was carrying two anti-tank launchers. Pedro took one off him and they both took aim at the house.

The ambassador's wife was in the master bedroom when she was called by the maid, "Madame, your son has had a fall in the garden," she was shouting frantically.

"I'm coming," she shouted as she ran from the bedroom.

The maid was already back in the garden attending to the 4-year-old when the ambassador's wife came out of the house. She ran to the side of her son, who had a nasty-looking cut on his hand. They were being closely watched by his two older sisters, Marion—6 years—and Vanessa—7 years old.

"What happened?" she said.

Maria answered, "He was running and he fell on the garden rake."

The maid had him sitting up as she wiped the wound with a wet towel. To her surprise he just sat on the grass and let her wipe his hand, he did not cry once.

They heard the explosions in the house, the second one blasting out some of the upstairs windows in the back of the house, showering them with glass. The ambassador's wife covered her son's body with hers as she pulled the two sisters to the ground.

Pedro took aim at the first floor, Peli at the ground floor, they pulled the triggers, releasing the deadly grenades. As the missiles entered the house through the windows they exploded with amazing effect. They stood watching as the smoke billowed out through the broken windows. A fire had started downstairs and was already burning with fury. They returned to the car and drove off in the direction of London. In their hurry to escape they did not know they had missed their target, the ambassador's wife and children.

"What are we going to do now?" asked Peli.

"We will leave the car at a house that is owned by the man I work for, he has three grocery stores and lets me stay at this house. I only use it for entertaining women, if you know what I mean," said Victor.

"Up to your old tricks," said Pedro.

"Ah! You know these English women, they cannot resist a little Spanish charm, especially when I make the accent very thick." He loved to charm the ladies.

"He was always like that at Madrid University, he would have three or even four girlfriends going at once. I don't know how there is anything left between your legs," said Pedro.

"Jealousy is a terrible thing, but then I cannot blame you," said Victor.

They joked like this for almost forty minutes, it was as though the attack on the ambassador's home had never taken place. There could be people dead in the house, or at least that was what they hoped, and they did not have any conscience.

They left the car at the house selected by Victor and walked to the local underground station. On the train people were talking about the bombs that had been going off all over the country. As usual the media were quick to report any kind of terrorist attack. Pedro listened to the cackling of these people and realized how fast the public exaggerated terrorist attacks and the information they heard from the media. He enjoyed listening and watching them as they all gave their own version of the news releases.

Sebastián and Velasco drove past the Spanish Embassy Commercial office on Chiltern Place in West London, to check that there weren't any changes since their last visit. If their information was correct the Spanish ambassador would be visiting the office before going to the exhibition at Olympia.

"Why did we not wait to attack the ambassador at the exhibition center?" asked Sebastián.

"We did not have an exact time for his visit to the exhibition center. The commercial office is only very small and he would be a much easier target once he was inside," replied Velasco.

"Do you think that it will create a problem with the office being on the second floor?"

"No, the distance that the grenades have to travel is very small, and they will not have time to veer off course. As we discussed his security detail, except for the driver, will be inside with him. Circle around once more and his car should be there by then."

Sebastián did as he was requested and drove around the block again. It was now three minutes past nine and there was no sign of the ambassador's car. Velasco was starting to lose his patience.

"Where is he? They were supposed to be here by now, drive around again."

They came around a second time, only to find that there was no sign of the ambassador's car. There was a black Ford motor car outside with a driver sitting in the front.

"That must be his car, he is using a different car," said Velasco. "Quickly, stop across the street as planned. I am going to stand outside the car and fire the grenades, it is too awkward to fire them out of the sunroof."

Velasco climbed into the back of the car and checked that the Light Anti-tank Weapon was ready to fire. The car stopped and he was out of the vehicle with the LAW on his shoulder. He aimed at the second-floor window that Sebastián had identified as the Spanish Commercial Office and pressed the trigger. To his surprise, nothing happened—it did not fire, he pulled the trigger again, nothing. He immediately threw the weapon onto the backseat of the car and took out the second LAW. By now people in the street had noticed what he was trying to do and were running around screaming and shouting. Velasco did not like this, nor did Sebastián, who was getting very nervous. He heard the second weapon discharge the grenade, an explosion occurred almost immediately at the building across the street, he had hit the target.

Velasco was amazed at the power of the 66mm shell as it left the LAW. He did not have time to take his eye away from the sight before the shell hit the target. He dropped the LAW in the car and jumped into the backseat.

"Get out of here," he said to Sebastián.

He did not need telling twice as he pressed the accelerator and drove away. As the car sped down the road Velasco was cursing at the fact that the first grenade did not work.

"I thought that those weapons were supposed to work."

"I am sorry, but there is no way that we can test them, once they are fired they are no longer useful." Sebastián was very scared of Velasco.

They drove the rest of the way back to the safehouse without speaking.

The first Algerian team members set out before midnight in individual vehicles, Mustafa to the town of Wilmslow and the City of Manchester and Zaki and his brother for the City of Birmingham. Magreb left for Gatwick airport at 7.00 a.m. and Sami left for Wapping 8.00 a.m.

Tarek was driving around aimlessly, he had left the garage far too early. Sweat was running down his face, the stress was beginning to show.

Mohammed was in place at Trafalgar Square at 8.30 a.m. waiting for the French foreign minister to pass on his way to the conference at the Tower Bridge Hotel. His driver always took the same route out of his apartment due to the one-way street system, an easy target. Behind him some teenage boys were kicking a soccer ball back and forth to each other and it reminded him of his youth in Algeria when he used to do the same thing. The Square was already very busy filling up with tourists, all eager to take photographs and feed the pigeons. The traffic was as busy as ever, with a relentless stream of vehicles going past the tourist spot. Adel was about fifty yards away watching for the car to appear, he would signal to Mohammed when it was coming. They did not expect it to show up until about ten minutes to nine.

Mustafa, Magreb, Zaki and his brother had all planted their devices and were already heading back to the house in London.

It was 8.50 a.m. when Tarek stopped the van outside the French Embassy as planned. The minute he got out of the van a uniformed policeman approached him.

"You can't park that there," he said.

"I have come to do an estimate for painting the window frames and doors for Messier La Roche." He showed the policeman his writing pad with the name written on it.

"Stay here while I check with his secretary," the policeman said. He turned and went into the Embassy.

Tarek did not wait any longer, he walked quickly to the corner of the street and disappeared.

The policeman came out less than a minute later but could not see the painter. He walked over to the van to see if he had gotten back inside, he wasn't there. He could not see him anywhere, he was not happy—something was wrong. He called his dispatch and requested a tow truck to have the van removed. One of the Embassy staff arrived for work, she was a young twenty-year-old dark-haired girl who always took time to say hello to him.

"Morning George," she said in her very strong French accent.

"Good morning Michelle, how are you today?" he asked.

"I am very happy. I go to Nice in two days for my twenty-first birthday." She was very excited. "Is that your new police van, George?" She smiled, pointing at the painter's vehicle.

"Very funny, no it belongs to a painter that was here a moment ago. His clothes had more paint on them than the van," he said, smiling.

"Were they dirty white?" she asked.

"Yes, have you seen him?" he replied.

"I just saw a man around the corner taking off dirty-looking white pants with paint on them," she said.

His response to what she said was immediate. "Michelle, go into the Embassy and press the evacuation alarm. Tell everyone to leave via the rear exit NOW." He shouted the last part to make her realize that he was not joking.

She ran inside as he tried to open one of the doors, they were locked. He put his face to the glass on the passenger door and looked inside, nothing unusual in the front. He strained to look into the rear but could only see a wooden board acting as a partition. The police officer could hear the siren going off inside the Embassy as he hurried to the back of the van. There were no windows in the doors, he turned the handle on one of the doors and to his surprise it opened. As he pulled the door open he stepped back in surprise.

"Christ almighty," he said to himself as he saw the large metal drums inside, he knew that it was a bomb. He ran into the Embassy screaming at people to hurry out of the building. He did not want to use his radio for fear that it may detonate the bomb. He picked up the telephone in the lobby and dialed the police station that he reported to, someone answered.

"Hello, police."

He recognized the voice, "Sally, this is George at the French Embassy. I have a car bomb outside the building."

That was all he got to say, as the bomb detonated, completely demolishing the Embassy building.

Mohammed and Adel were still waiting at Trafalgar Square, but there was no sign of the minister's car, Mohammed looked at his watch, it was 8.58 a.m.—only two minutes to go before the bombs went off. At that moment he heard a loud boom in the distance. He knew that it was the Embassy bomb, he saw Adel start to walk towards him. They had to go, the minister was not coming, he picked up his oversized canvas bag and saw Adel start to wave his arms at him, *he is coming*. He put the bag on the wall in front of him and unzipped it, placing his hand inside, ready to pull out the anti-tank weapon at the precise moment the car was level with him.

Adel disappeared into a crowd and made his way back to the car to wait for Mohammed.

Mohammed could see the minister's car slowly making its way along the road in the heavy traffic, an easy target. The car was almost level with him on the far side of the road with two lanes of traffic between him and the car. He climbed onto the low wall next to an ornamental streetlight and lifted the anti-tank weapon out of the canvas bag. He extended the barrel, flipped up the sight on the end. He pulled the trigger as something hit his arm, moving the launcher slightly, the rocket was on its way. It flew through the air, missing the target, striking another car, causing it to explode in a ball of flames. People were running everywhere, screaming in total panic as he jumped off the wall. He turned to grab the bag when he was knocked to the ground. He felt someone's arms around him and struggled to get free, it was a policeman. Mohammed swung his elbow backwards into the policeman's face, the blow caused him to loosen his grip. Mohammed rolled over on the sidewalk in an attempt to get away but the policeman grabbed his ankle, he lashed out with his feet. The policeman again lost his grip but was up on his feet as Mohammed started to run. Two men came running towards Mohammed, he pulled out the pistol from behind his back and fired two shots, hitting both men. He turned and fired a third shot at the policeman, hitting him in the chest. Nobody else was going to be a hero, he ran across the road between the cars through the smoke from the burning car. He ran along the sidewalk screaming for people to move, he waved his gun around as people jumped out of his way. Adel was ready with the car when he arrived, he could see that Mohammed was sweating profusely.

He got into the car, "Drive, Adel, drive," he said.

As he drove he noticed that Mohammed did not have the canvas bag, "Where is the bag?" he asked.

"I had to leave it, a stupid policeman tried to stop me I shot him and two others." He sat back in the seat panting as he tried to get his breath back.

Fear spread throughout the country, particularly on the rail systems. People that normally took the train home from work now arranged for a friend to give them a ride or took a bus or taxi. The public were getting worried that they would soon become a casualty of a new attack, the combined attacks of the Gahi and Basurto groups had the desired effect.

The British government made a public announcement on the national news asking for the public to remain calm and assist the police in their inquiries. They pleaded for witnesses to come forward.

The police and emergency services were stretched to the limit, particularly in central London. The barrage of phone calls to the police by the public was choking the system. There were those that were genuine eyewitnesses, others who just wanted information about the bombings and of course the crank callers claiming responsibility.

Strain had spent most of the morning on the telephone with the Prime Minister trying to help him understand who could have done this and why. The attack in Liverpool was obviously the work of the IRA, but it had been four hours since the other attacks had taken place and nobody had claimed responsibility. There had been several crank callers, the police traced them and were in the process of trying to identify who they were.

Strain watched the news on the television in his lounge, he had only slept for an hour since the bombing of his team the night before and was starting to feel weary. All he could think about was the dead team members and was there anything that he could or should have done different to prevent them from losing their lives. He kept thinking about the families of his dead team members and how they would cope with the deaths of their loved ones, especially as there wasn't much left of one of them to bury. He focused on the television screen, the TV cameras showed the Prime Minister walking out of the front door of number 10 Downing Street, to a frenzy of camera flashes. To his right stood Simon Fletcher, head of MI5, and behind him were two of the PM's protection detail. As always he did not have any notes with him, he had already studied them in private and had memorized what he was going to say. Strain leaned forward in the chair to listen, turning up the volume with the remote control.

The Prime Minister began, "You are all aware by now of the explosion which occurred last evening at approximately 11.30 p.m. in the Pier Head area of Liverpool, which resulted in the loss of several lives and scores of injured. Our investigation, though in its preliminary stages, has uncovered conclusive evidence that the explosion was the result of a terrorist bomb. Prior to the bomb exploding a local newspaper received a warning from someone claiming to be from the IRA, this has not been confirmed.

"You may also be aware that this morning other bomb attacks occurred in London and several other locations across the country, and that assassination attempts were made against the French and Spanish ambassadors, both of whom escaped unharmed. Not so fortunate were over eighty members of the public who lost their lives in these attacks, and over two hundred more who were injured, many of them seriously.

"We cannot at this point confirm with certainty that these horrendous incidents are related, but the timing and method would, of course, suggest that such were the case. I have placed our armed forces and police departments across the country on a high state of alert and can assure you that we will pursue those responsible for these dastardly acts to the ends of the earth in order to bring them to justice."

He was transfixed to the television screen as the Prime Minister turned and walked back into number 10. He could not help notice that the PM looked particularly pale and tired, this was most unusual, he never allowed the pressure of a situation to get to him. He drifted off to sleep with the television still switched on.

The telephone rang, shaking Strain out of his sleep, he answered it.

"Hello," he said.

"John, I need for you to come to London." It was the PM.

"When do you want me there?" He never thought of questioning the PM or asking why he wanted him.

"Today, I am sorry, I know that you have been through a lot in the last day, but I need to talk to you," he replied.

"I will catch the first plane to London from Manchester airport." He really did not want to do this, as he needed the rest.

"Thank you, John. I knew that I could rely on you. You will not need to catch a plane, a government Learjet will be waiting for you by the time you get to the airport." The PM had already arranged for the plane to leave London, it was only ten minutes from Manchester Airport as they spoke. "A driver will meet you at this end, see you soon." That was all that he said as the phone went dead. Strain was in no mood to go to London but he had no choice, he had to go.

He arrived at Manchester airport and went to the security gate next to the domestic terminal. The security guard gave his ID a thorough check and opened the gates, allowing him into the restricted area of the airport. Strain was impressed with the private jet, as it was very expensively furbished inside. He refused a drink from the co-pilot and chose a large reclining leather chair to sit in. The pilot wasted no time and closed the door of the plane and prepared to take off. Strain was only on the plane two minutes when he fell asleep, forty minutes later the plane touched down at Heathrow, waking him up. He felt better for the sleep and was somewhat refreshed. As the plane taxied to a private terminal building he looked out of the small window, there were a car and driver standing by. He thanked the pilot and got into the car, the driver whisked him away to Downing Street. As the car drove through London he noticed that the driver was not going towards Downing Street.

"Where are we going?" he asked.

"I have been requested to take you to the Houses of Parliament sir," the driver replied.

"Whose request?" Strain replied.

"Sorry, sir, I don't know. I was told to tell you that someone will meet you when you arrived. I do not know who made the request and they did not say who you were to meet." The driver had many years of experience and knew not to ask questions—just drive as instructed.

"OK, thank you"

Houses of Parliament, that meant that the PM did not want him to be seen arriving at Number 10. It was not surprising, as the press would be hanging around there for days waiting for the slightest hint of a break in the news about the bombings. The car entered the private parking area at the houses of Parliament, it looked like a police convention, there were officers everywhere. The security had been upgraded to an incredible level, with firearms support everywhere. As he got out of the car he was met by Brian Harper-Jones, the PM's political advisor and Mask committee member.

"Hello Brian," Strain said.

"He's waiting inside for you, please follow me."

He followed him inside and turned down one of the corridors leading away from the PM's chamber.

"Where are we going?" Strain stopped walking.

Harper-Jones looked around very quickly, "He is in a side office that I use, he didn't want you to be seen together. John, he is very concerned about what happened to your team last night, he wants to talk to you about it." He started walking again, followed by Strain. They entered a small office, the PM's secretary was sitting behind a desk, Harper-Jones left him there and walked out. Laura was on her feet the minute he left and practically ran around the desk, throwing her arms around Strain's neck.

"Thank God you are safe," she said.

"Easy, Laura, you are going to pop my eyes out if you squeeze any tighter," he was trying to make light of the situation, but he could see that she was very emotional.

"I am glad you are OK. The PM is waiting in the next room." She gave him a smile that he would remember forever, and he kissed her firmly on the lips. He left her standing with a shocked expression on her face as he opened the door to the office where the PM was waiting.

"Hello sir," he said as he closed the door behind him.

The PM had his back to him. "Sit down, John." He swiveled around in the chair. Strain took one look at the man's face and realized that he had been crying.

"Are you all right, sir?"

"No, John, I am not and nor are you. We have both lost people very dear to us in the last twenty-four hours, I am sorry about your friends that died last night."

"Thank you, sir, I still don't believe that it happened."

"Yes, quite."

"What do you mean we have both lost someone close to us?" Strain asked the question without really thinking about it; after all, it was none of his business.

"My nieces were casualties in one of those attacks this morning, the one at Trafalgar Square, they were both killed and their mother was severely injured." His eyes started to fill with tears.

"The twins." Strain said it in total disbelief.

"Yes, they were going to a choir practice for a diplomatic dinner that we were going to hold this Christmas. I requested their church choir to sing a number of Christmas carols for the diplomats attending."

He was already blaming himself for their deaths and Strain could see it. "I am very sorry." He did not say any more.

"John, I want the bastards that did this, not just for my nieces but for the rest of the innocent people that were killed and injured. It is time that we took the gloves off and gave these terrorist organizations a taste of their own medicine. I don't want them to be able to harm anyone again, ever."

This was a new side of the PM that he had never seen before, hatred was in his eyes. "We will find them and bring them to justice, every last one of them," he replied.

"I want you to do that and swiftly, you have my authority to do whatever is necessary. You will receive special funding, which will be handled by MI6. I know that this is an unusual way to fund your group, but we have to operate in a different manner if we are to see justice, as you put it. They will provide you with as many vehicles and as much air transportation as you need, the plane that brought you down here is at your disposal twenty-four hours a day. If you require additional manpower they will arrange that also. They have received direct instructions from me that nobody is to know of your new role in this investigation. Everyone, including MI6, believe that you are still operating as the Mask Team leader. MI6 believe that I have involved you because of your present and past record of catching terrorists, and because you now have a stronger interest because of the loss of your team members. They will provide you with whatever information they receive on the suspects involved in the attacks. I do not want MI5 to know that you are involved with MI6, you can play them along as you see fit. This was not an easy deal to sell to MI6, you may have to tread carefully around them, let them think that they have control of you, John. Your contact is Sir Gregory Talbot, the head of MI6. Here is a number that you can call him on." He pushed a card across the desk with a telephone number typed on it. "You have wanted to do this for a long time, John, don't fail me. I don't want to know anything about the operation, this conversation and meeting has not taken place, remember what you told me in the past, accidents only. If we talk in the future it will be about the Mask Team or very general issues regarding these attacks. That is all I have for you, ask Laura to come in as you leave."

He didn't say anything, he just shook hands and walked out. "He wants to see you, Laura," he said as he walked into the next room.

Strain went back to the chauffeur-driven car and headed for the airport to return to Manchester, he could not believe that he had been given the authority to eliminate these terrorists, a license to kill.

He used a public telephone to call the number on the card that the PM had given him, a male voice answered, "Hello."

"This is John Strain, I have been asked to contact you," he said.

"Yes, Mr Strain, I understand that you are going to assist us."

"That is correct," he said but wanted to add, *you pompous bastard.*

"I take it that you will have a shopping list to provide to me, when can I have it?"

"I will call you back this evening and give you a full list of people and equipment, sir." He threw the *sir* in for effect.

"Jolly good. I look forward to hearing from you, good-bye."

Strain knew who he wanted to add to the team, he just hoped that Sir Gregory could arrange it. He made several other calls, mostly to his surviving team members. He arrived back home to see that there were a number of messages on his answering machine, he pressed the play button. All of the calls were from people that knew him and wanted to give their condolences.

He sat down with a large malt whiskey and put the telephone on his lap.

He dialed George Barton's home number.

"George, it is Strain."

"Christ, John, I am sorry to hear what happened last night in Liverpool, how are you doing?" The concern was clear in his voice.

"I'm fine, I need you and Chalky to work for me for about a month, are you interested?"

"Why yes, we are interested, I say we because I know that Chalky would say the same. What about clearance with our present boss?"

"You will both be going to a special terrorism training class at the Home Office, very hush hush, or so they will be led to believe. I will explain everything when we get together, will you contact Chalky?"

"Yes, when will we be needed?"

"Two days from now, after the funerals of my team members. I have a lot of other things to organize in the meantime."

"We will be ready, John. I have one question for you."

"What is it?"

"We are still collating all of the information that you requested on the Bowles job, we haven't quite got all of the airport stuff together. Are we to continue with this? I say we, as Chalky is the one cross-referencing all of the information we receive."

"Yes, keep that going as best you can for now, we may need it."

"OK, see you soon." He was going to the funeral and knew that he would see him there.

"Speak to you soon." He suddenly felt tired again and took himself off to bed.

He woke up feeling totally washed out and got into the shower to try to liven himself up. The hot water felt good, it did the trick, he felt alive again. He had no idea what time it was and didn't really care as he walked into the kitchen to make a pot of coffee, the clock on the microwave oven showed him that it was 6.30 a.m. With the coffee brewing he took a walk to the local store and bought a newspaper, the headlines were all about the previous day's terrorist attacks. As he approached his home he saw a car stopping outside, it was Bulldog.

Bulldog was not looking forward to this visit with his friend and boss, but he was the most logical choice. As he got out of the car he saw John walking towards him with a newspaper in his hand.

"Morning John."

"Morning, what brings you around so early?"

"You got any of that good coffee brewing inside?"

"Sure have, come on in." They both entered his home.

Strain took two mugs out of one of the kitchen cupboards and placed them on the counter top. "Come on, Bulldog, spit it out, why are you here?" As usual he got straight to the point.

"I don't know how to say this but Ann is pregnant, she was going to tell him the morning after he was killed in Liverpool." He watched Strain as he poured out the coffee, he did not flinch at the sad news.

"The news just gets worse as we go, I know how much they both wanted kids, how is she? Forget I asked that, stupid fuck that I am, I know how she is." He was trying to put on a brave face but Bulldog knew that he was hurting.

"Let's sit down and drink our coffee," he said.

They did not say anything to each other for a couple of minutes, it was Strain who eventually broke the silence.

"Do you want to stay on the team?" he said to Bulldog.

"What do you mean, do I want to stay on the team? Of course I do, why do you ask?"

"I need to discuss this with the rest of the team members but I want to know what you think they might say. Remember a couple of years ago we had the discussion about finding a way to stop terrorism by using terror, we where practically castrated for even thinking about it? Well, I have received the authority to proceed with the project. I want you and the rest of the team to be involved but it is a completely different game and I will respect any decision that you or the others make. I don't want an answer today, give yourself time to think about it." He hoped that they would all agree when he spoke to them.

"I don't have to think about it, John, I am in, I want to be a part of the process that gets back at those bastards, I think the rest of the team will feel the same. When do we start?"

"Always eager to get started, aren't you, Bulldog? We will gather some intelligence over the next couple of days and really start on finding out where these people are hiding after the funerals. I have asked George Barton if he and Chalky will help us out, he said yes but he does not know what we are going to do. I am not going to tell them what we are getting into, just that they are to provide technical and surveillance assistance. I do not want them involved in the dirty end to this job, the less they know the better. What do you think?"

"They have a right to know what they are getting into, John, you cannot expect them to do their job and not tell them what the result may be. At the end of the day they will put two and two together and will not thank you for keeping them in the dark. You can trust them to keep their mouths shut, tell them that this may finish in a bloody result, then let them make their own decision."

"You are right. We have been given an open checkbook and the freedom to target who we want, when we want. There is only one requirement from the authorizer, all those that we target are to die of accidental deaths. I do not know how long the authority will last. Once this starts and the blood flows people may not be bold enough to stick with the decision. We could be pulled off the job as quickly as we were put on it."

"Whoever made the decision to go ahead with the job knows what may happen, they are not going to pull us off that easily."

"OK, we need to include an explosives specialist, you and I are pretty good at the basic stuff but we need a true professional, any suggestions?"

"Yeah, one person comes to mind straight away."

"Well, who is it?" Strain asked.

"Remember Major Hartley at Hereford when we were being trained by the SAS, he would be ideal. He has a great deal of active experience and I am sure that he would welcome the challenge."

"He would be perfect, you're right, but he retired about two months ago."

"Technically yes, but he will never retire, John, he and I got to be good friends, he is sitting at home bored to death. I spoke to him last night, he called to see if it was our team that was hit in Liverpool. John, if you can get him authorized he would be more than happy to join in the party."

"I will make some calls and get him cleared, talk to him and make him the offer, see what he says." Strain was excited at the thought of Hartley joining them, he had a wealth of experience and would be an excellent addition to the team. "Give me a call later, tell me what he says."

"I am going to get a couple of hours sleep, I will call him when I wake up, see you soon." He got up and left.

Strain did not trust MI6 and had the use of Hartley cleared directly through the PM's office, Laura made the call herself, and as usual when she made a request on behalf of the PM to MI6 nobody would argue with her. Not only did she not get questioned, it was automatically accepted that the conversation never took place.

George Barton and Chalky White had the order to attend the Home Office granted by their respective bosses. They were immediately ordering additional state of the art, technical equipment through Sir William, the head of MI6.

15

SEPTEMBER 30TH, IRELAND

Foy was back in Ireland, his search for information on Strain and verifying his address had proved to be fruitful, he had returned for the funeral of his sons and Maureen Donnelly.

The funeral for their children went as smoothly as one would expect. A lot of old friends and family attended to pay their respects and a great number of IRA supporters. Like any other funeral there were family members that had not seen each other for years and most probably would not see each other again until the next wedding or funeral. Foy and Donnelly stood with each other outside Foy's home discussing what they were going to do next.

"They are having their funerals tomorrow. I want to go over to the mainland and visit with this man Strain. I will need you to take me in that flying machine of yours if you can," he said to Donnelly.

"That won't be a problem, but I would like to leave when it is dark. How did you know when the funeral was going to take place?"

"I called the police headquarters in Chester and told them that I was with the Greater Manchester police and we were sending some uniformed officers to the funeral, they told me everything." Foy was quietly pleased with this stroke of genius.

"It was that easy, eh! Nice one, Alan. What are we going to do about him, don't you think we should both be talking to him, he could be a handful?"

"I think that he needs to know that we are all being used here and if he cooperates with us we can find out exactly who is behind this and why."

"You want to join forces with this man? He will kill you as soon as he sees you. I say we just kill him and take care of Eamon ourselves." Donnelly did not like the idea of working together with the people that killed his daughter.

"I understand all of the reasons why we should not work with him, but we have a lot of unfinished business here and he can help us and we can help him. If we just kill him and Eamon we may never find out who else is behind this. We will be wanted men for the rest of our lives and I don't think that either of our wives or we want that. We have to come out of this clean and the only way we can do that is if we involve Strain. He has to agree to some of our terms and one of those is that he ensures that our names are kept out of this. Once he knows that he was set up like us he will want to find out who did it as much as we do."

"I know what you say makes sense I just don't like the idea of working alongside the bastards that took our children's lives." The pain of his daughter's death suddenly visited him again as tears filled his eyes.

"We have to agree on this one way or another, how do you want to do this?" He hoped that his friend would go with his idea, if he didn't he would be on the run for the rest of his life.

"This is hard for me, Alan. I know what you say makes sense but I have just attended my daughter's funeral, as you have your sons'. Either way, I see us going to England in the morning is that right?"

"Yes, whichever way we do this we go to England." He wanted him to know that whatever decision he made, he was behind him one hundred percent.

"I will decide before we leave," he replied.

"What is the latest on Eamon?"

"I was told this morning that he flew to London again, I have somebody finding out where he is staying in London. When I drop you in Southport I will fly back here and try to get the information to find him. We have the use of a safehouse in London when we need it, I don't have the address yet, I will give you the details when I get them."

"He will be running scared, but I am sure that he has heard about Fagan's death and I would not be surprised if he has a bodyguard looking after him. Find out as much as you can, especially who is protecting him, it is bound to be an IRA member, whoever it is they are going to be good."

"I agree, the police are not saying if Fagan and the other bodies have been found, not publicly anyway, they will tell the families first. We will leave around four a.m. I will call you later to confirm the time. Our wives are not going to like it when we leave so soon after the funeral but it can't be helped."

"I know, but it will be over soon." Foy was going to say that hopefully they would still be alive, but he did not want to tempt fate.

"I am going home. I will call you later." Donnelly felt drained and needed to sleep if he was going to be alert for the flight in the morning.

OCTOBER 1ST, ENGLAND

During the flight to England they said very little to each other, both of them thinking of what was ahead of them. Donnelly eventually broke a particularly long period of silence. "There are a couple of extra guns in a box behind your seat if you would like to help yourself."

Foy turned around and found a wooden box with three nine-millimeter handguns inside. "Which one do you want?" he asked.

"I want one of the ankle holsters, I already have my favorite gun with me." It was very rare for him not to carry a gun of some kind.

He strapped one weapon to his ankle and put the other in his jacket pocket. "Have you heard where Eamon is yet?" Foy asked.

"No, I don't think that I will know for a little while yet, he is not going to be easy to trace."

It was time for him to ask the fatal question of his involvement with Strain. "Have you decided if you want to be involved with Strain?"

"Yes, you are a terrible man for making the voice of reason talk to me, but we will do things your way. However, I want to come to an agreement that if Strain does not agree to cooperate we eliminate them all."

"Agreed." He did not hesitate in his reply because he would kill them all if they did not want to work with them. He had no idea how things would go with Strain, but he was prepared for the worst.

The plane touched down in Southport in the northwest of England, where Foy was dropped off, and Donnelly immediately turned around and headed back to Ireland.

A member of an IRA active service unit had left a car at the airport for Foy's use. The drive to Liverpool from the airport only took Foy thirty-five minutes. He was too early to go to the cemetery and stopped at a McDonald's restaurant. It was close to the famous horse race track in an area of Liverpool called Aintree. He had two and a half hours to kill and did not want to bring attention to himself. After spending thirty minutes in the fast food restaurant he drove to the Seaforth area of the city and parked the car. He sat and watched the waters of the river Mersey estuary for over an hour and then made his way to the cemetery. He needed this time to think of how he was going to approach Strain, it wasn't long before he knew what he was going to do. He had to take a chance and confront Strain at his home. He would be at his most relaxed there and hopefully off guard, especially after the funeral.

As he arrived at the cemetery he could see that there were parked cars scattered everywhere. Many of the cars were marked police vehicles, a policeman in uniform was standing in the middle of the road directing traffic. Foy switched on the turn signal on the car, showing the officer he wanted to go into the cemetery, he indicated for him to park across the street. Foy gave the officer a quick salute at which he saluted back, he obviously thought that he was another police officer. He parked the car, leaving his mobile phone on the front seat, he made his way across to the cemetery.

Foy stood in the cemetery clutching a small bunch of flowers he had bought at the cemetery gates, watching the entrance to the Chapel as the coffins were carried out. The scene was no different to the one the day before when he had buried his two sons and his good friend Donnelly had buried his daughter. Everyone was dressed in black, women crying, men holding back the tears and in some cases failing. He was totally numb to their grief and to the loss of their loved ones, he had lost his own and seen many others before him lose friends and family. The cemetery looked even more dismal as the rain fell and the gravestones stood like bleak concrete soldiers standing guard over the graves of the dead.

The rain intensified and he repositioned himself on a wooden bench under a tree. On the back of the bench was a brass plaque with an inscription on it which read, 'In loving memory of our son' he did not read any more as he felt the pain of his own loss coming back.

The mourners followed the coffins through the graveyard. Some put up umbrellas, shielding themselves from the rain. On man walking closely behind the cortege was supporting a woman who looked as though she had lost control of herself. She was crying uncontrollably and was finding it very difficult to walk. *She must be one of the wives,* thought Foy. The man supporting her looked across the lines of gravestones, his eyes making contact with Foy's, he looked back at him and engaged his stare. Neither man looked away for what seemed like an eternity, Foy knew that this was Strain.

Strain held Ann by the arm as they left the chapel, she had been hit particularly hard by her husband's death. She had planned to tell him when he returned home from work the day of the bombing that he was going to be a father. They had been trying for eight years to have a child, and had almost given up on the idea of becoming parents. Her sister told Strain and the other team members about the pregnancy earlier that morning, which only added to their grief. Strain and Bulldog did not admit that they already knew. The rain was soaking everybody and everything, the scene looked totally miserable.

Strain was struggling to hold back his emotions as he looked at the coffins ahead of him, why had this happened? He had asked himself that question a thousand times since the bomb had exploded. He looked to his right, sitting on a bench under a tree was a man holding a bunch of flowers, he somehow looked familiar. The man never looked away, he just stared straight back at Strain. Someone held an umbrella over them, blocking out the rain. Strain looked up at the umbrella. He looked back across the graveyard—the man on the bench had disappeared.

When the man looked up at the umbrella Foy got up from the bench and quickly slid behind the trunk of the tree out of sight. At the grave site the mourners all had their backs to him and he walked away unnoticed. The policeman directing traffic saw him coming as he walked through the gates of the cemetery and stopped the traffic to allow him to cross the road. He gave the policeman a thankful nod of the head and made his way to the car. As he approached the car he saw that one of the windows had been broken, he knew straight away that the car had been broken into. He opened the driver's door and saw that the mobile phone was missing. He cursed himself for being so stupid as to leave the phone in the car, he should have turned it off and taken it with him. He did not have time to go looking for a store that sold mobile phones—he had to get to Strain's house.

It was two hours before Strain showed up at home, he drove right past Foy, who was parked at the end of the street. Foy waited for him to park his car in the drive and enter his house. He slowly drove down the street and parked the car about thirty yards from the house. Foy knew that this was the most dangerous part, as he had to get into the house quickly before any nosey neighbors saw anything. He quickly walked up the drive and knocked on the front door, he was glad that it was solid wood, he heard movement inside and the door opened. Before Strain had time to even see who was at the door Foy struck him on the side of the head with the butt of his pistol. He stepped inside the house and closed the door behind him. Strain was lying on the floor unconscious with a small trickle of blood running down the side of his head. Foy dragged the unconscious body into the lounge at the back of the house and left it on the floor.

He looked at Strain lying on the floor and felt like shooting him where he lay, but he was not going to achieve anything by doing that. There was a telephone on a table in the corner of the room and he decided to call Donnelly.

"It's me," was all he said when Donnelly answered.

"What happened to you? I have been trying to get you for hours?"

"It is a long story, but I have to buy another mobile phone. As soon as I do I will call you with the number."

"Speak to you later," said Donnelly.

Foy was getting the feeling that they were being set up again, but why? He didn't have a clue. He looked around the room and saw that there was a bottle of malt whiskey on the shelf by the television. It was a little early in the day but why not, he thought, and helped himself to a crystal glass and poured himself a drink.

Next to the television was a music center with a selection of CDs on top. He browsed through the selection and saw that there was a varied selection of music. Strain obviously had a wide-ranging taste in music, there was Led Zeppelin, Jimmy Hendrix and a lot of Opera. Foy selected a CD by Luciano Pavarotti and inserted the disc into the player. The first track played it was 'Della Mia Bella' from Verdi's *Rigoletto.*

"You like opera, Mr Foy," said a voice behind him.

He swung around with the gun in his hand and saw Strain still lying on the floor touching his forehead.

"Yes, it is an acquired taste, Mr Strain."

"Well, now that we have got the pleasantries out of the way, why are you here, other than to kill me?"

"If I was going to kill you I would have done it by now." He turned his back on Strain and poured a second whiskey, he knew that he was still too groggy to do anything. "Trust me, I do want to kill you for killing my two sons, but I realize that you are not totally to blame, have a drink." He handed the glass to Strain and sat on the sofa.

Strain could not figure out what was going on or what the hell Foy was talking about. He slowly got to his feet and took a large drink of the whiskey. He looked at Foy with hatred in his eyes.

"You are the one responsible for the bomb that killed my friends."

"And you are responsible for murdering my sons and my friend's daughter." The fury sprang out in his voice, the hatred filled the room between them.

"Murder? They were armed to the teeth, what did you expect us to say, 'Stop, police'?"

Foy jumped to his feet and pressed the weapon into Strain's face, "Don't get fucking smart with me because I would truly enjoy spreading your brains all over this room. God help me, I want to kill you more than I have wanted to kill anyone."

Strain lost his temper at the thought of his team members being blown to pieces by this man. He pushed Foy away from him. "Fucking shoot me if you're going to and let's get this over with, because if you think that I am going to sit here and let you fuck me around or torture me you can forget it."

Foy came closer at this point than he would ever come to killing Strain. He sat back in the chair, the now empty whiskey glass in one hand and the gun in the other. He suddenly felt exhausted and realized that he wanted to know who was behind this more than he wanted to kill this man.

Strain walked to the other side of the room and sat in a chair opposite Foy, he looked at the man and saw how tired he looked. "What the fuck is going on here, you have come here for some other reason, what is it?"

Foy stood up and helped himself to another whiskey, "You want another?" he said, offering the bottle to Strain. He took it and poured a very large measure.

"You and I have been used by members of a splinter group of the IRA and members of your government. My son Alan, God bless his soul, was used by a member of the same splinter group to derail peace talks between the IRA and your government. He was told to kill a policeman and his wife a number of years ago and like a good soldier he did not question why, he just obeyed the orders." He took a drink of the whiskey.

"What has that got to do with me and my team? We have never operated in Ireland," said Strain.

"You may not have operated in Ireland but you are responsible for the arrests of many IRA members and now the death of my son Alan. My other son and his girlfriend were never members of the IRA, and I deliberately kept him out of the trouble." His anger was building again and he took a drink, trying to control himself.

"For now we can agree on one thing—we both hate each other and all we want to do is kill each other. I am willing to listen to what you have got to say, but then again you are the one with the gun. What is this about being used by the government and the IRA?" Strain still felt that if he got the chance he would try to disarm Foy.

"Very good, play at being a friend now, try to build a relationship with your captor. Don't treat me like I have just walked out of one of your police academies, I know all the psychological games. For now we agree to nothing, I will tell you what I know. You can tell me what you know, without each other we will not get to know the whole story. So you can try to get the gun off me now, that is what you are thinking, or we can exchange information." He watched as Strain stared at him and realized that the music was still playing, 'Recondita armonia' by Puccini played in the background.

"You were at the funeral today, did you want to see what your handiwork had done? It may please you to know that the woman that I was supporting didn't even get chance to tell her husband that she was pregnant for the first time."

"Guilt trips will not work with me if that is what you are trying to do, I have seen too much death to feel guilt for anyone. Pleasure in other people's grief—I don't get that either. Don't you understand that we are as sick of the violence as you are? We live every day of our lives with violence around us, yes, I have been a part of that but times are changing and we need to find solutions not breed more violence."

Strain held his head in his hands and listened to the music, trying to calm himself. He knew that he wanted to hear what Foy had to say, it might give answers to why his team was targeted.

"OK, tell me what information you have and let's try to see if there is any sense to all of this." He stood up, at which Foy raised the gun. "Just getting another drink," he said.

Foy watched him as he poured himself a drink, this was a dangerous man and he knew that he had to stay on his toes. Strain sat down again, wondering if he was going to survive this meeting, did Foy have some other reason to be here or was he telling the truth that they had both been used?

"If you believe what I have to say and we agree to work together on this I have a request."

"What is it?"

"If Kevin Donnelly or myself end up being arrested on the mainland you must agree to have us released to return to Ireland."

"You must be fucking mad, you have murdered two of my team and you expect me to repatriate you back to Ireland? I am the one that is hoping to arrest you and so is the rest of my team, not to mention every policeman in England. I don't believe you have the balls to ask me that." Strain looked at Foy and saw that this was a very cool character, a true professional terrorist, and a hard man. It was as though something switched over in his head, Foy was here to get answers, not for revenge, not yet anyway. "I don't believe I am saying this, but I will do whatever I can to help get you repatriated, if what you tell me turns out to be true."

"I want a guarantee that we will be sent home."

"There are no guarantees in our business, you should know that."

"Very well," Foy replied and then he did something that shocked and surprised Strain. "Here," he said. He threw the gun to Strain, who caught it and immediately pointed it at Foy.

"What the hell are you doing?" he asked.

"My way of showing you that I am here for genuine reasons and if we are to help each other we have to have a certain amount of trust."

Strain didn't know why but he threw the gun back to Foy. "I am going to make a pot of tea, you want a cup?"

"Yes, I think I will, this whiskey is starting to taste too good," Foy replied.

He followed Strain from the lounge to the kitchen and back to the lounge. They did not trust each other on their own.

"So what is your story?" he asked Foy.

"It is a bit long winded but I need to tell you everything so that you can understand what has gone on. This goes back a number of months and starts with Bowles. I talked to him one day and he suggested that I convince my son Alan to return to Ireland and have him captured by the police on the way. He stated that the government was serious about starting full-blown peace talks and he had inside information. The government was going to agree, as one of the terms, to offer a release program for political prisoners. He said that if Alan was captured before the peace talks took place then he would be eligible for release under the peace agreement. I did not trust this information at first but I was eventually persuaded to contact Alan to see what he thought. He wasn't particularly happy at the thought of being incarcerated for a year, but his future freedom made it worth trying. The wheels were set in motion and Alan made his way back to the UK, where he would eventually meet me. This is where everything started to go wrong. What I didn't know was that a leading member of the IRA was also in touch with my son, he told him that I was being set up by the British Government. He was told to be armed in case something happened before he met me."

This made sense to Strain. "That was why he was so heavily armed at his brother's apartment."

"What do you mean by heavily armed? I don't know what happened." He wasn't sure that he really wanted to hear how his son died.

"He and your other son had a small arsenal in the apartment, automatic and semi-automatic weapons, but now that I think back I believe that Alan arrived with them, they also had Flash Grenades. They were definitely prepared for the worst. All I can tell you is that my information was that he was to show up at his brother's home, sometime that night. I had my team keeping surveillance on the place, it was so secretive that they did not even know that he was supposed to show up. It was just another stakeout for intelligence gathering to them. When Alan arrived the plan was to have team members at the back and others with me at the front. It was supposed to be a simple entry and arrest.

"When we got into position at the front door, we heard an explosion from inside. One of my team members, on my word, blew off the lock on the front door with a shotgun. We didn't know at the time but we believe that Maureen Donnelly was walking past the door at that point and she was hit by the shotgun blast. A terrible accident, there was no way we could have known that she was there." Foy saw genuine regret in Strain's face. "As we entered the apartment all hell broke loose, there was gunfire everywhere. Somewhere in the firefight your son Peter was hit, Alan escaped through a rear window and was confronted by the rest of the team. It was a fucking mess. We were led to believe that it was to be a simple arrest, he wasn't supposed to be armed. What you have just told me explains why he was armed, somebody planned this very well."

They both remained silent for a minute, everything that Strain had just said was running through their minds.

"Why would the IRA set up your son this way and how did you people get Bowles involved in all of this?"

"Bowles has been working with the IRA for years, we caught him in one of his perverted sexual acts and used it against him. He would feed us information about government and military activity against us and for this we agreed to keep the videos of him secret. He was also on the take with the IRA member that set my son up."

"You keep mentioning this IRA member that set your son up, who is he?"

"Not yet, you will get to know who he is eventually."

"Somehow I get the feeling that I will get to know his name when he is a dead man." Strain knew that he wasn't going to be told the name.

"He was involved with a small group of IRA members who secretly split away from the organization. Everyone else thought that they were still loyal soldiers—boy, were we wrong. They were running their own operations including drug deals, gun running and extortion. They were making a lot of money at the expense of the leadership and our cause. We got this information from two of the members and I have no reason to disbelieve them. There is someone else that they deal with in the British government and this other IRA member is the only one that knows who it is. This is why we need each other's help."

"Tell me who the other IRA member is and I will have him arrested and he will tell us who his contact is."

"This man will not talk to you or me. We will have to try to find some other way of getting the information. You have access to many electronic sources that I do not, this may help us locate those involved. I know that you are running around like chickens with your heads cut off at the moment trying to find out who committed the other bombings around the UK. I will help you find out who did this in exchange for your assistance in locating who was responsible for the death of my sons and the Donnelly girl. After all, the same people set you up as well."

"Why would they do all of this?" Strain knew that he had the answer to that part of the puzzle.

"Money, nothing else, just old-fashioned greed. I don't want revenge, I want justice for the deaths of my sons and Maureen Donnelly. You can exact some justice for your lost friends at the same time, we can do this together or we can carry on the way we are and try to kill each other, this way they win and everybody else loses."

"Was it you that attacked members of my surveillance team in London, the night Bowles died?"

"Yes, it was me, but I did not kill Bowles, I was in London to find out what happened to my sons. I made a telephone call from a friend's house when I heard the news of the shooting in Birmingham. The friend is one of the splinter group members, I obviously didn't know that at the time. He recorded the conversation I had with Bowles, I told Bowles that I was coming to London to get answers as to what happened to my sons. They got panicky because they thought that if I got to Bowles I would find out what was really going on. When I arrived at Bowles' address you and your friends were already going inside. I saw that you had a surveillance point across the street and I took the opportunity to see what information you had, that was when I found out that they had already killed Bowles. I see that you all covered up the truth about how he died and announced that he had a heart attack."

"Yes, as you said, he was murdered, but we had to keep it quiet, we did not want anything to screw up the investigation. They have got us playing right into their hands, haven't they?"

"Yes, they have until now. They are going to continue to upset the potential for peace talks as long as they are making money. That was another reason why they wanted me involved, they had my sons murdered just so that I would go crazy on the mainland seeking revenge. They almost succeeded, I started by killing your team members and you were next. My attack on your team was personal, unfortunately I did not find out that we had been set up until after the death of your team members."

Strain wanted to find out who was behind this as much as Foy. "You have got me convinced, I am willing to work with you."

"Good, I will call you tomorrow with information on who was responsible for the bombings and attacks that took place around the country. I will hopefully be able to give you names and addresses. I will also track down where the IRA member is and try to get some information out of him. He is my responsibility, Donnelly and myself will take care of him. Do you have a mobile phone that I can contact you on?"

Strain opened the drawer in a sideboard where there were several mobile telephones. He looked at the back of the phone where there was a piece of paper taped that had the number on it. "This is the number where you can get me, what is your number?"

"I will have to call you when I buy a mobile phone."

Strain took another phone out of the drawer and gave it to him. "Here, use this one."

Foy did not say anything, he just took the phone and left.

Strain called Shadow and asked him to arrange two alternative safehouses that they could use in London other than Canary Wharf. This was no problem, Shadow had at least six at his disposal.

Donnelly was working hard trying to find out where Eamon was hiding in London and was getting nowhere. The telephone call from Foy was a welcome break to the silence he was experiencing at home.

"Take a drive for half an hour into the country and call me back on this number." Foy gave him the number of the mobile phone that Strain had given him, as always using the one-short system.

Thirty minutes later he called Foy. "How did you do?" he asked.

"It was a little tense for a while but he agreed that we are all being used and that for now we will work together. I need you to find out who is responsible for the attacks that took place in London. I also need to know where they are hiding in London."

"You don't want bloody much, do you? I should be able to get it from one of the lads who is living in Spain. What did he have to say for himself?" He was referring to Foy's conversation with Strain.

"A lot, especially about the deaths of our children. Maureen was in the wrong place at the wrong time, Kevin, her death was a complete accident."

"That's what that bastard told you, was it?" He was enraged at the thought of his daughter being killed by this policeman.

"He had no reason to make it up, I believe that he was telling the truth. He wasn't expecting Alan to be heavily armed either, Alan showed up ready for a war. We have got to find Eamon, he and someone else from the British side are up to their necks in this. They had their fingers on the triggers as much as these policemen."

Donnelly listened to every word that Foy was saying and for the first time did not solely blame Strain and his team for the death of his daughter. "I will find out what you need to know, I will call you when I have something."

"Thank you, Kevin, we will get those responsible, you have my word." He pressed end on the mobile phone and put it back in his pocket.

OCTOBER 2ND, LONDON

The next morning the team went to work, they took the private plane to London, Strain and Bulldog went straight to MI6 headquarters, the rest went to the safehouse on Canary Wharf by the River Thames.

There was a mountain of information coming in from the public and far too many leads for them to pursue on their own, thankfully there were a lot of other police and intelligence officers working behind the scenes. Members of the Mask Team spent the whole day going through the information without finding any solid leads.

"Come on, let's go and meet the others. I think that we deserve a meal," he said to Bulldog.

"I'm ready," he replied.

A young lady walked into the information room as they were about to leave. "Are you Mr Strain?" she said.

"Yes," he replied.

"Sir William would like a word with you. If you would follow me please." Before Strain could answer she turned around and walked back down the corridor.

"I will be right back," he said to Bulldog.

Sir William, as the young lady called him, had a nice office that was expensively decorated. "Come in, Mr Strain," he shouted.

Strain did not hesitate, he went straight into the private office.

"Take a seat, this won't take a moment. Our agents at Gatwick airport received information from the immigration office that Osama Ali Yousef arrived an hour ago. He entered under a false name and passport and was allowed to pass through as instructed. We have been waiting for him to arrive here for several months. A contact of mine informed me that he would be coming today, he is to be the guest speaker at a private fund raising in the Cumberland Hotel by Marble Arch. We have several addresses of his known associates here in London and four other locations around the UK. The real interesting part is that he was not met by anyone at the airport. He is a well-known figure with various left-wing fundamentalist groups and a very high-ranking member of Islamic Jihad. Why would nobody meet him? A team of my agents followed him after he cleared customs and immigration. He stopped at a couple of stores and kept looking around, obviously trying to check that he was not being followed. After about a half an hour of this kind of activity he made his way to the Le Meridian Hotel, which is connected to the airport terminal via a covered walkway. He sat and drank coffee at the café in the lobby area, read a newspaper, and eventually left the hotel and walked back towards the terminal. By this time I had as many as twenty agents and immigration officers scattered around the airport and parking garage. As he walked back through the covered walkway he made a sudden turn into the parking garage and disappeared."

"So you lost him," said Strain.

"For a very short time, yes, but luck was on our side. An elderly lady took a fall walking down one of the ramps in the parking garage, one of the plain clothes immigration officers was helping her up when he saw a man getting into the backseat of a car on the parking level below him. What was unusual about this was that he lay down on the backseat and the driver of the car covered the man with a blanket. He made a mental note of the license plate and we ran a trace. The car was registered to an eighteen-year-old white female with an address in Stoke, she was contacted and stated that she had sold the car two years ago in part exchange for another car, her story checked out. During the interview she stated that she was always being contacted by the police, for non-payment of parking tickets, that was the break we needed. Whoever drives that car does not care where he parks it, as there are eighteen outstanding parking tickets, mostly from the London area.

"Ten of these tickets have been issued in the same three roads in London, three by the same parking warden in one road. We talked to the warden and she knows the car and knows which house the driver goes into when he parks the car illegally. She even saw the car at the back of a garage when she was getting petrol one day on her way home from work. Apparently she got into a right screaming match with the driver on one occasion and has never forgotten him or the car since. We asked her if she could pick the driver out from a photograph, she said yes and we brought her here, you passed her coming into the office. We went through the usual procedures and showed her lots of photographs of many of our Arab friends and this is the one that she pointed out." He showed him two 10" x 8" photographs of a bearded Arab-looking male.

"Who is he?" Strain asked.

"He is Tarek Ragab, we have suspected him of being involved with terrorist organizations for some time but we had no proof. He apparently lives at the address where several parking tickets have been issued, one was issued outside the address the day before the bombings and attacks took place. The owner of the petrol station where the parking warden saw the car also rents the garages at the back of his property, he is also an Arab. I have six surveillance teams in place at the house, petrol station and garage. MI5 do not know about this information yet, but it will not be long before they do."

"Where did Ragab take him the man in the car?"

"To the Cumberland, it was obviously Yousef, he will give his speech in two days."

"Can I have the addresses that you have in connection with Ragab and Yousef's followers?" Strain knew that this was as good a place to start as any, these looked like solid leads.

"My secretary already has a copy for you at her desk, is there anything else?"

"Not at the moment, thank you, sir."

"Don't mention it, good luck." For the first time Sir William seemed to give his blessing to Strain.

Hartley agreed to join the team, especially after Bulldog had told him what they were going to do. He joined them at the safehouse and they all discussed how they were going to take care of the terrorists once they located them. It was agreed that to kill them all with explosives would look a little suspicious—they had to be a little more creative. Two detonations of bombs was acceptable as accidents did happen when terrorists handled explosives. They would ensure that the investigation teams found enough evidence to prove first of all that they were terrorists and secondly that they were possibly accidental detonations.

"I will do a quick tour of the Cumberland Hotel and see what the layout is like. Can you contact C10 and ask them if they have any information on the hotel that may come in handy?" C10 was the hotel collation unit that gathered information on crimes and criminals that operated in and around the hotel industry.

"No problem," said Strain. "Bulldog can get that for you." He smiled at Bulldog.

"Gee, thanks for that dangerous detail, boss," he said.

"I can see that I am going to enjoy working with you lads," Hartley laughed.

As the head of MI5 Simon Fletcher was a very powerful individual and was used to operating outside of the rules. In his business you almost had to work this way to get anywhere. His men were stretched to the limit already, especially as a result of the recent terrorist attacks. He had eight two-man teams operating directly for him, the rest of the teams worked for his subordinates. The head of these teams was Carl Weir, a twelve-year veteran of MI5. Carl was particularly good at his job and stood head and shoulders above his peers. Fletcher was convinced that he had a mole in his organization and had been trying to find out who it was for a number of weeks. Fletcher had confided in Carl about his suspicions. He had spent many hours searching through personnel files and family histories but had come up blank. Fletcher knew that it was only a matter of time before he found out who it was, but time was what he could not afford. The only black mark that Fletcher had against him was that Carl had heard about the Mask

Team when it was first being developed. He went to Fletcher requesting to be considered, which he said he would be. Unfortunately he had no intentions of recommending him for the job. He knew that he would not only be accepted but would most probably end up as the team leader and he could not afford to lose him.

Six months after the Mask Team was in operation Carl saw his personal file sitting on the secretary's desk. He knew that he should not review it without Fletcher's permission but he bluffed the secretary into letting him read it. His application for the Mask Team was in the file on the back of the application was a space for the recommendations of his superior, Fletcher. To his shock it was blank, Fletcher had never even filled out his part of the application and had not submitted it.

He was furious when he read the file and confronted his boss with his finding. Fletcher tried to talk his way out of the situation but failed miserably. Carl requested an immediate transfer or Fletcher could have his resignation. Fletcher eventually talked him into believing that the position was already allocated at the request of the PM. He told Carl that it was the PM's decision that Strain was going to get the team leader job and nobody else, it was purely political. This of course was a total lie but it seemed to bring Carl back into the fold. He accepted the excuse and wasn't surprised because that kind of old pal promotional bullshit went on all the time. Carl never, from that day, had any time for Strain or the Mask Team, his bitterness was in the open for all to see. He had several opportunities to embarrass Strain and tried to on every occasion but failed, he despised Strain and the rest of the team. His sole goal was to become the team leader and the minute he did he would replace all of the present members loyal to Strain.

Two weeks earlier Carl had submitted a second request for consideration to be included in the Mask Team. Fletcher did not submit the application and attached a non-eligibility notice on the front, Carl found the notice in the inner office mail. This did not please him and he stormed into Fletcher's office. "Is he in?" he said to his secretary.

She was taken aback by his temper. "No, he is out, what is the matter?"

"Do you know that he did not even submit my request for the Mask Team again? He sent it back to me in the inner office mail. I will see that bastard when he returns." He walked out, leaving her in a state of shock.

He went to the file room to try and cool down, his way to relieve tension was to work. Fletcher's secretary brought in the telephone records for the previous two weeks and slammed them down on the desk in front of him.

"You do not need to take out your petty quarrel on me," she said and left the room.

He had been requested by his boss to scan the telephone records to see if there was anything that would give away the mole. He always gave the records to one of the junior office lads to review as they had very little to do. He called the office pool number and requested someone to pick them up. He threw the files to one side on the end of the table, a brown envelope fell to the floor. The office grunt arrived within a couple of minutes, he picked up the envelope off the floor and left it on the desk and took the telephone files away.

He had taken thirty minutes to cool down and decided that he should apologize to Fletcher's secretary; after all, it wasn't her fault. He picked up the envelope on the table and thought that he had better return it to the secretary, it obviously wasn't part of the telephone records. Curiosity got the better of him on the way out of the door and he looked inside the envelope, inside was a print-out of a telephone record. He looked at it a little closer and saw that it was Fletcher's telephone extensions.

Fletcher's secretary was surprised to see Carl back in her office, "Do you have the latest contact number for Strain?" He was very abrupt without realizing it.

"Yes, of course I do."

"I need it," he said.

"Come on, Carl, this is none of his fault, don't start any trouble, it's not worth it," she said.

"Just give me the number." He was raising his voice again and she was scared of him. She wrote the number down on a piece of paper and gave it to him. He marched back to the file room and then to his office. He worked on his computer for a few minutes and then called Strain on his mobile phone.

"I have some information for you. I need to meet you as soon as possible."

Strain did not recognize the voice as he had never met Carl or even spoken to him, he did know of him but that was all. "Who is this?" he asked.

"Never mind who it is, I have information that you need on the IRA and something else."

"I am not meeting anyone without knowing who they are." For all he knew he was being set up by the IRA or anyone else.

"You name the time and place and I will be there, that should satisfy you. Look, I have got to give you this information. I cannot trust anyone else with it."

Strain was very curious at this point and decided why not meet whoever this was, "Meet me at the Red Lion pub on Parliament Street in two hours."

"Red Lion Parliament Street, I will see you there in two hours, Strain," he replied.

Fletcher's secretary was even more concerned now about Carl, she decided to try and talk to him to see if she could calm him down. She walked down to the file room where he was before, she was about to walk in when she heard him on the telephone. She knew that she should not be listening but when she heard him say the Red Lion in two hours and heard Strain's name she did not go in, she quietly scurried back to her office.

Strain was in the offices of MI6 when he received the call on his mobile phone. Bulldog was sitting across the table from him, listening to what Strain was saying.

He waited for Strain to finish the conversation, "What was all that about?" asked Bulldog.

"I am not sure, someone wanting to meet me to pass on information, but they would not identify themselves. As you heard I am going to meet him in two hours at the Red Lion."

"It could be a setup, boss, we are getting closer to these terrorists."

"Yes, I know, that is why I want you inside the pub in an hour, and Shadow will arrive a minute behind me. This guy reckons that he knows me, let's be careful. I want you to be armed."

Fletcher returned from lunch in a happy mood for a change. "Any calls?" he said to his secretary as he walked into the office.

"Only a couple. I have put the messages on your desk," she replied.

"Can you get a hold of Carl for me?"

"I don't think he is in his office, I saw him leave earlier. There is something that I need to discuss with you about Carl."

"You look worried, what is it?" He could tell that something was wrong.

"This is awkward, Carl got his application for the Mask Team back in the internal mail and he was very upset about it."

"Yes, I thought that he would be upset but it is not a problem."

"No, sir, that is not all of it. He was absolutely furious he came looking for you, I have never seen him so angry. Well, I took the telephone logs down to him and he was still very upset and I wasn't very happy with him because of the way he had spoken to me. Well, a little later he came to my office and asked me for Mr Strain's latest contact number, which I gave him, he was still angry. I decided to go to the filing room where he was working to try to calm him down. When I was outside I heard him arranging to meet Mr Strain, I think that he may do something silly."

"You are right to be concerned, where was he meeting Strain?" He didn't know what was going on but he did not like it.

"I didn't mean to listen in on the conversation, he was talking so loudly and I could not help but hear. He is meeting him at the Red Lion on Parliament Street in about an hour."

"I know you would not deliberately listen in on a conversation, do not worry about that, I am just glad that you told me. Who is working today from the emergency response group?"

"Joe has just come in, I thought that he would have gone with Carl."

"Good, have Joe come up immediately, have a van and a car ready to go downstairs."

"I do hope that he is not going to do something stupid," she said.

"I will take care of him, I am going down to the file room." He walked into the file room to see what Carl had been working on but the only thing left out was an empty brown envelope with his name on it, he went back to his office.

"What was in this envelope? It was in the file room," he said to his secretary.

"I put your monthly telephone calls in it, I must have given it to Carl with the others by accident."

"No problem," he said coolly, he walked into his office and closed the door behind him. His intercom buzzed. "Yes," he said.

"Joe is here to see you, sir."

"Send him in," he replied.

Joe had worked with Fletcher for six years and had a great deal of loyalty to him as well as Carl. He went into the office. "You called for me, sir?"

"Yes, Joe, I think that we may have a serious problem with Carl. He requested to be moved to the Mask Team again and I refused his application. I sent the request back to him and he has gone off the deep end. My secretary told me when I returned to the office that he had called Strain and arranged to meet him. She said that he was incredibly angry when he called Strain. I am sorry to say that I think that he has gone to take his anger out on Strain."

"Christ, sir, you know that he hates Strain. What are we going to do?"

"I have asked for a surveillance van to be brought around and a car. We have to try to stop Carl getting to Strain. This could not only destroy Carl but also destroy a lot of good work that this department has done. I have just discovered that you and the rest of Carl's group went to Chester recently and had a bit of a confrontation with Strain."

"Yes, Carl said that it was not to be discussed with anyone, he put a great deal of emphasis on anyone."

"Well, I assume he meant that I was not supposed to find out, that was an unauthorized operation."

"He stated that we were to keep Strain under observation, he told us that you were concerned that Strain was turning into a vigilante after the Birmingham job."

"I am promoting you to second-in-command, Joe, effective immediately, Carl is suspended. We will discuss how we are going to handle this on the way."

He had Joe completely off guard with the promotion, it was something that he thought that he would never get while Carl worked in the same office. Joe was ecstatic with the promotion and it showed.

The surveillance vehicle and car were waiting in the basement for them.

"I will drive the van. Joe, you get in the passenger side, have the car follow us and tell him to park about three blocks away from the Red Lion on Parliament Street." He got into the van and saw Joe through the rearview mirror talking to the driver. He checked his Browning automatic, releasing the magazine he checked that he had a full clip of bullets. He replaced the magazine and slid his hand across the top of the gun, putting a bullet in the chamber. He knocked off the safety and put the Browning back in his shoulder holster, he took out his mobile phone. Joe returned and got into the van.

"Carl, please listen to me for a second, you don't want to do that, Carl! Carl!" He dropped the phone from his ear, he had a totally frustrated look on his face.

"What did he say?" Joe asked.

"He said that he was going to kill Strain, I tried to talk some sense into him, but he wouldn't listen. This is my fault for rejecting his application. We have got to try and stop him, let's go the Red Lion on Parliament Street.

They had been parked outside the Red Lion for almost fifteen minutes, much to the disgust of a traffic warden who tried to move them without success. They saw Strain walking towards them. Joe looked into the rearview mirror on the side of the van and could see Carl walking towards Strain from the opposite direction.

"Here comes Carl, sir," he said.

"I will watch Carl, you watch Strain. Let's see what happens."

Carl was only about ten yards from the van when Fletcher said, "Oh! Christ he is going for his weapon, warn Strain." They both jumped out of the vehicle at the same time.

"Strain, get down," shouted Joe at the top of his voice as he ran to the front of the van.

Fletcher was incredibly quick, he was out of the van and had the Browning in his hand. He was immediately into a solid shooting stance and shouted, "No!" He then fired two shots at Carl, both striking him slightly below the left nipple on his chest. Both bullets tore into his heart, one lodged in his spinal column, the other exited through his back, he fell to the floor.

Carl was only about fifteen feet away from Fletcher when he appeared out of the van, he could not believe his eyes. He saw the weapon in his hands burst into life as Fletcher fired two shots at him. That was the last thing that Carl ever saw.

Joe was running towards Strain, shouting, when he heard the shots being fired, he and Strain both drew their weapons. Strain threw himself to the ground and rolled once, coming up onto one knee with the weapon extended in his hands.

"Who are you?" he said, pointing the weapon at Joe.

He was also kneeling but he had his back to Strain and was pointing his weapon towards Fletcher. "I am with Fletcher."

Strain immediately refocused his weapon on the area where Fletcher was standing, totally confused as to what was happening. As they approached Fletcher he was checking the body, he turned and looked at them and shook his head, indicating that he was dead.

Bulldog was sitting in the bar of the pub when he heard the gunfire outside and raced towards the door. The patrons in the pub had mostly ducked down in their seats or dropped onto the pub floor at the sound of the shots outside. As Bulldog got to the door of the pub he could see Strain and another man with their weapons pointed at somebody. He dropped to a cover position in the doorway and watched the street behind Strain. He could see some people running away from the scene and others stood around, mouths gaping in disbelief. Others tried to move a little closer to get a better view of what was going on, hoping to get a glimpse of the blood so they could tell their excited version of the day's events that night at home or in the pub with friends. People that had been drinking inside the pub had got up off the floor and were now looking through the pub window at the scene outside.

Fletcher turned around to Joe and Strain and said, "Help me get him into the back of the van." They both obliged as a police officer came running over. Shadow was now on the scene and watched as they put the body into the van.

A police officer arrived on the scene, "What is going on here?" said the police officer as they put the body into the van.

Fletcher pulled out his ID and said, "Move all of these spectators out of the way, Officer, I will take the body to the morgue."

"I am sorry, sir, but you have to stay here until my sergeant arrives."

He could tell straight away that this was a new recruit and very wet behind the ears. "I will take care of your sergeant and any reports, just keep these people back. Do not talk to anyone other than your supervisor as to what went on here, especially the press. This is a national security issue, do you understand?"

He snapped to attention at the national security part. "Yes, sir." He went to work diligently, giving instructions to members of the public that were standing around watching.

"What the fuck is going on?" said Strain.

"Meet me at the office, we will discuss this there," said Fletcher, he and Joe climbed into the van and drove off.

Bulldog and Shadow joined Strain. "What's happening, boss?" said Shadow.

"I don't know, lads, but we are going to Fletcher's office to find out."

"That man that he just shot, he was one of the blokes that we got into the car chase with at the Wheatsheaf in Chester when you met the Chief," said Shadow.

"Are you sure?" said Strain.

"Positive, he was one of them," he replied.

They arrived at Fletcher's office to be greeted by his secretary, this was Strain's first visit to the office.

"Hello Mr Strain, did you see Mr Fletcher? He was rather anxious to see you." She had not heard about what had just happened.

"Yes, thank you, I did see him. I don't suppose that there is a chance of a cup of tea, is there? I know that Mr Fletcher will want one when he gets here." Strain was as polite as ever.

"Certainly, right away, please go in and make yourselves comfortable," she replied.

"Shadow, find out which morgue they took that body to and snoop around a little, see what you can find out about him. I will call you when we leave here."

"I'm on it," he replied.

Bulldog was impressed with the grandeur of Fletcher's office, very posh indeed. He wandered behind his desk, having a good look around, the thought of him snooping around the office of the head of MI5 gave him a smile. He picked up one of Fletcher's business cards that was sitting on the desk and admired the gold letters.

"They don't give us business cards, especially as snooty as these." He heard the secretary talking to someone outside the door and returned to the correct side of the desk. He slipped the business card into his pocket.

A minute later the secretary arrived with the tea, followed by Fletcher and Joe. Fletcher took off his coat and waited for his secretary to leave the office, she closed the door as she left.

"John, sorry about that incident in the street, let me introduce Joe, he is my second-in-command." Joe shook hands with him and Shadow.

"This is Bulldog, one of my team members," Strain replied.

"This is a long story, but I will make it as short as possible. Carl, the man I shot in the street, was one of my employees who had applied for the Mask Team when it was first thought of. I did not want him to be considered because he was more valuable here in MI5 than he would be on the team. He recently submitted another application, which I also declined to consider. He has held a great resentment for you since the team first went into action and it boiled over today."

"You mean he was out to get me because of the Mask job?"

"In a nutshell, yes. He found the application and refusal to be considered for the team in his mail tray today and according to my secretary, he went totally out of control. He made her give him your mobile phone number and went to the file room. She went down there to try and calm him down when she overheard him on the telephone arranging to meet you. When I returned to the office she confided in me about Carl and she thought that he was going to do something silly. She told me what had gone on and I got Joe here to go with me to the pub to try and stop him from meeting you. When I got into the van to leave for the rendezvous that you had, I called Carl on my mobile phone and talked to him. I asked him to meet me back at the office to discuss the matter. He refused and became very abusive. He said that he was going to kill you and nobody was going to stop him. I pleaded with him not to meet you, to talk this over and not to do anything that he would regret."

"I heard the boss asking him on the phone not to do it," said Joe.

"When we were in the van outside the pub I saw him approaching and when he saw you he went for his gun. I had no choice but to shoot him, John, he was going to kill you. I cannot believe that I had to kill one of my own men."

Strain and the others could see that he was getting emotional about it and sat quietly.

"Have you got any whiskey in here?" asked Strain. "I could do with one."

"That is a good idea," replied Fletcher and he turned around to the filing cabinet behind him and took out a bottle of whiskey and four glasses. He poured four generous measures out, emptying what was left in the bottle. "I am going to conduct an internal investigation, I will try to keep your name out of it as much as possible. I don't want anyone to know about this, he was a good man and I want him to be remembered that way. I will make the necessary arrangements for the story to be squashed in the press or at least fabricate something believable. I want to be left alone when you have drunk up, gentlemen." Fletcher was in no mood for them to be sitting there watching him. They all drank up and left the room.

Outside the office Strain stopped Joe. "Joe, how come nobody saw this coming, I mean you guys work closely together like we do?"

"I don't know, one minute the boss is telling me that Carl is going off the deep end, then I get into the van and hear him pleading with him on the mobile phone, the next thing I know is we are at the pub and Carl is dead."

"Thanks, Joe." Strain was totally gutted by this turn of events.

"There is one other thing, we were the people that were keeping you under surveillance in Chester. We lost another one of our lads that day, as you know. Carl was running that operation without authorization. Mr Fletcher has only just found out about it, he wasn't very pleased." He left.

"What makes a bloke go over the edge like that, boss? He must have really lost control," said Bulldog.

"I don't know, but if I ever get the chance I am going to find out."

16

OCTOBER 3RD, LONDON

Foy received the call from Donnelly with the information on who was supposed to be behind the ETA bombings. He wasn't too surprised to hear that it was the younger of the Basurto brothers. He called Strain. "I have some of the information that you requested on the London job."

"You fellas don't hang about, do you?" he replied.

"We have our sources, the same as you. The man who is heading the ETA operation is Velasco Basurto. He is a real lunatic. He is at an address in London, do you have a pen?"

"Yes, go ahead."

He gave Strain the address. "I don't know if we will be as successful with your Muslim friends, as this could be one of several groups that are capable of carrying out such a job."

"How is your end of the job coming along?" asked Strain.

"Not so good at the moment, but don't worry, we will find out where the goods are located." Foy knew that time was against them, but he would find Eamon eventually.

"I am sure you will, thanks for the info." He hung up.

MI6 was doing a good job of filtering most of the messages coming in to the information hotline set up as a result of the bombings around the country. Several calls got the interest of the intelligence gatherers, one in particular was from a woman in her late twenties. She stated that she was going out with a Spanish man who she had met at a party. Over a number of months she had been out with him several times. He had mentioned to her that he would not be able to see her for a week as he had some friends coming into town. She thought that it was unusual for him not to try to see her for more than a week. He had called her every day at work and at home since they had met at the party. He was very persistent in his pursuit, especially in trying to get her to go to bed with him. She thought that there was something very odd going on and felt that she had to report her suspicions to the police. She had provided two addresses that she knew he frequented and nothing much else.

MI6 passed the information on to Strain and his team, mainly because they thought that there was nothing in this other than a jealous girlfriend. Strain could not believe it, one of the addresses was the same as the one given to him by Foy. The information supplied by MI6 and Foy had to be verified and Bulldog came up with a scheme to perform a false market survey.

Shadow and Hartley went to one of the addresses only to find out that the young Spanish man who lived there hadn't been seen for a couple of days.

Strain and Bulldog chose the second address, Bulldog started on one side of the street and Strain started on the other. They worked their way from house to house asking questions on behalf of the local council about the trash collection service. Once they started they wished that they had found a less volatile subject. It amazed them both that so many people could be so upset at the trash collection performed by the council. Basically the service was poor to nonexistent at best. Strain got to the ETA safehouse and rang the bell, he couldn't hear anyone inside but his peripheral vision caught the curtain moving to his right. He rang the bell again, this time more than once hoping to annoy the occupants, it worked.

The door opened, "What do you want?" Sebastián said.

Strain smiled, "Good morning sir, I am performing a survey on behalf of the local council about the trash collection service."

"I am not interested," replied Sebastián and slammed the door shut.

Strain walked down the path, scribbling some notes on his clipboard, and went to the house next door, realizing that he was being watched from inside.

Sebastián walked into the front room where Velasco was looking through a gap in the curtains. "He has gone to the house next door, it looks genuine." He watched as Strain talked to the neighbor.

Peli came down the stairs, "There is another one across the street doing the same thing going from house to house."

"They are just survey people, we get them all the time," replied Sebastián.

It took Strain and Bulldog another hour to get to the end of the street.

"How did it go?" asked Bulldog.

"The fella that answered the door is definitely Spanish and he was in no mood to talk to me. It could be them, how did you do?"

"Good, there is a house across the street almost directly opposite, it is for rent. I had a good talk to the neighbor, she tells me that it is furnished. I made out that while I was doing the survey I was looking for a new place to live, she gave me the number of the estate agent. We could set up a surveillance point from there."

"Get in touch with the agent and let's take a look inside." Strain knew that this was the group.

The next morning the surveillance team was in place and Chalky White was enjoying every minute of the new operation. He had new equipment and was not sitting behind a desk, it was all a bonus.

The only window in the house where there weren't closed curtains was the bathroom window upstairs. The glass was frosted but someone had left the window open and he could see anyone inside that used the toilet. Chalky had one camcorder and one long-range camera focused on this window. He had taken shots of two different people in the first ten minutes and had nothing since. George left with the negatives to develop them at MI6 H.Q.

George had developed the film and called Strain. "John it's George."

"What have you got, George?"

"You won't believe it, the photos that Chalky took, they are of the ETA leader Velasco Basurto and one other male that I cannot identify."

"Thanks, George," he replied calmly. "Can you get a listening device on the property tonight when it gets dark?"

"Yes, no problem, we can attach a couple to the windows at the front and rear."

"Good, do it as soon as you can without being seen. I will meet you at the surveillance point this evening. Good job, George." He was convinced that this was the group that they were looking for, they had a solid sighting of Velasco at the address. He called Bulldog and arranged to meet him at the surveillance house.

George showed up at the surveillance point a little later than they expected, it was already dark.

"Where have you been, George?" asked Strain.

"I have some information for you that I think you will like." He opened the briefcase that he was carrying and took out a brown folder. "Have a look at those," he said and handed the envelope to Strain.

Strain pulled out some photographs that were inside, as he looked at them he could not help his surprise. "Fuck, it's him," he said.

"It's who?" asked Bulldog.

"Velasco Basurto, one of the most wanted ETA terrorists, the same man that George has taken a photo of in that window over there." He handed one of the photos to Bulldog.

The photograph showed a man with a Light Anti-tank Weapon on his shoulder, the side of his face was very clear.

"Where did you get these, George?" asked Bulldog.

"A tourist took the photograph when he was firing that grenade at the Spanish Commercial Office. I was at the office picking up some bugging devices when I saw this envelope in the tray marked for transfer to MI5.

Well, you can't help but look, can you, so I did, now you have it." George was very proud of his little piece of skullduggery.

"It looks like we have our culprits," said Strain. "Let's get the bugs in place on the windows, George."

"Already done, John, that was one of the reasons why I was a little late."

"You sneaky little bastard," said Bulldog.

"He's not that sneaky, I have a couple of nice photos of you, George," smiled Chalky.

"Nice to see that you were paying attention for once." Chalky knew that that was a little dig at him for the situation at Bowles' house.

"Here is the receiver." He handed a bag to Chalky.

Chalky went straight to work and listened in on what was happening inside the house. He enjoyed this because he was about to show off one of his greater skills, languages. He spoke several languages, one of them being fluent Spanish, and he had a very good knowledge of the Basque tongue.

OCTOBER 4TH, ENGLAND

The next day was very uneventful, with the recording of conversations going on throughout the morning and afternoon. It was most definitely the right house, as many times during the day they recorded conversations about how the attacks took place. The terrorists were watching everything on the television and laughing about the chaos that they had caused. Strain listened to several of the recordings and knew that he had to get to these men before they escaped.

"These fellas smoke like chimneys, I just heard one of them say that they had gone through a box of two hundred between them. Wait a minute, they are going to go out for some cigarettes." Chalky waved Strain over to him. "They are talking about going to a local Greek restaurant for a meal and getting some cigarettes while they are out."

"When are they going?" asked Strain.

"Tonight at about seven," he replied.

Strain took Bulldog into the next room, leaving Chalky to listen to the rest of the conversation.

"We are going to set everything up tonight, Shadow and Hartley can do their thing and you and I are going to take care of these bastards. Hartley is already set to go on the Cumberland hotel job, we may as well do them all at once."

"How are we going to get these guys? Another accidental bomb isn't going to look good." Bulldog knew that this wasn't what Strain wanted to hear but it was true, they could not afford another bomb.

"I hate it when you talk sensible, Bulldog, it just doesn't feel right. If we get inside the house tonight we may find something that we can use. Let's play this by ear, if we do not find a way we may have to wait them out. We may even get the opportunity to isolate them and take them out in a shoot-out. The latter is not good because that increases our risk of a team member being killed or injured." Strain knew that he had to find a way of erasing these ETA members.

Strain requested the MI6 teams to be pulled off the surveillance of the petrol station, garages and Garab's house. Sir William was not very pleased about the request but Strain assured him that he had enough team members to handle the surveillance. The real reason was that he wanted his team to be able to operate without being under the watchful eye of MI6.

Seven o'clock did not come around soon enough for Strain and Bulldog as they listened to Chalky giving them a blow-by-blow description of what was being said inside.

"They are getting ready to leave," said Chalky.

"We give them twenty minutes, then we go," said Strain.

They all watched as the men left the house in twos and walked along the street out of sight.

"They have left the lights on in the house, they obviously don't pay the electricity bill," said George.

"You call us if you see them coming back, George, let's test the communications." Everything worked fine. Strain and Bulldog were both dressed in all black and looked very menacing.

"When we get outside, how about we just ring their doorbell and if nobody is home we go in through the front door. I have my lock picking kit with me, it won't take a second," said Bulldog.

"Sounds good to me," replied Strain.

They double-checked their sidearms and both men set off into the darkness.

George and Chalky watched them as they walked across the street and straight up to the front door. They stood at the door for no more than fifteen seconds, the next thing George and Chalky saw was them disappearing inside.

Strain rang the doorbell and waited, listening closely with his ear to the door. "No noise, let's do it," he said.

Bulldog had his lock picks already in his hand and went to work on the lock, five seconds later they were inside.

"You check upstairs, I will check down," Strain said to Bulldog.

Both men cautiously made their way through the house, first checking that it was in fact empty. Search teams around the world had made many a mistake by not checking that the bed was not occupied or someone was hiding in a closet.

There was nobody home. They performed a thorough search of the property, both men finding semi-automatic weapons and cash hidden in various places in the house. There were cigarette butts everywhere and the stench of stale cigarette smoke filled the air.

Bulldog made his way downstairs to Strain, who was searching the lounge for a second time. "Anything, John?" he whispered.

"No, just weapons and used cigarettes everywhere, what about you?"

"Same thing, they sure smoke a hell of a lot."

"No kidding, look at the bars on that electric fire, they must light their cigarettes on it." Strain pointed at the fireplace. "I think that is all they use it for, as the house is heated with hot water radiators."

"I am going to take a look in the kitchen," Bulldog replied.

Strain joined Bulldog in the kitchen. "We had better leave I don't see any way of getting these bastards."

"Yeah! Sorry to say I agree."

They both started to walk out of the kitchen when Bulldog looked at the stove. "Wait a minute, I have an idea." He walked over to the stove. "John this is a gas stove."

Strain was totally lost as to what Bulldog was getting at. "What are you thinking?"

"If we can loosen the main gas pipe on the stove and turn the gas on we could fill the house with gas. These old stoves are renowned for having faults as they get older. The gas company sent my mum a note about two years ago to have hers inspected, it was exactly the same type. She had to change it because it was so old. If my idea works when one of them lights a cigarette—*boom*, they all go up."

"If they walk into the house smoking a cigarette we will not get them all." Strain thought that it was a good idea though.

"How about we can switch off the gas at the main inlet next to the meter by the front door. Loosen this pipe here and the one on the gas water heater upstairs and leave them like that. They are old fittings and we can make it look as though they have come loose with time. We will come back in the middle of the night when they are asleep and turn the gas back on again. The house will fill with gas while they are asleep and as soon as one of them tries to light a cigarette, they are toast."

"It sounds like it might work, what if they turn the electric fire on when they come in?"

"I will blow the fuse on the plug so that it doesn't work, they have been using matches as well and there are plenty lying around. It is the only chance we have, John, with minimal risk to the public. Everyone will be tucked up in bed, these fellas are not going to be able to go all night without a smoke. They are certainly not going to use the stove to cook, as they have just gone for a meal. They boil the water to make their coffee with an electric kettle." Bulldog was convinced that this would work.

"We may just make them sick or kill some of them with the fumes, we have to be certain that the gas is ignited." Strain liked the plan but it needed to be foolproof. "The houses either side, I don't think that they will be affected too much, maybe some broken windows. Thankfully they are detached and are built like fortresses. We will have a lot of broken windows, but not much else damaged," Strain replied.

"It is a shot in the dark, John, but we don't have any other way."

Strain looked at him with a big smile on his face. "A shot in the dark is right and that is what we need. I'll loosen the pipe upstairs while you go and turn off the gas, I will explain later."

It didn't take them long to disconnect the pipes, extinguish the pilot lights on the stove and hot water heater and fix the fuse on the electric fire. Bulldog was right about the main valve for the gas going into the house; it was outside in the meter cupboard.

Bulldog had finished when he saw Strain stood in the hallway writing down something.

"What are you doing John?"

"The telephone number is on the front of the phone, if my other idea doesn't work, we can call them in the night in the hope that someone hears the call. He will hopefully get up and light a cigarette."

Chalky spoke to them on the headsets, "You two had better leave by the backdoor they are coming down the street and you don't have time to leave by the front door."

"Roger that," said Strain.

They both headed towards the backdoor and left the house, Bulldog just managed to lock the door as the ETA members opened the front door.

They made it back to the surveillance house after a quick jog around the block, entering through the rear door.

"You like to live dangerous, don't you?" said George.

"It was a bit close. Where are your listening devices on the house, George?" said Strain.

"Two on the bottom front window and one on the rear, why?"

"We need to pack up and leave, and I don't want to leave anything behind for MI5 to find. You and Chalky pack up your gear and we will see you at the safehouse."

"Let's pack our things, Chalky, we don't want to be around for the firework display."

It took them thirty minutes to pack all of the equipment and leave.

Strain and Bulldog checked that they hadn't missed anything and left.

"So, are you going to tell me what you are going to do to ignite the gas?" asked Bulldog.

"They always seem to leave a light on, I would bet money that they will leave the toilet light on upstairs. If I shoot out the light bulb with the .22 caliber rifle that we have in the back of the car, the filament in the bulb will ignite the gas before it dies out."

"That might just work but I like your telephone idea better, if that fails shoot. Where would you shoot from?"

"The wall at the back of the surveillance house gives me a clear view of the bathroom and lounge windows. It is only a sixty-yard shot at the most and it keeps me far enough away from the blast."

"Let's hope that it works, I don't want to have to walk in there with a match."

The Cumberland Hotel, which was located close to Marble Arch in London, was like most hotels around the world they had minimal security and anyone could walk off the street and enter the hotel without being questioned. What else could hotels do? Certainly not check every person going through the doors to see if they were a guest or legitimate visitor. Inconvenience the guest as little as possible, make them feel welcome, service their needs quickly and efficiently, but do not put obstacles in their way, and that is what security checks at the hotel entrance would do. Some hotels restricted access to the guestroom elevators at night but that was about all they would do to inconvenience the guests. This lack of security in hotels had helped many a criminal go about their business relatively safely and undetected. Hartley, amongst others, always appreciated these security loopholes but had a certain amount of sympathy for the head of security. After all, he was the one who had to answer the questions from management after the crime was committed and explain why his security was letting the side down.

This was the third time Gordon Hartley had entered the hotel, he was now getting to know all of the entrances and exits, as well as where the conference rooms were located. He was using a different disguise to the last two visits, this one included a full facial beard matching his hair, which he had dyed a dark rust color. He was dressed in a business suit, shirt and tie, carrying an oversized briefcase, this helped him blend in with the other hotel guests. It was 9.45 p.m. as he made his way to the reception desk, he had chosen this time because the reception was less likely to be busy and at that time of night they only had one person working the desk. The young blond receptionist behind the desk looked attractive in her hotel uniform with the obligatory badge showing her name, 'Olga'. *She looks like an Olga,* thought Hartley.

"Good evening. I wonder if you can help me?" He was using his best Canadian accent, which was so good that it had even fooled some Canadians in the past.

"I will certainly try, sir," she replied in broken English.

"What a nice accent, where are you from?" Flattery will get you most places and always seemed to work for him.

"Thank you, I am from Denmark. How can I be of service?" she replied.

"I am supposed to attend a conference tomorrow which *Al Hayat* Arabic newspaper is holding here in the hotel." He took out a piece of folded paper from his inside jacket pocket and held it up for her to see, but not long enough for her to read it. "My office sent me this fax but forgot to put in what time it started and which conference room it is to be held in. Can you look it up for me please?"

"Certainly." She tried to access the information in the computer but it was not cooperating. "I am sorry sir my computer is not working properly today, I will see if it is in the Conference Book." She opened a drawer behind her and took out a large book with the words 'Conference Rooms' written on the front. She turned the pages to the correct date. Hartley was reading the entries in the book upside down from where he was standing, he saw an entry marked, 'Confidential' in red.

"I am sorry, sir, but the meeting is marked confidential and I cannot release the information to you." The receptionist had been trained well, because she immediately closed the book and returned it to the drawer.

"But I will be attending the conference, that's obvious, otherwise I would not know about it," Hartley complained weakly, he did not want to pressure the receptionist, as he had the information he needed by reading the book upside down.

"I am sorry, sir, but I cannot help you."

"Do you think I could be given the information in the morning if my name is given to you by one of the organizers that have invited me?" That should let her off the hook and give her a way out, he thought.

"Yes, sir, I am sure that would be OK," she replied.

"Thank you for your help, goodnight." He walked towards the elevators.

Hartley took the elevator to the first floor, where the conference suites were located. He took the folded piece of paper out of his jacket that he had held up for the receptionist, on the back was a floor plan showing where each conference room and suite was located. The conference floor was totally deserted, thankfully there were no late events taking place. From his observation of the entries in the receptionist's book he was looking for the Argyle suite, it was easy to find from the elevators. When he tried the door handle the room was locked, *no problem,* thought Hartley. He took out his lock pick set and went to work, opening the door within seconds. He stepped inside the room, locking the door behind him. The room measured about twenty feet deep by forty feet long and was already laid out for the meeting in the morning, the tables and chairs set out in a 'U' shape. At the front of the room was a lectern, with a small table and two chairs on either side. The streetlights outside gave him enough light to see his way around the room but not enough to do his work. Hartley walked over to the lectern and placed his briefcase on the floor. In the dim light he could see that a digital clock illuminated the top of the lectern.

"How thoughtful of you to provide a timing device for me, alas I won't need you this time," he said to himself. He placed a small pen flashlight between his teeth and switched it on, allowing him to see underneath the lectern. He removed the screws underneath the lectern which held the top of the lectern in place. It only took him two minutes to attach the one pound of Semtex explosive and detonator to the inside of the lectern. Hartley tested the small receiver that he had with him by pressing the button on the transmitter. The tiny red LED light came on the instant he pressed the transmitter, it seemed to light up the whole room, it was so bright. Connecting the receiver mechanism to the detonator always gave him a slight chill as bombs had been known to explode by accident at this point. Sometimes it was a fault in the wiring or manufacturer's assembly, or just negligence on the bomber's behalf. This was one reason why he always stripped the parts down that he was going to use and rebuilt them himself, no mistakes this way. There were many other ways that remote control devices had been known to detonate bombs prematurely, one was when someone used a radio close to the bomb, and the signal from the radio would detonate the device. The biggest problem in finding out why a bomb detonated prematurely was when the bomb exploded the reason why was normally destroyed with it. Next he unscrewed the head of the microphone on the lectern and removed it from the flexible stem. Inside the head of the microphone he placed a listening device and replaced the microphone head.

Hartley replaced everything the way it was, double-checking that he had not left anything out of place. He took four different explosive mechanisms from his briefcase and carefully placed each one in a different position above the tiles in the false ceiling above the tables. In addition to the devices he placed a small piece of paper next to one of the devices. The paper was crumpled and had obviously been folded and unfolded many times. On the piece of paper was a rough hand-drawn wiring diagram of an explosive device showing the wires connected to what looked like a car battery. When the lectern device exploded the shock wave would tear out all of the ceiling tiles, dropping the mechanisms to the floor, where they would lie amongst the debris. Because of the explosion and the following panic and stampede for the door nobody would notice the mechanisms dropping. Satisfied that this part of his work was complete, he left the room, locking it behind him. He slipped quietly out of the hotel unnoticed and headed for the rendezvous with Shadow.

The petrol station closed at ten p.m. and the owner went directly to the garages at the rear, he checked that they were locked and then made his way home as he had done so on the two previous evenings when MI6 had watched him.

Shadow and Hartley watched him as he walked around the back to the garages and checked that the locks were secure on the garage doors.

"Glove time," said Hartley as he handed Shadow a pair of surgical gloves. "No prints and no static, I prefer these to any other kind of glove. You can feel everything through the material, very little sensitivity lost to the fingers." They put the gloves on.

"Those locks won't help you, my old son," said Shadow, smiling as he watched the garage owner check the locks.

"You think you can pick them locks?" asked Hartley.

"Watch me." He was out of the car and across the street before Hartley could ask him any more. He watched the street to make sure that the owner did not come back. As he looked back at the garage Shadow was gone, he scanned the area around the garages but could not see Shadow. He got out of the car with his oversized bag and walked over to the garages. As he got close to the one where Shadow was trying to pick the lock the garage door opened slightly.

"Come on, get in here," Shadow said.

"You weren't kidding when you said you could open it, I have never seen anyone open a lock so fast." Hartley was truly impressed, as he was very good at picking locks himself.

There was a car in the garage and various boxes and tools scattered around. They searched the garage with the aid of two small pocket flashlights, which they held in their mouths. After he had a good look around Shadow said, "I am going to see what is in the garage next door."

Hartley gave him a thumbs up and continued to scratch around inside the car. He worked at a fast pace but he was very systematic in the way he did things. He would always teach in his classes at Hereford that you never rush explosives, if you do you will make a fatal mistake one day. He took the Semtex plastic explosive out of the bag and squashed it into place under the driver's seat. There was a lot of explosive and he only just managed to fit it under the seat. He tugged at it several times to make sure that it would not dislodge.

The beauty about plastic explosive was that it was very safe, as you could do almost anything with it; Something else he demonstrated to his students at Hereford. He especially liked the part when he would throw a piece of plastic explosive across the room at someone and watch them jump with fright. It wasn't long before he had them all squashing, molding or rolling out the explosive in the classroom.

He lifted the carpet on the floor of the car and removed the rubber boot around the floor-mounted stick shift. He moved the stick shift around to find out where it stopped in the reverse gear position and then put it into neutral. Next he very carefully placed a small trigger mechanism, with a plunger on one end, exactly where the stick shift would strike it when it was put into the reverse gear position.

The trigger mechanism was made of a hard cardboard tube with a small wooden plunger through the center, both of which had been previously soaked in pure alcohol. Once the heat from the explosion touched the cardboard tube and wooden plunger they would practically disintegrate. On the bottom of the plunger was a contact, this would complete the circuit with the wires to the power supply.

He moved the stick shift into reverse several times to see that it pushed in the plunger on the trigger mechanism. One more check to see that the device was secure and the plunger was not obstructed, it worked perfectly. Next he connected the trigger mechanism to a power supply, which was a small battery and a detonator. He double-checked everything and then embedded the detonator into the plastic explosive. He carefully replaced the rubber cover around the gear lever, making sure that he did not move the lever backwards and left the carpet as he had found it.

He then removed a timing device from his bag and placed it under the driver's seat next to the plastic explosive.

The plan was that parts of the timing device would be found in the debris after the explosion by the police anti-terrorism search team. The evidence that they found would then point to an accidental detonation of the device. The result of the inquiry into the explosion would prove that the bombers were about to transport the car bomb to an unknown location, when it prematurely exploded as they were leaving the garage.

Ten minutes had passed when Shadow returned. "There isn't much in the other place, but it definitely looks as though they put the bombs together in there. I saw several fertilizer bags stuffed into a plastic trash bag and pieces of wire all over a bench. You should have a look and see what you think."

"I will, I have finished here. Make sure that we have left nothing and lock up, I will be next door."

Shadow was about to look in the car when Hartley put his hand on his shoulder making him jump.

"I wouldn't touch the stick shift if I were you." He gave a big smile and left.

That was enough for Shadow to gently close the car door and not touch it again. He had another quick look around and then locked the garage door, leaving it as it was before they had entered. He went into the garage next door, where Hartley was snooping around.

"What do you think?" he asked Hartley.

"This was definitely one of the places where they prepared the explosives, if not the only place. This is a real find, we have struck a pot of gold, I hope that they enjoy our gift next door."

They searched a little more and five minutes later they were in the car driving away.

"Let's hope that John is right—that they do not try to drive that car before we are ready," said Shadow.

"I think that he is right, they will not move for several days or until something scares them out. I would bet money on it that they will try to run when they hear the news, your boss is smart to come up with this scheme. Let's head for their safehouse and fix the car outside."

"On the way," replied Shadow.

They arrived at the fundamentalists' safehouse as the lights started to go out inside.

"They must be bedding down for the night," said Hartley.

"I hope they sleep heavily," replied Shadow.

"I think we will give them an hour or so before we approach the car, what do you think?"

"Sounds good to me." Shadow lay back in the driver's seat and watched the house.

Slowly the lights on all of the houses in the road went out one by one as people retired for the night. The hour seemed more like two hours for the both of them, now it was time to move.

"Let's to go to work," said Shadow.

"I will watch your back, don't get spotted by them," said Hartley.

Shadow moved out of the car and quietly walked down the street towards the house. Hartley watched him as he approached the car.

Shadow knew that the car did not have an alarm fitted, opening the door of the car was easy. As the door opened the interior light came on, he immediately switched it off. The hood release lever was on the driver's side of the car by the door hinge, he pulled the handle and the hood popped up. Shadow quietly opened the hood on the car just enough to where he could squeeze his upper body inside. There was enough light from the street lamps to let him see part of the engine. The spark plug leads showed up nice on the top of the rotor cap. He pulled the center lead out that led to the ignition coil. Very quickly he placed a piece of paper over the end of the lead and put it back into place. The engine would turn over but would never start when the driver tried to start the car. He quietly closed the hood and disappeared into the night, back to the car and Hartley.

"It's been a busy night. Let's go to the safehouse and have a drink." Hartley was ready for one.

"Sounds good."

OCTOBER 5TH, ENGLAND

It was one o'clock in the morning when Strain and Bulldog returned to the observation house. They could see that the light was left on in the bathroom at the terrorists' house across the street. Bulldog got out of the car at the end of the street and walked down to the house. He went up to the front of the house and opened the gas meter cupboard and turned the gas back on. He quietly worked his way around the front and rear windows and removed the listening devices, then returned to Strain. They re-entered the surveillance house by the rear door and watched the ETA safehouse.

"We will give them an hour, there should be plenty of gas in there by then. What do you think?" asked Strain.

"That should do it."

They had been watching the house for twenty minutes when Bulldog said, "I could murder a cup of tea, do you fancy one?"

"Tea? Where are you going to get tea from at this time of night?"

Bulldog tapped the side of his nose with his index finger, "I have a flask in my bag by the backdoor."

"You could have told me sooner, I am gasping for a brew, I will come down with you," replied Strain.

They drank the tea and decided that it was time to make the phone call. Strain dialed the number and let it ring for a very long time.

"Nobody answered, we will try again in a few minutes." Strain said.

Inside the house Peli woke up to the sound of the telephone ringing. He was coughing and choking. He realized that something was wrong but didn't know what. The telephone had disturbed his sleep and he needed to use the toilet. He got out of bed and made his way to the bathroom he felt nauseous and heady, then he realized that it could have been the wine that they had drank at the restaurant, they did drink a lot. He visited the toilet and walked back to the bedroom, still feeling very giddy. He picked up his jacket and took out a packet of cigarettes and a box of matches. He put the cigarette in his mouth and struck the match on the side of the box. It didn't work, he tried a second time and the match gave off a huge glow.

The whole house erupted into a fireball, blasting out walls and windows. The house shook with the might of the explosion, causing one side of the house to collapse. Part of the roof and the first floor followed and crashed to the ground. Within seconds the fire intensified and engulfed the whole house as it leaned over to one side.

The ETA members inside the house didn't know a thing. By the time the fire department arrived and extinguished the fire, their bodies would be burned beyond recognition. Identification would be the job of the forensic scientists, identifying them by dental records.

Strain and Bulldog were standing in the kitchen at the rear of the house when the gas ignited.

"What the fuck was that?" said Bulldog, momentarily forgetting what they had planned, they waited a few seconds before moving.

"It must be the house," said Strain.

They both ran to the front of the house, stepping on broken glass in the lounge from the windows that had been blown out. The looked across the street to see the house in flames as it collapsed to the floor. The fire broke the darkness of the night, making it look like daylight outside. The main gas pipe at the front of the house was burning like a flare from an oil rig, throwing out a giant stream of fire.

"The houses either side look OK, apart from broken windows, no real damage from what I can see. Hopefully no injuries, just a few shocked people." Bulldog was genuinely concerned that no innocent members of the public were hurt.

Strain was surprised by Bulldog's concern for the people in the other houses.

"Do you realize how stupid we were? A minute ago we were sitting by this window. Christ, what a pair of brainless bastards, we would have been shredded by the flying glass. We had better get out of here before the emergency services arrive," said Strain.

"Right behind you, boss," replied Bulldog.

Thirty minutes later they were at the safehouse, ready to try and get some sleep. They knew there would be a full day ahead of them.

Hartley arrived at the Cumberland Hotel at 8.00 a.m. and went to the restaurant and ordered a full English breakfast. He did not really expect to see Bin Yousef, but it was worth a try. With the breakfast in his stomach and no sign of Bin Yousef, he decided to walk up to the conference floor. There were people standing around at various locations talking and drinking the free coffee provided. One man went up to a registration table by one of the conference rooms and introduced himself and wrote his name on a piece of paper, which he stuck to the front of his jacket. Hartley followed his example and wrote down a false name and stuck the name badge on his jacket, now he looked like all of the others around him. As he made his way to the room where Bin Yousef was to speak he saw him appear out of a door marked 'fire escape'. He was closely guarded by two men, both were watching everything around them. They moved him quickly and discreetly into the conference room before anyone saw them. Hartley had seen enough and left the hotel.

He walked into the pedestrian subway outside the hotel in the direction marked Marble Arch. He worked his way through the subway system, finally arriving at the corner of Hyde Park. He took an earpiece out of his coat pocket and placed it in his right ear, switched the receiver on in his pocket and could hear the background noise of the people in the conference room in the hotel. He had to be sure that he could identify that the target was in the room before he triggered the bomb.

Thankfully the conference started on time, and after a short five-minute speech Bin Yousef was introduced. Hartley waited fifteen minutes listening to what Bin Yousef was saying, he was hoping that he might pick up some intelligence. To his surprise Bin Yousef started to wind up his short speech, he had only been talking seventeen minutes. He could not wait any longer and pressed the transmitter button in his pocket.

The audience was mesmerized as they listened to Bin Yousef. He was a great speaker and admired by all present. He apologized for the shortness of his presentation but assured them that the time would come when he could meet them again in more favorable circumstances. He was wishing them all well when the podium exploded. Bin Yousef was killed instantly as the explosion shredded his body. The room was totally devastated by the explosion, two of the organizers of the conference who were on the stage with Yousef were killed instantly. Some of the attendees struggled to their feet after the initial blast and tried to find the exit door. There were bodies scattered about the room, many of them severely injured. It was total chaos as the settling dust and debris continued to fall onto the people in the room. The injured cried for help, but their cries were ignored by their associates, as self-preservation took over as they tried to escape the carnage. Some were still in a state of shock from the blast and were in no position to assist them. The ceiling tiles had, as planned, all fallen out of the light metal frame that held them in place. The bomb mechanisms that Hartley had planted were scattered around the room amongst the debris.

Hartley watched the whole thing take place from where he stood in the park. He was watching the windows of the hotel as he pressed the button on the transmitter. He could not help but jump slightly as the windows in the hotel conference room were blown out, scattering glass all over the street below. There would be some minor injuries to pedestrians in the street, but nothing that concerned him. He did not have to wait around to see any more, he knew that he had eliminated the target and walked away across the park.

Mohammed and his extremist supporters were watching the television in their safehouse when the news flash came on the screen. The picture showed a very attractive woman sitting behind a desk looking at some papers in front of her, she looked up at just the right moment and started to speak.

"We have just received a news flash of an explosion at the Cumberland Hotel, Marble Arch, on the corner of Oxford Street and Park Lane in central London. We do not have pictures at this time as our news crews are still on their way to the scene. Apparently the explosion happened approximately fifteen minutes ago on the first floor of the hotel, which is mainly a conference and exhibition area. We have no news of casualties at this point, but we will keep you up to date as the story develops. I am Cindy Smith reporting this breaking story for BBC News."

Tarek was stunned, as were the others watching the television as they knew that Osama Ali Yousef was scheduled to be at the Cumberland hotel, he was to give his fund raising speech that morning.

"We must pray for our brother and ask Allah to watch over him," Tarek said.

"Do you think that he is dead?" someone said behind him.

"How do I know, you have the same information as me," he replied.

It was an hour before the phone rang. Tarek answered it, "Hello."

"He is dead, so are several of the others, I spoke to a hotel worker who was on that floor and he told me that the explosion was in their conference room. You must move to another place, you are not safe there, Allah be with you." The caller hung up.

"He is dead. We have to go to another house, bring your weapons and whatever money you have. We leave in two minutes." Tarek went upstairs to wake Mohammed and give him the bad news.

Mohammed was greatly shocked at the news, "Who called to tell you that he was dead?"

"A contact from the *Al-Hayat* newspaper, he said that we were not safe here we have to leave."

"You trust this contact?"

"Yes, Mohammed, why would they lie, they requested the fund raising meeting. The editor of the newspaper was there, he is the main organizer."

"Have you got another place for us to go?"

"Yes, we have several safe places to hide outside of London."

"Get the others ready, we will leave as soon as I am dressed." Mohammed was as always suspicious of anyone he did not know that supplied information. His internal warning system was working overtime.

They gathered in the lounge waiting for Mohammed to join them. Tarek sent Magreb outside to start the car.

Mohammed joined them, "We will leave for another safe place, when we are there we will decide what we are going to do next."

Magreb entered the room, "Tarek, the car will not start."

"Ah! That infernal vehicle, we can go to the garage and get the other car." Tarek turned to Mohammed. "If that is OK with you?" He suddenly realized that he was not in control as usual.

"Yes, if I remember it is not very far, we will take two taxis. Tarek and I will go to the right out of the house, the rest of you go left, we will see you at the garage." They left two minutes apart.

By the time Mohammed arrived at the gas station the others had already arrived and were waiting for him in a backroom, out of sight of the street.

"It is good to see that you made it safely," said Magreb. His nervousness was showing through.

Mohammed could smell the fear in the air. They were all looking at him to lead them to safety and to provide words of wisdom. They wanted to know that everything was going to be OK. He walked up to Magreb and patted him on the back gently, giving him a little reassurance and support with a smile. "We are all going to move to another town. We will stay in two different houses, we will split up into two groups. Tarek and I will go to one place, Magreb will drive us, the rest of you will go to another address that Tarek will give you. I do not want any of you trying to contact Tarek or myself, we will contact you when we need to tell you something."

"The house that you go to has plenty of food, enough for you to live for a month. I will call you in a week and let you now what we intend to do next. Do not worry if you do not hear from me or Mohammed, be patient." Tarek knew that this was easier said than done as they would all be very anxious to leave England. "Our good friend here at the garage has given us another vehicle that we can use. It is a green van parked by the garages that we have been using at the back of this petrol station. Here are the keys, it is full of petrol and there is a ten-gallon can of petrol in the back. The can of petrol is there so that you can fill up the tank when you arrive at the house. This means that you will not have to stop at a petrol station when we tell you where to go when we leave for Algeria." He handed the keys to Hassan.

"When will we go back home to Algeria?" asked Mustafa.

"We will leave when it is safe to do so. The police will be watching all of the airports, seaports and trains leaving the country for the next several days. You need to be patient, my brothers, we must leave now." Mohammed wanted to distance himself from the rest of the group as he knew that he had a better chance of surviving without them.

"Leave through the backdoor," said Tarek.

They all wished each other well and left by the rear door.

"Tarek, give them a couple of minutes before we leave." Mohammed was being as cautious as ever.

"Yes, Mohammed, I will ask Magreb to get the car out of the garage."

Mohammed was still feeling uneasy, something was not right but he did not know what it was. He was going to wait inside the petrol station until they had all left before he made his move. On the way to the safehouse he would tell Tarek to change to another address, one that he knew, he did not trust anyone.

Outside Hassan was holding the rear doors of the van open as they all climbed inside. Magreb was saying good-bye to Zaki, who was getting into the front passenger seat.

"Magreb, get the car out of the garage." Tarek handed him the keys to the padlock and the ignition keys.

"Yes," he replied and walked back to the garage where the car was stored.

Tarek went around to the back of the van and helped Hassan close the doors. With the doors on the van secure, he walked back towards the garage where Magreb was getting the car. He heard the van start up and drive towards him as he got level with the garage, he turned to wave good-bye to the van as it passed him.

Magreb was very nervous about having to drive Mohammed and Tarek, it was a great honor for him to be selected. He opened the garage doors and stepped inside, where the car was parked. He opened the car door and sat in the driver's seat, he fumbled with the ignition key as he put it into the ignition, his nervousness was getting the better of him. He turned the key and started the engine. As he pressed down the clutch pedal he turned slightly in the seat and looked over his shoulder to see that it was clear for him to reverse the car. He saw Tarek outside and the front end of the van appeared as he slipped the gearshift into reverse.

The explosion was immense as the Semtex explosive detonated. Magreb and Tarek were killed instantly, as was Mustafa in the van. The force of the explosion totally destroyed the car and the garage. In one move the blast picked up Tarek's body, shredding it in midair as it spread over the passing van.

The van was severely damaged by the explosion, having been blown fifteen feet by the explosion onto its side. Zaki was still conscious but severely wounded, part of his face and scalp missing. The rest of the group in the rear of the van were dazed or dead. The ten-gallon petrol can inside the rear of the vehicle had been ruptured by a piece of wood, it was spilling its contents. The smell of petrol was suffocating as Sami realized what was going on. He heard his friends moaning in pain, he screamed out loud, "Get out, get out, there is petrol everywhere."

He could not open the doors of the van and started to crawl over his friends towards the front of the van. His clothes were soaked in petrol, as were the clothes of his colleagues. He saw that there wasn't much left of Mustafa and Zaki was in a bad way. He crawled out of the hole left by the broken windshield and reached back inside to pull out Zaki. He should have tried to save himself, the van burst into flames instantly engulfing him.

Inside the petrol station Mohammed was pouring himself a drink from the coffee machine when the bomb exploded. The explosion destroyed the windows of the petrol station and sent shrapnel and pieces of glass flying everywhere. He was knocked over by the shock wave as it tore into the back of the petrol station, showering his face and neck with scalding coffee. He got up off the floor and picked his way through the debris in the petrol station. He saw the owner lying on the floor in a huge pool of blood. His head had almost been severed by a piece of glass from the window. There was smoke everywhere. He stumbled out of the petrol station onto the road outside. He looked around and saw someone bent over by the front of a van that was lying on its side, he was trying to pull a body out. He was not going to help, his only thought at this point was to get as far away as possible before the police arrived. As he went to turn away the van burst into flames and the man outside, who he thought he recognized as Sami, became engulfed in fire. He watched as he saw him spinning around, he fell to the floor and was rolling, trying to put the flames out, he would not succeed. Inside the van he could hear others screaming as the fire consumed their bodies. Mohammed turned and walked away as if they did not exist.

17

OCTOBER 6TH, ENGLAND

Alan Foy had just arrived at his hotel in London when the mobile phone in his jacket rang. He took it out of his pocket and stepped into a public telephone booth in the hotel lobby. He closed the booth door behind him as he answered the call.

"Yes," he said.

It was Donnelly on the other end, "Where are you?" he asked.

"I am in London at the hotel. Where are you?"

"Stay there, I will be with you later today, I have good news."

"I am in room 242, see you soon," he replied.

Strain and the rest of the team were having a well-deserved rest at the safehouse. They had received instructions to lay low for a few days as the heads of MI5 and MI6 were getting very suspicious of the deaths of the various terrorists. The Mask Committee was called to the Prime Ministers office for a briefing to discuss the previous day's events.

Strain somehow managed to account for his actions by explaining that he called off the surveillance of the Muslim location by MI6 so that his men could continue. Unfortunately he was a little premature in requesting MI6 to back down, as two of his team were not available. He was so busy following other clues he forgot to request that MI6 resume.

The Prime Minister stepped in at the end of this explanation and gave Strain a very severe reprimand, so severe in fact that the other committee members thought that he was going to relieve Strain of duty. The PM recovered his composure and dismissed Strain, telling him that he was suspended for three days and he was to report back to his Chief Constable.

Strain was totally impressed with the PM's outburst, *a great politician at work*, he thought. *He not only makes the others believe that he was angered by my actions but he gets me out of the room and away from any awkward questions by suspending me.*

After Strain left the Prime Minister told the remainder of the committee that he did not want the suspension of Strain to become public. He ordered

MI5 to perform a full investigation into the deaths of the terrorists, the results to be reported to him alone. Fletcher knew that it was useless to argue with the PM and gave an obedient nod of the head, showing that he understood.

The Chief Constable was sitting in his office at police headquarters in Chester when he received the call from his contact on his private line.

"Hello," he said.

"We have a problem, Strain has become a real problem. Call him and tell him that you need to meet him in private, and nobody else is to know of your meeting. As of today he is suspended for three days, he is to report to you as soon as he arrives later today. He will assume that your call will be in connection with his suspension. Meet him somewhere completely private and I will join you. Where will you tell him to meet you?"

"Why do you want to be there, surely you cannot be seen together?"

"Never mind why, I will explain when I meet you, now where are you going to meet him?"

"How about my daughter's house? It is totally isolated."

"Good, arrange it for tomorrow and I will see you there, let me know what time, I already know where the house is. Remember, this is a matter of national security. Nobody is to know of our meeting." He hung up the telephone before the Chief could ask any further questions.

Strain explained to the team that the PM had suspended him for three days and told them to stand fast at the safehouse until they were released by Fletcher at MI5.

"When is he going to call us? I for one would like to go home." Shadow like the rest of the team were ready for a break from London.

"It will be today or tomorrow, as the PM wants to close this quickly. I suggest that you call the MI5 office as soon as I leave and get things moving along. Foy has one of our mobile phones, this is the number, give him a call, Chalky, and arrange to pick it up for me. I don't want anyone else going with you. I don't need any more exposure by one of you trying to kill him or Fagan. We will have our showdown with those two some day, I just can't afford for it to be today. Chalky, collect all of the information that you have on the Bowles job and we will destroy it."

"Great, I spend all that time putting in the info and now it is a waste of time, I was still working on it this morning."

"Stop moaning, Bulldog will help you."

"Wow, thanks, boss, don't do me any more favors, will you. What have you heard from Foy and Donnelly?"

"Nothing at the moment, they are still trying to locate their man. They haven't called so I guess they are not being very successful. See how they are doing in the morning when you try to get the mobile phone back, not that we really need it." He said his farewells to the team and left for the airport and took the private jet to Manchester.

The flight was totally uneventful and arrived at Manchester airport on time. He drove his car out of the airport and headed towards home. As he turned onto the M56 motorway he switched on his mobile telephone and laid it on the passenger seat. Two minutes later the phone rang.

No prizes for guessing who this will be, thought Strain. He answered the call, "Hello."

"It sounds like you have got yourself into a real mess this time, John." It was the Chief Constable.

"Yes, sir, he wasn't very happy with my report." He assumed that the Chief knew about his suspension.

"Three days suspension from the PM no less, by God, you don't do anything in a small way, do you?"

"Sorry about that, sir. I have been told to report to you, when do you want to meet?" He was hoping that he did not say straight away.

"Well, I am having dinner with the police committee at the moment and I don't expect this to finish before midnight. Can you meet me at my daughter's house in the morning at say, 10 o'clock? I want to meet in private, John. We will have your official meeting at my office late tomorrow afternoon."

"Yes, sir."

"I will explain everything when we meet, try to keep out of trouble until then, would you?"

"Yes, sir, see you in the morning." He was curious as to why the Chief wanted to meet at his daughter's house and not the office. He did not give it much more thought and continued driving towards home.

Donnelly arrived at the hotel and went straight to Foy's room, he knocked on the door.

Alan looked through the door viewer and saw Donnelly on the other side. He opened the door, letting him into the room.

"Well, you sounded all excited about something on the telephone, what have you found out?" Foy poured them both a drink of Jamesons whiskey.

"Remember I told you that I was waiting for the address of the safehouse that we were going use in London?"

"Yes."

"Well, I was given the safehouse address last night by Sean, I used him for the sniping job when I interrogated Fagan."

"Yes, I know him."

"Well, this morning I get a call from someone at the house who asked for my mobile phone number. After a little persuasion I gave him the number and he said he would call me back. Thirty minutes later the same man calls me on my mobile and told me to be ready to take down some information. He then gives me an address in London and states that what we are looking for is located there. Well the address is only the same one that Sean gave me the night before as a safehouse."

"I get the feeling that we are being used to do someone else's dirty work again or we are being set up. Did you recognize the voice on the phone?"

"No, it could have been anyone. Whoever it was he had a strong Belfast accent."

"Any ideas what we do next?" Foy knew that they had to go to the address, but he wanted to go with a plan in mind.

"They will be expecting me, but I don't think that they will be expecting you. I was thinking that I could go to the address and let myself inside, there is a key under a plant pot by the front door. I would leave the door unlocked and you could sneak in after me without being seen. I am sure that Eamon will be there and you could get the jump on him."

"Sounds good to me, but he will not be alone, why don't we take a good look at the place before you go in?"

"Yeah! Let's do it."

They left the hotel and took the underground to Monument Station and walked a half mile to the address. They could not see any vantage points to watch the house, as it was situated on a bend in the road and it was very difficult to keep the place under observation.

"There was a car hire place down the road, let's hire a car and we can park close to the house and keep it under observation." Donnelly noticed that they had several vans parked outside the hire company, one of them would be perfect.

"Good idea," replied Foy.

Thirty minutes later they were in the back of the van watching the house. The tinted windows on the van helped them see out but nobody could see in.

It had been dark for three hours and there was no sign of anyone in the house, it was in total darkness.

"I think that I should go in, Alan, and you can watch my back. If he is not inside you can come in after me and we will wait for him."

"I am with you but be careful, he could be in there. I will go around the back and see if there is another way in."

They both got out of the van and headed towards the house.

"Give me a couple of minutes to get into position around the back," said Foy.

Donnelly nodded his head, his eyes were totally focused on the house ahead of him.

Foy found the correct gate to the back of the house and tried to open it, but it was locked. There was a six-foot brick wall surrounding the back of the house and no other way to get inside, he climbed the wall. He dropped into the rear garden and scurried across the grass towards the rear of the house. He stood next to a garden shed and watched the windows of the home. He could not see anything from where he was and quickly ran to the rear window. He carefully looked into the house as a light came on inside, he ducked down out of sight.

Donnelly walked very slowly towards the house, giving Foy plenty of time to position himself at the rear. As bold as anything he walked straight up the path of the house to the front door. He could not see any movement inside the house, he saw the plant pot by the door and bent down to see if the key was underneath. It was very dark and at first he could not find the key and then realized that it was stuck to the bottom of the pot. He placed the key in the lock and opened the door. He quickly stepped inside, his gun in his hand, he closed the door, being careful not to lock it. He could not see anything inside the house, it was so dark. As he walked towards the first room on his right he heard a floor board behind him creak, he turned.

Eamon moved without making a sound as he came out of the small cupboard under the stairs. As he stood up a floor board creaked and Donnelly started to turn, he was too slow. Eamon smashed the butt of his gun into the side of his head, knocking him down. He dragged the unconscious Donnelly into the rear lounge dropping him on the floor in the middle of the room. He turned the light on to see his catch more clearly. He did not want to waste any time and picked up a vase of flowers that were on the table and emptied the water onto Donnelly's face to wake him up.

Foy peered through the corner of the window, trying not to be seen, he could see Eamon with a vase in his hand. He stood up a little more and could see that he was pouring water onto Donnelly, who was lying on the floor. He took a step back from the window and pointed his gun towards Eamon. He was about to pull the trigger when he felt something being pressed into the back of his head, he froze.

"Now don't do anything heroic, Mr Foy, as I would hate to have to shoot you. Give me your gun very slowly."

Foy could see Eamon stood by the window looking at him, he was waving at the man behind him to come inside.

Foy felt the pressure of the gun on his neck, "Who are you?"

"You will find out soon enough, now move towards that door and let yourself inside."

Foy opened the back door and stepped inside.

"I have another visitor for you," the man shouted as they walked through the kitchen towards the room where Eamon and Donnelly were.

Eamon stepped into the hall. "Welcome, Alan, it has been a long time since we saw each other, come in." He pointed towards the lounge and Foy walked inside.

Donnelly was sitting up, rubbing his head, when he saw Foy walk in. "Well, they got you as well, Alan, I don't feel quite so foolish now."

"We walked into this one, didn't we?"

"Sit on the floor next to him," said Eamon.

His sat next to his friend, giving him a slight smile.

Eamon sat down in a chair opposite them, pointing his gun at them. "I suppose you will want to know who it is that is helping me. Step around here and let them see who you are."

A man stepped between them and turned, it was Sean.

"What the fuck are you doing with him, Sean?" shouted Donnelly.

Sean said nothing and walked back around behind them.

"To be sure you can't trust anyone anymore, can you?" Eamon said and burst out laughing.

"You will be laughing on the other side of your face when I get a hold of you," said Donnelly.

"And what makes you think that I am so stupid as to let you live that long?" Eamon was very sure of himself and was confident that he was going to close the final chapter of this episode.

"Why did you have to kill our children, Eamon?" asked Foy.

"I didn't kill them, the police did that, and you know they did."

"Your finger was on the trigger as much as theirs. You set up my boy from the beginning, using him for your own greed. He had the chance of coming home and starting a new life with the new peace talks and you had him murdered."

"Oh! Stop crying, you know as well as I do that our business is bloody and that there are casualties on both sides. There will never be a true peace in

Ireland and you know it, there is too much to lose financially. I am sick of listening to all the bleeding hearts about peace and what a bright future Ireland has, we have no future. The war will go on with or without the likes of you and it is people like me that will keep it going that way. Christ, man, have you forgotten the atrocities that the English have committed against us and our people? They have murdered hundreds of good IRA men and women and for what, to keep the politicians happy."

Donnelly screamed at him, "You bastard, you murdered our children for money, not for any cause, for money. Fagan told me all about it you fucking bastard." He tried to get to his feet but was knocked down by Sean. "What are you doing with this murdering bastard, Sean, you helped me get Fagan, what is going on here?"

"Why don't you tell us who else is involved, Eamon, I mean you have nothing to lose now as you are going to kill us next. Who is the other person in the government that helps you?"

"You will be most surprised when I tell you, I—" The window shattered, showering them with glass. Foy and Donnelly rolled flat onto the floor as they saw Eamon's body fall sideways into the chair, blood sprayed out onto the floor from his chest.

They both lay still on the floor as they heard the sound of breaking glass once more. Sean fell on top of Donnelly, he had a huge hole in his back where a bullet had exited.

"Get to the window, the brick will give us some protection," shouted Foy.

They both rolled on the floor and lay against the wall under the window. Next to Donnelly was Sean's handgun, he picked it up as Eamon stood up in the chair. He was about say something when a second bullet hit him in the middle of his forehead, he fell to the floor dead.

Donnelly fired the handgun once at the light bulb, smashing it and putting the room into darkness.

"We have to get out of her. Make your way to the front door," said Foy.

They crawled across the floor on their hands and knees heading towards the hallway. Donnelly felt something grab his leg and he put his hand down to help himself break free. It was Sean, he had a hold of his ankle, he was trying to say something.

"Donnelly, wait a minute," he whispered.

Donnelly stopped. He could hear Sean saying something.

"I am sorry about your sons, I want you both to know that I did not have anything to do with that. I have been working with the IRA leadership to find out what Eamon was up to. They were hearing rumors about him starting a splinter group. I reported back to them that you found out that he had a contact in the British government. I was supposed to find out who it was and report it back so that our political wing could expose the person involved. They were going to use it as part of the bargaining power for a peace agreement." He made a gurgling sound and died.

"God be with you, Sean," said Donnelly.

Both men managed to escape from the house without any further incident. Whoever the shooter was that killed Sean and Eamon, he had completed his task.

"Let's head back to the hotel and have a drink, I need one," said Foy.

"So do I, we could have a few hours' sleep and drive to Southport, then head home on the plane early in the morning."

"That sounds good." Foy was ready to go home to his wife. He knew that there was no way that he was going to find out who the contact was in the British government. Whoever he was he had cut off any trails that would lead to him by killing Eamon.

Strain had a restful night and woke up at six a.m. He was unusually hungry and decided to have breakfast at Frank's cafe on the dock road. On the way to the café he called Bulldog at the hotel. "Morning, how are you feeling this morning?"

Thankfully Bulldog was already awake. "I am glad that I didn't decide to have a sleep in this morning. It is only six forty-five, what are you doing up so early?"

"I had a good night's sleep and decided to go to Frank's for breakfast."

"Thanks very much, John, we are down here working and you are relaxing, having a good time."

"Not really, I have got to see the Chief this morning—sorry, I am not supposed to tell anyone, forget I said that, officially I don't see him until this afternoon."

"What do you mean officially, are you going for your ass chewing for getting suspended?"

"I spoke out of turn, forget I said that I was meeting him."

"Come on, John, what is the problem, don't you even trust me now?"

"You know I do, you pushy bastard, he said he was worried about something personal and he wanted to meet somewhere away from the office."

"Sounds very odd, where are you meeting him?"

"At his daughter's house, now drop it, we haven't talked about this."

"OK. I will have a beer with you when we are done here and you can tell me all the gory details."

Strain's phone started to make a bleeping sound, he recognized it as the warning that the battery was about to run out of power. He realized that he had left the cigarette lighter cord at home and could not charge the battery. "As if I would tell you anything, got to go, my battery is flat, see you soon."

"Yeah, good-bye."

He arrived at the café at seven and was greeted at the door by the familiar smell of bacon and eggs cooking. He picked up a *Herald Tribune* newspaper on the way in and decided to take his time as he did not have to meet the Chief for three hours.

OCTOBER 7TH, CHESTER, ENGLAND

The Chief Constable was waiting for his contact at his daughter's house as planned. He had been pacing up and down for almost an hour when he heard a car outside on the drive. He walked to the front door to see him arriving, he pointed to the garage, "Put your car in the garage," he shouted.

The driver did as he was told and closed the garage door behind him. The Chief Constable was showing his usual nervousness, which normally came out as anger.

"Where have you been? He will be here soon, you should have been here a long time ago."

"Don't worry, we have fifteen minutes or so before he arrives. Come on, let's go into the house," he said.

He noticed that his contact was carrying a heavy-looking brown bag. "What's in the bag?"

"Rope, we are going to make it look as though Strain committed suicide." He walked through to the kitchen.

"Suicide, I don't know if anyone would believe that."

"This is the story, Strain called you and said that he wanted to meet with you. He was having problems coping with the deaths of his team members and really needed your help. You say that he sounded very depressed when he called and you were very concerned about him. He wanted to meet you somewhere quiet where you could both talk and you suggested this place because he knew it was empty. Pull that chair over here." He pointed to one of the wooden chairs by the kitchen table.

The Chief dragged a chair over to where they had been standing. There was a series of four old wooden beams that held up the cathedral-style ceiling above their heads.

The contact took the thick rope out of his bag, which had a noose at one end. He positioned the wooden chair under one of the beams and stood on it. He threw the noose end of the rope over the wooden beam. He struggled with the rope for a moment. "Can you get another chair and help me? I think the rope is caught on a nail or something."

The Chief did as he was told and pulled another chair over and positioned it so that he could see the opposite side of the beam where the noose was. He stood on the chair and pulled on the noose. "Yes, it seems to be stuck on something," he said.

"Keep hold of the noose and let me move over, see if I can see what it is." He moved his chair and stood it next to the Chief's. He still had a hold of the opposite end of the rope, he stood on the chair.

"I don't see it caught anywhere," said the Chief.

"Here, give me the noose, you get on your toes and get a better look at the top of the beam."

The Chief handed him the noose and grabbed the beam with both hands and pulled himself onto his toes. "No, don't see anything, perhaps we should move it to another part of the beam."

"That's a good idea," the man replied.

The Chief lowered his feet back onto the chair, giving himself a firm footing. He turned towards his accomplice and felt the noose being thrust over his head.

As fast as he could the man pulled the noose over the Chief's head and pulled the knot tight. He jumped off the chair and held on to the rope, keeping it tight so that the Chief could not loosen the noose.

"What are you doing?" The Chief could feel the pressure of the rope around his throat. "For Christ's sakes man, stop playing games, this isn't funny." He was more terrified at this point than he had ever been in his life.

"I am not playing games, you have become a liability, Chief Constable just like Bowles. You will be committing suicide because of the debt you were in. Your debt plus the fact that your daughter is in a very expensive drug rehabilitation center in America, which you could no longer afford, pushed you to take your own life. Your bank account will show that you are in a great deal of debt. You may want to know that I got your daughter addicted to drugs. It was so easy, I arranged for a handsome man at a party to give her the drugs. After the party she was gradually fed the drugs to the point where she became addicted. How else was I going to be able to control you, your problem is you are too clean. You should have had some kind of extra marital affair and it would have been easier." The Chief summoned strength from somewhere and lashed out with his foot at the man. The heel of the shoe caught him under the nose, breaking it. The man fell to the ground cursing as blood poured out of his nostrils. He held on to the end of the rope and got back on his feet. He knocked the chair away from under the Chief Constable's feet.

The Chief was choking as the noose tightened around his neck, he fought frantically, his hands clawing at the rope as he tried to lift the weight of his body off the noose. He was frantic, his eyes wide with fear as the strength in his arms started to desert him.

His accomplice tied the end of the rope to the oven door. He tried to stop his nose from bleeding by holding his head back and pinching the bridge of the nose, it stopped bleeding temporarily. He walked over to look at the Chief as he swung by the end of the rope. He was still fighting to keep his weight from tightening the noose.

"You are supposed to die quickly, you are supposed to have a broken neck, stop fighting it." He could see that this part of his plan was not going the way he had expected it to. "Stop fighting it, you useless bastard." The Chief wasn't going to die easily. He had to do something else and so he jumped up at the Chief, grabbing him by the waist, and wrapped his legs around his victims legs. "Now I have got you, hahaha."

He hung on to him, both of them swinging as though it was some kind of sick circus act, he was laughing out loud. There was a loud crack and the Chief's arms dropped to his sides, his neck had snapped.

"About fucking time," he said.

He carefully laid one chair on its side on the floor under where the Chief was hanging and replaced the other chair under the kitchen table. He heard a car coming up the drive outside and hid himself in the kitchen storage room.

As Strain drove up the drive he saw the Chief's car parked by the front door. He was curious as to what the Chief wanted to discuss with him, something very personal, he had said. He parked the car alongside the Chief's and walked into the house. There was no sign of the Chief in the lounge so he walked through to the kitchen. The Chief's body was still swaying slightly as he walked into the kitchen.

"Oh fuck no, what have you done?" he said out loud.

He picked up the chair that was lying on its side and stood on it. As he looked at the Chief's face and saw the position of his head, he knew that his neck was broken.

"Why did you do this? Nothing is worth taking your life, damn you," said Strain as he looked into the vacant eyes.

He got down off the chair and walked over to the oven door to undo the rope and lower the Chief's body to the floor.

"I wouldn't do that if I were you." The voice startled Strain, he turned around to see who it was. "It is a shame that he had to take his own life, isn't it, John?"

He could not believe his eyes as he saw Fletcher step out of the storage room. "What is going on here, Fletcher?"

"I thought that it was obvious, he has committed suicide. A tragic end to a very promising career."

"If it is such a tragic end, why do you not sound very distressed by his death? Why do I get the sudden feeling that you have something to do with it?" Strain stepped towards him.

"Stay where you are, Strain. I am more aware than most people how dangerous you are, especially when you are pissed off. He had become a liability, something that my little group of investors could not afford. Why do you care anyway, he was up to his elbows in our money making scheme, yes, he was crooked just like the rest of us. Oh! Except you of course, the great John Strain and his wonderful Mask Team." He could not hold back the sarcasm and hate in his voice.

"So you make money out of killing him and others, I expect." Strain was looking for a way of getting him into a more relaxed state as Fletcher was as nervous as a cat in a dog pound. Strain moved towards the kitchen table and sat down.

"You won't be sitting there very long, we are leaving."

"I suppose you will tell me where we are going eventually, in the meantime why don't you tell me what this is all about? There is obviously a lot more behind his death and the death of others. I suppose you and Eamon Callaghan are behind a lot of the extra activity that my team and I have been through over the last few weeks?"

"Ah! You know about Eamon, you have been busy. You see, Strain, you have to learn that there is a higher pecking order in life, where people like you are not included. Your job is to follow orders and not to question them, that is where Carl went wrong. He was a good man when he worked for me, but like you he was expendable."

Strain was surprised to hear Carl's name. "He tried to kill me and you stopped him, or at least that is how you made it look. I take it he wasn't going to kill me after all?"

"You see, that is what I mean by a higher pecking order, he was going to warn you that he thought that I was involved with the IRA, so I killed him. That is something that you could not do in your high and mighty standards with rules to obey and play by. There is only one fucking rule and that is personal survival."

Strain pointed at the Chief's body hanging by the rope, "I suppose he didn't play by the rules, the same as Bowles, did you kill him as well?"

"He got caught up in this because I needed to keep an eye on you and the

Mask Team. Getting him involved was the easiest. As I told him just before his neck broke, I got his daughter involved in drugs, and keeping her addicted was simple. She was just like her father, weak. Bowles was simpler in many ways because he had a vice, he liked having sex with young girls and the ultimate vice, greed. Like all of the others he eventually outgrew his usefulness. If Alan Foy had gotten to him before Eamon he would have told him everything and we couldn't have that, now could we?"

"You know that Alan Foy will hunt you down when he finds out that you set up his son. Just like you set up my team." He stood up.

Fletcher knew that Strain was going to try and attack him at the first opportunity and decided that it was time to end the discussion. "Time for us to leave. You have found out everything you need to know. I have to return to London and start to get my financial affairs together. Next month I will be announcing that I am going to retire, make your way to the front door." He waved the weapon at Strain, who obeyed his instruction and walked out of the kitchen.

Outside Strain could not help but notice how blue the sky was, *a good day to be alive*, he thought and he was going to try and keep it that way.

"Here." Fletcher tossed his Ford car keys to Strain. "Open the trunk."

Strain did as he was told as he caught the keys and opened the trunk, the lid raised by itself on the two hydraulic rams.

"What now?" asked Strain.

"Now you bend over into the trunk."

This was his last chance to try and save his own life. He bent over with his head and shoulders inside the trunk. He turned his head slightly so that he could see Fletcher's feet.

Fletcher moved towards Strain, the gun pointed at his head. He was more on edge than he would have liked to admit. He extended his arm forward so that the gun was approximately a foot from Strain's head.

The feet moved towards him and Strain decided that it was now or never. He turned to his right, swinging his arm in an arc upwards to where he thought Fletcher's arm was. He felt nothing, no contact with Fletcher or the gun, as he spun around to face upwards.

Fletcher was not surprised at how fast Strain moved and was glad that he was ready for the move. The arm missed his gun by a fraction of an inch as he swiftly lifted it out of the way of Strain's attack. He saw Strain's eyes look at him and he brought the gun down on the side of his head, the butt smashed into his skull.

It was too late for him to make a counter move, the blow to his head was brutal, splitting the skin on the hairline above his right ear. He fell to the floor, dazed but still conscious.

"You are wasting your time, John, you are no match for me, I am ready to anticipate your every move." He kicked Strain viciously on his right side, fracturing one of his ribs. Strain covered his side with his arm as he felt the pain surge through his side and into his chest. The next kick caught him on the right hip and the third in the small of his back. Fletcher was enjoying himself as he knew that he had the man at his mercy. "What's up, John, don't you like this?" He kicked him in the back again.

Strain felt the kick to his lower back more than any of the other blows, it caught him off guard as he winced in pain. He curled up in a fetal position to try to protect parts of his body, but it wasn't helping much. Another blow to the lower back. He let out an involuntary cry of pain.

Fletcher was working up quite a sweat kicking Strain, and sweating was something that he detested. He was a little out of breath as he grabbed Strain by the shirt collar. "Get up, get up," he said in anger as he pulled on the shirt collar.

Strain was feeling the pain from the blows but knew that he was not finished. He slowly got to his feet, using the back of the car to pull himself up. He made it look as though he was in worse shape than he really was. He let Fletcher tug at his shirt once more and he thrust his fist into Fletcher's crotch. The blow to his groin knocked him to his knees as Strain brought his knee up into his face.

Fletcher felt the bones in his jaw and face grind together as the lower jawbone snapped against his cheekbone. The pain was excruciating and he fell backwards screaming in pain, his mouth unable to move. The muffled scream echoed in his brain as he pulled the trigger on the gun. Two rounds were released in Strain's direction as he hit the ground.

The sound of the gun being fired was deafening at close range Strain instinctively ducked. One of the bullets tore into his shoulder, missing the collarbone and exiting out of the back of his shoulder. He didn't really feel the bullet, as the adrenaline pumping through his body masked the pain. He was slumped over the trunk of the car his upper body holding him up.

Fletcher was back on his feet, the pain in his face was incredible. He fell against Strain's back, using his own weight to keep him hanging in the trunk. He put the gun against the back of Strain's head.

The gunshot was loud, the bullet entered the back of the neck, missing the spinal column, and smashed into the collar bone, blood splattered all over the side of Fletcher's face and Strain's head. Fletcher fell backwards onto the concrete drive, shock and pain written all over his face. Fletcher was trying to scream again, the sounds muffled by the frozen jaw.

Strain heard the shot and felt the blood spread over the side of his face, the wetness a sign of his death, but he wasn't dead. He suddenly realized that the blood was not his, he looked around and saw Fletcher lying on the floor, his face disfigured from the broken jaw. He had shock and horror in his eyes and blood all over his face and jacket. Strain quickly looked for the gun and saw that it was out of Fletcher's reach.

"Did you think that we were going home before we finished what we had come here to do?" said the voice behind him.

Strain turned to see Alan Foy and Kevin Donnelly both pointing guns at him and Fletcher as they walked across the driveway from the hedgerow.

"You are in a bit of a mess, Mr Strain," said Donnelly, as he walked towards him. He had his gun pointed in his direction and fired it once.

Strain thought that he felt the bullet as it passed him and he heard Fletcher's muffled groan of pain. He turned and realized that Fletcher had tried to get to his gun and Donnelly had shot him in the arm.

"Am I next?" he asked.

"You should know by now that we do not blame you for the deaths of our children, we blame him," said Foy.

"I agree with Alan, but it does not mean that I do not want to kill you," said Donnelly.

"Well, do I live or do I die?" asked Strain as he spat a mouth full of blood onto the floor.

"You live, he dies," replied Donnelly, pointing at Fletcher.

"I would prefer it if the both of us lived." Strain could see that Donnelly did not like this response. "I think that he should live the rest of his days in prison to regret his actions and wish for the day that he finally dies. In prison he would be in a living hell when the prison population find out who he is and without a doubt they would have their fun with him." Strain hoped that this would give both of these men a reason not to kill Fletcher, as he really did want him to live and spend the rest of his life in prison.

Foy walked over to Fletcher and grabbed him by the jaw, the screams were unmerciful. "What do you want to do with him, Kevin?" he said.

Donnelly walked across and stood on his wounded hand, again he screamed. "I like what the policeman says, let him live, let the boys in prison use him for their bitch."

"Live it is then," said Foy.

"How did you know that I was here?" asked Strain.

"One of your smart boys called me on the mobile phone, he told me that he had found out who was involved from the government. He thought that you were being set up by your boss and that you were to be eliminated, as you had gotten too close to the real players. It is kind of ironic that we save your life, when we had come to the mainland to kill you. The rest of your team was not close enough to help and they could not get you on the phone to warn you. We were heading for the airport to fly home when we got the call for help. It was worth the detour, here we finally found out who was responsible for the murder of our children."

Donnelly spoke, "Last night we tracked down Eamon, we were in the house with him when a sniper shot him. He was dead before we could get any information out of him." He left out the fact that they were being held at gunpoint at the time. "The one called Chalky explained that he was closing up an investigation when one of your men recognized a phone number that was on the computer. Apparently the phone number was on the back of a business card that was picked up by someone called Bulldog in his office." He pointed to Fletcher. "The phone number belongs to a private airfield outside of Heathrow. When your lads checked the phone log that they had requested for that airport it showed that a call was made from there to his home. They told us that you were going to meet privately with your Chief Constable and one of them made a wild guess that you would meet here. You are one lucky bastard, it was a good guess."

"I guess I am, it would appear that we have all of those responsible."

"Be thankful that you are to live," said Donnelly.

Strain was struggling to stay conscious at this point and said, "Trust me, I am thankful. I think that both of you had better be leaving, someone may have heard the shots. I will call the ambulance and police, leave quickly."

Both men looked at each other and walked away. "No offense, but I hope we never see you again," said Foy.

"Likewise," replied Strain as he watched them walk away. Strain had to call for help but could not trust the local police to take care of Fletcher, as he would most probably convince them that he was the one in need of help. He picked up Fletcher's gun and walked over to the Chief's car and called Laura at the PM's office. Twenty minutes later the first ambulance arrived, closely followed by the Deputy Chief Constable and two plain-clothes officers. The Deputy Chief took control of the situation and reassured Strain that he was acting under the orders of the PM, he was safe.

18

OCTOBER 7TH, SPAIN

Albi Basurto knew that he had to rest overnight before he could go to England to try to stop his brother. The injuries that he had received in the car crash were much worse than he realized. What he did not know was that his brother's campaign had already taken place. He made it to a safehouse and lay on the bed to rest, he would sleep for sixteen hours.

It was early in the morning and he did not realize that he had slept so long. He woke up feeling like he had been run over by a train, the pain in his shoulder combined with the headache he had was almost unbearable. He had to find a pharmacy to buy painkillers. He made a pot of strong coffee and drank half of it before he ventured outside. He disguised himself and made his way to a local newspaper shop that was owned by an ETA member. He would be able to talk to him and find out what the latest news was.

As he walked into the newspaper shop the owner saw him and recognized him immediately.

"Albi, what are you doing here? The police are everywhere looking for you." The shop owner was a great believer in Albi's ability to bring peace to the Basque country. He too had seen enough bloodshed and pain, he had lost his youngest son when he was beaten to death in a Spanish jail. This was one more reason why ETA wanted all ETA members that were serving time in Spanish prisons to be transferred to prisons in the Basque region. This would be a fundamental part of their peace deal.

"I was in a car crash trying to evade a police roadblock, I need to get some painkillers, I was in a coma at the hospital for I don't know how long." The pain from his injuries was increasing.

"Come into the back, I have some very strong ones that will help you." The shop owner lifted the hinged part of his wooden counter top to let Albi inside.

He sat down and was already starting to feel tired again. "I need your help, I have to get to England."

"It is not a safe place for you to go at the moment. The English are hunting down anyone with any connections to Spain and any known affiliation to ETA. I am sorry but perhaps you do not know what has been going on because of the coma."

"What do you mean?" Albi was starting to fear the worst.

"There has been a great number of bombings and assassination attempts in England. There were attacks on the French Embassy, the ambassador's home and several other locations that we believe were carried out by Muslim extremists."

"Mohammed Gahi," said Albi.

"Yes, as always you seem to know who is doing what. There was an attack on a Spanish government office and at an exhibition set up to encourage business with Spain, amongst other attacks. I am sure you know that it is Velasco behind those attacks. He was also behind the bombings in Logroño."

"I don't believe that he would go through with it, what is he thinking about?" Albi was furious at his brother.

"It has not been very popular with the rest of the organization. The police and anti-terrorism units have been hitting every known business and criminal group known to have ETA connections. The criminal elements are the most upset at this time, as they have lost millions in goods that have been confiscated by the authorities, not to mention drugs. We have lost three of our major arms caches in the raids, we estimate about half a million dollars in value. You and your brother are not very popular at the moment."

"I can see why, but I did not have anything to do with the attacks in Logroño and England. I was trying to stop Velasco and make him realize what he was doing, you know that I am dedicated to finding peace. I was with that traitor Carlos when we tried to stop Velasco leaving for England on the boat, we were too late. We were going to get a plane to take us to Ireland to try and cut him off when we had the confrontation with the police."

"What did you mean when you said Carlos was a traitor?"

"He was an undercover agent for the police, we were totally fooled by him."

"I can't believe it, he was always so active. I hope that he is dead, if he isn't we will kill him." The shopkeeper meant what he said.

"I need to contact Velasco, I have to find out where he is staying in England."

"You are the second person that has asked where he might be staying, Eneto called, he wanted to help get him out."

Albi was surprised at this news, as he knew that Eneto did not normally care if his brother lived or died. "When did he call?"

"He didn't, someone else did and they told me, confidentially, that Eneto was the one that wanted to know. That was three days ago, for all we know your brother may be on his way home."

"I need to find out where Eneto is and what he is up to."

"I have one of my most loyal soldiers already watching him, I know that he did not like your brother, I was suspicious when I heard that he was asking where he could find Velasco. Let me make a couple of telephone calls and see what he is doing."

Albi was starting to feel sleepy again, he lay down in the storeroom at the back of the shop, the strong painkillers were working and he drifted off to sleep.

He had been asleep for two hours when he was woken by the shop owner.

"Albi, you have to wake up."

"I am awake," he said.

"Here, drink this coffee, it will help." He gave him a very large cup of coffee.

"What have you found out?"

"It is not good news, Eneto has been drinking heavily the last two days and he has bought himself a new car. I think that he found out the information that he wanted from one of the other ETA members. They gave him the address of one of our people in London. He did not know that Eneto was up to something, he thought that he was requesting the information for you. There was an explosion at the address that Eneto was given in London, it was in the early hours of this morning. Our sources tell us that it looks as though it was a gas explosion, probably some kind of fault on the gas system. Four or five charred bodies have been taken out of the rubble so far. I am sorry, Albi, but I think that one of them was your brother and the others were all ETA."

He stayed silent for a moment, controlling himself. "Where is Eneto?"

"I have three people watching him as we speak, do not worry, he is not going anywhere. What do you want us to do to help you?"

"I will take care of him, can you take me to him?" Albi was without emotion, cold blood ran through his veins.

"I have a car and driver waiting outside, he will take you wherever you want. You can trust him and the other two that will help you, they are my sons."

Albi stood up, no longer tired, the hatred had him wide awake. "Thank you, I owe you a lot."

"You owe me one thing, peace for our people, you can do it, Albi."

"I want this to be my last act of violence, then I give you my word I will work for peace."

He had the driver stop and buy a five-gallon container and have it filled with gasoline on his way to meet Eneto.

Eneto was in a tailor's shop being fitted for a brand-new suit, he stood in front of the mirror admiring himself and how good-looking he was. The IRA contact had paid him handsomely for the information on where Velasco was staying in London. He didn't care why the IRA wanted the information, it would have pleased him greatly if he had known that the information was being passed on to Strain's terrorism team. He had purchased a new car with his ill-gotten gains and had parked it outside the tailor's store. He planned to leave early in the morning and drive to Athens to start a two-week vacation.

The bell on the door of the tailor's shop rang, announcing that another customer had entered. "I will be with you in a moment," shouted the tailor without looking up.

"I am in no hurry, am I, Eneto," said the customer.

Eneto looked into the mirror and saw a man standing by the door wearing a ski mask and holding a sawn-off shotgun. He did not wait for introductions. He knocked over the tailor and ran through the back of the store. The man gave chase and saw him leaving by the backdoor, he closed the door behind Eneto and locked it. He walked back through the store and pointed the shotgun at the tailor and said, "You have seen nothing." The old man nodded his head in agreement.

As Eneto entered the alleyway outside he went to run to the left but realized that it was a dead end, a ten-foot brick wall blocking his way. He turned to the right and saw Albi stood there.

"Albi, thank goodness it is you."

"Why did you give them the information on where to find my brother?" Albi also had a sawn-off shotgun in his hand.

"I didn't give anyone information, I—" He was suddenly drenched by something from above. "What are you doing?" he shouted as he smelt gasoline.

On the roof above an ETA member emptied the five gallons of gasoline over Eneto.

"You told them where my brother was in London, didn't you?"

Eneto looked at Albi and saw that he was holding a cigarette lighter, "Albi, wait please, I didn't know what they were going to do. I thought that they wanted to talk to him about more arms deals." He could not take his eyes off the cigarette lighter.

"For this information they paid you enough money for you to buy a new car and clothes. It is blood money, the blood of my brother and other ETA members, you sold their lives for material things." His anger poured out as he flipped the top of the cigarette lighter, causing the flint to light the wick. He held it where Eneto could see it and tossed it at his feet.

Eneto jumped back and turned to run, he was too late, the gasoline ignited. Flames swept up from his feet and within a second he was a ball of fire. He screamed in agony, his attempts at putting the flames out with his burning hands were useless.

Albi stood watching Eneto spinning in circles, screaming in agony. A car entered the alley, the driver sounded the horn. Albi turned, "Get in," shouted the driver, "The police will be here soon." He got into the front seat and they drove away, leaving Eneto to burn.

OCTOBER 8TH, LONDON

It was only a forty-minute flight from Manchester on the private plane but Strain slept all the way. He woke feeling like somebody had recharged his batteries while he was asleep. The rest had obviously done his body some good. At the terminal the driver was waiting for him and transported him straight to Downing Street to meet the Prime Minister.

Laura was anxiously waiting to see him as she had heard a whisper that somebody had tried to kill him, this on top of the bombing in Liverpool was too much for her.

Strain walked towards her office, "Morning Laura."

"Good morning John, how are you feeling?" Concern was written all over her face.

He gave that reassuring smile of his and said, "I am fine, in great shape, and you?"

She blushed slightly, "I am doing OK, thank you. I will let the Prime minister know that you are here."

"Thank you." He sat down as she dialed the PM's extension. "He is ready to see you, please go straight in."

Strain knocked on the PM's office door and let himself inside his office, "Morning Prime Minister."

"Yes, morning John, please take a seat," he replied. "I am leaving in two days for the United States to meet the President, I want you to go with me. He and I had a conversation yesterday about terrorism and how we handle things here. As you know they are suffering from terrorism more now than they have ever experienced in the past. I have offered your expertise on how you think things could be handled over there. The President is sick and tired of the terrorists committing these bombings that they are having. I think that your recent success will be at the top of the agenda. How do you feel about going with me?"

"I would be more than happy to go." Strain was rather taken aback at the invitation and at the news that the US President was thinking of doing the same thing.

"Thank you, John, we leave the day after tomorrow. Laura will give you the details." He called Laura into the office. "Laura, please make sure that Mr Strain is on the flight manifest for my trip to the United States. Would you be so kind as to give him all the details?"

"Yes, sir, right away," she walked out of his office back to her desk.

"Thank you, John. I knew that I could count on your support."

"You're welcome, sir." He stood up to leave.

"Take her out to dinner sometime, she would like that." He pointed in the direction of Laura's office.

Strain adjusted his jacket and mumbled, "Mmm, yes, sir."

Laura had all of the information waiting for Strain at her desk.

"Here is everything that you need for your trip. You have a room booked at the Sheraton Park Tower again for the next two nights."

"Thank you, Laura, I guess that I will see you on the plane."

"Yes, see you then," she replied.

Strain got to the hotel and lay down on top of the bed. He could not get what the PM had said out of his mind, "Take her out to dinner," he whispered to himself. He lay there looking up at the ceiling, it was four o'clock in the afternoon, he felt very sleepy. Perhaps the PM was right, he should take her out to dinner.

He picked up the telephone and called Laura at the office.

"Laura, John Strain. I was wondering, would you do me the honor of joining me for dinner this evening?" He really was hoping she would say yes.

She was taken completely off guard by his invitation. "Yes, that would be very nice, where are we going?"

Strain hadn't thought about where they would go, "I would appreciate it if you would choose a restaurant, you know all the good ones in town."

"I will make the reservation for eight o'clock, is that a good time?" she asked.

"Perfect, where will I pick you up?"

"Seven thirty at my apartment, 26 Partridge Gardens off Knightsbridge."

"Seven thirty it is."

"Good-bye." She was totally flustered when she put down the telephone, she could not believe how she had kept her composure.

Strain picked Laura up at exactly seven thirty, she looked stunning. The restaurant was only a twenty-minute drive from her home. Laura chose an intimate restaurant in the trendy Belgravia area of the city. Strain was very surprised when they walked into the restaurant, it wasn't what he had expected. The waiter was very attentive and the seven-piece band playing on stage was very good. He really liked the fact that they played a variety of musical pieces and not so loud that you could not hear what the person at your table was saying.

Laura could not control herself all evening, she smiled at Strain like she had not smiled at anyone for years. The meal, the wine, the music, the company—everything was perfect. She felt like she had waited for this evening for a lifetime.

Strain was swept away by the whole evening as he listened to the band start to play again. He looked at the small dance floor across the room and stood up. "Would you like to dance?" he said, offering his hand to her. Laura accepted and took his hand and walked to the dance floor. The big band sound of Glenn Miller filled the room, 'Moonlight Serenade', perfect for the moment. They floated around the floor as if they had done it a thousand times. Strain held her closely as he realized that there was something special about this woman, this was going to be a long relationship.

The band was coming to the end of 'Moonlight Serenade'. Strain looked into Laura's eyes. Her body suddenly went limp and her head fell to one side. He felt something wet sprinkle his face. He heard people in the restaurant screaming as he tried to lift her limp body to its feet. He held her with one arm and gently moved her head. "Laura, what is the matter?"

He could now see what was wrong—she had been shot in the head, his hand was covered in blood. He looked across the room towards the band and saw Velasco Basurto facing him, he had a semi-automatic gun in his hand, he had shot Laura. He looked back at Laura and from deep inside his body came a blood-curdling scream, "Noooo!"

The sound of his own scream jolted him out of his nightmare as he sat upright in bed in a lather of sweat, realizing that he had been dreaming. He got out of bed and showered, ready for the trip to America.

*

Printed in the United States
49032LVS00003B/124-132

9 781413 711097